Book 2 of The Halcyon Cycle

The Battle for HALCYON

Peter Kazmaier

THE BATTLE FOR HALCYON
Copyright © 2015 by Peter Kazmaier

All rights reserved. Neither this publication nor any part of this publication may be reproduced or transmitted in any form or by any means, electronic or mechanical, including photocopying, recording or any information storage and retrieval system, without permission in writing from the author.

This is a work of fiction. Names, characters, places and incidents either are the product of the author's imagination or are used fictitiously, and any resemblance to actual persons, living or dead, businesses, companies, events, or locales is entirely coincidental.

For more information or to order additional copies, please contact:
Wolfsburg Imprints
2421 Council Ring Road
Mississauga, Ontario, Canada
L5L 1E5
http://www.wolfsburgimprints.com/

ISBN: 978-1-4866-0853-9

Word Alive Press
131 Cordite Road, Winnipeg, MB R3W 1S1
www.wordalivepress.ca

Library and Archives Canada Cataloguing in Publication

Kazmaier, Peter, 1951-, author
    The battle for Halcyon / Peter Kazmaier.

(Book 2 of the Halcyon cycle)
Issued in print and electronic formats.
ISBN 978-1-4866-0853-9 (pbk.).--ISBN 978-1-4866-0854-6 (pdf).--
ISBN 978-1-4866-0855-3 (html).--ISBN 978-1-4866-0856-0 (epub)

    I. Title. II. Series: Kazmaier, Peter, 1951- Halcyon cycle ; bk. 2.

PS8621.A96B38 2015   C813'.6   C2015-900782-8
    C2015-900783-6

Dedication

To my parents, Karl and Lilo Kazmaier, who first taught me to follow the Master, to cherish a sense of humour, and to know that even when we disagree, we still love one another.

Contents

Books by Peter Kazmaier   vii
Map of Eastern Feiramar   ix
The Halcyon River Region   xi
Map of the Island of Halcyon   xiii
The City of the Dead   xv

Chapter 1	The City of the Dead	1
Chapter 2	Council of War	7
Chapter 3	The Halfmen	10
Chapter 4	The Ruined City of Arkand	20
Chapter 5	The Hidden Way	40
Chapter 6	Eleytheria	46
Chapter 7	Down River	50
Chapter 8	Playing with Fire	66
Chapter 9	The Aberhardt Constant	73
Chapter 10	Beserkers	79
Chapter 11	Pursuit	86
Chapter 12	Rebirth	95
Chapter 13	In the House of Kelldor	100
Chapter 14	A Narrow Escape	115
Chapter 15	The Giant Steps	129
Chapter 16	Besieged	138
Chapter 17	Kelldor	150
Chapter 18	Hanging in the Balance	158
Chapter 19	Goose's Neck	167
Chapter 20	The Bladewood	176
Chapter 21	Hide and Seek	184
Chapter 22	Romulus and Remus	190
Chapter 23	Trouble in Halcyon	202
Chapter 24	Disappearances	211
Chapter 25	The Winds of War	223
Chapter 26	Traitor for a Higher Cause	231
Chapter 27	Unleashing the Dogs of War	235
Chapter 28	Chaos	237
Chapter 29	War	240
Chapter 30	Rescue	251

Chapter 31	Commando Raid	260
Chapter 32	In the Eye of the Hurricane	266
Chapter 33	Fugitives	280
Chapter 34	The Battle for Halcyon	286
Chapter 35	A New Life	298
The End		301
Glossary		303
Acknowledgements		311
About the Author		313

Books by Peter Kazmaier

The Halcyon Cycle
The Halcyon Dislocation
The Battle for Halcyon

An Apologetic Prequel to *The Halcyon Dislocation*
**Questioning Your Way to Faith. Learning to
Disagree without Being Disagreeable**

Northern Wild

Pishon River
(also called the Halcyon River)

The Great Gorge

Giant Steps

Skull Desert

Lake Tolbar

Skull Mountains

Ruined City of Arkand

Westport

Arlana's Home

Erand Gabur

Southern Wild

Map of Eastern Feiramar

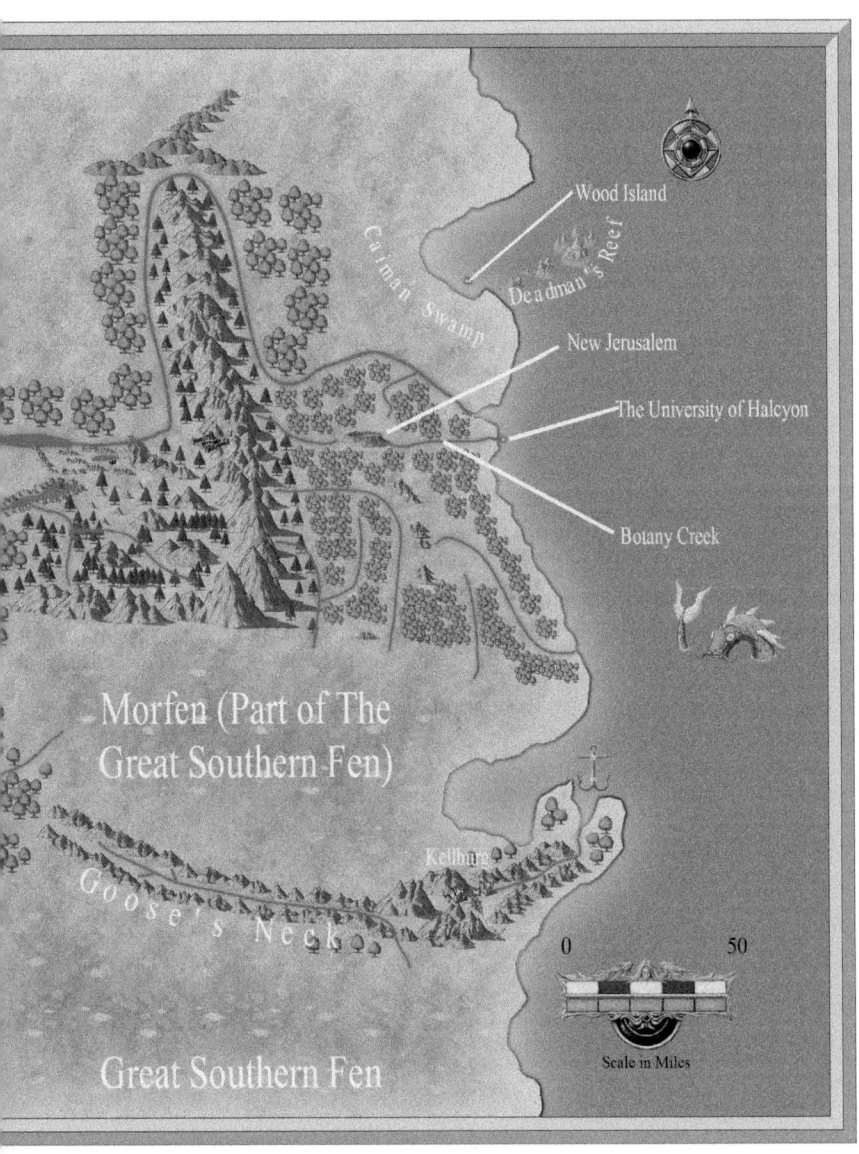

The Halcyon River Region

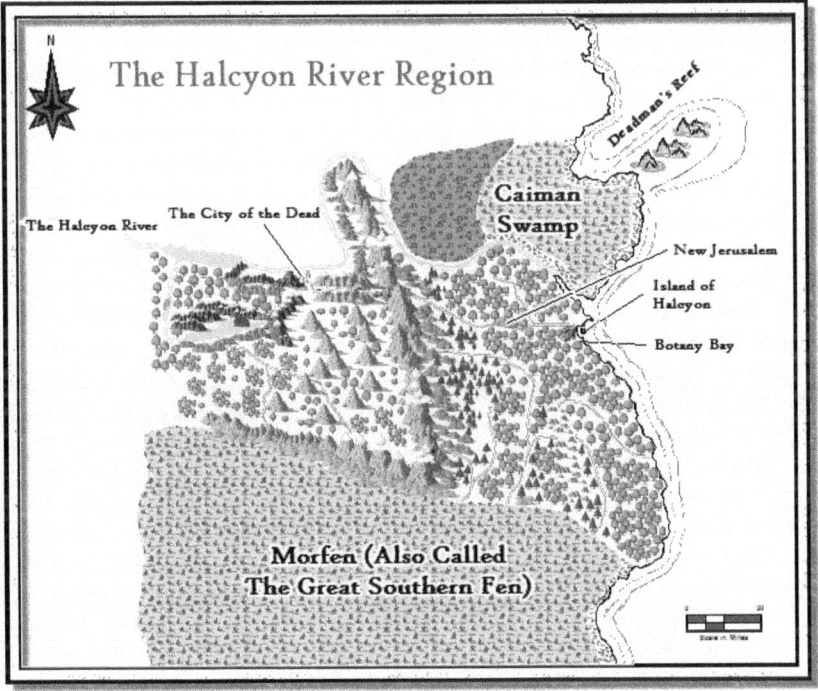

Map of the Island of Halcyon

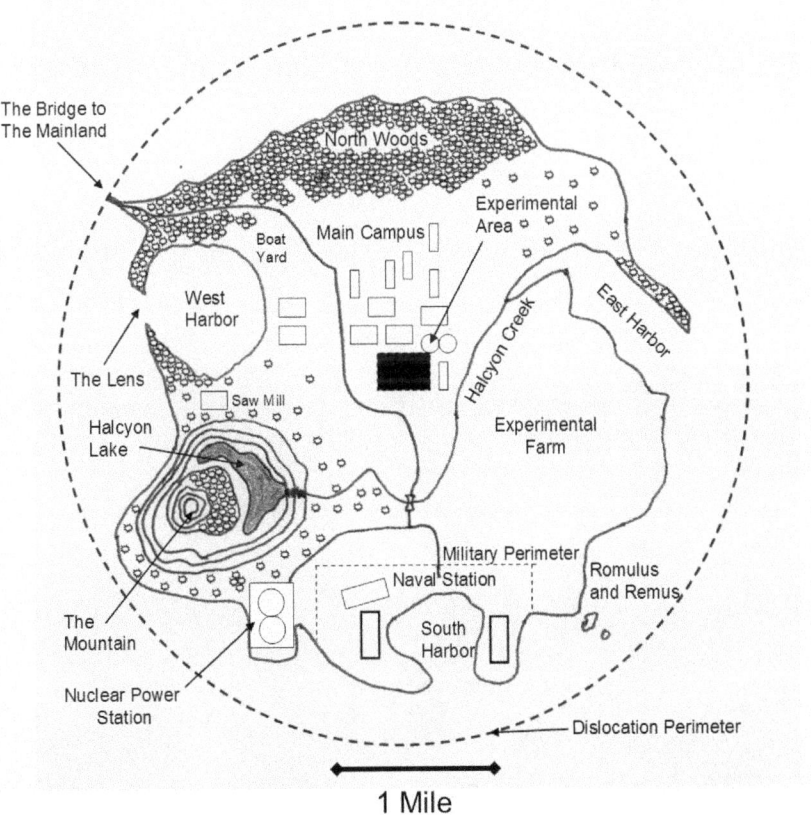

The City of the Dead

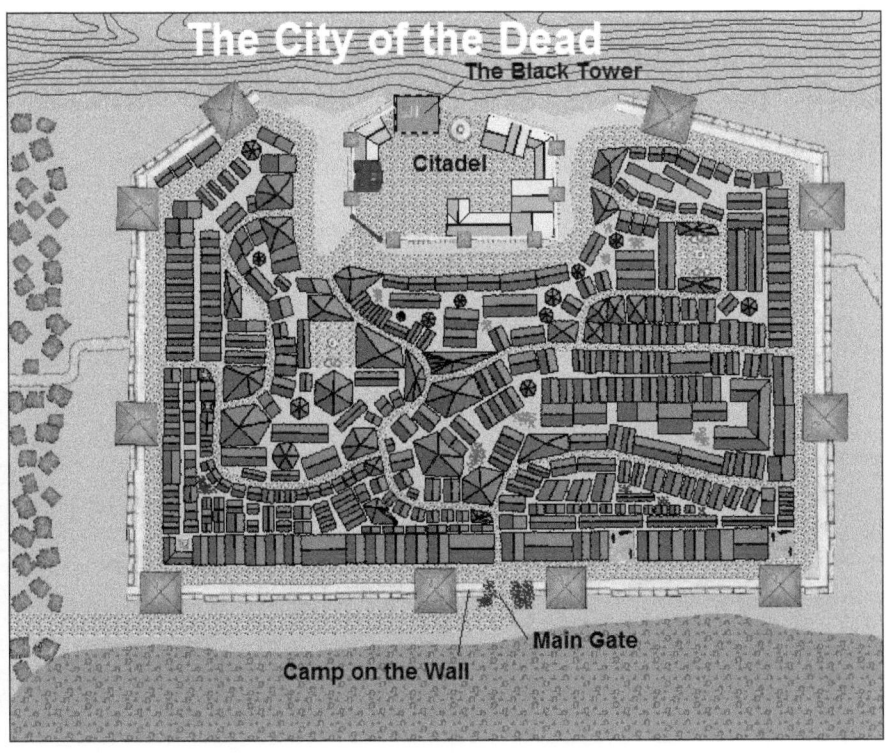

Chapter 1

The City of the Dead

Dave Schuster looked up the cave tunnel at his companion. The green luminescence from the lumi-lichen covering the wall provided just enough light to see that his friend had stopped before a dark crack leading off to the left.

"Is this the way, Hanomer?" Dave asked.

Hanomer, a badger-like creature, turned toward him. "Yes, friend Dave, I think it is. I'll take a closer look."

Hanomer had a third hand at the end of his prehensile tail and used this hand to search in his haversack. He produced a gourd about eight inches long, narrow at one end and bulbous at the other. Hanomer stroked the plant with his hand and the plant began to glow with a yellow-white light. With each successive touch, the light grew brighter. Apparently satisfied with the light intensity, Hanomer thrust the light gourd into a notch in the rock with his third hand. Dave could see the bright light of the gourd throw the ragged edges of the crack into sharp relief.

"I'm sure, friend Dave, this is the right way. It should be wide enough for you." Hanomer, tall for a *Hansa* at four feet, led the way as Dave turned sideways and squeezed into the crack to follow him. Dave whistled in relief to see that this side passage widened after the initial opening. Hanomer led him down the narrow winding passage for several hundred steps until they came to an open space. Hanomer stopped and raised his right fist in warning.

"Friend Dave," Hanomer whispered, "I still don't think this is a good idea. We're very close to Meglir's Citadel and there will be many Apemen guarding this place, and now that Meglir has taken over Hoffstetter's body, Meglir could be anywhere in these passages with an army of Apemen. Won't you reconsider and go back?"

"I know Hanomer," said Dave. "We have discussed this before. We came all this way because we have to know if Meglir is planning to attack us at our colony of Eleytheria or if he's going to head down river to attack my home island.

"You told me Hanomer, this passage was rarely used. So we should be safe. We only need to have a look to see if Meglir is preparing to march, then we'll know what to do.

"As you will, friend Dave," said Hanomer sighing, "Everything I said about this passage is true. We won't be directly over the Citadel but farther to the west and high up so you can still look into the citadel square. We'll be close enough that you still should get the information you seek."

Hanomer resumed his stealthy advance down the passage, and soon the tunnel ended at a narrow opening high up on the mountain side. Far below them, off to their right, Dave saw the high walls of the rectangular citadel, towering above the deserted City of the Dead. From the inside of the citadel wall, buildings jutted out, opening onto a large parade square in the center. Although the city no longer had people, it did have Apemen—soulless caricatures of humanity. Dave saw the square was filled with Apemen. With their lumbering gait they carried supplies to fill a line of wagons that crowded the center of the square. Dave also saw some of the Turncoats who had been part of the Halcyon expeditionary force, but had defected to Meglir, the power under the mountain. The Turncoats didn't help with the loading, but sat around the periphery. Most had rifles but a few had switched to crossbows.

I wonder how many bullets they have left. They'll all be using crossbows soon.

"They're definitely planning something Hanomer," whispered Dave, "but which way are they going to go, that's the million dollar question. Are they going to go east to Halcyon or west to Eleytheria?"

"What is a 'million dollar question?'" asked Hanomer.

"It means a very important question." Dave watched silently for a few moments more. He had seen enough. "I guess, Hanomer, we have the information we need. Meglir's about to move and we have to assume he's going to move against us at Eleytheria. If he moves against

Halcyon, there's nothing we can do to help them anyway, but if he moves against us, we need to be ready and we need to have an escape plan, in case he overruns us. Let's head back.

Dave followed Hanomer as they retraced their steps back down the tunnel. They finally reached a part of the tunnel labyrinth that Dave had remembered from his previous visits and he realized that they were heading back to Hanomer's deserted village on Knife Lake.

"Hanomer, we're not heading out the way we came in. You're taking us back to your village."

"Yes friend Dave. I'm glad you are remembering the passages. Since Meglir and the Apemen are so busy loading their wagons, I wanted to stop by my village to recover some gifts and heirlooms my father had left me. When we abandoned the village in desperate haste at the attack of the Apemen and Turncoats, I didn't have time to collect all my valuables to take them with me."

Dave could hear the roar of a waterfall and they entered a cavern with a sandy floor and a stream of water gushing out of a crack, high in the rock wall, and plunging into a lake at their feet. Ahead of them, the lake narrowed to a channel. In the distance, Dave could see the subdued sunlight of early evening as the channel opened into the Knife Lake. The last time the *Hansa* had paddled into the long, narrow lake from the underground pool, Dave had just been rescued from certain death at the hands of the Apemen by the *Hansa*.

"What do we do now Hanomer? There are no boats. Do we swim?"

"We could swim friend Dave, but there is a better way, not as fast as the paddle, but it will keep us dry." Hanomer led the way to a narrow passage at the left side of the cavern.

They came out in the long, steep-sided valley that housed Hanomer's village on the edge of Knife Lake. Night had fallen and the overcast sky made the night dark. Nevertheless, Hanomer unerringly guided them across the meadow that sloped down to the fijord-like mountain lake when they came to the village. The huts seemed like dark mounds and Dave could smell lingering smoke and taste ash from the burned village in the gentle breeze. Hanomer's third hand tugged at Dave's jacket as Hanomer wound his way around the debris of the village. Finally he stopped.

"I will go in friend Dave."

Hanomer dug his way into the wreckage. Dave decided to follow him. Since most of the dwelling was underground and only 'the veranda' was burned; the main part of Hanomer's home and belongings were intact. Hanomer activated his light gourd.

"Friend Dave," said Hanomer. "I thank the Creator they were very hasty when they burned the village. They did not go into our underground dwellings and only burned the entrance. I hope that which my father gave me, has not been disturbed."

Hanomer disappeared into a back room and came out with a small pouch which he strapped to his belt.

"Now we can go friend Dave." They were moving towards the entrance, when Hanomer put his hand on Dave's arm.

Dave heard Hanomer's voice in his mind. **Stop friend Dave. I hear someone outside.**

Dave stopped and strained his ears.

Faintly he heard the words, "I tell you I saw 'em go in here."

"Okay, I believe you, but we're not going in. We have 'em trapped. We'll wait for them to come out."

Hanomer pulled on Dave's arm and led him back into the deepest part of his home. Using his light gourd, Hanomer searched the back wall. He found what he was looking for and then moved a cupboard to reveal a small tunnel. Hanomer entered the tunnel and motioned for Dave to follow. When Dave had squeezed in and found a small room, Hanomer reached back and pulled the cupboard into place. Hanomer's third hand grasped Dave's *Hansa* buckskin jacket and then guided Dave down the passage. Hanomer extinguished his light gourd and climbed out of a trap door that led to the burned-out hulk of a wooden shed not far from his home. Dave joined him and looked back. It was too dark for him to see clearly until he saw one of the men light up a cigarette. "They're Turncoats," he whispered. A bullet kicked up the dirt at their feet. With the rifle report ringing in their ears, Hanomer, clasping Dave's wrist with his third hand, began running down the path. Dave heard the men curse and begin pursuing them.

How can they see in the dark?

Still this was Hanomer's home and he led them, using all available cover, unerringly to the edge of the forest high up on the hill.

Once in the woods, Hanomer abruptly changed direction. After another hundred paces, Hanomer clambered across a ridge of rock and pulled Dave under some hanging vines into a cave. Breathlessly, Dave listened. He could feel the pounding of his heart. There was no sound of pursuit.

Have they given up the chase? Dave wondered.

A twig snapped.

"Quiet you lummox," a gruff voice said. "Stop and use your ears. Are they still runnin'?" After a short period of silence, another voice said, "I don't hear anythin', boss."

"I don't either. They're either bein' quiet or have gone to ground. Jenkins you take your group and head up the path. The rest of you are with me. Spread out, look under every bush and shoot anythin' that moves. With our night vision goggles we should have an advantage."

Hanomer's third hand pulled Dave further into the cave. He touched Dave's arm and Dave heard Hanomer's voice in his mind:

Now we wait!

Hanomer returned from his third reconnoiter to the cave entrance.

"Friend Dave, I think the Turncoats have finally given up the search. They have built a fire in the meadow at the edge of the forest. We can get away now."

"Get away? Friend Hanomer, we should creep up to the campfire and overhear their talk."

"Friend Dave, what if this is a trap? What if someone is waiting for us?"

"I want to hear what they're saying. Sitting that close to the fire, their night vision goggles won't help them…"

"Friend Dave what are 'night vision googles?'"

"They are machines that help men see in the dark."

"This is very dangerous, friend Dave."

"But worth the risk. We will learn more from their words than we learned from watching the preparations in the square. Let me go by myself. There is no point in both of us risking our necks."

"No, friend Dave, I will guide you in. Follow my direction."

Hanomer led Dave to the edge of the forest about one hundred paces from the fire. He then climbed a large pine to look for a possible trap. Hanomer made no sound. After about ten minutes he returned.

"There are eight men around the fire and eight haversacks," said Hanomer. "I think they have all returned. Follow me."

Hanomer led Dave back into the forest until he found a brook. He followed the channel of the brook to the edge of the forest.

I've learned a lot from Hanomer. A year ago you would have heard me stumbling through this creek bed a mile off.

Hanomer stopped Dave and guided him over the edge of the creek bed to a cluster of bushes near the campfire. Ahead of them, eight men were just finishing their rations.

"No Jenkins, Meglir is not goin' to complain because we ain't goin' to tell him we lost 'em. This was ordinary—nothin' special to report see. Otherwise we'll catch it for losing 'em and our fat will be in the fire."

"So boss, which way is he goin'? East or west?"

"Don't rightly know. Meglir doesn't tell us anything, even though we jumped ship and joined him. Still I can use my head and I think west. Why else would he send us to scout this route? We need the practice of a simple operation before we tackle Halcyon. Those Apemen zombies can't handle boats. Still Hoffstetter—I should say Meglir—needs to use boats so he's waiting until our boys have built two boats for him. My guess is that he'll lead the Apemen up the coast while we ferry supplies up for him as he takes that island. Those guys in that splinter colony have had lots of time to grow comfortable. Taking it should be a piece of cake."

Dave had heard enough. He gave Hanomer a tug indicating he wanted he wanted to go back. They backtracked and then headed off through the woods for Eleytheria.

Chapter 2

Council of War

Dave and Hanomer had been pushing hard since they had left Hanomer's village to get back to Eleytheria. When they finally reached the shore of Lake Tor, after a grueling week of bushwhacking, Dave wearily waved for a boat and collapsed on a rock. The weather had turned to a late August rain. He and Hanomer, soaked to the skin despite their rain gear, were too tired to talk.

When the boat eventually arrived from the island of Eleytheria, they threw their packs into the stern, and stretched out for the short ride. Floyd Linder and Al Gleeson were waiting for them on the shore, wearing their ponchos. Several of the *Hansa* had joined them, and sang a song of greeting to Hanomer and Dave. The song, in deference to Dave, recalled his slaying of the Rokash and his earning of his *Hansa* name, Rokomer.

Dave looked at Al, every inch the scholar, standing beside Floyd. Even though at 5' 11", Al was only slightly shorter than Floyd, Floyd's athletic physique accentuated the difference, and along with his shaven head, made him look much bigger.

Al cleaned the water off his glasses and said, "You fellows look exhausted, why don't you come back to my house, get out of those wet clothes and have something to eat?"

"We are wet and hungry," said Dave. "However, we have some important news and so we busted our tails to get back here. We need to hold a council meeting right away."

Half an hour later, after a brief snack, and a change into dry clothes, Dave and Hanomer went to the building at the foot of the towering rock mesa call the Torburg, where the council had gathered. The council consisted of equal numbers of refugees from Halcyon and *Hansa* that had come from Hanomer's deserted village. Dave related their story in detail.

"So you think they are likely coming for us, as we had long feared?" asked Al.

"Yes," said Dave.

"The question is what to do," said Floyd, "fight or flee."

"We could load up our boats and head up river," said Al.

"But we know from the *Hansa*," here Floyd nodded to Hanomer, "that the Halcyon River enters a deep gorge not far from here. Will we ever get out?"

"Friend Al, said Bandomer, another one of the *Hansa*, "we have not explored beyond the entrance of the gorge, so we cannot say. Still we could head up Lake Tor and climb the Spray Falls and so make our way to the City of the Trees, as a way of escape."

Al leaned forward over the table and placed his hands on his chin as if considering Bandomer's suggestion. Finally he said, "The City of the Trees is even closer to the City of the Dead than we are, and then Meglir would have us all trapped in one place. What if he burns us out? I think we need to keep all of our options open. Meglir can only move his Apemen if he goes along to control them. It seems to me the last thing we want to do is get everyone into one place."

"We don't yet know what other options we have available. I also think that moving to the City of the Trees so soon, would be a mistake and would make life easier for Meglir," said Dave.

Al looked out the window at the towering mesa at the back of the island. "We also chose this place because of the old fastness, the Torburg. A long siege by Meglir would buy everyone time. I would rather be up on that mountain fighting Apemen who cannot climb very well than be surprised by them, as we try to find a trail to safety through unknown territory with our families."

"Still," said Floyd, "since the Apemen can't handle boats, the escape to the City of the Trees is one option. I wish we had one that would draw Meglir further from Halcyon."

Dave stood up. "Come on Hanomer, we need to get going."

"What are you thinking?" asked Al.

"I'm hearing that plan A is to get ready to retreat to the Torburg. I suppose plan B is to head up Lake Tor, haul our stuff up past the Spray Falls and go to the City of the Trees. We need a plan C that would force Meglir to follow us further away from Halcyon and so buy everyone else some time.

"Hanomer, we need to cross Lake Tor, and head west. We could scout the gorge and see if that route is open to us. We may also be able to move west or south. If we leave right away, it should only take us two weeks or so. We'll be back in plenty of time before Meglir can move his force up here."

Chapter 3

The Halfmen

"What are they, Hanomer?" Dave whispered.

He peered cautiously over the edge of a bluff from his hiding place under a stunted elderberry bush. The bluff dropped about sixty yards straight down and then leveled out into a sandy, undulating desert. The desert stretched before him to the south and west until it became a brown smudge shimmering at the horizon, where a cluster of mountains arose.

Dave turned to his companion. Hanomer did not speak, but stretched out his long prehensile tail through the brush. The clump at the end of the tail spread into a hand. Dave offered his arm so Hanomer could touch him.

They are Halfmen, friend Dave. Very dangerous. We must stay very still. Look ahead, to that haze on the horizon. Those are the Skull Mountains in the middle of this desert, or so the Lore Masters have told me. The Halfmen live there. It is troubling that so many are so far from their home.

Dave stifled his questions and turned back to examine the creatures below. At the bottom of a steep cliff was a group of the creatures Hanomer had labeled "Halfmen."

About twenty of them sat in a circle while a couple were standing and facing west toward the desert. They were over five feet tall and their foreheads had a pronounced slope which gave them an ape-like appearance.

They did not seem to be particularly attentive to their surroundings, but rather taken up by an argument. Their loud speech, which seemed to be all snarls, reached even to the top of the cliff. Dave could make out the occasional word, so they spoke the Common Speech. Some of them amused themselves by tearing up foliage and throwing it away. Others simply spent the time throwing stones at a large cactus just outside the circle. One stone fell short and glanced off a rock, hitting the nearest Halfman in the leg, who howled with rage and hurled himself at the thrower.

Something is not right. The eyes of the Halfman at the edge of the semicircle keep wandering to the top of the bluff.

Dave again felt Hanomer's tail appendage touch his arm.

Friend Dave, I am very uneasy. Let us go back; these Halfmen have sharp eyes and they must not see us.

The two fighting Halfmen were rolling on the ground and the whole group had sprung up to surround them and egg them on with jeers and laughter.

With all this commotion, now would be a good time to leave.

As Dave turned to suggest this, he saw Hanomer had already begun to creep quietly out of the elderberry bush. Dave carefully did the same. Although a big man, he was able to extricate himself from the bush, without making a sound.

A year ago I would have chosen my spot less wisely and shaken the whole bush as I tried to leave. I've learned a lot of woodcraft from the Hansa.

Staying low to the ground, Hanomer crept back from the cliff edge to a hollow where he rose to his full height of four feet. He straightened his vest, which was lined with pockets and pouches, donned his food pouch and picked up his bow and quiver. Looking to make sure they had left nothing behind, he began to retrace the path through the woods to the east. Dave belted on his sword and picked up his backpack and crossbow. Looking over his shoulder one last time at the cliff edge, he followed Hanomer into the woods.

The animal trail they were following descended gradually toward the northeast. The edge of the forest consisted of stunted oak trees which grew larger as they penetrated further into the woods.

"What were those things, Hanomer? They didn't look like Apemen," whispered Dave.

"No friend Dave, they're different from *Kilk*. The Apemen that captured you had nothing inside them to talk to. No spirit inside to give an answer. They're just empty shells. That's why Meglir or another

Bent One need to be nearby to use them as tools. These Halfmen have also been corrupted by the Bent Ones, like the Apemen, but they breed like other animals and think for themselves. Still they're altogether bent. The Lore Masters have told us they hate all living things and kill without reason or cause."

"Are they under the control of Meglir?" asked Dave.

"Maybe. The Bent Ones corrupted all things to control them. If a Bent One were here, they would be doubly dangerous because the Bent One would give a purpose and strategy to their actions—an ability they normally don't have. Thankfully there have been no Bent Ones here other than Meglir for many long years. Still, the Halfmen had better not see us or we could be meat for their pot. They would eat *Hansa* or even you, friend Dave, if we give them the chance."

"Do you think they saw us?"

"I'm not sure, friend Dave. Still one of them seemed to look toward the top of the cliff."

Dave was filled with a sense of foreboding. He loaded a steel-tipped quarrel onto his crossbow and held it at the ready. Hanomer broke into a quiet trot and sped back, retracing their trail. After about one hundred paces, they rounded a curve and came to an area dense with young pine trees.

As Hanomer loped by a large boulder, a dreadful figure with the horned head of a buffalo on broad shoulders like a Minotaur, leapt out and swung his club at Hanomer. Hanomer ducked and flattened himself against the ground. The club cracked against the boulder face as it went wide.

The man-sized figure raised the club again to crush Hanomer, prone on the ground. Dave's bolt struck the monster in the chest and the second blow missed Hanomer's head, scattering dirt as the club bit into the earth. As the stricken figure collapsed, the buffalo mask fell away, revealing the head of a Halfman.

Hanomer immediately sprang to his feet and set off in a new direction, waving to Dave to follow. They had not gone more than a hundred paces when they heard a terrible howl of rage behind them. Hanomer redoubled his pace. They heard another howl off to their left. Dave concentrated on placing one foot in front of the other and not stumbling.

By early evening, the sweat poured down Dave's face after eight hours of being chased. If it hadn't been for Hanomer's ability to sense where the Halfmen were, they would have run into a trap on at least four occasions. Despite all of their efforts, they were still heading west and south. They wanted to head east and get back to familiar terrain, but instead, they were relentlessly driven away from home and toward Halfmen territory and The Great Desert. Sunset could not be too far off now. During the night, Dave hoped that with Hanomer's unerring guidance, they would be able to double back and head for home.

Hanomer moved stealthily ahead of Dave down a narrow path. The evening sunlight dappled the ground, and the pungent smell of pine sap hung in the air. Hanomer had chosen densely clad terrain so they might remain as inconspicuous as possible. He stopped. Ahead of them the game trail descended into a shallow ravine. A brook trickled under the dense foliage at the bottom. Hanomer peered up and down the ravine and sniffed the air as if faced with a difficult choice. Finally, coming to a decision, he crept down into the ravine and turned left. They headed upstream. The brook ran in the general direction of the great river to their right and eventually plunged over a precipice into the Halcyon River in the canyon far below.

Hanomer stopped suddenly. He frantically signaled for Dave to go back. Just then came the sound of many feet ahead pounding toward them through the brush. Dave raced back down the path away from the sound. Hanomer followed him. After a quarter mile down the path Dave saw a dozen Halfmen crouching on the ground holding their clubs ready to strike. The Halfmen leapt to their feet and howled. Dave looked right and left for a way of escape. On both sides the ravine was too steep for him to climb. He knew he would be caught.

Clenching his teeth, Dave pulled out his sword and rushed forward. The leader gave way in surprise, and Dave was able to grab his raised wrist and give him a blow to the head with his sword hilt that sent the Halfman reeling.

Two more assailants grabbed Dave's arms.

Grunting, Dave threw one attacker off and delivered a blow to the second one before he was borne under by the weight of the Halfmen. With his face pressed into the ground amid the general guttural howl of his assailants, he saw Hanomer lying quietly facing him, his arms and legs tied.

When Dave's wrists and ankles had been tied, he and the Hanomer were thrown onto their backs. The Halfmen brought two stout saplings, and passed one each between their tied hands and feet.

"*Khar dash*," said the leader.

Two Halfmen hoisted Dave's pole onto their shoulders, staggering under the weight and began toiling up the ravine in the general direction of the desert. Dave, hanging from the pole like a slaughtered buck, felt the jolt of every step on his wrists. Twisting his head, he saw Hanomer being carried on a pole behind him. Dave's wrists bruised, then bled. Every stumble and jolt by the carriers wrenched his shoulders.

It was the second night since Dave and Hanomer had been captured. The Halfmen had stopped by an oasis that had some hardy vegetation and a shallow pool of water in a rock depression in the center. They were now crowded around the watering hole and for once during a stop, Hanomer and Dave had been left alone at the fringe of the encampment.

"Why haven't they killed us?" whispered Dave. He had been meaning to ask this question from the outset, but the beating he had received the first time he had tried to talk to Hanomer, had discouraged him from trying again.

"I do not know, friend Dave," said Hanomer. "I am sure they do not have anything good in mind for us. They do not care for their own folk so they would not care about us, especially since we killed their chieftain."

"Oh great!" said Dave. "There's still something I don't get, Hanomer. Why didn't you make a break for it at the ravine? I couldn't have made it up the side, but I think you could have with that handy tail of yours."

"I could have escaped, friend Dave but it was my duty to stay with you. I am here to cheer you up so to speak." Hanomer smiled.

"Hanomer, knowing you were following me, ready to help me escape would have given me a lot more comfort that being tied up with you now."

"Escape's no problem."

"What do you mean?"

Hanomer wrinkled his muzzle in a grin. "The Halfmen haven't tied my tail!" He unclenched and clenched his third hand on his tail for emphasis. "These Halfmen don't know *Hansa*, so I kept my third hand hidden. Still, even if I untied us now, we would not escape. We are two days into the desert and have no water. Even if I knew where to find an oasis, unless we had a big head start, they'd have us again before the next sunset."

He flicked his tail over and touched Dave's wrist to emphasize the significance of his words.

The moon would not rise for many hours yet and it would be a dark night. As light faded, the two guards returned. The first stopped by Dave and kicked him in the ribs.

"Are you comfy, big fellow," jeered the guard in the Common Tongue. "I'm goin' to enjoy cracking your bones with my teeth."

He then went on and did the same to Hanomer. Tiring of his sport, he joined his comrade and they argued loudly in the Common Tongue. Still their speech sounded full of gutturals and hisses. Their tirade dwindled and the guards fell asleep as night descended; the clear sky was broken by the evening stars.

Dave was just drifting off to sleep when he woke with a start to find Hanomer's third hand covering his mouth.

Wake up Dave and lie quiet. Someone is coming.

Dave shifted his eyes to look toward the fringe of the oasis. It was very dark and he could see nothing. Then he noticed that some of the blackness was moving. As the shadowy figure approached, Dave realized it was tall, much taller than a Halfman–almost as tall as he was, but slender. He saw the glint of a knife and then Hanomer was free. Hanomer struggled free of the pole, bowed courteously to the figure, and then crept back behind Dave to see if anyone was coming from the main camp of the Halfmen.

The dark figure then crouched over Dave and cut his bonds. Dave tried to use his hands to get to his feet. He had to bite back a yelp as pain shot up his arm when he put weight on his wrists. Without a word the stranger clasped Dave's shoulder and helped him to his knees and then his feet. Without letting go, lest Dave stumble, the stranger helped him out of the oasis into the desert. Dave looked around for the sleeping forms of the guards, but evidently they had returned to the main camp.

After about two hundred paces, they entered a depression in the sand where two horses stood.

"Can you ride?" said a soft voice in the Common Tongue. It was the voice of a woman.

"Yes!"

"Good, then I want you to ride my mount. She will not let you fall. I will carry our little *Hansa* brother with me on the pack horse."

She helped Dave into the saddle and placed the reins into his swollen hands. She picked up a sword leaning against a rock, strapped it under her cloak and then lifted Hanomer onto the pack horse. She leapt up lightly behind him and urged her mount out into the desert. Dave's horse followed without any urging.

They travelled at a fast trot for about an hour. The pack horse stayed about ten paces ahead. Dave's mind was full of questions, but he knew the last thing he wanted was to let Halfmen hear him if they were already on their trail.

Finally, the stranger slowed her horse to a walk and fell in beside Dave.

"When I first followed you and Hanomer, I thought you were one of us, even though you speak the Common Tongue with a pronounced accent." she said quietly. "However, Hanomer and I have been speaking Mindtalk and he has made me realize that you are not an Ancient, although you look like one. I have never met one of the Lesser Men."

"Lesser Men?" said Dave puzzled.

"That is our name for you. I mean no disrespect."

"You mean you've seen people like me before?"

"Seen? No. On our continent of Feiramar, your kind were all killed by the plague unleashed by Meglir about half a millenium ago."

Dave had to think about this for a while.

"By the way, my name is Arlana and I am one of the Ancients."

"Do you mean that you are very old?" Dave asked.

She laughed gently, without condescension.

"No, not at all. Indeed I am only twenty years old—much too young to take on the duties of a Guardian or Ranger. Our people are called the Ancients by Hanomer's people, because we live for many years and have remained unchanged for a long time."

"I thought Hanomer's wise ones said that you had all left?"

"They said that did they? That's a long story, which can be told, but not now."

"So how did you find us, and why did you rescue us?"

"I came across the Halfmen carrying captives. I know what the Halfmen do to captives so I followed until I had a chance to rescue you.

"So where are we going?"

"Ahead is the Ruined City of Arkand. You must be special captives indeed, to avoid immediate death at the hands of the Halfmen, and be carried back to the Skull Mountains, in the center of the desert. Since you are great prizes, they will follow us, but if we reach the Ruined City, they have such fear of that place, that we will be safe.

The moon came up. In the moonlight, Dave could see that Arlana had light, braided hair that hung almost to her waist. Her complexion was dark and even in the moonlight he could only see her bright eyes on her dark face. No wonder she had almost been invisible when she had crept up to the Halfmen's camp.

She turned to Dave. "Friend, how did you come to be here? As I said, we have not seen a Lesser Man in about five hundred years. Did you come from the continent of Abaddon, across the Eastern Sea?"

"No, I've never heard of Abaddon. Our coming here is a long story," said Dave.

"We have many hours of riding ahead of us. We will ride and then walk to give the horses a rest, but we will not stop until we reach Arkand. Your tale will help to pass the time."

"I'm curious," said Dave. "Tell me about Abaddon and then I will tell you my story."

"Hmm," said Arlana. "I will tell you the little I have learned. To learn more, you will have to ask someone who knows much more than I.

"Abaddon is a large continent across the eastern ocean. It is a land, surrounded by very high mountains. Curiously enough, the main part of the continent is far below sea level. The air is thick and so supports many beasts that could not survive here. In the center is a deep chasm to an even lower part of the continent which we call Sheol or the pit. The whole continent is inhabited by corrupted Ancients we call the Bent Ones. Sheol is even worse. I have heard that even the Bent Ones don't go there.

"That's all I can tell you. Now tell me your story, Dave."

"I come from another world," said Dave.

"Another world? Did you come by yourself?"

"No, there were many thousands of us on an island. My people have many machines and tools and one of our new machines unexpectedly brought us here."

"I see," said Arlana thoughtfully.

"I was part of a university," continued Dave.

"What is 'university'?"

"It is a school and a place where we try new things that we call experiments. One of those experiments that used new machines brought us here. We say it 'dislocated' us."

"So your machine created some kind of portal or door between our worlds."

"I guess so." Dave had expected her to be surprised by the Dislocation and the presence of another world, but she seemed thoughtful rather than surprised, as if a portal were not all that unusual.

"Our island appeared on the coast at the mouth of The Halcyon River, the river Hanomer calls the Pishon. We met no people, so we spent our first while exploring the coast. Eventually we headed up river and found the City of the Dead."

"The City of the Dead," said Arlana in a whisper. "We are forbidden from going there. That's why Hanomer's people think we have disappeared."

"I can see the reason for the prohibition. I was captured by Apemen and only survived because Hanomer and his people rescued me."

"I took him back to my village, and taught him the Common Speech," said Hanomer.

Dawn looked to be near.

"That is quite a tale, Dave. I think there is much more to tell and I will ask for more details later." said Arlana.

She stopped her horse and dismounted. Dave looked at her in the morning light and could see her clearly for the first time. She was just under six feet tall, slender, with long golden hair and grey eyes. Her skin was dark chocolate brown. Facing the sun, she spread her arms and Dave saw her skin color lighten before his eyes to white in a matter of seconds.

Dave swallowed hard. There were, of course, many races and ethnicities in Halcyon and so different skin colors were not given a second thought, but this! This was uncanny. This was beyond uncanny!

His surprise showed on his face. As Arlana turned from the sun, she looked at Dave, laughed gently and then turned grave.

"I see Dave, that you were surprised by my ability to change my skin color. I remember my lessons now. Your people have lost that ability. I am sorry I startled you."

"But your hair and eyes."

"No, those do not change color, but my people can change their skin color from light to dark as needed." Her skin color darkened to chocolate and then lightened again. Finally she returned to her dark complexion.

"The dark hue will protect me from the sun. Since your people have lost our ability, here you will need a blanket to protect you."

What does she mean my people have lost this ability? We never had it, Dave thought to himself.

She untied a blanket from behind Dave's saddle and Dave draped it over his head to keep off the blazing sun. They had a brief drink, watered the horses from the water skins, and then set out again. Arlana kept looking over her shoulder with concern on her face.

We've been moving so fast. Surely those Halfmen can't overtake us at this pace.

Chapter 4

The Ruined City of Arkand

It was the evening of the second day, when Dave woke with a start. He felt so tired. He had been falling asleep all day and only the fear of falling off his horse had kept him struggling to stay awake. They had walked and ridden for almost 48 hours, with only the shortest of stops. Arlana had found two small oases to water their horses and replenish their water skins.

As Dave looked around, he noticed they had left the desert behind and were descending a broad, gentle slope that was mainly grass with the occasional stunted tree. Ahead he saw a river in the valley and beyond that a series of rocky outcroppings.

"Something is not quite right." He mused, struggling to get his torpid thoughts in order.

No, the rocks were too regular, and some of those features must be the remains of walls. He was looking at rubble and partly collapsed structures that once were a city. But what a city! He could see the ruins climbing up from the river to a plateau, but he could not see where the city ended. Even the small part he now saw, dwarfed the City of the Dead.

Arlana had also been looking across the river. The bank descended steeply to the water. She urged her horse upstream searching for a place to cross. Dave's horse followed her. After about three hundred yards, she descended a shallow slope and then began to cross. The river was deep, but had little current at this point and soon her horse was swimming. Dave's horse did not hesitate but splashed into the water. It stopped in the shallows, bent down to drink, and then also stepped into the deeper water.

The cool water on Dave's hot, sweaty legs felt so good. He leaned over and with his free hand, splashed water on his face as the horse began to swim. In about fifty paces, the horse touched bottom and began to clamber up the shore.

Arlana stopped and dismounted. "Praise the Creator, we made it! The Halfmen will not dare to follow here." She took her water skins off her horse, and with Hanomer began to fill them in the river.

Dave was too tired to speak. He slid off his horse and sat down. *I ought to help.*

"Wake up! Wake up!"

Dave could feel himself being shaken roughly, but it seemed that even if all the Halfmen in the desert were attacking, he could not rouse himself. He felt a cool cloth on his forehead. Arlana was mopping his face.

"I know you're tired, Dave, but we only have a little way further to reach the heart of the city where we'll be safe. The Halfmen could still shoot us with their arrows here." Her voice was compassionate and understanding. She hid well the extreme exhaustion she was feeling.

Dave struggled to his feet and mounting his horse once again, began a slow climb up a rubble-strewn street. After a mile, they reached a crest, and he saw the city lying before them. They were on a flat table of land that stretched about ten miles to three jagged mountain peaks, which rose sharply from the floor of the plain to a height of perhaps six thousand feet, so that the tops were snow covered. Several streams plunged down the steep sides of the mountains, and disappeared among the ruins of the city.

"Tragund, Arkand, and Elecor, the three peaks of Arkand," said Arlana. "It's not much further and then we shall find water and shelter. If we're fortunate, I'll remember where the storehouses of the Guardians are and then we will also have a good meal."

"All I really want is a good sleep," mumbled Dave.

Arlana paused at a fork in the road. She led them to the right. Ten minutes later, she breathed a sigh of relief and dismounted in front of a heavy gate before an intact building. Arlana pushed on the gate. It swung open. She led her horse in. Dave urged his horse to follow, bending low to avoid the lintel. After passing through a short tunnel, they came to a courtyard.

"No one is here," said Arlana, with a disappointed edge to her voice. "Still, we have many safe houses in the city and the Guardians may be using the others."

Dave slid off his horse and Arlana took the reins and led the horses into an enclosure on the far side of the cobblestone courtyard. She returned a minute later, and led the others up a stairway to a room. Dave found a pile of heather, collapsed into his bed, and was asleep before he could even say "good night."

Dave woke to a ravenous hunger. A delicious aroma wafted up through an opening in the wall, which had once been a window. Leaving his sleeping room, and descending the stair to the courtyard, he saw Hanomer with his back to him, tending a small fire in an open-air, stone fireplace. Three large fish were roasting on the metal grating.

"Where did you get the fish, Hanomer?"

Hanomer turned and smiled. "The Creator provided them. There is a creek to the west of us, that runs through a wooded green in the middle of the city and I speared them in a pool." Hanomer showed Dave a crude spear he had made by fastening a knife onto a pole.

"It sounds more like you provided them rather than the Creator."

"Friend Dave, I didn't put the fish into the creek. The Creator also made it possible for me to learn the skill necessary. Just because I had to work hard to catch the fish, doesn't mean the Creator had no role in it. Many of his gifts go unnoticed if I don't train myself to see them."

"Have it your way," said Dave absently, thinking about the delicious fish.

Dave, seeing it would take a few minutes until the fish were ready, pulled his thoughts away from the them and his hunger. "Let me ask you something, Hanomer, when you and Arlana speak of this Creator, are you talking about a person or something else?"

"I'm sorry, friend Dave, I don't really understand your question. By 'a person' do you mean someone like you or like me?"

"I don't mean the Creator has to look like one of us, but is the Creator someone you could talk to, who would listen and might even talk back."

"What else could the Creator be?"

"Well," said Dave. "Some people believe the Creator is a Life Force, a Law or a Principle that's behind everything. You know like the Law of Gravity."

"Law of Gravity?" said Hanomer.

"The rule or principle that makes your bow drop to the ground when you let it fall out of your hand. Instead of making your bow fall, this law would bring everything around us including us into being."

Hanomer thought for a long moment, clearly puzzled by the concept as he turned the filets on the fire.

"Friend Dave, when you pick up your bow to shoot it in battle, do you ask it for permission?"

"No, of course not!"

"But," continued Hanomer, "If you wanted me or Arlana to go into battle with you, would you ask permission?"

"Of course, you're people and the bow is an inanimate object. There's nothing even to ask of the bow."

"It seems to me if the Creator is not person, but like the bow, then it is a very small Creator. I don't think this world could come out of something that small."

"How is breakfast coming?" said a familiar voice.

Hanomer and Dave turned to the voice and saw Arlana leading her horse through the tunnel.

"We have fish," said Hanomer, "but no bread."

"I can help with that."

She led her horse into the courtyard. She looked exhausted. Untying a sack from the pommel she handed it to Hanomer. Without another word, she led the animal to the stables.

Dave stared after her. Her skin was a deep tan and her long golden hair was tied back in a braid that extended to her waist, swaying back and forth as she walked. She had taken off her curious green cloak and the simple white belt over her soft leather tunic accentuated her slender figure. She was the most beautiful woman he had ever seen, but he couldn't get over the changeable nature of her complexion. It seemed so unearthly. Dave didn't know whether to let himself fall in love with her, or be terrified of her. Perhaps the two were the same thing.

Hanomer handed the sack to Dave and picked up some makeshift twig and leaf dishes. He began lifting the filets onto the dishes using a knife and a branch that he had carved into a spatula.

"We have no dishes or utensils, friend Dave, so these will have to do."

"Hanomer, this smells so good I could eat it off the ground."

Dave opened the sack and found some bundles wrapped in a leaf he did not recognize. The leaves had an aroma like freshly baked bread.

There was also a pottery jar whose contents smelled like butter and made Dave's mouth water.

Arlana returned and washed her hands from a water skin. She smiled as Hanomer gave her a steaming plate of fish and sat down on a low stone wall. She extended her hands over the food and closed her eyes for a moment.

Dave watched her and her complexion darkened to a chocolate brown.

"How do you do that?" asked Dave.

"Do what, Dave?"

"Change your skin color so fast."

"I just think that I want the color to change and it does. When I was younger, the color would change without my wanting it to. Learning to control the change is part of growing up."

She reached over and touched his arm.

Dave heard a voice in his head. **Can you hear me?**

"Yes," said Dave out loud.

"Great Lady," said Hanomer. "Dave and his kin can only partly use Mindtalk. He can understand us mind-to-mind, but cannot speak. But he has the divine spark of the Creator in him, so he is not an Apeman or a Halfman. Still he is not an Ancient."

"Tell me about this place you described. I think you called it a 'verr-sit-tee.'"

"In our tongue, English, a university is a place of great learning."

"What sorts of things do you learn?"

"We learn—here he lapsed into English—chemistry, physics, biology, mathematics, psychology, and sociology."

"What are these things?" asked Arlana.

When Dave did his best to explain, Arlana said, "I have never heard of these things."

"Of course you haven't," said Dave smugly, "we're very advanced and have much knowledge and many weapons and machines you have never even dreamed of."

Dave could see Arlana's eyes flash as she stuck out her lower lip. "Your people have been weakened and broken by the Bent Ones, and you have the effrontery to tell me, after I rescued you, that your people's knowledge is like light to our darkness! You are an impertinent cub. I will have to help you grow up."

Dave could feel his face getting warm. He knew he should be conciliatory, but she had raised his hackles. "Sorry princess, sometimes the truth is hard to take. My people, in our books, know more about the universe than all the knowledge that could be found in all of your books. You do have books, don't you?"

"Of course we have books," she snapped. "You require some serious training. I will adopt you and help you learn some manners," she said with a satisfied smile forming on her lips. "Yes, youngling, I will take up your education."

"Lady Arlana," said Hanomer, "you have still not told us everything about how you came to find us."

Clever Hanomer, thought Dave, *always finding ways to keep me from getting into a fight.*

Arlana seemed to regain her composure. "No, I haven't told you that. Let me go back to the beginning and tell my story.

"My father is called Kelldor and he is Chief of the Council of Thirteen."

"What is the Council of Thirteen?" interrupted Dave.

"It is the ruling council of our people, the Gurundar which is translated as Guardians in the Common tongue. He set out two months ago for what was to be only a short trip to visit his closest friend, in the north. After he did not return, I, unwilling to simply sit by and wait, decided to look for him. I travelled to his friend, and found that he had been called away to the Ruined City of Arkand. Having lost my mother and only brother many years ago to the Halfmen, and unwilling to sit and do nothing if my father was in danger, I started near the great river Pishon, gave the Skull Mountains a wide berth by keeping to the northern edge of the desert and then cut across to go to the ruined city. It was there that I came upon this band of Halfmen carrying two captives to the Skull Mountains."

Arlana was thoughtful. She looked at Dave. "Youngling, you told me many things about your arrival here, your home, your home island, but you have not told me in detail how you met Hanomer."

As they continued to eat, Dave told her his story about how the university struggled to survive after the Dislocation, their expedition to the mainland, and his adventures in exploration, finishing with the details of his capture by Apemen in the City of the Dead. At this he saw Arlana's face turn very pale, but she said nothing.

Then Hanomer took up the tale and told about Dave's rescue by the *Hansa*, their growing friendship, and finally Meglir's release from the black obelisk by Hoffstetter.

At this Arlana started. "Our great enemy is free! My people must be told. And now Meglir has Lesser Men that he can control. I must find my father and warn him. We are no longer safe even if we stay away from *Tar-en-Gorg*, the City of the Dead, as you call it. I must find my father."

"What do you mean by saying 'now Meglir has Lesser Men that he can control?'" asked Dave.

Arlana looked searchingly at Dave. Finally, reaching a decision, she folded her arms and said, "It has been passed along in the histories of our people that many years ago, in previous ages, there were portals between our world and another. These portals occurred in special places that were marked. At that time, the Bent Ones grew strong and there was war between my forefathers and the Bent Ones. Through their arts, the Bent Ones changed and weakened the children of Ancients they had captured to make them into slaves that they could control. The Bent Ones cannot really make anything new, only bend, twist and weaken one of the creatures of the Creator. This happened here. It was said, the ability to change skin color was one of the things that was lost. They made several kinds of "Lesser Men" as we call them. Some like the Halfmen have been so corrupted that they have little, if any of the divine spark left in them. Still we do not readily kill them except under great need.

"Are there no people in your world, Dave, that can change their skin color?"

"No," said Dave. "We have people with many different skin colors, but none that can change their skin color at will."

"A world without Ancients," said Arlana to herself.

"Are there no people like me here?" asked Dave.

"There are none among us now here in our land," said Arlana. As I told you before, there once were, and they lived among us, but were all destroyed by the great plague. If there are some living with our western kindred, I do not know. For we, as the Guardians and the remnant, are not allowed to set foot in the western lands."

Dave put his hand to his head.

"Arlana how much of a color change can you achieve?" asked Dave.

Instead of answering, her skin gradually darkened to a rich chocolate brown and then began to lighten until her skin color was a pale white. The whole transformation had taken less than a minute. Dave stared at her for a moment.

How many times have I worried that I would be disliked simply because I was white? How many others with different skin colors have felt the same way? Here Arlana can be any skin color she wants and pretty well fit in wherever she wants.

Then Dave remembered his own reaction to her color change and how it had first struck him. It had been so startling.

Maybe I'm wrong, maybe she would be an outsider to everyone and no one would accept her.

Dave finished his meal in silence and didn't ask any more questions.

When Arlana finished, she set her plate aside. "I'm not a full Guardian and I only remember this safe house, because I was here on a trip as part of my education. However, at the storehouse I found a map that shows many safe houses all over the city. Since this is a base of operations for the Guardians, I should be able to find help."

"Do you want us to come along?" asked Dave.

"No," said Arlana. "I will show you the location of the storehouse and you can bring supplies here as you need them. There are also wooded greens, gardens if you like all over the city. We have taken trouble to plant them with edible foods so that we can replenish our supplies. Hanomer, perhaps you could see to provisioning us. I would like to leave the storehouse better supplied than when we found it, if possible. And another thing, do not go near the river. The Halfmen will not cross, but if they see you, they will try to kill you."

With that, Arlana led them to the stables, mounted her horse, encouraged Dave to carry Hanomer on his horse, and led their group out through the gate. A short canter brought them to a ruined building. The entrance to the storehouse was a stout, well-sealed cellar door, leading under a pile of rubble. Arlana dismounted, lifted the latch and went in. Dave also dismounted and then stooped and entered a cool subterranean chamber, filled with jars and boxes of provisions. Arlana left them to their work and returned to her search for the Guardians. Dave helped Hanomer collect and load the supplies onto the horse. They had enough to last for the next couple of days. They started the slow walk back to their temporary home.

After they had carried the supplies back and stacked them in the corner of their room, Hanomer and Dave sat down to rest.

"Is that pond you found this morning suitable for swimming?"

"Yes, friend Dave."

"Then I think I'll get cleaned up. Do you wanna come?"

"Another time, friend Dave. I am in need of some *tranquor* and I would prefer to go and explore the city alone for a while."

"Hmm, *tranquor*—time for reflection and composition. What are you composing?"

"A ballad about our adventure with the Halfmen. If I work my craft well, the whole village will want to hear it many times."

"I hope there aren't any stanzas to add to our tale. Those Halfmen give me the creeps."

"Lady Arlana is convinced they will lose interest in two or three days and go about their business," said Hanomer.

"I hope she's right. Well, while you're "tranquoring" in the city, I will tranquilize in the pond."

"I'm not understanding you, friend Dave."

"Never mind. I'm going for a swim. After all that time in the desert, there is nothing I would like better than to soak with just my nose and toes sticking out of the water."

After getting directions to the park from Hanomer, Dave followed the road that ran past their lodging for about two hundred yards where he came upon a low wall that enclosed a forested area. He found an arched gate just as Hanomer had described. The gate led to a straight, dark, tree-enshrouded tunnel, that burrowed through the dense growth. Mainly oak, maple, and beech, the ancient trees were covered with moss and the branches intertwined overhead like so many gnarled fingers. Dave stumbled. Steadying himself against the trunk of a beech tree, he saw in the gloom that roots crisscrossed the path and made footing treacherous. Despite the gloom, there was a wholesomeness about this wood. He sensed no danger; the trees appeared beautiful rather than ominous. The path bent to the left and the character of the wood changed. The trees here were of massive girth but there were fewer of them and the forest floor was carpeted in yellow star-shaped flowers. Shafts of sunlight made patches of brightness amid the blooms. Ahead a red squirrel chattered at him nervously and then darted up a tree as he approached.

The forest tunnel ended at the edge of an oval pond that was about the size of a football field. In the center of the pond was a small, heavily treed, circular island perhaps thirty feet in diameter. The shore of the pool was a rocky shingle bounded by tall sycamores. A flat tongue of rock extended across the northern boundary of the pond. He walked out onto the rock into the sunlight. The water looked clean, clear, and he could see minnows darting in the shallows.

Dave looked around. The place was secluded. He stripped off his clothes and gingerly stepped into the water. It was cold, but a delight to his desert-parched skin. He washed his clothes as best as he could with soap he had found at the house, and then spread them out on the rock to dry, while he went for a swim to the southern end of the pond. The water was so refreshing. When he dove he could see large fish in the depths. Smaller fish swam among the curving spiral strands of vallisneria. He used a leisurely side-stroke and looked at the island.

That island is unnaturally round.

He swam to the island and stood knee deep in the water on the rocky shore. The trees were a kind of oak he had never seen before with eight inch trunks spaced every four or five feet so that branches made a solid curtain like a cedar hedge along the edge of the island.

He climbed out of the water, bent the nearest branches, and wormed his way on hands and knees toward the center of the island.

"Ow!"

He had rammed his bare knee into a horizontal stem running along the ground. He swore at himself.

If you decide to go exploring, have the common sense to take some clothes along.

The horizontal stem connected the two nearest trunks. The center of the island was empty of trees but covered with a thick layer of oak leaves. He made his way to there; he saw that all the trunks were joined as if they were one tree.

He sat down on the leaves for a moment and studied the grove. There was no wind in the grove. He felt, rather than heard, very quiet voices.

Something was odd. The oak grove hedge was broken at one point. When he went over to look, he saw that the horizontal stem had been cut and an oak trunk has been dug out of the ground. The earth of the ground, like a wound, was still fresh.

This must have been dug up in the last few weeks. It looks like someone took a cutting?

Something else was odd—the oak grove should have been covered with acorns but there were none. He walked around the periphery and examined the trunks in greater detail. The third tree trunk had a very large acorn about the size of a mandarin orange hanging close to the stem. If he hadn't lifted the leaves, he would have never seen it. He thought of picking the acorn, but decided to leave it. He stepped through the gap in the oak hedge and swam back to the rock. He didn't want to leave the water yet, so he swam once more around the pond. After twenty minutes he climbed out of the water and stretched himself on the rock to dry in the sun. He heard the simple, three note whistle of a chickadee. The sun dappled the water. He thought with regret that the Halfmen had taken his New Testament. He had begun reading it and he associated these times of sitting in a quiet place in the morning most closely with that activity. He tried to remember what he had been reading.

It's a peculiar kind of a book—two thousand years old and about a carpenter who goes around talking in riddles and healing people, but now I'm missing it.

He remembered then that he had been reading about The Prodigal Son who had left home and wasted his father's money. The picture of the son's father waiting for him to come home came into his mind.

Is that me in the story? I'm far from home. I feel like that kid did. So where are you God when I need You? Why don't You come to rescue me?

There was no answer. It was time to go back.

Hanomer and Dave spent the rest of the day exploring buildings around them. Most were empty but had a wholesome air, not at all like the oppressive atmosphere Dave had felt at the City of the Dead. Late in the afternoon, they decided they should head back in case Arlana had returned. In the distance Dave saw an intact building more impressive than any they had seen so far.

"If we get a chance, we'll have to look at that one Hanomer."

Hanomer nodded in agreement. "Friend Dave, I will stop at the pond to fish and dig up some potatoes."

Dave went straight back to the safe house. Arlana had not yet returned. Dave set about selecting the supplies he needed for supper, coaxing the embers to flame, and preparing their evening meal. Arlana and Hanomer arrived at the same time. Hanomer had caught three fine trout so Dave and Hanomer began cleaning them for supper.

It still rankled Dave that Arlana had taken to calling him 'youngling.' When Arlana returned from looking after the horses, he gave her his best smile. "So how did your day go, Arlie?" asked Dave, peeling the potatoes.

"Arlie?"

"A term of endearment. In my culture we give people nicknames. Arlana, I think you're too serious and you need a nickname."

"Are all your people this silly, youngling, or is it just you?"

"It's probably just me," said Dave attempting again to put on his most disarming smile.

"I see," said Arlana, coldly. "As far as your question goes, my day did not go very well. I searched all the closer safe houses, and although I saw signs of habitation, no one was there. Everyone has vanished. *Kree ah na koo*, I can't believe it. Where is everyone?"

"*Kree ah na koo*?" said Hanomer. "I have not heard that before."

"It's from the Old Tongue and means 'may the Creator help me'," said Arlana, thinking intently.

She paced back and forth, her hands behind her back.

"They're supposed to be guarding the city! Where are they?" She tugged on her long braid and wound it absently around her index finger.

She seemed to reach a decision and looked searchingly at Dave. "I'll have to search further tomorrow. I'm very tired and not very hungry. I think I will get some sleep."

The next morning when Dave rose, Hanomer was already up, making breakfast. A gentle drizzle was falling and the rain drops were sizzling as they hit the hot stones of the fireplace. Hanomer had constructed a fan of sorts from leaves, to protect the food from the rain.

"Where's Arlana?" asked Dave.

"She has already left, friend Dave," said Hanomer as he turned the bread, toasting it over the fire.

"What do you say we check out that building we saw yesterday?" suggested Dave.

Hanomer sniffed the air. "I think it will rain like this all day. It will be a good day to spend indoors."

After cleaning up, they set off up the road. Although it was raining, it was not cold. The building Dave had spotted earlier was even more impressive when they approached it. A large plaza fronted the entrance and broad steps ran the full width. At intervals up the side of the building, plants were growing in patches on the wall. At the top of the steps large columns, ten feet in diameter supported the upper stories. Dave approached the heavy wooden doors. He pulled, expecting resistance and almost fell over when the door swung outward silently as he tugged on the brass handle.

"Wow," said Dave. "These don't seem old at all. I never expected them to be this well maintained." Dave entered a large foyer with a vaulted ceiling. Ahead was a broad staircase. The door closed slowly behind him with a muffled thud as the dull light of the day was extinguished behind them.

Startled, Dave went back half expecting to be locked in, but the door could be opened as easily from inside. There were no windows, but the walls glowed with a pale yellow-white light. At intervals, light gourds at eye level, provided stronger light.

"There must be someone around to keep the light gourds tended."

"I don't think so friend Dave. I saw the leaves and stems on the outside walls and so they are self-sustaining."

"Let's search this floor. The silence gives me the creeps so let's stay together."

Hanomer sniffed the air. "Friend Dave, this place has a wholesome air. It has been much frequented and tended by the Ancients. I don't sense any danger."

"Alright, let's see if we can find someone here then."

The building appeared to be a library. Every room they searched was filled with books, scrolls and tablets. Some were in jars, others in glass cases, while still others were neatly stacked on shelves. Dave's excitement mounted. He suggested they search the building systematically.

"What are you looking for, friend Dave?"

"I don't know. I can't help but think this place is important and will tell me something about the Ancients. You can learn a lot more about a people from their books than you can from their architecture. Let's go to the very top and work our way down."

They headed up the central grand staircase, which zigzagged back and forth as it climbed up. On the fifth floor, the stairs ended. Dave led the way from room to room. There were so many manuscripts that Dave began to feel it would take a lifetime even if he could read just a few of the languages. Every once in a while, Dave would pull down a manuscript or a book, briefly look at the script, and then show it to Hanomer. Some were in the Common Tongue and covered diverse topics such as memoirs, poetry, history, and legal documents. Dave made note of the history texts in the Common Tongue. Many were in strange scripts that even Hanomer could not identify.

After briefly scouting the top floor, they worked their way down—all the way down. There were also five floors below ground level. The many rooms on every level, just like the top level, were filled with written material. Each room also had benches and wooden tables. The place was clearly a library of unprecedented size. Impressive as the size of the building had been outside, he had nevertheless underestimated the room it had on the inside for books.

There were also many locked rooms. The fifth floor underground was filled with locked rooms. The wooden doors had no visible locks but didn't budge no matter how hard Dave strained to open them. After his third attempt at one of the doors, Dave felt more determined than ever to find out what was inside.

Along the ceiling, vines of light gourds ran from the outside of the building into the room.

Dave examined the ceiling again. "Hanomer, do you see that opening on the ceiling where the light gourd stems enter the room? Could you squeeze through it?"

Hanomer thought for a moment and then took off his tool belt and climbed up on Dave's shoulders. The opening was still out of reach.

"Hanomer, if you give me your hands, I'll extend my arms so you can grab the opening with your tail. Will you be able to pull yourself up?"

"My third hand is easily strong enough to support me."

Dave was impressed; Hanomer weighed at least sixty pounds. The hand on his tail was very strong. Dave took Hanomer's hands and extended his arms so Hanomer was just able to grab the light gourd vine with his third hand when his tail was fully stretched. Pulling himself up, he began to wriggle through the opening, feet first.

If he gets stuck or meets something in there, I'll never be able to help him, Dave worried.

Hanomer's head disappeared and Dave sat down to wait when to his surprise, the locked door swung open.

Hanomer stuck his head out. "The door only needs to be pushed to open it from the inside."

The room was about fifty paces long and like all the others, contained row upon row of shelves. Some of the shelves were filled with scrolls, while others had books with heavy leather covers and thick parchment leaves. Dave carefully opened some of the scrolls. The script looked familiar.

This can't be! How is this possible?

The letters were Greek, all capitals, run together without spaces or punctuation. He couldn't be mistaken. He used Greek letters all the time.

This world must be connected with my own. How else could the language and books cross over?

Shaken, he moved on and came to a different set of scrolls. These he recognized as Latin. Again all capitals, run together, without punctuation. Dave checked a third—more Latin in a book this time. He looked at the book in more detail. The first page was all capitals with no punctuation or spaces.

INPRINCIPIOERATVERBUMETVERBUMERATA-
PUDDEUMETDEUSERAT

VERUMHOCERAT ...

Dave wished he had studied Latin in high school rather than French. He had just made a discovery, perhaps more momentous than the Dead Sea Scrolls and he couldn't even figure out what it was saying. He turned a couple of pages and a name caught his attention.

ETSICUTMOSESEXALTAVITSERPENTEMINDESER-
TOITAEXALTARIOPORTET

FILIUMHOMINISUTOMNISQUICREDITINIP-
SONONPEREATSEDHABEATVITAMAETERNAM ...

Moses, how can this be a passage about Moses here in this world?
He sat down stunned. He wrung his hands as he grasped the implications of what he had just found. His world had turned a corner. Somehow he had not really believed what Arlana had told him about communication between their worlds until now. Moses! Here in a book.

"What is it friend Dave?"

"I think these scrolls are from my world. From a long time ago. How can that be?"

"Can you read them, friend Dave?"

"No, Hanomer, they're in languages I recognize, but don't understand."

Arlana would know. How will I get her to talk?

"Hanomer, let's check another of these locked rooms."

At the end of the hallway was another locked door. Again Hanomer wriggled through an opening and then the door opened easily when pushed from inside. They entered a landing of a spiraling ramp that went both up and down. Dave led the way down the ramp until they came to a large cavern. A green light from the lumi-lichen on the wall pervaded the chamber. Dave stopped.

"Not worm caves again?" muttered Dave. He felt a sick feeling in his stomach as he thought about his first near-death experience with the rock-boring worms he had encountered. He didn't want to meet another one of those monstrosities.

Hanomer stopped Dave and examined a section of the wall covered with lines and script.

"Friend Dave, here is a map of the caverns with inscriptions in Common speech."

Dave came and studied the map with Hanomer.

From the map, Dave could identify the river they had crossed when they came to Arkand. Judging by the three mountain peaks behind the city, the Mountains of the Skulls to the northwest, the tunnel ahead of them led under the river and then on for many miles to a small forested hill directly west of them.

"Let's check this out Hanomer."

"Wait friend Dave, there's some kind of warning here which I don't understand."

Dave paced a circuit of the cavern impatiently while Hanomer tried to make out the inscription. When he returned, Hanomer was still studying the script.

"Any luck?" asked Dave.

"There are many words from the Old Tongue that I do not understand. There seems to be a guardian or guardians in this passage which prevents the wrong people from using it."

"Are we the wrong people?"

"I don't know, friend Dave."

"Any idea who or what the guardian is?"

"No."

"Hanomer, this is a very old inscription. The guardian has probably long since left. Let's proceed carefully and at the first sign of danger we'll turn back."

"I agree, friend Dave. I don't think the Ancients would deliberately hurt us. Let's go ahead."

They walked through the rest of the chamber and for a hundred yards through an underground tunnel when they came to a second cavern with a stream running through it. In the green light the cavern was filled with plants with luminous leaves, like some of the artificial Christmas trees Dave had seen back home. Some were low bushes and others were the size of trees. Dave pushed ahead through the leaves and almost immediately the plants gave off a pungent smell.

How do they live down here with so little light?

"Ugh," said Hanomer. "This stench is unbearable."

Dave was determined to go on even though his eyes were watering. Holding his nose and breathing through his mouth he pushed forward hoping to reach the other side of the cavern. Things grew worse; much worse. Every time he touched a leaf a stinging sensation burned his skin. He gave up and decided to turn back. Red welts had appeared wherever the leaves had touched him. Hanomer was not affected as badly but the leaves caused him to itch wherever they touched his fur.

"Let's get out of here," said Dave.

They worked their way back through the plants, adding to their growing discomfort. Finally they reached the map and climbed the spiral ramp. At every floor there was a landing with a door that connected to the main library. Finally they found a door that opened in the other direction. Dave pushed it open and saw an unfamiliar rain-soaked plaza. Once the door closed, Dave tried it again, and found, to his disappointment, that it had locked again.

Maybe I should have propped it open, he thought with regret.

They walked around the outside of the library and made their way back to the safe house. Arlana was waiting for them. She took one look at Dave and went to get a salve from her saddle bags.

"What happened?"

Hanomer told her while she rubbed the salve onto Dave's boils. She handed the ointment to Hanomer.

"What were those plants, lady Arlana?" asked Hanomer.

"They were *Guria*, guardian plants in the Common Tongue. My people plant them in places that we wish to protect. Had I been with you, the plants would not have reacted to your presence. You should have left at the first warning."

She looked thoughtful, and said quietly to herself, "So you found the hidden road. I knew it existed, but it is shown only to recruits like me after we join the ranks of the Guardians. Our Rangers use it to access the city secretly without crossing the desert."

"There's something else." said Dave. "We found manuscripts in languages that come from my world. How can that be?"

"From your world you say. That's very interesting. I can't really say what our library contains. The books are the most precious part of our heritage. The Guardians stay here in this ruined city to protect that knowledge. Your world, Terramon and our world, Feiramon have been separated for a long time but it has not always been so. In the past there were times when portals opened between our world and yours and many peoples traveled back and forth. When these natural portals open, they stay open for many years. In ages past, large numbers of your people came into our world and I think ours went there as well, although I don't know if they ever stayed. They must have carried some of your writings back with them when they returned."

"Where are my people now?" asked Dave.

Arlana looked at her feet. "Many, many years ago, before even my father was born, the Long War raged over our land. Much was lost until finally the Bent Ones were driven away from Feiramar to Abaddon, the cursed continent to the east. Your people, the Lesser Men fought with us, but being weaker and more vulnerable, were killed in great numbers. Others were enslaved and dragged off to Abaddon, since your weak minds are easily controlled by the Bent Ones."

"Weak minds!"

Hanomer grabbed Dave's arm to stop the interruption.

"Yes, weak minds. The Bent Ones have great power to mold your thoughts. They cannot do so with us as adults and that is why they hate and fear us so."

"Were all my people killed in the Long War?"

No, some remained, especially in The City of the Dead. When Meglir corrupted himself, he enslaved all the Lesser Men he could get his hands on. They gave him an army to command and a measure of immortality since he could possess them and escape the trap of his obelisk prison for a while. Eventually, as I mentioned before, all the Lesser Men on Feiramar died in the plague that Meglir started."

There was stunned silence.

Is there something she is not telling me?

"Let's speak no more of it now," said Arlana. "It's time to eat."

"Just one more question, Arlana. Where does that tunnel lead?"

"My people live in comparative safety beyond the Barrier Mountains west of the Skull Desert. I suspect the tunnel would take us many leagues toward the Barrier Mountains, skirting the fringe of the desert. The Halfmen have ever been our enemies and these plants protect us from them.

Early the next morning Arlana wakened them.

"I will take you home today."

"Are you sure that the Halfmen have left?" asked Dave.

"Yes," said Arlana. "I looked over the desert from several lookout towers and there is no sign of them. They are not very intelligent and quickly lose interest when they have lost their quarry. Besides I will take you east and we will exit the city well away from the desert so I can send you on your way home. I am heading that way anyway, to find my father."

It took them two hours of travel through the city until they crossed a ridge and Dave saw the river before them. By now it was raining heavily. The river here was much larger than when they had crossed it before, since several streams from the city had swelled the flow and the heavy rains has further increased the runoff.

The banks on this side were very steep. A bridge spanned the river and Arlana headed her horse directly for it. On the other side, after a wide interval of grass, forest stretched ahead of them as far as the eye could see. After Arlana had crossed the bridge, she and Hanomer dismounted, and she led her horse down to the water for a drink where the bank had a gentle slope. Dave, eager to look ahead, urged his horse down the road to the edge of the forest. He smelled wet leaves and heard the steady splattering of the rain on the soggy ground. The road stretched out ahead of him. At the side of the road he saw a curious indentation. He dismounted for a closer look. In the mud he saw a distinct footprint.

Dave looked back. Arlana and Hanomer were coming up the bank. Fog was rolling across the ruined city towards him. Soon it would make visibility difficult.

Dave heard the bushes snap behind him. Turning around, he saw a masked form leap out of the undergrowth wielding a black, jagged blade. Dave's horse reared, pulling the reins out of his hand and pitching Dave to the ground. Dave rolled onto his feet and snatched his knife from his belt as he struggled to catch his breath. Howling with fury, the creature charged him, lifting its sword high over its head. Dave lunged to dodge the blow, stumbling again to his knees. The weapon descended, ringing as it struck a stone on the road. Dave tried to get up. The blade descended again and Dave deflected the blow aimed for his head with his knife. Shattering the knife, the terrific blow caught Dave's left arm at the elbow. Dave shrieked as the weapon severed his arm. With blood spurting from his wound, Dave fell again to his knees. He heard the thunk of an arrow hitting the Halfman in the chest, as he shuddered with pain.

The pain was unbearable; yet he persevered. He looked down on the road and saw his severed arm lying in the mud, blood oozing from the ragged stump. Faintly and far away he heard a voice.

"Get up Dave!" said a voice. "Please get up! I'm so sorry."

Chapter 5

The Hidden Way

Arlana stood in the pouring rain, desperation welling up inside her and threatening to overwhelm her self-control. She looked down the road, expecting to see Halfmen emerge from the wood at any time.

Hanomer, crouching over the body of the Halfman he had just shot, also watched the wood.

Arlana bent down and gave the tourniquet on Dave's stump another twist. The bleeding had stopped and a red ribbon of his blood was streaming away from his limp, prone body.

"Hanomer, help me get him onto the horse before more Halfmen come. We have to go back."

Arlana grabbed Dave's shoulders—they were muscular and he was very heavy. She managed to drag his dead weight to a sitting position as a groan escaped from his lips. The rain and the pain of the movement was beginning to revive him.

"Dave," pleaded Arlana. "Dave, you have to help me get you up on the horse. Please Dave."

Dave opened his eyes and looked up at her. Pain was etched on his face. Clenching his teeth and using his one good arm, he shifted to a kneeling position. Hanomer clutched his maimed arm while Arlana held his right arm and Dave managed to stand. A whistle from Arlana brought Dave's horse. Hanomer put Dave's foot in the stirrup and with Arlana's help, Dave pulled himself into the saddle and then slumped forward. Arlana leapt up behind him and kept him from falling.

The rain abated to a drizzle as they slowly made their way back across the bridge and through the winding roads of the city, the buildings and ruins appearing as indistinct, mist-shrouded sentinels along the way.

"What time is it, Hanomer?" asked Arlana.

Hanomer sniffed the air. "It is just after midday."

Ahead of them loomed the archway and gate of the safe house that had been their home for the past few days. Hanomer dismounted and opened the gate. Arlana rode through the courtyard to a corner sheltered from the rain and dismounted.

"I don't think we can get him upstairs to the bedroom."

Hanomer nodded in agreement.

She placed some blankets on the paving stones. With Dave's semi-conscious help, Arlana and Hanomer lowered him onto the blankets. She removed the bandage from the stump and blood oozed from the severed artery. A white patch of bone was visible amid the congealed blood of the wound. After going back to her horse for supplies, Arlana sewed the end of the artery together as well as she could and then sewed a flap of skin over the open wound. Dave moaned as he lapsed in and out of consciousness. She loosened the tourniquet and the wound remained closed. She washed her hands and then bandaged the stump again with fresh linen.

When she was done, she collapsed back with a sob and leaned against the wall. She had worked tirelessly to get them out of danger, but now the stress of the day's events overwhelmed her.

What am I to do? What a fool I've been. I should have stayed home as father said. I'm not up to this and I've gotten Dave killed with my foolishness.

She felt a hand on her shoulder.

"Do not be troubled Lady Arlana. You have behaved with great courage even in this difficult time," said Hanomer.

"I've killed him Hanomer. I've killed him!"

"We would be dead now if you hadn't come. I believe the Creator has a purpose for him and for us and I can't believe that it's over yet."

"It is said Hanomer, that your people can hear the Creator speak to you. What is He saying to you now?"

"I have asked, good lady, but I only meet silence."

"Why is He not giving us direction?"

"It usually means we already know what to do and no more words are needed."

Hanomer walked away from the safe house, his long tail swinging from side to side, and left Arlana to her thoughts. He returned in twenty minutes dragging two stout ten foot poles while bowed under a bundle of sticks and vines balanced on his back. He dropped his load and wiped his muzzle with his kerchief.

"Whew, that tired me out. I'm glad the roads are paved with cobblestones or else I wouldn't have made it."

"Hanomer you could have made two trips or asked me to help."

He smiled and began to untie the bundle of sticks and vines.

"Lady Arlana, you need to think about what we have to do next. I'll help us be ready to go when you've made your decision." Arlana sat down to think. She saw Hanomer work quickly to assemble the stretcher.

Finally she got up and went over to Hanomer. "I have badly misjudged the Halfmen. Something has changed. They are not behaving as we were taught. If the Halfmen have stayed this long," continued Arlana, "they will be guarding the whole perimeter of the city."

"I think," said Hanomer, "we have to try something. Things won't get better by waiting. There are probably no safe roads out, but you need to pick the best one and we ought to get moving. Could you help me get Dave onto this stretcher?"

After dragging Dave onto the stretcher and tying him to it, they brought over Dave's horse and lashed the long poles of the stretcher one on each side of the saddle. Arlana then lifted Hanomer onto her horse and mounted behind him.

"Take me to the ramp that led to the hidden way you and Dave found, Hanomer."

Hanomer gave Arlana directions as they traveled further into the heart of the city. The clop, clop of the hooves mingled with the scrape of the stretcher on the cobblestones, breaking the silence of the ruins.

In a few minutes, with Hanomer's unerring guidance, they arrived at the back of the library where Dave and Hanomer had exited from the underground passage after the *Guria* had blocked their way and caused them so much grief.

"Begging your pardon, Lady Arlana, I'll have to go to the front to open the doors for you from the inside. We only got out this way."

"Give me a minute, friend Hanomer, and let me examine this door."

She dismounted and walked up to the door, searched the surface intently, and then reached for a depression high up on the right hand side. She touched it, a click sounded, and the door opened silently as she pulled on the handle. She remounted and led the horses onto the spiral ramp.

At the bottom of the ramp they came to a stone sign post. She again dismounted, giving Hanomer the reins of the packhorse, and looked at the writing and the symbols.

"Is this the map you and Dave were talking about?"

"Yes, friend Arlana."

"This tunnel could take us home. See how it runs straight as an arrow west, and emerges here on this rocky mesa? I'm sure this was designed by my people."

"But Lady Arlana, what about the plants? Do you really think Dave and I will not be affected this time?"

"Hanomer, I am only a child when it comes to being a Guardian. I have been taught that we will be unaffected. However, let's be careful and make sure that I have understood correctly. We can't afford another attack."

She remounted and they continued on until they reached the cavern with the guardian plants. Even though there was little light to nourish the plants, the taller ones among them resembled trees. Arlana reached out and touched a delicate, luminous leaf.

"Let's give it a try. At worst, it could drive us away as it did you and Dave."

Arlana rode straight in, heedless of the branches she touched as she passed. There was no pungent smell. She saw Hanomer look back. Arlana followed his gaze and saw Dave's good arm brush against the foliage. In the pale algal light of the underground cavern, there were no welts on his arm.

She placed a hand on her companion's shoulder. "Don't worry Hanomer, these guardian plants were placed here by my people to keep this road safe. Just as I thought, these trees will not show their sting while I am with you."

For the next three days they followed a straight paved road that traveled through the underground passage. At intervals they stopped at a well or an underground stream to replenish their water. The unfailing glow of the pale green lumi-lichen lit their way. Every few miles they again encountered a forest of guardian plants where they had to follow a narrow path that wound through the dense foliage before they could rejoin the road.

"Friend Arlana," asked Hanomer. "Are these guardian plants natural or are they the creations of the Ancients?"

"I am one of the few women of my people who has asked to train as a Guardian," said Arlana. "From this training I have learned that these trees were created by our forefathers before much knowledge had been lost. This is how we protect the road and even our land from the Halfmen. With all of these patches of vegetation, even if someone destroyed the plants at the entrance and could travel onward, every few miles they would have to clear the guardian plants all over again to get through the string of caverns. This formidable defense has kept us safe for many gnerations."

"I don't think my people really understood, friend Arlana, how long the Ancients have worked to hold back evil. Our ignorance has made my people ungrateful."

Arlana smiled and Hanomer lapsed into silence.

On the third evening they encountered a ramp which ended in a roughhewn gate on a rocky mesa facing west. Ahead loomed the Gurundarian Mountains, also called the Barrier Mountains in the Common Tongue. Arlana looked around in the twilight.

"Stay with me Hanomer. These trees are the more familiar guardian trees that we grow on the Gurundarian Mountain slopes to keep the Halfmen away. If you wander in by yourself, they will attack."

Arlana went over to look at Dave. He seemed to have recovered from the initial shock of his injury and had regained consciousness a day ago. Now, he was able to rise occasionally when they stopped for a break.

"How are you doing Dave?"

"I have been feeling better, but my stump is hot to the touch."

"Let me have a look." Arlana carefully unwrapped the bandage. The stump had healed, but the skin was distinctly flushed and indeed, warm to the touch.

Dave attempted a laugh. "It must be bad, since you're not scolding me."

Troubled, Arlana tried to put on a brave face. "I need to get you to our healers since they have much more power than I. See those mountains? Behind them is my home. If we get there, we will be safe and you will get help."

With Hanomer's counsel, Arlana decided they would try travelling for a good part of the night on the plains below. The sooner she got Dave to the healers, the better.

When they finally stopped for one of their infrequent rests, it was late afternoon of the next day. They were on their fourth day traveling across the plain.

Dave had sunk into a fever and his condition had deteriorated. He moaned softly and his forehead was hot to the touch. Arlana unwrapped the bandage on his stump. The sickly sweet smell of decaying flesh greeted her.

"He's worse isn't he, Lady Arlana?" Hanomer asked, joining her.

"Yes, much worse," she whispered as she collapsed to sit on a rock.

Looking very grave, Hanomer put his hand on Dave's forehead. "Be brave, friend Dave. You have a tough road ahead, but my heart tells me it will end fair and right."

He turned back to Arlana. "Begging your pardon, Lady Arlana, he needs you now more than ever to think clearly and get us to safety." He sniffed the air and then pointed east.

"I see a dust cloud. The Halfmen are coming fast and closing in. We need to hurry or we won't make it."

Arlana rose in alarm. "Hanomer, I don't know what's going on. I thought we'd meet help by now but all the land and paths are deserted. If the Halfmen catch us again we are finished."

She paused, and raised her eyes to the distant mountains.

"If we can get there we will be safe."

But what about Dave? When the flesh begins to rot, there is no hope—unless... No my people will never allow it.

Chapter 6

Eleytheria

Al crouched on the rock promontory with his bamboo fishing pole. He unwound the line from the spindle and swung the float and bait into the deep pool just past his rock.

Keep low Al. The lunker will see you.

The hellgrammite on the hook wiggled as it sank into the depths. He waited. The float disappeared as the trout struck. With a whoop, Al gave the pole a jerk to set the hook. The trout bent the bamboo pole as Al tried to pay out line from his spool.

"Don't break, please don't break," he muttered under his breath.

The tension released suddenly as the line parted. A curse bubbled to Al's lips but he swallowed it and sat back down, running his hands through his short brown hair. He took his glasses off, cleaned them on his shirt, and then pulled in the line to look at the damage.

He heard steps on the rock behind him. It was curious how he could tell who it was from the sound. He turned and smiled as he saw Pam, her long auburn hair tousled over her face, scrambling toward him over the broken terrain.

She's a delight to watch! Whatever made her agree to marry a klutz like me?

She reached him, threw her arms around his neck and kissed him gently on the cheek. She settled down beside him, close enough that their bodies were touching, and looked across the lake from their island to the western shore of Lake Tor.

"Any sign of Hanomer or Dave yet?"

"No, hun. No sign of Floyd or Cordomer either."

She turned to him and caressed his cheek with her hand. As mayor …"

"Deputy mayor." He corrected.

"As deputy mayor you have to maintain your appearance."

"That's your job," he smiled.

"Don't make a joke out of it. I'm serious."

"Sorry." He kissed her gently on her cheek.

Smiling, she picked up a pebble and threw it into the pool.

"Have you thought any more about what we talked about this morning?"

Al shifted uncomfortably. He could feel Pam's eyes on him. Making up his mind about what to say, he looked her in the eyes. "Pam I know you want to go back to Halcyon and get Little Thomas from the Staycare Center, but I can't leave right now. Not with Floyd away."

"But I could go by myself. I've already talked to some of the *Hansa*. They could get me there safe and sound."

"Pam, Blackmore and his cronies will be waiting for us and this time, if we're caught, we we won't have any opportunity for escape."

"Al, please let me go. I'm a nobody to Blackmore and I could get Little Thomas out before they know what happened. Besides why would they care about one more orphan?"

Al put his arm around his wife and gave her a squeeze.

"Pam you know that I love you and that I care about Little Thomas. Just let me wait until Floyd gets back. I need to come up with a plan that gives us even a small chance to get him out. Let's talk about it then."

Pam was about to speak again, but bit back the words. She seemed to shrink within herself, as if a cloud had swallowed up the sunshine and left her world a drab and dreary place. Al felt Pam's disappointment wash over him like an ice cold tide and his heart raged against Halcyon for putting them into this position.

She thinks I don't really care about Little Thomas because he's not mine. But I do! It's just that we have zero chance to succeed. Can I throw her life away when there's no chance for success?. Lord, what do You want me to do? He prayed silently.

Pam rose woodenly and walked back to their cottage leaving Al to his thoughts. He had lost all interest in fishing.

A shout came from across the lake. Al looked up to see a figure waving his hat on the far bank. Al scrambled to his feet, raced down the shore to the boat, and shoved off as soon as he got there. When he reached the western shore of the lake, Floyd Linder waded out to help pull the boat up onto the bank.

"Did you find them?" asked Al.

"Nope," said Floyd shaking his head. He and his *Hansa* traveling companion, Cordomer, climbed into the boat.

Al cradled his cup of hot *Siph*, the drink *Hansa* made from the root of the sugar gum bush.

He looked up and saw Floyd staring at him.

"So tell me what happened on your expedition with Cordomer," said Al.

"Well, we spent a couple of days searching for Dave and Hanomer's first campsite. When Cordomer finally found it, the fire pit was cold—a week old, he guessed. Cordomer found what he callled a "trail talk" stick. On it, Hanomer had written their travel intentions for their next day; they were planning to head west in almost a straight line, where the land climbs up to a high plateau. Hanomer had also marked their trail, so we pushed it, hoping to gain on them."

Floyd paused to take another sip of his *Siph*. He described the carcass of the Halfman they found, how the trail led to the bluff overlooking the desert, the signs of a pursuit and, ultimately, a capture. "So it looks like Al and Hanomer were captured by Halfmen," said Floyd grimly. "Since Halfmen eat their enemies, we have to face the fact that they're probably dead."

Al, in shock at the revelation, ran his hands through his hair and bowed his head as the grief grew. A pit had opened at his feet and darkness washed over him as if his eyesight had failed and he could no longer see light. Unexpectedly, the picture came into his mind of the scene where he and Pam had watched Dave overcome by Apemen at the City of the Dead. He remembered his grief, but he also remembered that Dave had not died. Hope kindled in his heart and the darkness began to lift.

"I don't know why Floyd, but I don't think Dave is dead. I just have this feeling or premonition that Dave and Hanomer will be alright."

Floyd didn't answer. He just stared at Al with his lips pursed.

"Still," Al went on, "You are going to have to be doubly on your guard now that the Halfmen are to the west of us. We know Meglir, if he attacks us here, will come from the east. We had hoped to escape to the west but now that is cut off."

"What do you mean by 'you'?" growled Floyd. "Don't you mean 'we'? Don't tell me you've decided to carry out that fool plan we talked about before I left?"

"Yes, I just made up my mind."

"Gleeson, you're an idiot! You're not going to last three days back at Halcyon."

"Look Floyd I know the odds …"

"Then why the hell are you going?"

"I have to go even if it costs me my life," said Al quietly. He could feel tears misting his eyes.

"But why?" said Floyd. "I just don't understand."

"Floyd, there are some things a man has to do, or at least attempt, even if it looks as if there is no chance of success. Pam can't forget about Little Thomas and longs to have him out of the hands of Halcyon. She would go on her own if I didn't come along. I know we'll be caught. I know we have almost no chance of success, but I have to try. I'm going with my eyes open. I have no illusions about the danger…"

Floyd put up his hands in exasperation. He looked away for a moment and then looked Al square in the eyes, his mouth grim. "Have you told her yet?"

"No, I've been putting it off."

"Well at least that's a plus. It means you at least have the sense to see the impossibility of what you're doing." Floyd took a deep breath. "It's hard for me to stay angry with you Al. I think you're crazy to attempt this because you can't help but get caught, but I've said my piece so I'll shut up now. If you do end up sticking with your decision, you know you can count on me to help."

Al smiled, "I know Floyd."

Chapter 7

Down River

It was still dark but Al could not sleep. He could hear Pam's soft breathing at his side. *What is it about love that makes me walk bright-eyed into a trap that might cost our lives? It makes no sense and we have almost no chance of success. But I can see Pam's worry eating away at her and we have to try.*

He searched in the dark for his Bible and notebook, left their hut and walked down the well-worn path to his favorite reading spot on an east-facing promontory. It was still too dark to read so he sat down to collect his thoughts. He had been growing his beard and hair and his face felt itchy. Reaching up to scratch his chin, he lost himself in thought. He couldn't help sensing that there was another reason for going back to Halcyon, beyond his love for his wife, but he couldn't put his finger on it. *Is this God talking, or am I just talking to myself?*

The first rays of the sun fell on him and his heart lightened. He pulled out a poem he had written as this shadow had come over his relationship with Pam. He re-read it.

BRIDGES

I'm on an island in a torrent
Life passes by and by
Others at a distance
Darks shadows to the sky.

Words are like long bridges
Bringing joy or pain
Each morning we rebuild them
Then tear them down again.

Will enemies cross over?
Or friends that bring us grain?
We hope for friendly succor
But fear the enemy pain.

Our heart is deep in longing
For land shining in the sun
The span too far for building
Has construction not begun?

In Bethlehem a pylon
Was driven close to shore
At Calvary the final span
Was set for ever more.

Will stone and fence forever
Bar entrance to my isle?
Or will I open up a crack
To see a scowl or smile?

The smile is from my Father
Who'd built the bridge to me
His love has left me conquered
My capture set me free.

Now will I build to others?
Or will I stay alone
Risk joy or pain to crowd me
Or hoard for me alone?

Am I going to live for myself—do what's sensible and pragmatic, or will I risk it all in a rescue that I know is doomed to fail? At this moment, one of his favorite verses came into his mind from Proverbs 4:18:

But the path of the righteous is like the light of dawn, which shines brighter and brighter until full day.

At the beginning, with dawn far off, I expect it to be dark. As I do what the Master wants, I expect things will become clearer. Why am I focusing so much on getting caught or not getting caught? I know what the Master wants me to do.

He heard the snap of a twig behind him.

"I thought I would find you here," said Floyd.

He's going to try to talk me out of it.

Floyd sat down beside Al on the rock, pulling up his long legs and wrapping his arms around them.

"Al, you look like death warmed over. What's eating you? Are you worried about Dave and Hanomer?"

"I am. But I still believe in my heart that they'll be alright. No, I haven't slept very well. I've really disappointed Pam over Little Thomas. She doesn't say anything, but I can see it in her eyes."

"You see," said Floyd. "That's why I never want to get married. You two were so in love and now when you do the sensible thing, Pam is wounded and you're miserable."

"And you think that's a reason not to marry?"

"It looks that way to me. Isn't marriage making you miserable?"

"You're wrong Floyd. Before Pam and I were married we really didn't know each other—nor should we have expected to. The disappointments we experience now occur because we're getting to know the real other person. We're facing the test. Can we really love each other once we see what we're really like? That's what love is all about."

"Maybe you two should have tried living together to see if it would work out."

"Pam and I aren't cars that can be taken for a test drive to see if we'll be suitable and then returned to the dealer's lot if we're not. It's much better to be very careful before you commit and then stick with it. I have a lot of rough edges to rub off and Pam is just helping me do that."

"I was just jerking your chain, Al. I know you well enough to know that you don't think like that. So changing the subject, tell me you've had the good sense to give up your hare-brained scheme to try to rescue Little Thomas."

"I haven't given up on my plan—I just haven't told Pam yet because I wanted to think the whole thing through before I tell her. In fact I've thought it through all over again and I'm determined to go, but I can't bring myself to leave, if Dave and Hanomer are missing."

Floyd broke off a stalk of grass and began to chew on the end.

"With you growing a beard and all to keep from being recognized in Halcyon, I wouldn't be surprised if Pam already suspects what you're up to. I still think you're crazy, but if you're determined to go, you have to go now and not wait for Dave and Hanomer. You need to go early enough so the weather is good. I've said my piece and you've decided to go so I'll do everything I can to help. What's the plan?"

Al explained while Floyd listened, grunting assent or nodding every once in a while.

"Well at least you've thought this through. I'm glad you're taking some of the *Hansa* along."

"Let me show you something," said Al.

Al led him down a steep path to the east shore of Eleytheria. The path plunged into a thicket of sumac and emerged in a little cove, surrounded by dense cedars with a narrow entrance that faced north. Floating in front of them was a long mass of reeds about 30 feet long.

"What am I looking at?" asked Floyd his eyes scanning the cove.

Just then a furry head poked out of the reed mass.

"Good morning friend Al and friend Floyd," said the *Hansa*.

"What's this?"

"Show Floyd what it is Bandomer."

Without a word, two more *Hansa* appeared and began collecting the haphazard reed mats into sheaves and tying them together into bundles. Underneath the reed mats, the gunwale of a boat appeared. Slowly, as more and more of the reeds were bundled and tied onto the gunwale, the floating mass of reeds transformed into a boat. Along the length of a boat rested a mast. The three *Hansa* stepped the mast, secured it with stays so that the whole vessel looked quite seaworthy. The boat was broad of beam and looked like an ordinary boat that had been overgrown with vines.

"But it's alive?"

"Precisely," said Al, "apparently this reed vessel is made from a plant called boat weed, initially bred by the Ancients. The boat weed is grown on a frame of timbers that define the shape of the boat; the boat weed fills in the spaces and makes the whole thing water tight. They tell me it keeps the inside of the boat dry, even soaking up the bilge. If a side is punctured, after temporary repairs, the boat weed closes in and seals the hole up again."

"But the thing must have roots and provide for a lot of drag."

"Apparently not, but in any case we are aiming for stealth and not for speed."

"Yeah, but if you're spotted…"

"With the *Hansa* guides," said Al, "We'll only travel by night. During the day we'll tie up in a reed bed somewhere and unbundle the boat weed so the Halcyonites won't even know we're coming."

Floyd followed Al as he stepped onto the deck. Walking to the middle of the boat, Al stepped down to the hull and ducked underneath the deck.

"Pam, Little Thomas, and I will sleep here. The *Hansa* will sleep in a smaller cabin under the forward deck. There's only enough room to crawl in but we should be snug."

Al felt along the hull. Inside it was a solid mass of fibrous vines that covered the frame.

"They built the whole thing out of reeds and poles, gluing them together with this red resin. I'm going to have to find out where they get it since I think we could use it for fastening other things. Then they planted boat weed on it and trained it where they wanted it to grow. The red resin was painted onto all the surfaces where we don't want boat weed leaves."

"Where are you going to keep the food and supplies?" asked Floyd.

"The *Hansa* don't take up the whole bow compartment and at least half of the space is for storage. We have a small brazier for cooking or warming up the cabins, but we probably won't need that unless it turns unseasonably cold."

"Well it sounds like a good plan. Should get you there." Floyd said, though his eyes told a different story.

"Are you going to take my advice and leave right away?"

"Yes. I'll tell Pam."

The rest of the day was spent preparing the boat. Al fervently hoped that Dave and Hanomer would return, but there was no sign of them.

Pam was clearly excited by the news. She began to pack their few belongings immediately and noticed Al watching as she folded her medical uniform. Holding it up, she smiled. "This is how I get into the Staycare Center without being noticed," she explained.

"That's a good plan," said Al returning her smile, even though he could imagine five flaws that would have her caught before the day was out.

She rose, came into his arms and whispered "Thank you."

He ran his hand through her short hair. She had cut off her beautiful long hair this afternoon as part of her disguise, and he missed it.

As the sun cast long shadows from the west Al, Pam and their three furry companions boarded the boat. The *Hansa* in the boat along with their kinsfolk on the shore sang a song of farewell. The human Eleytherians just waved. With Bandomer giving directions from the bow, they poled the boat out of the narrow channel of the cove and into the lake.

Al took up his seat in the stern and worked the tiller while the *Hansa* put up the large mainsail and staysail. The boat began to gather way. Pam had been helping the *Hansa* unfurl the sails. She tied off the last rope, and made her way back to the stern and kissed Al gently.

"With all of your beard, there's hardly any place left to kiss."

"A definite disadvantage of this disguise." He pulled her close as she snuggled and laid her head on his shoulder.

After a time, she disentangled herself and went to the bow, where she sat, arms wrapped around legs, looking toward Halcyon. The boat, demonstrating surprising speed, cut a small bow wave even in this gentle offshore breeze. As darkness settled in, Al checked his chronometer which was still unerringly following official Halcyon time. The moon was past its first quarter and would not rise until after midnight. Sunset would be shortly after 7:00 P.M. They would have to make their way down the Tor river by starlight.

Rolomer offered to take the tiller from Al, since he knew this part of the river better than Al did. Bandomer stayed at the bow, occasionally giving quiet directions for course corrections. An opera bird gave its imitation of Verde somewhere on the eastern shore. The night passed slowly. Somehow Bandomer was able to find his way through the Thicket Islands into the Halcyon River main channel and their speed increased with the current. The moon rose and cast its pale light on the water. Since they were traveling by night and sleeping during the day, Bandomer had determined to stay up all night and navigate them through this tricky section of the river. The river had widened to a long lake which was inundated with hundreds of islands. Al, tired as he was, decided to follow Bandomer's example and stay up all night. With the rising of the moon, navigating would be a little easier.

Al found himself waking with a start. At about four o'clock in the morning, they were approaching Fort Linderhof. Bandomer had changed course to give Linderhof the widest berth possible and the course change had awakened Al. As they rounded a bend, Al could see the high mesa that was their old campsite, leering at them from the shore. They could not see the City of the Dead from the river, but a yellow glow was playing on the mountainside where the city would be. *What is that light?* Al scanned the top of the mesa. *Are any eyes watching from the fort?* The brooding silence and the light show were ominous, like the quiet of a predator before the pounce. Terror haunted this place.

Pam came out of their cabin and sat beside Al. "What do you think that glow on the mountain side is?" she whispered.

"I am not sure," said Al.

Bandomer came back from the bow on hearing Pam's question.

"Friends," said Bandomer. "I smell oil from torches. A great many torches. I think Meglir is marching his army."

I wonder where they are going—east or west? said Al to himself. For the twentieth time he asked himself if he had done the right thing in heading for Halcyon.

It had been six days since they had set out. The trip had been uneventful. Every morning, just before dawn, they had pulled into a reed bed, had taken down the mast, and covered the boat with reed mats like a tent. As the sun came out, the leaves of the boat weed mats unfurled and made the vessel look like a mass of vegetation.

It was Al's turn on watch. They were getting close to the mouth of the river and the reed bed on the northern fringe of the river bordered a large swamp that the Halcyonites had called The Caiman Swamp because of the large alligator-like creatures that had been spotted there. In the early morning, fog shrouded the boat, and Al could only see about ten feet to either side. He lay among the fronds on the weed boat and listened intently. The closeness of the fog, the smell of decaying plant matter, and a sense of being watched made him uneasy. The boat was close to a small cypress eyot.

Al heard the rustle of a large animal only a few feet away. The rustle was followed by a grunt. Watching intently, Al could see nothing, but experience told him that a boar was looking for roots on the island. Instinctively he checked the wind. He was downwind of the boar. He searched for his crossbow and loaded a bolt, hoping for a clean shot. Fresh meat would be a welcome addition to their diminishing fare.

A huge boar, perhaps four years old, emerged from the fog and approached the water for a drink near a root that barely broke the surface. Al carefully raised his crossbow and began to line up his shot.

Maybe the boar is too big? What if he charges?

As the boar's mouth touched the water, Al realized with a shock, that the root was the snout of an alligator. The alligator exploded out of the water seizing the boar's snout. Squealing in terror, the prey planted its feet and tugged with all of its might. The boar was very strong, and the alligator, about fifteen feet long, was slowly dragged out of the water onto the shore, while holding tenaciously onto the snout. The squealing had awakened the others and first Pam and then the *Hansa* gathered around Al watching the struggle.

The full front quarters of the alligator were out of the water now, clawing desperately to haul its prey off the eyot. The boar was also tiring as blood from the damaged snout ran in rivulets into the turgid water.

Suddenly, wrist-thick tentacles rose silently out of the water and like three snakes, arced over the body of the alligator. Within a heartbeat, the reptile was wrapped in tight coils.

"Oy," shouted Rolomer, "a *Krachodon*."

The alligator reacted with lightning swiftness. It released the boar, twisted its body and thrashed mightily with its tail to break the grip. The struggle carried the alligator close to their boat. The tail crashed onto the gunwale, ripping a large mat of the boat weed cover off the top of the boat and knocking Rolomer into the water.

Al reacted without thinking and leaned over the gunwale to grab Rolomer, just as large wide jaws, enshrouded by tentacles, closed on the hapless body of the alligator with a bone crunching snap.

In its death throes the alligator's tail tore shreds off the side of the boat and the hull was stove in. Rolomer bobbed to the surface. Al snatched his harness and hauled Rolomer out of the water. As he dragged Rolomer toward the boat, a tentacle wrapped around the *Hansa's* ankle, pulling him back. Al was wrenched off his feet and into the side of the boat. He braced his shoulder against the gunwale, clung grimly to the harness and looked over the side.

The Krachodon had a long narrow body like a crocodile about the size of a wagon, with tentacles surrounding its mouth. With the crushed alligator firmly in its jaws, it sent the wriggling tentacles toward the boat. Al cried out, his knuckles white with exertion,

"Help me!"

Pam grabbed Al's sword and hacked at the tentacle holding Rolomer's ankle. The sword sliced through the tentacle, spraying blood into the boat. The tentacle writhed, staining the water red. Rolomer, free of the tentacle scrambled to the stern to help Taromer pole the boat away from the island while Al, Pam and Bandomer slashed at any tentacles grabbing the boat.

The monster moved with them as the boat gave way, but was unwilling to release the limp alligator in its jaws. Finally, Al snatched up his crossbow and fired a bolt at the eye of the Krachodon. The bolt hit with a thud, lodging in a bony ridge around the eye. The monster sank into the water, its prey still in its jaws, leaving a trail of red.

Al sank down exhausted.

"What was that thing?"

"We call it a Krachodon which means 'snake jaws' in your tongue," said Rolomer. "I have never seen one that big, friend Al. Praise the Creator that it had its prey in its mouth since it could easily have destroyed our boat."

Praise the Creator indeed! thought Al.

The rain was coming down steadily as Al and Taromer, stood in the front of the boat, peering into the fog.

"Friend Al," said Taromer, "we could use some fresh water and camp for the night. Should we not put in to shore before we cross to your island?"

"No, we mustn't do that—it's too dangerous," said Al. "When we first arrived in your world, we tried to move to the mainland for food and wood. However, we found a plant with bright red fruit that we called Happy Berries. At first, as our people ate the plant they felt happy and strong, but as they continued to eat this plant, they lost their minds and became like very strong, wild animals. They killed many of us and even now will attack us if we land there. Perhaps they have died out by now, but I did not want us to be attacked."

Taromer thought for a while. "Friend Al," he said, "I still do not understand how you came to Feiramon. Is this island we are approaching some kind of doorway between our worlds?"

"No, my people have many complicated machines. We study the Creator's world, and use His rules to build very sophisticated devices. My people invented a new one and that machine moved the whole island from our world here.

"So what is on this island?"

"In our world we called this a university."

"A university?"

"Yes, it is a place of study. We had about sixteen thousand students here studying many kinds of knowledge."

"Sixteen thousand! That is more people than we have in all of our *Hansa* villages."

Al could hear the gentle wash of waves on a shore and could smell the scent of pine trees.

Taromer sniffed the air with satisfaction.

"We are close to land, friend Al."

True to Taromer's pronouncement, the fog cleared, revealing wooded hills and a rocky shore. Al peered at the familiar terrain. "I think if we follow the shore west, we'll find the creek I was suggesting as a good anchorage."

Al's prediction came true in a few minutes as the rocky shore opened up into a narrow bay. At the end of the bay was a narrow creek. A brook cascaded down to meet it. They poled the boat up the creek until they reached the point where the creek tumbled down from the heights above in a cascade. Taromer pointed to a small reed bed on the east bank. They poled the boat in, lowered the mast and covered it with the boat weed mats. Bandomer created a short walkway, out of oars, to the nearest clump of turf. Al and Pam clambered to the shore trying not to get their feet wet. The three *Hansa* followed. They stood on the narrow bank fringed by a steep hillside, covered with brush.

"Friends," said Bandomer, "we will tunnel into this bank and stay hidden while the boat repairs itself from the damage. We will also keep a lookout for your return."

"How long will it take until the hole in the side has grown over with boat weed?" asked Al.

"The hole is not very big and it should be done in a week. Will that give you enough time to bring back your cub?"

"Before we can attempt a rescue and return to the boat, Pam will need to find out how the Staycare Center is operating so that we can find a way to get Little Thomas away from them. I'm sure it will take more than a week even to come up with a workable plan."

Pam, in her eagerness, had already changed into her Halcyon clothes. She had covered her short hair with a broad brimmed hat. Much of her outfit was borrowed from her friends back at Eleytheria.

When Al had changed his clothes, he asked "How do I look?"

Pam examined him closely. "Not bad, I think. Still your voice gives you away, so be careful who you talk to. What about me?"

Al ran his hands through his thick hair as he looked at his beautiful wife. He took her hat off and looked at her again.

"The short hair helps, but I am afraid anyone who knows you well would recognize you. It's too bad you can't grow a beard."

Pam punched him in the ribs. "Albert Gleeson, I have never heard you make a joke about me before. You must be scared out of your mind. You're almost beginning to sound like that rascal, Dave. Growing a beard indeed!"

Al felt a pang of guilt at Dave's name. He hadn't thought about or prayed for Dave for several days. He kissed Pam gently.

"We should go and get away from the boat, in case anyone spots us."

Al led the way as they struggled through the brush until he came to the fisherman's path that led back to the Halcyon campus.

He pointed down the path to the shore. "Down there is the rock I used to fish from when I went for sea bass."

"Did you ever catch any?" asked Pam.

"I caught a few in my time. Well, sweetheart let's hope this fishing expedition for Little Thomas is equally successful."

Turning in the other direction, they followed the cascade as they climbed the hill. The rain had stopped, but the water dripped constantly from the trees. The air was so fresh it brought memories back to Al of fishing expeditions that had brought such peace to his soul even if they hadn't often added to his larder. Even in the midst of his oppressive duty serving the legalistic Dalyites, he had met God whenever he was alone in the wilderness and had time to think.

They reached the crest and saw the campus below them at the foot of the northern hills. The buildings, looking shabbier than even a few months ago, had been designed to be modern and futuristic. But without upkeep and cleaning, they were drab and forlorn. The cloudy sky only added to the oppressive desolation.

They followed the path into the valley and came to Socrates, the dorm where both Al and Pam had lived.

Al walked to a bench screened by bushes not far from the entrance. The bushes had not been cut back in months and hid the bench from the dormitory. They sat there watching the entrance. Al was hoping to see Tom or Dwight, but although some people he recognized left the building, his friends were nowhere to be seen. Finally late in the afternoon, Al thought he recognized a familiar gait.

"Wait here, hun. I see Tom. If everything is alright, I'll come back to get you. Go back to the boat at the first sign of trouble."

"But Al…"

"No 'buts'. You have to promise me this."

Pam looked Al in the face and her lips trembled in protest. But she seemed to change her mind and her expression relaxed. "Okay," said Pam quietly, lowering her head.

Al thrust his hands in his pockets and left the cover of the bushes.

He walked right up to Tom, so that they almost bumped into each other. Tom looked up in surprise.

"Oh, sorry man…"

"Tom, it's me Al."

"Al?" Tom peered at him closely. "Well I never would have—you look like a bear with that beard. Are you crazy? What are you doing back here?"

"No time to explain now. Is there a place to talk privately?"

"Sure—my room?"

"What about your roommate?"

"Dwight's my roommate," said Tom.

"Okay, let's get Pam and we'll go in with you."

Tom's mouth gaped open in surprise.

Tom followed Al to the bench where Pam was seated. As soon as she recognized him, she leapt up and ran to give him a hug.

"Your husband has quite the beard. How do you like being married to a hairy beast?" asked Tom.

"That would be telling!" Pam said, kissing Tom affectionately on the cheek.

Tom took them around to the side of the building and they began the long climb to the fifth floor. They came out of the stairwell close to Tom's room. He ushered them in quickly, watching to ensure no one saw their approach.

Dwight looked up from a dog-eared book he was reading at his desk, startled. He ignored Al, but looked at Pam with surprise.

"Pam? Is that really you?"

Pam went over and gave Dwight a hug.

"I'm glad to see you too Dwight."

"How is Al doing?"

"I'm fine thank you very much!"

Dwight's eyes widened in surprise. "Wow, with all that hair, you must have gone through puberty since I saw you last! Actually, you look better when we can see less of your face."

"It's been a while, Dwight. Good to know our relationship has lost none of its sparkle."

Dwight, smiling, jumped up and grabbed Al by the shoulder and they clasped hands.

"Have a seat," said Tom moving a worn out chair for Pam. "Would you like something to drink? We have Halcyon tea and our island beer, which by the way, hasn't improved much since you guys left for who knows where."

After everyone had something to drink, Tom asked about what had happened since they had parted company.

"We're on an island, which we call Eleytheria, derived from the Greek word for freedom," said Al. He talked about the trip up river, the hard work in the founding of their colony and their fear of Meglir attacking them. Finally he told them about Dave setting off on his exploration trip with Hanomer and their long absence. He could see the concern on Tom and Dwight's faces as they thought about Dave's disappearance.

"So much about us," said Al. "What about you?"

"Well," began Dwight, "we set off at the same time you did, and MacDonald kept pushing us to get back to Halcyon as quickly as possible. We never stopped once. That evening, when we passed the coastal mountains, we briefly put into shore and let off those of our crew that wanted to try to find New Jerusalem.

"We reached West Harbor without fanfare and MacDonald set off to report to Blackmore and his cronies. We tied up the boats and were told to remove our stuff and pile it on the shore and wait.

"I was expecting we would all be thrown into prison, but later that evening we were given instructions to return to our dorm rooms, resume our shore duties, and await further orders. They never came. The rumors about the catastrophe spread like a virus so that everyone was talking of nothing else for a week. They blamed Blackmore, they blamed Hoffstetter, and they blamed MacDonald. Then everything began to settle down and slowly the view emerged that it was mostly MacDonald and the traitors who had escaped that had brought the calamity on us. Those of you who set out west were included in that lot."

"That figures. So Blackmore with his Halcyon propaganda machine was even able to wriggle out of this one?" said Al.

"That's about it. They never threatened us. They just kept putting the message out there and eventually people began to believe it ."

"I guess," said Tom. "Your disguise means that you already know that your return will be viewed with the same enthusiasm as a fox at a hen party. You must have a pretty important reason for taking this risk."

"I think," said Dwight, "it would be more like a fawn wandering into the middle of a hungry wolf pack."

Al looked at Pam and she briefly met his eyes and then nodded.

"Tom, we've come back for Little Thomas."

"So that's it."

"Yes, Pam and I just can't leave him in the Staycare Center. He should be with his mother and father—I mean stepfather."

Tom said nothing but exchanged glances with Dwight.

"This is risky business," interposed Dwight. "How do you plan on getting him out? How will you get away?"

"To be honest," said Pam, "we don't have a full plan yet. Since I was in med school before the Dislocation, I'm going to pretend to be a nurse and sneak into the Staycare Center. Seeing a stranger in a medical uniform is a common occurrence in there. Once I learn their routine, I'll identify a time when we can get away with Little Thomas and back to our boat before they discover he's gone. We know it's risky. We really don't want to involve you two for that reason, but we were hoping you would just give us some guidance so we can get set up here and operate on our own."

"For example," added Al, "is there a room in the building we could use? Maybe there are other things we should know—we have been away for a long time."

Dwight pressed his finger tips together and said nothing while he thought. Finally he ran his hands across his forehead.

"Personally, I think it's providential that you came. Tom and I have a problem—a big problem. I think your coming can help."

"What Dwight and I are saying is that we can solve two problems at once. If things go badly for us, we'll hitch a ride out of here. We'll help you get Little Thomas out, of course, but we're hoping that your offer at Linderhof to take us with you to your new colony still stands."

Pam and Al breathed a collective sigh of relief.

"Of course the offer still stands," said Al. "So what is this problem you're trying to solve?"

"Well," began Tom, "Dwight and I have been hanging around together pretty much since we got back. We both work on the fishing trawler, and we work in the lab with Professor Sturgeon—do you remember him Al?"

"How could I forget him? He was there the first time I saw one of those Halcyon monstrosities—sharks with tentacles around their mouths. Sturgeon is the guy who looks like Charles Darwin with a hook nose."

"That's right—that's him. Well he disappeared a little over a week ago. The rumor is either that he killed himself or that he died in a sailing accident, although no one has seen the overturned sailboat or even a body. He's just not at the lab anymore. If you ask about what happened you simply gets rumors and speculation."

"How do you know the rumors aren't true?" asked Al.

"I don't know for sure, but there are a couple of things that don't add up and one that makes me downright skeptical."

"Let's hear it!" said Al.

"Well, I've known Sturgeon since before the Dislocation and he doesn't strike me as someone who's about to commit suicide."

Dwight nodded in agreement.

"Sure, Sturgeon goes out on the trawler frequently, but I've never known him to go sailing by himself. So it doesn't make sense to me that Sturgeon would go out by himself in a sailboat either. But here's the clincher: The last few days before he disappeared, he looked worried—not depressed—worried. When I asked him if everything was okay, he said he'd found something important, but he couldn't talk about it until he had more evidence. And the next thing I knew, he'd vanished."

"Any idea what it was?" asked Al.

"No," said Tom, "but Dwight and I are going to find out."

"Since Sturgeon disappeared, I've kinda had the run of the laboratory. When we find a new species, I help classify it and run toxicity tests on it. That doesn't take much time, so I also spend time on our research projects. Dwight helps me most of the time. We have lots of reason to go into Sturgeon's office and go through his papers. It sounds as if you have a few days of lying low while Pam figures out the routine at the Staycare Center. Rather than just sitting here, why not help us?"

Al looked at Pam.

"Go ahead, hun," said Pam. "I have to go into the Staycare Center to find Little Thomas. It will take me a while to get the lay of the land and figure out the best way to get him out of there. You can't really help me right now, so you may as well help Tom and Dwight. Plus, Floyd and Dave will love it if you bring back some information on the situation in Halcyon."

"Very good! I would much prefer to be active than to sit in a room worrying about whether or not you were discovered. When do we start?"

Chapter 8

Playing with Fire

Many of the rooms on the fifth floor of Socrates were empty, so Pam and Al set up house in a room near a stairwell, just down the corridor from Tom and Dwight.

About eight o'clock that evening, Al was pacing back and forth in their room, feeling like a caged tiger, when there was a knock on the door. Al felt his stomach lurch, but when he looked through the peep hole, he whistled with relief.

"Hey Tom," he said, opening the door.

Tom came in carrying several packages. He handed one to Al and set the others onto the table.

"What's this?" asked Al turning the heavy manila-wrapped object in his hand.

"Those packages are food that Dwight and I smuggled out of the cafeteria. This way you won't have to go down there. You'd probably be safe, but why take a chance?

"As for that second one, that's for you, Pam."

Pam eagerly unwrapped the parcel and then whooped with delight.

"A nurse's uniform! This is even better than the medical student uniform I had brought along."

"Now all you need is to make a fake badge, and then you can go almost anywhere, including the Staycare Center to find Little Thomas."

"Oh, I still have my badge. I kept my old one. I knew I was going to need it."

"Well, then you're all set," said Tom. "If you flash your badge, especially at night, no one will look at it closely or remember your name. After you guys have a bite to eat, let me steal your old man for a while so he can join me at the lab. Almost nobody is there this late at night but me, and if I take Al along, it won't cause a stir."

Al and Pam were ravenous. "This smells like chicken," said Al. "Halcyon finally has enough chickens to start eating them?"

"Yeah," said Tom. "Things have changed a bit since you were here last. Chickens are one example. We've also found an island up the coast that we use for lumber since we still can't use the mainland because of the Renegades."

"But doesn't that island also have Happy Berries? Won't the addiction start all over again and then you'll just have one more island full of Renegades?"

"The Navy guys went in and cleared out the Happy Berry bushes near the lumber camp. We haven't set up a permanent colony there—the lumber crews sail in, cut the wood and then float the logs back to Halcyon. It's a risk, but we need the resources."

Pam and Al ate in silence. Finally Al pushed himself away from the table. "Boy that was good! I haven't had chicken in ages! So what's happening tonight?"

"Well, Tom and I are going to take our usual shift in the lab. The plan is that we'll lock you into Sturgeon's office. If anyone comes in for a test result or brings new samples, we'll both be there as expected, our usual friendly, helpful selves. You should have no trouble getting an extended period of time to go through Sturgeon's papers. Maybe you'll help us figure out what's going on."

"So what am I supposed to do?" asked Pam.

"Do you want to help me?" asked Al.

"We'd better not," said Tom turning red. "With my, uh … history, I have a bit of a reputation, and if we brought a pretty woman into the building at night, I'm afraid we'd get the gossip tongues wagging, which is the last thing we want."

"Listen," said Pam, "I think I can move around campus at night with no problem. I need to check out the Staycare Center anyway, to make sure I understand what has changed on campus. When we get Little Thomas, we'll need to get away quickly and quietly. That will give me more than enough to do."

Later that evening Al, Tom and Dwight made it to the lab without incident. Al had begun to feel much better about their chances of successfully rescuing Little Thomas. He had not expected to get this far without detection.

Tom took the passkey out of the top drawer of his desk and opened Sturgeon's office. There were piles of papers everywhere.

"Oh man!" said Al. "This is going to be a huge job."

"Yeah, I know," said Tom. "I'll lock you in. In the unlikely event that someone comes and wants in, hide in the closet at the back. If you need to come out, peek through the blinds to make sure that we don't have any visitors, and then rap on the office door."

After Al heard the click of the lock, he turned on a small light by the desk and began to survey the office. He first checked out the closet at the back. It was much larger than he had expected. There was a row of lab coats in the front and a second row of blazers and winter coats at the back. He pushed the clothes to one side and put a box on the floor behind them.

"If someone comes in, I'll just stand behind the clothes on the box so they don't see my feet, then hope for the best." He decided silently.

A picture at the side of the closet caught his eye.

What an odd place for a picture! He thought.

Upon closer inspection he realized it was on a hinge. Behind it was a small recessed safe.

I bet that's where the answer lies, but how do I open it?

With a sigh, Al went back outside and began picking up papers on the far side of the room, carried them back to the light, read through them carefully and then placed them on the floor.

It had been a week of meticulous work reading through all of Sturgeon's papers. Al had learned a great many things. The Halcyon chemists had isolated the key component of Happy Berries which, with boring predictability, the natural product chemists had named the compound *Happenone*.

They had also made a number of derivatives of this drug, one of which was a *Happenone* antagonist and could be used to make users violently ill if used the narcotic. There was another derivative which they called *Hyperhap* which elicited a good deal of interest judging by the number of toxicology samples sent to Sturgeon, but Sturgeon himself was puzzled by the interest since *Hyperhap* had little efficacy for dealing with the addiction. However, the bottom line: Al was no further ahead in explaining Sturgeon's disappearance.

On other fronts things had gone much better. No one had recognized them and the danger period had receded, at least in their minds. He had made one trip back to the *Hansa* on the north coast and the repairs, or more properly, the regrowth of the boat was progressing well. Pam had been able to scout the Staycare Center and had even located Little Thomas, but she was discouraged; the children were never left alone during the day, and she had not been able to find a way into their sleeping quarters. But then, they had known this would not be easy. Seeing Little Thomas for the first time had given her such a sharp sense of regret at having abandoned him, that now she could not wait to get him out, yet she had to steel herself to keep from doing something rash.

Al had just emptied one of the drawers on Sturgeon's desk, when a thought struck him. He pulled out the drawer as far as it would go and felt underneath. Nothing! He pulled out each drawer in turn and checked underneath. When he felt the bottommost drawer, his hand touched a plastic sleeve. Excited, he tried to pull the drawer out, but it caught.

Searching carefully, he found a catch at the back that released the drawer. Turning the drawer upside down, he found a thin booklet in the sleeve. Pulling the booklet out, he began to leaf through it. It was entitled "Passwords and Personal Identification Numbers." He found three numbers, without any identifying description and tried them on the safe. It didn't open.

Maybe those were his gym locker numbers. He said to himself, half-amused by the thought.

He tried every combination of numbers he could find, but none worked. He sat down and rested his chin on his hands.

The combination for the safe has to be in here. But where?

He went over the little pamphlet again. He hadn't missed any numbers. However in the middle he found a curious limerick:

There was a young chemist from Illyium
Who thought he'd study Beryllium
He took a flask red
He believed contained Lead
But found that it was Selenium

It doesn't even really work. Why would Sturgeon put that in here? Beryllium, Lead, and Selenium? Suddenly, the message behind Sturgeon's code dawned on him.

Al went to the periodic table on the wall and picked out the atomic numbers for Be, Pb, and Se. With trembling hands he turned the dial: 4-82-34. Click, the handle moved, and the door opened. Inside was a stack of notebooks, a passport, and a small box containing a few keys.

He picked up the top leather bound notebook. The last entry was dated September 20th, the day before Sturgeon had disappeared.

> I've reached an impasse with the new narcotic *Hyperhap*. I know there's something going on in the Primate Department of Zoology. Why else would they have taken all the insulin pumps out of medical? I tried to get into Primate yesterday, but I was rebuffed. I bet I know a few things they don't. There's a small food service elevator from the food preparation area for delivering food to the various animal enclosures. It's just big enough to hold one person.
>
> If I'm right, that idiot Boyd is endangering us all. I'm going to go in tonight and find out what's going on. If it's what I think it is, I'm going straight to Blackmore to blow the lid off this thing.

Al went back to an entry dated September 12th and tried to get a picture of what had gotten Sturgeon so concerned.

> I told them that my cell cultures contain the active enzymes that reliably predict neuroprotein interactions in the human brain. My studies indicate *Hyperhap* is even more addictive than *Happenone* even though it doesn't have many of the long term physiological side effects. Why are they still asking questions about it and pushing me to do more *in vitro* studies?

And on September 15th…

> I was over at Zoology tonight about 1:00 am, in my other office and as I was leaving, a bunch of Bigelow's Special Forces came up. I went to investigate and my sudden

appearance so early in the morning obviously surprised them. They ushered me out very quickly with no explanation, but not before I saw what they were unloading. It looked like the comatose bodies of four people. There was enough light on the loading dock to see that they were still alive and their orange eyes indicated heavy *Happenone* addiction. They were Renegades. What are they doing with them here?

Tom gently rapped on the door to indicate it was time to leave. Al put the notebook in his satchel, locked up the safe and returned with the others to Socrates without saying a word about his discovery.

When they were all back at Socrates behind locked doors, Al showed the others the notebook they had found. Each read the final entries for himself.

"So what do you make of it Al?" asked Dwight.

"I don't know for sure," said Al. "But it is pretty clear that Sturgeon believed Jonathan Boyd was behind this and that it involves Renegades and Hyperhap. The other thing that caught me by surprise was Bigelow's return. He was last with Meglir. How did he make it back?"

"Somehow he returned to the island of City Point after we had driven the Apemen off. Tom and I didn't know about it until well after we reached Halcyon, since he travelled downriver in one of the other longboats. When we realized he was here, he had already started to organize his own Special Forces unit reporting directly to Blackmore. Tom and I decided to keep a low profile since we were known to be your associates."

Tom turned red. "I was scared. I didn't want Bigelow's personal grudge to come down on us. Al I'm sorry."

Al looked at Pam. She was white as a sheet. He went to her and put his arm around her shoulder.

"Don't worry honey, it will be alright."

"But what if he's been in to see Little Thomas? Bigelow would hurt him just out of spite."

"Bigelow may be Little Thomas' father," said Al gently. "But he's so full of himself, he probably hasn't given his son a second thought."

"Maybe you're right."

A wave of jealousy and anger swept through Al. He left Pam's side and began to pace up and down in an effort to keep the raging emotions from showing on his face.

Why couldn't Little Thomas have been mine? Now Pam is forever tied to Bigelow. How can I do the right thing when I'm so angry at Little Thomas' father!

Al sighed and thrust his hands into his pockets as he continued to pace back and forth.

Get a hold of yourself. Focus on doing the right thing. Pam has been forgiven and Little Thomas cannot help his paternity. He needs to be my son and my anger at his father must never be directed at Little Thomas.

Pam got up from the table, a look of concern on her face.

"Al, are you alright? What are you thinking?"

"I am alright, Pam. I am trying to figure out the right thing to do."

He squeezed her hand and came back to the table.

"I also need to figure out what is going on in the Primate Department in Zoology."

"Don't you mean 'we?'" asked Dwight.

"You fellows need to remain uninvolved since you are staying in Halcyon, while I am not. Besides, if I get caught, you need to help Pam get Little Thomas out of Halcyon."

"Al, no! No! You can't take a chance like this. Sturgeon was caught and you will be too," said Pam. "Why are you doing this?"

"Honey, this needs to be done. Bigelow is mixed up in this and I can't let him win. Failure of whatever he's doing would be best for you, for Little Thomas, and for Eleytheria. Besides, I think Sturgeon pulled off the break into Zoology and then made the mistake of confronting Blackmore, and Blackmore turned him in. I will not make the same mistake."

Pam's lips trembled and her eyes were moist. Her look said she didn't believe him. She said nothing but embraced him as the tremble escalated into a couple of shuddering sobs.

Wiping her eyes, she straightened her dress. "I know you're doing what you think is best. I'll pray that you'll be safe."

The rest of the evening was spent working out a plan. Al, Tom and Dwight went over it several times until they had it memorized. They worked on all of the contingencies that they could think of. Dwight had several keys to Hobbes, the dorm nearest the cove where the *Hansa* were hidden. They were to use a room in that dorm as a last resort in case everything else went wrong and they had to make a run for it.

Chapter 9

The Aberhardt Constant

"What's all this about Darwin?" asked John Hobbs, wiping his pudgy face with a handkerchief.

Darwin Blackmore considered his colleague for a moment. John Hobbs was short and his extra weight made him look as if he did not have a waist.

Blackmore caught himself stroking his goatee and put his hands down on the conference table in front of him.

"John, I don't really know what Aberhardt wants to talk to us about. He asked to meet with the Senate Executive Committee on a matter of some urgency. Since he's a member of the Senate I couldn't say 'no.' I have given him twenty minutes."

The door opened and Blackmore's pretty executive assistant, Bernice Le Blanc, entered and closed the door behind her.

"Professor Aberhardt has arrived for his appointment. Is it convenient for me to bring him in now, or do you need more discussion time?" asked Bernice.

Blackmore looked around the table. "Shall I have him brought in?" Everyone nodded. Blackmore turned and signaled to Bernice.

A few moments later, Bernice ushered Aberhardt into the conference room. Blackmore rose to shake his hand as Bernice left and closed the door behind her. Frederick Aberhardt was an austere man with a long thin face crowned with thin, wild, scraggly hair. His chin was defined by a brown goatee that was as wild as the hair on his head.

"Professor Aberhardt how good it is to see you," said Blackmore. Blackmore hoped he sounded sincere.

Aberhardt took his hand, but only nodded in acknowledgement.

"Please have a seat at the table," said Blackmore.

"I'm used to lecturing, so I'll stand," said Aberhardt.

Blackmore felt his face getting warm. *The pompous swine!*

Blackmore turned toward the others and cleared his throat as he tried to regain his composure. With long practice, he made his face impassive.

"Friends, it gives me great pleasure to welcome the distinguished Professor Aberhardt to our council chambers. He is one of the most eminent sociologists of our time. He has written the book The Sociology of Democratic Governance, which received the President's Award shortly before we were dislocated. Even before the award, the book had become obligatory reading in all serious sociology and political science courses."

He turned to Professor Aberhardt. "Welcome to our meeting, Frederick. Please tell us about the urgent matter you wanted to talk to us about." Blackmore sat down and leaned back in his chair.

Aberhardt had a surprisingly loud voice for a thin man and glowered at his audience with piercing eyes.

"As Darwin has said," began Aberhardt, "I am the pre-eminent sociologist at Halcyon. I'm here to warn you that you are taking a dangerous course. As I listened to our Senate deliberations over the last few weeks, it has become clear to me that we are contemplating taking more direct action to bring resisters or rebels into line. WE MUST NOT DO THAT."

The shock of Aberhardt's shout, made Hobbs, who had begun to doodle on his note pad, drop his pencil on the floor. He frowned at Aberhardt and shifted his position.

"I'm not sure I follow you, Frederick," said Blackmore in a soft voice.

"In my book, *The Sociology of Democratic Governance*, I go to great lengths to define what has subsequently been named the Aberhardt Constant.

"Perhaps you should explain, Frederick, since not everyone here has read your magnificent work recently."

Aberhardt's eyes bored into Blackmore, as if questioning whether or not he was being mocked.

Blackmore gave him his most reassuring smile.

Apparently satisfied, Aberhardt went on. "Many governments in the past have tried to direct the thinking of their subjects. They have used force and coercion. Although they appeared successful for a time, they ultimately failed. Why?" Here he thrust his index finger into the air.

"They failed because coercion achieved outward compliance, but had no control over what happened in the minds of their citizens. Thus, their thoughts unmodified, the subjects became increasingly rebellious until the opposition gained power to revolt."

"Through our empirical studies we know better. We encourage people to express their opinions. We welcome them. When they criticize us, the nature of their criticism tells us to what degree our persuasion is working. By using the media, the arts, and education, we can change the prevailing public opinion in the direction we want at a rate given by the effectiveness of these tools. I have measured that effectiveness. That rate is defined by Aberhardt's Constant. As long as we only make changes at a rate less than this time constant, then the average person, even though he grumbles about some of the things he sees going on, doesn't become alarmed enough to take action because the change is happening slowly. He doesn't realize that his opinion is being incrementally shifted for him by unending repetition in the direction of the next behavior modification step through school, through television and every other thing in his environment he sees or hears. We can study him, poll his attitude and opinions, and if one message doesn't work, we'll try another. We can always measure our effectiveness because he's willing to tell us what he likes and what he doesn't like."

Blackmore shifted in his seat uncomfortably. He heard Lydia Pendergast beginning to tap her foot on the floor.

Maybe I shouldn't have sat down. Now that Aberhardt has the floor he could go on and on.

Aberhardt continued. "This gradual thinking modifcation works splendidly *as long as we don't go too fast*. Some changes are so significant and so difficult, we actually have to wait for a new generation to grow up under our tutelage to achieve change. But, here is the critical point: if we try to go faster by coercion, then not only will we build up the subject's resentment, but by its very nature, coercion causes the subject to hide his true feelings from us. When that happens we no longer accurately measure public opinion." Aberhardt again stabbed the air with his finger for emphasis. "And so we will be governing in a vacuum, being forced to use stronger and stronger measures to maintain compliance until the system collapses in a revolt or an unwelcome opposition party.

"All of this is explained in my book …

"Yes, yes, yes!" muttered Lydia Pendergast. "We know all that."

Aberhardt glared murderously at Pendergast.

Undaunted Pendergast continued. "Halcyon is a closed, controlled environment. We have broken down many of the institutions that have caused us so much grief. We know that religion poisons everything and so we have been careful to make the practice of religion a private affair, excluded from all public discussion, and so thanks to our excellent management, religion has almost disappeared. We won't have any Martin Luthers rocking our boat…"

"Undoubtedly that has been an excellent development," said Aberhardt.

"We have suppressed the family," continued Pendergast. "Isn't that important?"

"It's true, that suppression is very important for sociological evolution. The stable family is a sociologically self-contained unit which means we don't really know what ideas are taking root there. They don't need us to care for them. In our new order, we create state dependency by ensuring there are almost no close familial relationships…"

"Exactly my point," interrupted Pendergast.

"Let me continue," interrupted Aberhardt in turn, "the subjects now look to Halcyon to raise their offspring. If they are sick they come to our doctors. If they are depressed they talk to our psychologists. At every turn we are able to influence them. These are all excellent steps, but with our current actions we are jeopardizing all of our progress…"

"Really Frederick, I'm sure you're right about the basic facts and your theory is brilliant," said Trevor Huxley cleaning his glasses. "But it will take twenty or thirty years to make the kind of changes we want if we follow your infinitesimal steps, even given the rather substantial control we have over the Halcyon media, the few artistic endeavors we have left and of course our educational activities. We simply don't have twenty years. This army of Apemen we have heard about could be here any day now and we need to make sure that everyone is on board. We can't have any disunity. We can't have our decisions questioned. Only the strong will survive and we need to govern strongly."

"Besides," added Pendergast, "your problem, Aberhardt, is that you're working through social influences. Biology is more fundamental than sociology. Give me the right neurotransmitters and I can make our people believe anything you want."

"Enough," said Darwin Blackmore. He stroked his unruly goatee. "Thank you Professor Aberhardt for your valuable and insightful discourse. I will weigh your suggestions as well as those of Professor Pendergast and Administrator Huxley carefully."

Aberhardt scowled. "You're not going to take my warning seriously, are you?"

"Nonsense," said Blackmore. "You have given us much food for thought. As I recall, Aberhardt's Constant is a constant in name only and can be increased; perhaps you and Dr. Pendergast should have more discussions. With the right kind of psychopharmacopeia one could make the changes much sooner and so modify the magnitude of the Aberhardt Constant. Thank you for your time."

Blackmore's best smile was wasted on Aberhardt's back as he stomped out.

As the door slammed, Pendergast muttered, "When I make this work, we'll have to rename it the Pendergast-Aberhardt Constant."

Blackmore, ignoring Pendergast's mumblings, went on:

"I have one more item to discuss. Do you remember after the first Halcyon River expedition returned and reported about the City of the Dead? There was a fellow on that expedition, Albert Gleeson. Subsequently, because of his bizarre religious ideas, Jonathan Boyd, the psychiatrist at Halcyon Medical Center, decided he was delusional and needed to be protected. Boyd sedated him because of his illness, but then Gleeson mysteriously vanished from Halcyon. He reappeared on the Second Halcyon River expedition, and then after that disaster, joined the rebels in the new colony. Well I have reliable information that he has secretly returned to Halcyon."

"Is this a problem?" asked Huxley. "After all he is only one person. I presume there is only one, am I right?"

"No, he's not a problem," said Blackmore. "Indeed, now that we know he's here, he's even less of a problem, but still this colony he and his fellow rebels have set up is an annoyance. Furthermore as Professor Aberhardt has so eloquently pointed out, we persuade people to our way of thinking through the media, the arts, and through education. But this colony is beyond our reach on all three fronts. We want to mold and shape our society by controlling the story that everyone believes. Who knows what peculiar ideas, indeed, what dangerous and inimical ideas they may come up with, in the absence of our guidance.

We can't lose control of our conditioning program because of these uncontrolled upstarts."

"So what do you propose?" asked Pendergast.

"Propose? I propose we watch him discreetly. That way we can locate all of his contacts. We may not need to do anything, but if he does cause trouble, we'll pick him up. Now if we have no further business, I still have some excellent wine in my cellar that I think we should try."

Chapter 10

Beserkers

Al, Tom and Dwight had been watching the Zoology building all day. Tom had identified a group of men with red armbands carrying stunners that were going in and out as members of Bigelow's Special Forces. But Al had not seen Bigelow.

Not stunners! The sonic blast from a stunner would make its target feel like they had received a concussion. *They're useful only at twenty to thirty feet, but the Special Forces would have much less reluctance to use those than they would a gun or a crossbow.*

Finally twilight settled in and from Tom's description, the evening feeding of the caged animals in Zoology had passed. Dwight remained as a lookout. Now that the local Halcyon cell network was operational again, they would use it as a warning system. If there was any unusual activity at the entrance, Dwight was to phone Tom on his cellphone asking if he wanted to go to the Seaside Pub. That coded message would tell them to abort.

Using a passkey from Sturgeon's safe, Tom and Al entered Zoology through a back entrance and took the service elevator to the feed storage area. The large room was dark except for a dim light from a distant hallway.

Tom handed Al a spare cellphone.

"Okay, let's do this!" whispered Al taking off his jacket and handing it to Tom. "Call me only if it's a genuine emergency. If I'm not back down here in twenty minutes, make your way back to Dwight, wait another ten minutes to confirm I've been captured and then head to the safe room in Hobbes. God be with you!"

"And also with you!" Tom placed his hand on Al's shoulder.

Al looked at Tom in surprise and smiled. Then he climbed into the dumbwaiter used to transport the feed to the animal area and assumed the fetal position. Tom closed the door. It was absolutely and utterly dark. Al fumbled for the latch and the door opened.

"Okay, I think this could work. Send me up." Tom closed the door and Al, feeling the first twinge of claustrophobia, felt himself rising slowly.

The dumbwaiter stopped; Al fumbled for the latch. The door sprang open with a soft click. The room was almost as dark as the inside of the dumbwaiter. There was a little light coming from a curtained window to the corridor. He could just see the outline of a sentry guarding the outside of the door through the window to the hallway.

There was something wrong! It was too quiet. If there were animals in cages, Al would have heard something.

But he heard nothing. He had a flashlight but couldn't risk using it, not with a sentry outside the door. Instead he got down on all fours and crept along the floor. Cupboards and lab benches shielded him. Ahead, light came through a small window set into a heavy door. He approached it, peered through, and saw a large fabric tent in the middle of a well-lit room. Curious, he decided to go inside. He glanced back at the hall window. The guard was nowhere in sight. Al quietly opened the door a crack and slid inside. The room was much bigger than he had thought. He entered the tent. It was a fully equipped operating room with clamps, a laser scalpel, and anesthesiology equipment. In one of the trays he saw insulin pumps and implant hearing aids in sealed, sterilized packaging.

He left the tent and went to the back of the large room. This part of the room was lined with large cages. Each cage held a hospital bed with straps and an IV pole. But the beds in the cages were empty.

Al walked around the tent to next side of the square room and saw four beds in cages. These had occupants. He moved closer and saw that they were strapped in and had IVs running. Two of the occupants had no bandages, while the other two had bandages on their heads and around their chests.

At the corner of the room, beside another door, was a work station with a log book and a cabinet that contained a series of keys. He found the keys for the four occupied cells and went into the first. As he approached he saw orange-tinged eyes staring vacuously at the ceiling.

Oh no! Happy Berry users—Renegades!

The occupants of the other three beds had the same eyes.

Whatever Boyd was doing, he was working on Renegades from the mainland. If they get free, they'll go on a killing rampage. Scenes from Botany Bay—and their fight to rescue the last few Halcyonites before the raving mad, but incredibly strong Happy Berry addicts killed them all—came to his mind. He could smell the acrid smoke from guns being fired, hear the deep throated yells of the Renegades, and recalled the slow motion quality of battle when every thought was focused on staying alive.

He forced his mind back to the present. He locked the cell doors, returned the keys and went back to examine the log book. He read:

> Pump insertion and audio implantation completed October 2nd. Bandage removal and initial command response test to be completed at 16:00 October 7th. Do not attempt to discontinue sedation unless backup staff and Special Forces are present.

He looked at the door next to the work station. It was directly across from the door through which he had entered, and led to another room. He peered through the glass and carefully opened the door. Beyond the door was a large cage and inside were about twenty naked individuals, all male. They milled around aimlessly. The cage smelled of urine and excrement.

Al looked at their eyes. They were all deep orange.

They're all Happy Berry users! Why aren't they attacking me and trying to get at me through the bars of the cage?

He looked at the control panel in front of him. On a large display there was a table of numbers and a data entry box that read "Select subject." On a sheet of paper beside the panel were a series of instructions.

In order to control the subjects:
    1. Key in the subject's number.
    2. Press the injection icon.
    3. Open the audio link and speak a command (such as "come here", "eat", or "shower").

4. To select another subject, key in a second subject number.

The numbers represent the Renegades!

Al typed in the number '1" and hit the inject button. There was no sound, but one of the Renegades gave an involuntary shudder. Al switched on the audio and said into the microphone "Come here!"

The same Renegade separated from the others and lumbered toward the front of the cage. He had a large "1" tattooed onto his chest.

Just then Al heard the noise of a door opening in the outer room. He looked around in panic.

I'm trapped!

He looked frantically for a way out or a place to hide. Spying a door to his right, he crept through it into a dark room. Quietly closing the door, he stepped away a safe distance, then turned to look back through the door's small square window. He watched as a man in a lab coat walked up to the control panel, punched in a few keys, then spoke into the microphone. The technician watched the Renegades for a few minutes and then left.

What are they doing with the Renegades? He thought again about the ferocious attack they had fended off at Botany Bay as they had rescued a couple of hundred people from a village of fifteen hundred. Then it hit him. He knew with a certainty what Blackmore was up to.

Al found a light switch to see where he was—a small corridor with two doors. One door led to a small change room full of coveralls. He took one coverall down from a rack of hangers labeled "Spares" and pulled it on and then turned off the light.

The other door had a sign:

A21 Do Not Enter Without Authorization

Al went back to the small cabinet on the wall in the change room. Finding it unlocked, he opened it and found a set of keys. One was marked A21. Taking it, Al unlocked the door and quietly pushed it open a crack. The room was occupied by a single individual lying in a bed asleep, hooked up to an IV, his long beard stretching over the sheets—it was Sturgeon!

Al approached the bed. He lifted Sturgeon's eyelid. The eye had an orange tinge to it.

Hyperhap! They're converting him into a controllable Renegade. Should I try to wake him? No, we'd both be caught. I can't get him out of here.

He looked at his watch. He had to get out. Backing out of the room, he once again peered through the door at the Renegades: they were lining up.

Now what? If that technician is sitting in the outer room, as soon as I open the door, I will be captured. Better to wait.

He got down on his knees listening for any sound of movement in the outer laboratory. He heard the clang of a cell door. He waited longer. The noises went on interminably.

He's checking the four Renegades in the cages.

Finally, Al thought he heard the sound of an outer door closing. He waited for two more agonizing minutes.

No sound! I cannot wait any longer.

Saying a quick prayer, he walked into the outer lab as if he had every right to be there. He expected to hear "Who are you?" but there was no sound. The lab was empty.

He moved and punched in the code for the feed preparation area and then climbed into the dumb waiter with difficulty. It took several tries for him to pull on the latch from the inside until the door snapped shut. When the latch snapped, the dumb waiter began to move. He arrived at the feed preparation area, but Tom was no longer there. Al glanced at his watch and left quickly. Walking rapidly to the little park, he saw Tom and Dwight waiting anxiously for him.

"Whew!" said Tom. "What took you so long? Where did you get that coverall?"

"I was almost surprised by a lab technician. The operative term is 'almost.' This coverall is a spare from the cage area."

"Did you learn anything?" whispered Dwight.

"Yes I did, but let's not talk here."

On the way back to Socrates, Al started the conversation. "Have you ever heard of Berserkers?"

"No—can't say I have," said Tom.

"Me neither," added Dwight.

"Berserkers were Norse warriors who fought with uncontrolled fury, cutting everything down in their path until they were killed, hence our term 'going berserk.'"

"Okay," said Tom. "Thanks for the history lesson, but what has that got to do with what you saw?"

"I don't think you're going to believe this, but Boyd has captured some Renegades. When he injects them using a remote controlled insulin pump, he can give them commands through an audio implant that they make from a hearing aid. Thus he gets Renegades to obey his commands. I'm guessing he plans to use them as Berserkers, as human fighting machines that never quit until they're cut down."

"So that's where all the Hyperhap has gone!" said Dwight.

"Start from the beginning and tell us everything!" said Tom.

Al told them everything he had experienced after he had climbed into the dumb waiter.

"Whew!" said Dwight. "So that's what got Sturgeon into trouble."

"What are we going to do about Sturgeon?" asked Tom.

"I don't know," said Al. "Whatever we do, we had better do it fast. I don't know how long he's been on Hyperhap, but it can't be long before they complete the whole procedure. I think I need to make an attempt to get him out."

"You'll never manage it on your own," said Dwight. "It will at least take two of us to handle him and three would be better."

"Bigelow has the place well-guarded," said Al. "The dumb waiter allows one person to go in, but not three."

"Wait a minute guys," said Tom, "Boyd or Blackmore will never turn Sturgeon into a Berzerker. He's too well known. Why spend all this bandwidth blathering about his death or suicide and then have him marching around Halcyon with Berzerker troops. One of his students will recognize him. My guess is they'll just leave him sedated, like they did with you, Al."

"Maybe you're right," said Al. "One thing's for sure, it's going to be very tough to get him out."

They returned to Socrates and went to Tom and Dwight's room.

"Let me show you something," said Tom.

He took out his pocket knife, unscrewed a cold air return vent in the corner of his room, and reached in as far as he could, pulling out two small packages. They were hand stunners.

"Good grief, where did you get those?" asked Al.

"I have my connections," said Tom.

"I've never handled one of those things before," said Al.

Tom showed him a smooth stainless steel cylinder with a fluted end. "They emit a sonic pulse that has the temporary effect of causing a person to black out at short range." Tom said. "You have to hit them in the head though. You can't see the sonic blast although it sounds like a low rumble. They black out for maybe twenty minutes and wake with a splitting headache."

"So if we need to, we could surprise the guards and get Sturgeon out."

"Let's go back to my room and talk it over with Pam," said Al. "Maybe she'll have some ideas on how we should proceed."

They walked to the couple's room, but it was empty. On the night table was a note in Pam's handwriting:

I've gone to catch a bit of fresh air.

It was their code that she had gone to check out the Staycare Center. Al looked at his watch. Fear put its clammy hand on Al's chest.

Something is terribly wrong! Shes should have been back by now.

Chapter 11

Pursuit

Pam heard the door close as Al, Tom, and Dwight left. She was filled with foreboding.

Sometimes men are so stupid! Al has to prove he's more of a man than Bigelow and now he's going on this risky, pea-brained adventure. I know he's going to get caught. I just know it!

She paced back and forth for a while hoping that they would come back. Finally she couldn't stand being cooped up any longer. To take her mind off her worry, she took a deep breath, then pulled out her Bible, looking for familiar passages to take the sting off her fear. She turned pages and found an underlined section:

> Rejoice in the Lord always; again I will say rejoice. Let your reasonableness be known to everyone. The Lord is at hand; do not be anxious about anything, but in everything by prayer and supplication with thanksgiving let your requests be made known to God. And the peace of God that surpasses all understanding, will guard your hearts and your minds in Christ Jesus.

Resolving to do what the passage said, she prayed fervently for Al and for Little Thomas. Her mind had been going a mile a minute, but now the act of prayer calmed her down.

Think clearly. I need to think about Little Thomas and decide on a course of action. Lord, if you're with me, give me some sign, some opportunity to get Little Thomas out!

Al seemed to think that it would take them some time to come up with a workable plan to get her son out. In contrast she had a foreboding that they did not have much time. What if she needed to be there tonight even without a workable plan? It was late. Should she go? She made up her mind. She couldn't bear the thought of just sitting around, waiting for other people to take action.

If I go to the Staycare Center and there's no chance to get Little Thomas out, I'll just come back, but maybe if God is in this ...

She didn't know how to finish her thought. She left a cryptic note for Al, put on her uniform and made sure she had her identification badge.

She walked briskly in the twilight toward the Staycare Center. A few of the street lamps had burned out, but the building was brightly lit. She had developed a routine in which she would walk to Little Thomas' floor and find an odd job to do. Sometimes she would tidy toys, other times she would put away books—anything as long as she seemed to be busy and have a job so that she wouldn't arouse suspicion. Idle workers in uniform were often conscripted for tasks—a situation she had to avoid.

When she arrived at his floor, she began to walk with decided intent from one end of the floor to the other. No sign of Little Thomas. *He may already be in bed.* At the end of the corridor she stopped to tidy up some books while she thought about where to go next.

Perhaps he's in the play area.

She headed briskly down a side corridor and felt relief wash over her as she saw him with about a dozen other children and two attendants. Pam didn't approach too closely, but rather found a spill on the floor she could clean up. She brought back a mop from a nearby storage closet and set to work. Whenever she could, she would glance in his direction, hungry to know how he was doing, and how he interacted with the other children

At three years old he seemed to be getting on well with the others, although he looked moody. He has Bigelow's eyes. How will Al ever accept him if Bigelow stares back at him every time Al looks at the child?

The loud blaring of the fire alarm began and several of the children began to cry, adding their screams to the din. The attendants began to move the children to the fire escape door at the back of the room. There were too many children.

This is my answer!

Pam immediately stepped in and picked up Little Thomas who had sat down on the floor with his hands clamped tightly over his ears. The two attendants continued to herd the children to the stairwell. One of the attendants gave Pam a grateful smile. Leading the way to the stairs, Pam held the door until the children were all on the landing. Then she followed down the stairs which were already beginning to fill up with other children and their attendants.

In the human stampede, Pam became separated from the rest of her group as she carried Little Thomas down the stairs. Pam wondered if this was a real or a false alarm. She couldn't smell any smoke. She continued down to the ground floor and out onto the grounds. The Fire Department had already arrived and the children were being gathered into groups well away from the building.

Pam walked resolutely toward a section of the parking lot where the streetlights were out and then continued walking along the deserted street. She heard footfalls behind her.

Someone is following me!

She increased her pace, but did not want to be seen running. The Socrates Residence appeared in front of her through the trees. Little Thomas began to whimper when she went in the side entrance.

"Shush my darling," she whispered stroking his hair.

She reached their room and collapsed onto a sofa in exhaustion.

"Nursie!" said Little Thomas as he stuck his bottom lip out.

"No, darling, I'm not your nurse, I'm your mother."

"Nursie," repeated Little Thomas, beginning to whimper.

What am I going to do? If he begins to cry everyone who hears him will know something is wrong.

"Would you like a cookie?" Halcyon cookies were not very good, but Little Thomas would have no basis for comparison.

"Cookie?" said Little Thomas brightening.

While the boy munched cookies, Pam thought furiously. Little Thomas must by now have been listed as missing by the Staycare Center. If she had roused suspicions by carrying a child around late at night, then they would soon be searching Socrates room by room. She had to go to their safe room in Hobbes and wait for Al. They had to head back to the boat and leave for Eleytheria tonight.

Pam picked up her note. They didn't have a code for Hobbes. She was panicking and wrote:

"Left for the other place" underneath her previous note, hoping that Al would look for her at Hobbes next. She picked up the Hobbes key, and then headed off with Little Thomas. She walked to the other end of the dormitory and went down that stairwell in case someone watched the entrance she had used.

When she emerged into the dark, a fog had begun to roll in. This made walking easier as long as she didn't get disoriented. Just when it seemed to be taking too long, the glow of the ornate entrance to Hobbes appeared ahead.

She hurried up the stairs and closed the door behind her as she sank onto a bed clutching Little Thomas to her bosom. She sang to him and fed him cookies until his eyes began to close. She laid him gently on the bed.

Hours seemed to have gone by and still there was no sign of Al.

What has happened? Is he waiting in Socrates? Is he hurt? Now that I have Little Thomas, what am I going to do?

Just as the idea was half beginning to form in her mind that she had to go back to Socrates, she heard a faint knock at the door and her heart froze.

They've found me. Like a fool I have waited too long.

She went to the door and looked through the peep hole. Three figures waited by the door: Al, Dwight and Tom.

She opened the door. With a cry of relief, Pam, rushed out and wrapped her arms around Al.

"I was so worried!" said Pam.

"So was I, my love," whispered Al as he hugged her to him fiercely. He gently disentangled her, looked up and down the hall and urged her back into the room.

"Didn't you get my second note?" asked Pam.

"We arrived to your first note and then went over to the Staycare Center which was in some kind of an uproar. They were looking for someone, so we took the long way home and found your second note. And here we are."

A whimper came from the bed room. Al's eyes widened. "You got him. How did you manage that?"

"There was a fire alarm and I just walked out with him."

"Were you seen?"

"I don't know," said Pam, her voice beginning to quaver. "I thought I was being followed, but I lost them after I left Socrates."

Al began to pace back and forth while Pam sat down to sooth Little Thomas back to sleep.

After the tenth circuit of the room, Al evidently had made up his mind. He turned to Dwight and Tom.

"Pam and I have to leave tonight with Little Thomas. You two have to decide if you're coming back with us or if you're going to stay…"

Tom and Dwight looked at each other. I don't think we tripped the alarm, so we need to stay here and maybe we can figure a way to get Sturgeon out. What about you guys, do you need our help getting back to the boat?"

Al drew a deep breath. "If the three of us make it back to the boat tonight and we set off, we'll be alright. If there's trouble, I doubt you two will be able to help us enough to make a difference. Besides, since you're staying here, there's a chance you could rescue us if we're captured."

"At least take this!" said Tom handing Al the stunner.

Al took the stunner, balanced it gingerly in his hands and handed it back.

"No, you need it more than we do. You know, as soon as Bigelow finds out Little Thomas was taken, he will figure out that Pam was here. Knowing Bigelow, he will put enough of his men on our trail that the guard covering Sturgeon will be depleted. If you're going to rescue him, tonight might be the best time to try."

"You could have something there," said Dwight thoughtfully. Tom stuck out his hand. Al took it and pulled Tom into a bear hug. Dwight hugged Al too and after he and Tom had kissed Pam good bye, they left quietly.

Tears welled up in Pam's eyes.

"Those two are true friends, Al."

Al held her close and wiped the tears away and kissed her.

"Yes, they are."

He went to pick up Little Thomas' sleeping form.

"We had better leave too if we don't want to get caught. That would waste all the help they've already given us."

Al led and Pam followed as quickly and quietly as she could.

When they reached the outside of Hobbes, the fog had lifted a little. Pam felt conspicuous.

"THERE THEY ARE!"

Pam realized the shout was some distance away.

"Follow me!" said Al. He headed toward the fishing path he knew so well, running as fast as he could with the dead weight of the sleeping boy in his arms. Pam followed. She knew what he was doing. Al had once told her that every escape consisted of two parts. First you had to get separation from your pursuer. Then you had to go to ground, making your way to safety. Al was hurrying to get separation.

The plan worried her. What if the boy woke up with the jostling? How would she keep him quiet?

As the path began to climb, the fog again enveloped them. Instead of fear, it gave Pam a measure of security. After a few minutes, they crossed a sheet of bare, flat rock. Al turned off the path and headed along the rock until he came to a thicket of bushes.

"We'll hide here."

"What if Little Thomas cries out?" whispered Pam.

"He must have been dead tired. He's still sound asleep. Now shush! I think I hear them coming."

They heard the tramp of feet, the sound of harsh shouts and saw lights vainly trying to stab through the fog. The men stopped.

"We've lost them," said Bigelow's voice.

"They can't be far," someone else said gruffly.

"We'll never find them in this soup."

"They can't go far. We'll just wait them out."

Bigelow cursed.

"They came by boat," said Bigelow. "If we let them get to the shore, they'll be gone and we won't see them again. Henderson you patrol this path up and down since we don't know exactly where they're hiding, but don't go too far. I'm going back for the dogs. We have one of Gleeson's shirts. Once they get his scent, this fog and the dark won't be a problem."

The sound of snapping twigs and scrapes in the silence of the night told Pam that Bigelow was returning to campus and that Henderson had moved up the path.

"Honey we're going to have to move," whispered Al. "I don't like travelling through the bush at night—there's too much danger of falling into a ravine or poking an eye out—but if we wait for Bigelow to return with the dogs, we'll be lost."

"Let's give it a try—we've got to try!" said Pam, fear edging into her voice.

Al handed the sleeping child to Pam. She could hear him taking his belt off.

"Hold onto this!" Pam felt him thrust the belt end into her hand. "I guess I'll take Little Thomas—he'll be too heavy for you to carry." Pam felt the belt tighten as Al moved off.

How can he even know which direction to go? Lord protect us all from a misstep.

Their progress was agonizingly slow. Al seemed to be testing every step before he put his weight on it. Finally he stopped and came back to whisper into her ear.

"I've found the creek that I was looking for. Unfortunately this creek doesn't join the one that leads to our boat. However, if we follow it down the hill, it will run under a path that cuts across the hill parallel to the shore. If we go right on that path, we'll rejoin the path we left, hopefully while Henderson is out of sight. Once we rejoin the path, we simply need to hang a left and go down the hill and we'll find the inlet where the boat is."

Al helped Pam down to the small stream. The sound of the brook splashing over rocks filled the air. She could tell from the shadows and the smell that this part of forest was covered with deciduous trees. The fog had cleared and starlight finally penetrated the canopy.

Al had them moving faster now. The bed of the stream was a series of flat rock shelves and the low water levels allowed them to walk in the shallows. Al stumbled once on a slippery rock, but did not go down. Pam stumbled two or three times.

The sound of baying broke the stillness of the night air.

They've found us.

Al increased his speed even more. After five more minutes he halted.

"Pam we're at the bridge. Stay here. Let me go up and make sure it's safe."

Pam let go of the belt and took Little Thomas. She saw Al's dark shape as an even greater darkness, climb out over the bank and disappear up the path. Little Thomas was sleeping peacefully.

Al was back in less than a minute. "I think it is all clear. I looked down the other path and saw no sign of Henderson. Let's make a run for it."

He took Little Thomas again and helped Pam climb over the bank with his free hand. She clung to him. Al took her hand and redoubled their pace. The baying of dogs behind them was noticeably nearer.

They're following us down the creek bed and they're close. She thought she could see stabs of light illuminating the trees.

They came to the crossroads and Al turned left.

Just then a whistle shrilly rent the still air. "I see them. They're back on the path," came the shout.

Al again handed Little Thomas to Pam. The boy began to whimper.

"You've got to run for it now. Get over the crest. If Henderson tries to follow by himself, I'll deal with him. Otherwise, I'll sneak back to the other side and lead them off. But you have to go."

"Al, please no! The dogs …"

"Pam you have to go."

Sobs began to shake her chest as she ran. Fear made her run faster than she ever thought she could. Her sobs woke Little Thomas again and he began to whimper even louder than before.

"There he is!" The shout was quite a distance behind her now. The baying of hounds picked up again.

Pam kept running. The path grew steeper and she had to slow down to keep from stumbling. Finally the path flattened out again.

Little Thomas was crying in earnest now. There was nothing she could do to quiet him.

Where is that creek? I have to find it.

"Friend Pam, is that you?" said a *Hansa* voice.

"Am I glad to hear your voice! Is that you Bandomer?"

"Yes friend Pam. Where is friend Al?"

"I don't know. We're being pursued. Al went back to lead them off."

Pam felt Bandomer's prehensile hand clasp hers and he led her off the path toward the shore. Soon he was leading her along a plank bridge onto the boat and she settled into her former cabin in exhaustion.

Bandomer came in and patted Pam on the hand.

"I will go ashore and wait for Al. Taromer and Rolomer will put the boat out near the mouth of the inlet where you'll be safe. When Al comes he and I will join you."

"What if they catch you?" said Pam.

"They will not, friend Pam. I will stay close to the shore and swim out to the boat if they come. They cannot catch me in the water. I am like a fish with hair!" chuckled Bandomer.

A moment after Bandomer had left, Pam felt the boat moving. After five minutes they stopped and she could feel the boat pull on an anchor cable as the wind shifted. Thankfully Little Thomas had fallen asleep again in her arms. She went up on deck.

What have I done? Thought Pam. *Al knew all along we had no chance of success, yet he came along to help me, and now he's paid the price.*

What will Bigelow do to him? Was I wrong? No! When I look into the sleeping face of Little Thomas, I know we had to get him out of that place. God if you can hear me—protect Al.

Pam was cold. The land breeze was blowing strongly. She rocked her sleeping child and hugged him to keep him warm and to still the anxiety in her heart for Al. Nothing happened for a long time, although she told herself it was probably less than thirty minutes. She heard the baying of dogs close to shore. A few minutes later, Bandomer, water dripping from his fur, pulled himself into the boat.

"They have captured Al," said Bandomer. "I overheard them. We must go now."

"No!" said Pam. "We must rescue him."

"We must get you and your cub home. In a few minutes they will see us. What if they chase us in boats? Friend Al put himself in danger to save you and the little one. Friend Pam, do not throw away your husband's gift of freedom."

Pam was going to insist, but she knew the *Hansa* too well. When Bandomer spoke about Al's sacrifice, there was no dissuading the *Hansa* from carrying out their duty and bringing her to safety.

With that the *Hansa* pulled up the anchor, stepped the mast, and hoisted the sail to catch the land breeze on their larboard quarter.

It was dark and the fog, which still clung close to the water, muffled every sound. She heard the snapping of branches and a voice alarmingly close by called out. "Pam, I know you're out there." It was Bigelow. "I have your lover boy. I can be really nasty when I'm angry. You've taken what belongs to me and I mean to get him back. If you don't come back with my son, Gleeson's going to have a very unpleasant time of it."

Pam was about to answer, when she felt Bandomer's hand on her arm. "Friend Pam, don't say anything. If he finds where we are he may shoot us."

She knew he was right and bit back her reply. Al was gone and subject to Bigelow's wrath. What would she do now? Bigelow never cared about Little Thomas when he was at the Staycare Center, after all he had wanted her to get rid of him when she was pregnant.

Now that Little Thomas is with me, suddenly he cares about the loss as if I had stolen his hat or his coat. The boy is nothing more than a possession to him.

Chapter 12

Rebirth

Arlana looked at Dave with concern. He seemed much worse. She could smell the sickly sweet stench of gangrene on the stump of his arm. He was delirious but sometimes called the name 'O'Reilly' and other times he talked about "following the master," but it made no sense. Just ahead in the cool of the night, a stream gurgled over a moss-covered rock. Hanomer was replenishing their water skins.

Arlana thought: *What am I going to do? If I remember my lessons, Dave has been the first Lesser Man who has come to our country for many hundreds of years. He must be important. He has come for a reason. He must not die.*

Hanomer came, poured water over his kerchief, and wiped Dave's brow. Arlana felt Dave's upper arm. It was hot.

He does not have much time before he dies. I wish I could give the horses more rest, but we have to push hard.

"We must keep going, Hanomer," said Arlana.

Hanomer sniffed the air. "Yes, my Lady. The Halfmen are close now."

Arlana spoke softly to the horse pulling Dave and began to walk. Hanomer took up his position behind her with his bow ready. The trees' fragrant smell of vanilla and the touch of the leaves on her cheeks felt like home.

She smiled grimly to herself. *The Halfmen won't find these trees nearly so friendly if they try to pass!*

The stings and the smell would warn them first. Then the pungent defensive vapors would suffocate them and make their eyes sting. But she had to be through the trees before the Halfmen came. They climbed the increasingly steep mountain path, one plodding step at a time. The horses were snorting with fatigue, their cold breath visible like four plumes of smoke.

She could hear the howls behind her. The trees were repelling the Halfmen.

Finally, the winding trail reached a broad stone shelf, the Barrier Mountains rising steep and impassible ahead of her. Directly in front of her a sheer rock wall rose unbroken one thousand paces. She approached the wall in the twilight. A mountain fragment, the size of a small hill, had fallen from the heights ages ago and cracked the weathered stone of the shelf. She led the horses to the very back of this massive tower of cracked stone where it leaned against the mountain wall. Behind the leaning buttress of stone was a narrow fissure.

"Hanomer, the Guardian Forest is our first protection, while the Cave of Kelarond is the second. Stay close since the path is perilous.

The way grew dark and then the familiar green glow of the lumilichen began to light their path. Arlana took out a light gourd and so did Hanomer. The light from the gourds played off the passage walls. They were confronted by three passages: one ran left, one straight ahead and one right. Arlana examined the wall for the cryptic inscriptions that were used by the Guardians or Gurundar in the Old Tongue for safe passage. She found them.

What do they mean? I wish I had paid more attention to my lessons! If I make a mistake now, I will lead us to the ice caves or the furnace cavern. May the Creator help me!

She took the passage to the right. It ran level for a while and then began a gentle descent. She almost turned back, before the tunnel began to climb again. Relieved, she pressed on more quickly.

Several hours later, Arlana began to recognize stone work on the walls.

I'm approaching the habitable parts.

The trail, which had passed through several large caverns, had now entered another one. The roof was so high that the light from the gourds did not reach the ceiling. The road beneath her feet, paved with cobblestones, ran straight to some distant end. They crossed the cavern swiftly. The prospect of an end to their ordeal drove Arlana on. An arch twenty paces high loomed ahead and the road ran beneath it.

The cavern they entered was just as large as the one they left, but in the distance Arlana saw a yellow-white light and breathed a sigh of relief. Straight across the cavern floor she ran and the horses sensed her urgency and pulled Dave along, his stretcher scraping and bouncing on the road bed.

Arlana halted and stared. Ahead of her was a long, straight bridge with a parapet on either side. It ran for three hundred paces across a wide chasm and ended at a heavy wooden gate, bound with iron, set into a high wall. Light streamed out of a window far up the gate tower set on top of the wall. This was the light she had seen when she entered the cavern.

Arlana led the horses across the long bridge as Hanomer walked at her side. About the middle she looked over the parapet into the depths below. A green sheen filled the chasm, but she could not see the bottom.

"They call it The Endless Chasm for good reason. No one has ever breached this gate."

Several streams on the far side ran off the rock wall and splashed into the void but she could not hear the water strike the bottom. Finally she reached the massive door at the far side of the bridge.

"Who goes there?" boomed a voice from the battlements above.

I know that voice!

"Ferris ap Hollidor do you not recognize your neighbor and cousin?"

"Arlana da Kelldor, is that really you?"

"Yes Ferris, it's really me. Come down quickly, and open the gate. I have one sorely hurt with me."

Arlana heard footsteps on the stone stairs and soon the sound of heavy bolts being drawn. The gate swung outward. Ferris rushed forward from a group of surprised guards and looked first at Arlana, then at the wrapped bundle on the litter.

"Ferris I beg you for a stretcher since my friend is badly hurt. I'm afraid if I don't bring him to Sirona within the hour, he'll perish."

"Cousin, I have a wagon with fresh horses, which we use for hauling provisions. I will hitch up a team and take you to Sirona as quickly as the mountain paths allow." He gave orders to his men who carried the stretcher through the fortification.

Arlana walked as one dead through the courtyard of the tower to the stable at the back. Dave had already been placed into the back of the wagon and Hanomer was beside him talking gently and giving him water to drink.

Arlana tied her horses to the wagon and climbed up beside Dave. She took his hand. It felt warm to the touch. The wagon began to move. In a short time Arlana felt the cool breeze of her country of Gurundar and saw the bright stars in the sky. It felt so good to be home. For the first time since she had left to search for her father, she felt safe.

In about thirty minutes they entered a courtyard through a gate in a tall hedge and stopped before a large house built into the side of a cliff that faced west. She saw a dark form in a nightdress and a shawl, holding a lantern waiting for them.

"No one comes to the house this late except in great need. Is someone hurt Ferris?" asked Sirona.

"Yes, my lady Sirona. He's in the back."

Sirona brought her lantern around.

"Arlana, my child!" she gasped as the light fell into the back of the wagon. "Where have you been? I've been beside myself with worry."

"There's no time for that now dearest Nana. There's a man here who's dying. We haven't a moment to lose."

Sirona looked at Dave with concern.

"Ferris, help us bring him inside."

With Ferris at one end of the stretcher and Sirona and Arlana at the other, they struggled to carry Dave into the house.

"We will take him straight to the arboretum." said Sirona. "He needs to go into the healing plant right away."

Dave moaned softly as he was carried.

"I want to follow the master," he mumbled.

They put the stretcher on the ground beside a large green mound the size of a small wagon. The plant gave off a pleasant scent similar to the sharp, earthy smell of marjoram. Sirona went around the room and lit several lamps and then came back to the plant. Sirona stroked the side of the mound with her hands and the large green leaves opened like a fan, each leaf the size of a bed sheet.

Dave turned and saw the plant and became very agitated.

"No, no—not this!" he moaned. He tried to get up.

Arlana rushed to his side. "Be calm. You are safe now. Be calm."

"What's wrong with him? He seems afraid of the Healing Plant," said Sirona.

"I don't know," said Arlana.

When the leaves were fully open, Arlana and Ferris carried Dave on the stretcher into the center of the leaves. Arlana rolled Dave, groaning, off the stretcher and then made him comfortable on the soft leafy interior. He seemed to have fallen into a coma. Small green appendages, like tiny vines on a stone wall, attached themselves to him. Arlana caressed Dave's forehead and then rose and walked out of the center of the plant.

Sirona again touched the side of the plant and turned white with shock.

She gulped and turned to Arlana trembling, "Child, what are you doing, he's not one of us."

"I know Nana, but he needs our help."

"We are forbidden to use the plant on Halfmen…"

"He is not a Halfman, Nana, dear. I think he's a Lesser Man, but he is not a Halfman!"

"Arlana, he may be a Lesser Man and so be closer to an Ancient than the Halfmen, but it still means he has been changed by the Bent Ones and we are forbidden to work on him. I will kill him with this plant if I try to heal him. I will not do it!"

"Nana, then I will do it! He needs my help and I will not just let him die. He is a child of the Creator, just as we are!"

Arlana stepped into the plant. Sirona seized her arm.

"No dearest, please don't. You are not a healer. You will not only kill him but also harm yourself as you try to undo the damage that has been done to his people by the Bent Ones."

Arlana resisted the pull on her arm. Sirona set her face as she came to a decision. "Arlana, I promise I will do my best for him and save him if I can. Only don't put yourself at risk. I couldn't bear it."

Arlana relented and stepped out of the plant. Sirona took her place in the center of the plant, laid down beside Dave and placed her hand on his right shoulder. The leaves closed. Arlana walked back and sat down in a chair tugging on her braid determined to remain awake.

Chapter 13

In the House of Kelldor

Arlana woke with a start. Sunlight bathed the room. A movement in the plant leaves had roused her from her deep sleep. She rose from her chair, smoothing out her riding outfit anxiously, as leaf after leaf unfolded. Finally in the center she saw Sirona and Dave lying side by side. The vines had all detached. He was sound asleep. With a start, she realized that his arm had grown back.

Sirona stepped out of the plant, haggard and badly shaken.

"He is—or I suppose I should say was—a hybrid, but not nearly so twisted as the Halfmen. I undid what I could and it was a near thing. I almost lost him four or five times. Still I don't know what I have made of him. I will have to go before the Council for judgment."

Arlana was stricken to the heart. *What have I done to her? Healing is her life and I manipulated her into actions that went against her oath as a healer!* "Forgive me Nana!"

"What's done is done, child." She reached up and touched Arlana's cheek.

"I need to rest. Sit with him until he wakes up. But be careful—I don't know what I have made of him!"

Arlana pulled a chair over and watched Dave. He seemed to be resting peaceably.

Except for the repaired arm he doesn't look very different.

After ten minutes Dave began to sir and stretched his arm. Then he sat bolt upright. His complexion changed rapidly to a dark chocolate brown. He looked around at the plant in panic.

He tried to rise quickly, toppled and then staggered out of the plant and stood panting with his back to the wall and sweat beading on his face.

"Arlana? Where am I? What is that Death Plant doing here?"

Surprised, Arlana said, "Death Plant? What's that?"

"In Meglir's cavern there were plants like this except they converted dead bodies into Apemen."

"You have seen these?" said Arlana, her voice trembling.

"You haven't?"

"No, I've learned about them though. Meglir made them by twisting the Healing Plants to his own ends."

Arlana stood up and held Dave at arm's length.

"How do you feel, youngling?"

A troubled look came into his face and he clutched his left arm with his right.

"I remember the fight with the Halfmen. I was wounded—I lost my arm!"

"Isn't it wonderful that the plant could heal you? But how do you feel?"

"I'm a little shaky. I feel different—like I've been reborn."

"In a sense you have," said Arlana. "The healing has made you a new person."

"It's more than the healing. I think I have finally come home. I have decided to follow the Master."

"What do you mean?"

"I can't really explain it. Besides you wouldn't understand."

"The healing hasn't improved your temperament, youngling. Your talk still makes little sense. Perhaps you ought to sleep as Sirona your healer commanded."

"No I don't think so. Where are we?"

"We are at my home in the borderlands on the shore of Lake Tolbar."

She looked into his eyes.

"You don't remember, do you?"

"I have hazy memories of an underground passage and a lot of pain."

He rubbed his left arm again.

"Well let me tell you what happened." Arlana recounted their journey back since the terrible fight that led to the loss of Dave's arm.

Dave put his hand to his brow. "I can't believe it. My arm growing back! Who ever heard of such a thing. They'll never believe it."

"By the way," he said, "what's all this youngling business?"

"Well," said Arlana, "I just saw you change your skin color like an Ancient, but you can't control the change, just as our children can't. I will have to adopt you as my little brother, and teach you the same things we teach our children."

"Little brother?" said Dave. "No way. You already have great difficulty acknowledging my intellectual and tactical superiority and find it very difficult to take my excellent advice."

"Hmm as I said before, Sirona was able to heal your body, but pity she did nothing for your temperament."

Dave flexed his left arm again. He seemed to remember something. "We've been away so long! They're going to miss us and send out search parties. What if they stumble into the Halfmen who have been stirred up like a hornet's nest? I've got to get back."

"Dave what you need to do is rest."

"No I feel fine. I need to get back."

"Without me you can't go anywhere. You need to rest."

Dave stood up and his complexion changed rapidly from dark brown to tan. Arlana watched him as he paced back and forth, wringing his hands.

"My friends are in danger. I have to go. If you won't help me Arlana, I'll have to go on my own."

Arlana became alarmed. *He would really attempt it wouldn't he, the dim witted oaf!*

"Youngling, if you will be patient and rest, I will take you home myself. And your journey will be shorter on account of my help."

"How can you make it shorter? I know how far we have to travel."

Arlana put her hands on his shoulders. *He is tall and strong!*

"We came by horse over the desert. That way is watched. That way is dangerous. However there is another way. At the head of the Pishon River, there is a huge cataract that we call The Giant Steps. At the foot of this cataract, we have boats. Since your home is on the river we can reach it by boat. Boats travel day and night and we will have the current on our side. You will reach your home in half the time."

Dave was about to protest, but changed his mind. "Promise me we leave tomorrow."

Arlana hesitated. *He needs more rest than that after all that has happened. He doesn't know what I have done to him.*

"Promise me or I'm leaving right now!"

Arlana made up her mind. "I promise. We leave tomorrow. But now you must take your rest."

Dave rose again in the late afternoon. His room faced west. On the western wall there were large balcony doors. He walked out onto a stone balcony which extended the width of the house. He rested his hands on the rough stone work and inhaled the fragrance of many flowers. He had never smelled such a riot of fragrances. He had enjoyed the delicious smell of a garden before, but now for the first time in his life he was sure he could distinguish every flower in the garden.

The house was part house and part castle. A stout stone wall, about ten feet high, bordered the courtyard below him. To the west, a lake stretched to the horizon. Outside the wall, a terraced garden, surrounded by a large meadow, bordered by a thick hedge, ran down to the lake. A wharf stretched far enough out into the water to allow a large boat to anchor. A brook meandered diagonally through the middle of the meadow. A white stone path ran west from a small postern gate, in the garden wall, straight down to the wharf, crossing the meandering brook at a stone bridge where the brook curved north emptying into a small pond. Dave turned away from this beautiful scene and looked north. A laneway from the courtyard passed through a large gate in the wall and after passing through the encircling hedge, met the road that came down from the high pass. He could see the pass road snake up the side of a wooded hill, heading north. *I wonder where that road from the pass goes?*

He walked along the balcony and saw that it continued along the south face of the house. He looked south. In the distance a stone fortress nestled against the mountain side about five miles away. The fortress was much larger than Arlana's home. He heard the rustle of clothing and Arlana, dressed in white, came around the corner of the balcony. She had a star-shaped flower in her hair. She saw him and smiled.

I forgot how beautiful she is!

"It is good to see you up youngling. You are looking hale."

"Hi Arlana. What a beautiful place you have here! Just to look over the meadow is like food to a starving man!"

She beamed with pleasure.

"What is that structure on the mountainside there?" continued Dave pointing at the fortress.

Arlana's face clouded. "That fortress is called Erand Gabur which means "Tower of Strength" in our tongue. It is the home of Arachodor, the second in command on the Council of Thirteen, after my father Kelldor."

Arlana seemed troubled at the name Arachodor, and Dave didn't know what to say.

"I am glad you like this house," resumed Arlana. "It's my home. It has so many dear memories—of my childhood, my mother and brother, as well the happy times I have spent here.

"You speak of your mother and brother with such sadness. What happened to them?" asked Dave.

Her eyes filled with tears. "When I was very young, when the Halfmen were thought to be so cowed that they never left the Skull Mountains, my brother, who was already a Ranger, took my mother to Arkand to see the home of our ancestors and to study at the Grand Library. That had been her fondest wish. They never made it back. They were killed by the Halfmen and so our war with them started anew, with them growing ever bolder."

She wiped away her tears. "I cannot speak more of it. Let's think of more pleasant things. Come let me show you my garden!"

Pulling on his sleeve, Arlana led Dave down a stair to the courtyard below and then out the postern gate to a small garden just under the west wall. The garden on a terrace was filled with roses and a vine with beautiful star-shaped flowers that climbed on an arbor in the center and over the low wall that marked the boundary of the garden.

"What is that flowering vine, Arlana? I've never seen the like before. It's so beautiful and fragrant. I could smell it from the balcony."

"That vine is called an arlana. I am named after it. The delicate white flowers like five-pointed stars are my favorite and the sweet scent always reminds me of home."

"Your parents named you well." There was an awkward silence.

Arlana led him along the walkway through the garden and described some of the flowers she had planted. After a few minutes, she looked at him with concern as if remembering something.

"You must be hungry. Hanomer is anxious to see you. He is also hungry and has fasted to eat with you. It's quite a feat for a *Hansa* to forgo a meal to eat with a friend."

They went inside where a large table, set against the wall, was already covered with bowls of vegetables and platters of meat. Another table in the center of the room was empty except for dishes, cutlery, and a centerpiece of an arlana bouquet.

"Are you expecting an army?" asked Dave.

"No, just Hanomer," said Arlana laughing. "We have invited a few guests and the rest of the household will eat with us."

A familiar voice made Dave turn his head. "Friend Dave, it's a joy to see you up!"

"Hanomer, I have missed you. Have they been feeding you well?"

"Friend Dave, on our journey from the desert, I was afraid that I would return to my kin in poor condition, looking as thin as a leafless bush in winter, but thanks to the Lady Arlana and her excellent cook"—he bowed to a tall, thin woman who was bringing in the food with two helpers—"after this meal I will be much more presentable."

"Your friend has excellent manners, Master Dave," said the cook.

"Whatever courtesies he may have shown," said Dave, unwilling to be outdone by Hanomer's compliments, "they are insufficient to honor the culinary delights I see before me. You have prepared a meal fit for a king in quality and an army in quantity."

Dave gave his best bow and the cook beamed.

"You will learn from our people that we value a cook more highly than warriors," she said. "For you and for the Lady Arlana's long hoped-for return, we have done our best."

Sirona arrived as well as several men in working attire. Finally, a young man in chainmail also came in.

Arlana put her hand on Dave's elbow and urged him over to the young man.

"Dave, let me introduce you to my cousin, Ferris, son of Hollidor."

"Greetings Dave," said Ferris. "I must say that you look much better than the last time I saw you. The Creator has watched over you. Among our people, warriors greet each other like this." He grasped Dave's right arm at the elbow and guided Dave to clasp his right elbow at the same time.

Dave looked at Ferris. He was tall, slim, clean-shaven, a young man who looked to be in his mid-twenties (although as an Ancient, Dave knew he could be much older). Although Ferris appeared tall, with his slender build, he was a couple of inches shorter than Dave. He had dark curly hair, in contrast to Arlana's blonde hair, yet Dave could see a resemblance around the eyes.

"Come, let us sit down," said Ferris motioning to a chair beside him.

When everyone, including the cooks, had sat down, Arlana said, "Before we eat, we honor the Creator with our thoughts and remember our estranged kinsmen across Lake Tolbar." Arlana rang a chime and looked west bowing her head in reverence. Dave sat quietly and watched her while Hanomer followed Arlana's lead and bowed his head. After about a minute, Arlana rang the chime again and rose to go over to the side table. She looked at Dave expectantly.

Ferris pulled Dave towards him and whispered in his ear. "Rise, man, and carry the platter for her! She's waiting for you."

Dave rose and walked over to Arlana. She smiled and indicated a large platter of white meat that smelled like turkey. Dave picked it up and followed Arlana. She went first to Sirona and gave her meat and then went around the table. As soon as they had moved on, Sirona and Ferris rose to pick up the second dish. When Arlana and Dave had made the round of the table and placed their half empty platter on it, almost everyone was up serving food. Dave sat down and watched Arlana. She thanked the servers as they came by but ate nothing. Finally everyone returned to their places.

Arlana picked up her fork and knife and said, "Friends eat as much as you like, giving thanks to the Creator." She began to eat. Around the table Dave heard "Thanks to the Creator" as a rolling rumble of sound, and then everyone began to eat.

Dave was famished and ate some of the turkey first. He turned to Ferris. "What was that all about?"

Ferris finished chewing a piece of bread. "It's our custom that we are one another's servants from the highest to the lowest. Kelldor is our Chief and this is his house, so he would normally serve the first dish, helped by Arlana. Since he is not here, Arlana served the first dish helped by you, her honored guest."

"Okay, but why me?"

"She hasn't told you then?" said Ferris, more to himself than to Dave. "Dave, it's not my place to tell you much about what has happened to you. You will need to speak to Arlana, but I will say this: you are not the same person you were when you arrived. Arlana is working to make you fit in with our people."

"Fit in? Why do I need to fit in?"

"Quietly, quietly, Dave. Do not begin your sojourn in Kelldor's house by embarrassing his family in front of the servants at your first family dinner. Servants' tongues have been known to wag. You have a great deal to be thankful for. Talk to Arlana."

Dave could see concern in his eyes. *What's going on? What haven't I been told?* He looked down at his hands. They were chocolate brown. They had been white a minute ago. *What's happened to me?*

Just then there was a yapping of dogs in the courtyard. One of the servants rose and left the room. Loud voices were heard in the hallway and a moment later the servant returned with three men, all clad in chain mail.

The servant bowed and said, "My Lady, the Lord Teledon ap Arachodor, hearing of your unexpected return, has come to pay his respects."

"And to express my delight at seeing you again," said the foremost of the three men.

The leader was tall and slender with full shoulder-length blond hair and blue eyes. He moved with the ease of one used to commanding others. Dave could feel himself already beginning to dislike the fellow. Teledon came around to Arlana's place and offered to take her hand. Arlana, pale with astonishment, rose smoothly, clasped his elbow as a warrior would and with only a slight quaver in her voice said coldly, "My Lord Teledon, what an unexpected pleasure. I would beg that you would allow me to offer you and your men a place at my table to celebrate my safe return."

Chairs were quickly found and the three men sat across the table from Ferris and Dave. As hostess, Arlana continued to provide food for the additional guests. Hoping to assist her, Dave began to rise, but Ferris clasped his forearm in restraint. Instead, Sirona rose and helped Arlana. When the guests' wine goblets had been filled, Teledon raised his for all to see.

"A toast to the safe return of the Lady Arlana!" The others around the table raised their goblets and the chorus of "Lady Arlana" rumbled around the table.

After a few bites, Teledon fixed his eyes on Dave and said, "Lady Arlana, I see you have another guest to whom we have not been introduced."

"Forgive me, my Lord. With the unexpectedness of your arrival I did you an injustice by omitting the introduction. This is Rokodor, the son of my father's good friend Celyddon at Northborough."

Dave was stunned by the lie, but tried not to show it.

"I did not know Celyddon had any living son," said Teledon.

Dave saw Arlana turn pale in her anger at Teledon contradicting her in public, but her voice was icy calm. "Rokodor is adopted. His parents are no longer with us and through the generosity of Celyddon, Rokodor now has a family to replace them."

Teledon looked as if he was going to ask another question, but changed his mind after staring at Arlana. Instead, he said, "Greetings, friend Rokodor. Blessed be the Creator for your good fortune after the loss of your parents."

"Thank you," said Dave.

The buzz of conversation resumed, and Teledon did not again ask questions or address himself to Dave. Finally, Teledon rose and excused himself, saying that he needed to see his father about an important matter. When the three unexpected guests had left, the dinner party quickly broke up. As Dave was about to leave with the others, Sirona pointed out to him that he was no longer a guest in the household and therefore, was expected to help with the cleanup. He followed her back to the table.

"Okay, will someone explain to me this fabrication about me being the adopted son of some guy I don't even know called Celyddon?" said Dave.

"It's not nonsense," said Sirona. "It was my idea, but I didn't think we would have to put it into practice so soon. Be thankful Arlana is quick on her feet. Furthermore, you had better show me some respect before I put you over my knee, you ungrateful whelp."

Dave burst out laughing as he looked at Sirona, who was frail and eight inches shorter than he was.

He bowed gravely to Sirona. "Unfortunately, Lady Sirona, I think my considerable weight would do fearful damage to your slender legs if you ever managed to get me across your delicate knees."

Sirona's mouth showed a trace of a smile as she turned to gather up the bowls, handing the larger ones to Dave.

"That's quite possible. All the more reason for you *not* to put an old woman to the test and put her 'slender legs' in jeopardy." She picked up another bowl. "I suppose I owe you an explanation. Come, and help me wash up, and I'll try to answer your questions. Don't think just because you are now the adopted son of Celyddon that you are entering a life of ease."

She picked up a stacked pile of the smaller dishes and walked to the door. Dave followed, carrying his load into a long kitchen and came to a washbasin. Water flowed continuously from a clay pipe and then into a drain. He carried hot water from the fire, and along with cold water from the pipe, filled a large basin and began washing dishes.

Sirona began to dry the dishes. "I was planning to talk to you about what happened, but I've delayed because you are supposed to be convalescing. However, Teledon forced our hand and we have little time."

"Okay, I'm listening."

"The simple truth is that when you arrived, you were close to death. The gangrene had spread and the poison was coursing through your body. Had you been one of us, I would have simply taken you to the Healing Plant and healed you."

"What's a 'healing plant'?"

"Let me show you." Sirona wiped her hands on a towel and led Dave up the back stairs to the arboretum that held an enormous green mound.

Dave caught his breath and cringed. "That looks like a Death Plant!"

"You have seen one of those? Of course you have, you have been at the City of the Dead. Long ago, Death Plants were made from Healing Plants by twisting and corrupting them. Healing Plants were either given to us by the Creator long ago or were made by our forefathers from other living things using their gifts—I don't really know which is true. The plants were meant to heal us from severe trauma. The Bent Ones, and especially Meglir, twisted the Healing Plants so they could make new creatures that were open to being enslaved by them. They perfected the abominable practice first introduced by the Bent Ones long ago, mixing Ancients with other creatures and so weakening them and leaving them open to control. I know you have seen the Apemen. Ancients were warped and twisted by the Death Plants into the abominations we call the Apemen. The Bent Ones also bred the Halfmen by their corrupt arts. That is why we have fought against them all these years."

"Who are the Bent Ones?" asked Dave.

Sirona beckoned Dave to come back to the kitchen.

"The history of my people would require many years of study. As Celyddon's adopted son, it would be well to undertake that course of study. I am not the one to instruct you however. Let me say what is known by all of our people. Long ago, our histories say, we came to Feiramon out of another world that we call the World of the Four Rivers or Naharamon. One of our gifts was the stewardship we exercised over living things and as part of that gift we had the ability to heal, even modify living things. Much has been lost, our gift has diminished, but the Healing Plants we have now come from that time. But early in our history our people were sundered. Some wanted to use their gift to achieve mastery over their fellow men, indeed over all living things, and so they twisted many organisms to their purpose using the gift they had been given. Their great plot was to develop slaves such as the Apemen, Halfmen, and others that were weakened and diminished so that they could easily be controlled. The more they diminished them, the more they imparted to them their own evil and corrupt nature. They took the good the Creator had made and twisted it beyond recognition for their own purposes.

My own people, the Ancients who still love The Good, fought against this ..."

"And you won?" interrupted Dave.

"Won? No, we did not win, but we have also not lost."

Dave moved a load of platters into the water and began scrubbing again. "So how does this apply to me?" asked Dave.

Sirona picked up some bowls and dried them vigorously. After a few seconds she put the dishes down and looked at Dave and turned him to face her. "Dave, when you came to me, you were not one of us; not an Ancient. Normally, we do not attempt healings on—on *others*. It is too dangerous. It almost always results in death."

"But you tried it on me and it worked out, right?"

"Yes, it worked out." Sirona dried her hands upon her apron. "You see the plants can heal an Ancient without my help, but in trying to heal you, because you are different, it would simply have killed you. Since I am a healer, I entered the plant with you, and in that bonded state, I used the plant to show me the map or a plan that defines your body and makes it function. I know how it should look and, using my own body map as a guide, I changed all the bits that made you different from an Ancient. Thankfully, there were not too many, and I did it well enough for you to be healed."

"So what's the problem?"

"For one thing you will notice differences."

"You mean like my skin changing color like yours does."

"Like that, but you are like an infant and you can't control it yet. But there are other problems. One of our strictest rules forbids healers from changing organisms, as the Bent Ones have done. Although I was healing you, some may say I broke that rule. One reason Arlana has said that Celyddon, her father's friend, has adopted you is for your protection. If Teledon even suspects what I have done, we would all be in grave danger. Arachodor, Teledon's father, could rally the Council against Kelldor, Hollidor, and Celyddon. They could conceivably even have us all killed. I think it will be best for you to leave as quickly as possible. I am almost certain Teledon saw that you could not control your skin color and although you speak the common tongue reasonably well, you do speak it with an accent."

"What about you? Aren't you in danger?"

Sirona smiled, reached up, and touched his cheek.

"I'm glad I listened to Arlana and healed you. I'm over three hundred years old and the best healer we have in Gurundaria so I'm sure the Council will have the good sense to be lenient. But go now; get ready to leave. You have a long trip ahead of you."

Dave walked back up to his room and found Hanomer waiting for him.

"Hello friend Dave. That was a splendid meal we had."

"Yes, Hanomer, I can't remember when I've had better. What are you doing here?"

"Lady Arlana is anxious to leave right away and I have come up here to pack and to take you to the stables for us to set off."

"When Sirona said we were to leave right away, she wasn't kidding." Dave grabbed his pack. "We'd better go then."

Arlana and Ferris were already in the stables saddling their horses.

"Youngling," said Arlana, "we need to leave. You must pick a horse."

"What do I know about horses? You pick one for me."

Arlana put her hands on her hips and looked at his face. "Just do what I say and come see these horses at this end of the stable."

Arlana took him to the nearest horse, a beautiful roan mare. She put his hand on the horse's neck and the horse turned its head to look at him.

"Close your eyes and concentrate on the horse."

Dave closed his eyes and thought of the horse and suddenly he was seeing himself through the horse's eyes. He sensed how the horse felt about him. The emotions flooded over him."

Shaking his head and removing his hand, he steadied himself against the stall. "Wow! She won't do. I'm much too heavy for her light frame on long distance travel. I couldn't put her through it."

"I agree," said Arlana. "Let's try another."

Stall by stall, Dave went through the stable. After several horses, none of which proved suitable, he came to a large, shaggy, bay stallion that snorted and tossed its head as Dave approached. He put his hand on the horse's neck and concentrated. Again he looked through the horse's eyes and felt the animal's emotions wash over him. He sensed raw, wild power, and an attitude of opposition. He had to fight with the horse. This one was unlike any of the other animals. Then calm set in, and Dave knew that the horse would bear him well. They had a certain kinship.

Dave pulled his hand away. Arlana was watching him closely. "I'll take him," said Dave. "I think I'll call him Traveller after a horse I read about. Traveller was always loyal to his master and I hope my Traveller will be the same."

"Hmm," said Arlana. "Has he agreed to carry you?"

"He doesn't think like we do at all but we seem to have an understanding."

"Good!" said Arlana. "Traveller, as you call him, has not found a rider he would carry well. Are you sure about him?"

"Yes, I'm sure Arlana."

She seemed unconvinced. "He is the strongest horse in the stable. Perhaps you are meant to ride him." She called one of the servants to saddle Traveller.

"I can saddle him," said Dave.

"Before we go, we have something else that can't wait." She led Dave out of the stable into the garden at the back. "Since you are now a son of Celyddon, you have to have a living cloak."

"What's a living cloak?"

"Come and see," said Arlana.

She took Dave outside the garden through a southern postern gate to a grove of ancient oak trees. On the trees hung masses of fibrous material like Spanish moss on the branches of the live oaks Dave had seen back home.

"Do these plants kill the trees?"

"No, they only use the trees for support. When our children are young, each is given one of these plants as a blanket. The plant grows used to him or her, and adopts the child as its companion. Later, the blanket is made into a cloak, like the one I'm wearing now."

"How do you wash it?" asked Dave.

She laughed her delicate laugh, like a chorus of birds singing. "We're on an urgent journey and I have to answer laundry questions?"

"I'm curious. These questions just sort of pop out."

"Do you wash the plants in your garden, Dave?"

"No," growled Dave, "but I don't wear them either."

She smiled again. "You ask such childish questions. I sometimes forget you're an infant in an adult body."

Dave was getting grumpier the longer this conversation went on.

"Perspiration, body oils, and even dirt are nutrients for the plant. It drinks water from the rain. It uses sunlight for energy. It needs nothing else. Now it's time for you to have one."

She sprang lightly into the tree, and climbed rapidly to the higher branches. He was amazed at her agility. She reached a large mass of fiber, detached it gently from the oak branches, and carried it down. She spread the plant out as a large irregularly shaped mat. Pulling a pair of scissors from her satchel, she carefully cut the mat into a rectangular shape.

She handed him his blanket, and then carried the remnant back up the tree and draped it carefully over a branch. When she reached the ground again, Dave hadn't moved, still astounded by her tree-climbing ability.

"Don't stand there gawking youngling, try it on!" She took the blanket from his hands and draped it over his shoulders and then turned him around to gaze at him from all angles.

"It will do well enough," she said. "Use it as a sleeping blanket for a few days and then when it has become acclimatized to you, I will sew it into your cloak."

"But I already had a blankie," said Dave petulantly.

"What do you mean?" said Arlana, surprise in her voice.

"Never mind," said Dave. "It's something from my childhood you wouldn't understand."

"I see," sniffed Arlana. "But you will use it?"

"Yes, I'll use it. Ever since I first saw your cloak, I wanted one like it."

They walked back to the stable in silence. Dave thought back to his earliest years and the blanket he had carried everywhere. *Maybe the blanket I had as a child was really a foreshadowing of something real, that I was meant to have, like this living blanket. Maybe a lot of things I dismissed as childhood fantasies are really reminders of something real and important.*

They arrived back at the stable. Ferris looked at Dave's blanket and exchanged a look with Arlana. Without another word, the others saddled up and headed out the gate. Dave went up to Traveller and patted him on the neck. He felt the same sensation of bonding he had felt before.

"You'll carry me Old Fella, even though you'll know I haven't ridden for a while and don't really know what I'm doing?"

Traveller swung his head around and nuzzled Dave's hand. With a sigh, Dave swung into the saddle, and Traveller trotted out of the stable after the others.

Chapter 14

A Narrow Escape

They rode out of the main gate of Kelldor's house. The road to the left bent around a mountain spur and headed north toward a small village nestled in a narrow bay. After they had skirted the spur, instead of heading for the village, Ferris turned right, leaving the road, and led them on a track up the side of the steep foothills, toward the mountains. Hanomer rode with Arlana and soon they were in animated conversation. Ferris rode on ahead, anxiously looking back to see if anyone was following them. They rode through a heavily wooded forest, only occasionally catching a glimpse of the mountain peaks through the trees. As the trail continued to climb, the solid expanse of the forest was broken with jagged rocks that reared up out of the ground like the teeth of a carnivore. At last Ferris found what he was looking for and guided them to a small glade, asking them to rest a moment. He dismounted and climbed a tower of rock that rose out of the forest ahead of them.

He came back, breathlessly. "No one seems to be following us. I'm sure if Teledon pursues us, he will expect us to leave the area as quickly as possible. That means he will head down to the town of Rickets and ask about us at the port, thinking we left there by boat. When Teledon determines that we never entered Rickets, he will head back to the caves to see if we have left Gurundaria through the passage under the mountain. When he finally realizes his mistake, we will be long gone to Westport. My plan will only work if no one sees us."

They mounted. Ferris picked a narrow path that was all but invisible as it left the north side of the glade. After a few hundred yards they reached an overgrown road that headed north. In silence they skirted the mountain valleys and the main road through dense pine forests, crossing the occasional stream. Late in the evening, just before sunset, they reached a broad road which bent up from the west. Ferris halted for a breather. "We've made good time and traveling will be much easier now on the open road." Urging them onto the road again, he let Arlana go on ahead and came alongside Dave.

"Are you coming with us on our journey or are you heading somewhere else?" asked Dave.

"No I think I'll go with you. As Arlana's cousin, I need to look after her. She's not supposed to leave our lands, but in view of the potential trouble and the fact that Kelldor is not here to protect her, she's probably safer away from here—at least until Kelldor returns."

"If we're trying to get away, why are we not heading back through the tunnel? Wouldn't that be a lot faster and put us out of Teledon's reach quicker?"

"You remember that trip down from the tunnel do you? You have a good sense of distance and direction, even though you were near death when we brought you in. No, the tunnel is too dangerous. Arlana proved that. The Halfmen are behaving strangely. I'm sure they are waiting outside the Guardian Trees for us to come out. No, we're heading north to the village of Northborough and the Giant Steps. Your, ahem, father lives there and will provide us some measure of protection. Even more importantly, we have boats at the bottom of the Giant Steps, the huge series of waterfalls at Northborough, and we'll take the river back to your home. Halfmen don't travel in boats. Still, we're traveling *incognito*. Let Arlana and I do the talking. Pretend you are sick and cannot speak for a time."

"But what's going on?"

"Dave didn't you listen to Sirona? Arachodor is a very ambitious man. With your healing, and Kelldor's absence, this is the perfect time to attack Kelldor by claiming Arlana and Sirona have broken our ancient law by using the Healing Plants in a way that is forbidden."

"Well what about Sirona?"

"As long as Arachodor doesn't have you, he has nothing. He would not convene an emergency council session with no evidence. Even if he accused Sirona she would appeal to Kelldor and Arachodor would have to wait. For him you would be the golden prize." They traveled on in silence, pushing to cover as many miles as possible.

Dave was very tired and dozed off several times. When he touched Traveller's neck with his hand, he could sense the horse's concern for him. *I'm not a very good rider. I think Traveller has kept me from falling off on numerous occasions.* Dave thought gratefully.

The clouds had moved in and the night was very dark. Dave suddenly became conscious of a number of things he had not noticed before. He could see even with just starlight, better than he had ever seen with a full moon. The second he noticed was his sense of smell; he could smell plants and animals all around him. He could even distinguish every one of their company by smell. When he talked to Ferris, he could detect by smell alone whether Ferris was angry, exasperated or pleased. Anger had a slightly pungent aroma, exasperation a hint of the sour, while Ferris had a floral tang when pleased.

I have a lot to learn about my new body.

Finally Ferris called a halt and led them off the main road. He, Arlana, and Hanomer pulled out light gourds since the night had become black like a coal mine under the trees with the clouds rolling in. Dave pitched himself onto the ground and was asleep at once, only to find himself roughly shaken awake by Hanomer.

"Friend Dave, it be time for us to be going," said Hanomer.

"I just fell asleep!"

"Begging your pardon friend Dave, you've been asleep about three hours."

"You're kidding. What time is it?"

"It's an hour before dawn."

Dave got up. He was cold. A very pale light indicated that dawn was on its way. Traveller was chewing fresh grass right next to Dave.

He realized that his living blanket was gone. Arlana was sitting on a fallen log in dim light working on his blanket. She looked up and smiled. "Before we get to the next town of Westport, you need to have a living cloak. A blanket simply will not do for a grown man. Come here, let me see if it fits."

He came over and she hung the cloak about his shoulders. She looked at the cloak critically. "Your shoulders make it hang a little high. I should have cut more material. Still, the living cloak will grow to the right length in time. It will have to do."

Dave was grateful that she had given up her sleep to complete the cloak. "I don't know how to thank you, Arlana. This is a wonderful gift you've given me."

She smiled and said, "Come and have some breakfast. I'm sure Ferris will be anxious to leave."

Ferris wanted to leave right away and eat in the saddle. Dave remounted and followed the others back to the road. As the sun rose, the haunting call of an opera bird filled the air, and Dave savored the lush grass of the meadows and the deep green of the pine woods. The scent of pine needles filled the air.

This realization of the beauty of the land and a sense of belonging brought a peace to his soul. Dave's thoughts turned to the trip out of Arkand and he shuddered. But he realized in that terrible time, Arlana had stuck with him and it turned the shudder into the warmth of committed friendship.

Dave's reverie was broken as the sun came out from behind a cloud. The road was paved with smooth, square stones so that not even a blade of grass grew between the joints. The day rapidly flew by as Ferris pushed them to keep going, allowing only a short respite for lunch. They encountered only the occasional rider coming toward them. Although they often greeted Ferris, he did not stop to chat.

Toward evening, they came upon a rise and Dave saw the road before them snaking toward a walled town that surrounded a harbor on Lake Tolbar. The harbor was filled with ships. Ferris called a halt and came back to Dave with Arlana, who had Hanomer in the saddle in front of her. Ferris pulled up his horse and leaned over his pommel. "Friend Hanomer and cousin Rokodor (here he nodded at Dave, emphatically), I must ask you a favor. We are about to enter the town of Westport. I want us to remain as inconspicuous as possible. It has been many long years since our *Hansa* friends have been among us." He bowed briefly to Hanomer. "Also, Rokodor, you are not yet skilled in controlling your skin coloration. I would ask that you both bundle up in your cloaks."

Hanomer did not answer, but pulled his hood over his face and withdrew his tail inside the cloak. Dave was annoyed but could not argue against the wisdom of Ferris' words and so also pulled the hood over his face.

If we're really worried about being seen, we should wait here until it's darker. Anyone who takes a good look at Hanomer will recognize that he's not a child. Whoever heard of a child carrying a bow and arrow?

Satisfied with their compliance, Ferris went to the front of the band while Arlana rode with Dave. Soon they came to the open gate of the town. Many townsfolk were about, but Ferris wrote straight ahead without asking directions.

At least he knows where we're going.

Ferris angled left and headed toward the harbor. Finally, entering a side street, he stopped under a large sign which had the image of a goose sitting on a nest of bottles.

"What does the sign mean?" asked Dave.

"The inn is called The Golden Goose," whispered Arlana. "Be quiet and wait here until Ferris comes to get us. Your accent will betray us."

Ferris returned and took them around the side of the inn through a tunnel into a courtyard. They put their horses in a stable and then carried their supplies up the courtyard stair to a large room overlooking the street in front of the inn.

Ferris ushered Dave and Hanomer into a side room.

"The innkeeper and his servants are bringing us water to let us wash and supper will be served in our room. Stay in here until they are gone."

Hanomer sat down and began going over his supplies. Dave did the same. Within minutes he heard a commotion in the outer room. Ferris came in and brought them out to a sumptuous feast with basins of water to let them wash up. The aroma of venison filled the air. There were potatoes with gravy, and leeks smothered in a cream sauce. Special meat pies had a seasoning Dave had never tasted before but would remember ever after as the best meat pie he had ever tasted. Unfortunately there was no *Siph*, but the heated wine, diluted with water and seasoned with spices, was superb. Long afterwards, when he and Hanomer had a particularly good meal, one of them would say to the other, "This was truly a Golden Goose feast!"

The superb supper had lifted Dave's spirits and he felt full of energy and a desire to explore the first real town he had seen in Gurundaria.

"Arlana, would you like to explore Westport with me?"

Arlana was just finishing a mix of greens. She looked at Dave with a scowl. "Youngling, with Teledon after us, why would you want to wander around town when every word you speak will reveal that you don't belong here?"

"Arlana, you and I both know we gave old Teledon the slip. He's probably still up in his fortress home, licking his wounds after the dressing down you gave him at dinner."

She smiled at his comment then forced her face into a scowl. "*Kree ah na koo*, you're seriously trying to joke your way into a rash ramble through this town. I will have none of it. Would you like me to ask my friend the innkeeper to have his men take you to your room?"

Dave could feel himself getting angry. *Why does she always treat me like a child?*

"I think it would be wise for us to do what friend Arlana says, Dave. She's right, you would stand out if you walked around and if Teledon does come, your walk around town would make it easy for him to find us."

Dave looked from Arlana to Hanomer. He was about to argue, but changed his mind. Instead he said, "Maybe you two are right. It's been a long day, perhaps we should turn in early."

"A wise decision, youngling. For my part I'm looking forward to a soothing bath."

Dave could tell she looked skeptical despite her words. He saw her watch him closely as he left the room with Hanomer.

Ferris excused himself soon after the feast to return to his room. He was worried. Although he had tried to remain positive, he was not at all convinced that Teledon would not follow them. He quietly knocked on Arlana's door. The splashing stopped.

"Who is it?"

"Cousin, I am going out for a bit. Please stay alert while I'm away. I have an uneasy feeling I just can't shake."

"Of course."

She's thinking the same thing I am. She's too smart to think Teledon won't be following us.

Ferris went out the back way to the courtyard so that he wouldn't have to go through the inn's common room, and took a side street to the harbor. He walked along the wharf examining each of the boats. He was about two thirds down the row of moored vessels, when he found what he was looking for: a two-masted ship called The Eagle. The gangplank was out, but a chain indicated that the crew was away and they were not open for business. Nevertheless Ferris went on board. There was a quarterdeck at the back with a couple of cabins. Near the bow was a very large hatch flush with the deck consisting of what looked like two doors. When he opened them up, there was a long ramp into the hold. *This has been designed to carry horses.* There was no cargo on board, although there were provisions and the water casks had been filled. Two horses were there with enough fodder to last for a short voyage.

Good! Very good. Tomorrow I'll stop by bright and early and see if Falcor can repay a favor.

Ferris went back to shore and walked to the south gate of the town. He had to think this through carefully. This was no time to make a mistake.

If Teledon does come, he won't come until late tonight. First, he'll have to wake the guard to get in and second, it will be too late to search the inns. I have to find a street urchin to keep an eye on the gate for him and then make arrangements to get the information from the watcher. I can't let the watcher know where we are though.

He arrived at the gate and sat down in a pub by an open window. He hid in the shadows and watched the well-lit gate. There were very few likely candidates about. There were some older busy bodies on the lookout for news or work guiding the unfamiliar to a good inn, but he wanted someone younger.

A group of twelve horsemen rode through the gate. The horses were lathered and the men were past weary. His hands clenched onto his beer mug. *This is bad, very bad.* It was Teledon.

They walked their horses right toward his window. He cowered. *They've seen me. Now I've done it.*

Ferris heard Teledon's voice. "My good man, we've ridden hard hoping to catch some friends with an urgent message. Can you help us?" Ferris heard the tinkle of a coin.

A raspy voice from outside under the window answered. "Thank 'ee kind sirs for taking notice of a poor fella like me. I would like to help yee gentle folk, but many have been through the gate this long day."

Another coin clinked. "I'm sure, friend, many have come by, but this party consisted of three adults and another who may have been the size of a child but who was one of the *Hansa*."

"A *Hansa*!" said the raspy voice. "That's quite a tale. I am growing quite parched watching all day. Would you kind gentlemen buy a poor man a beer?"

"I will do better than that," said Teledon. "With this you can buy many beers."

"Thank 'ee kind sir! Perhaps two hours ago four strangers rode in. The man and the woman, although tired, had the air of royalty. The other two were hooded. The smaller, who I thought a child, had a bow across his shoulder so my curiosity was piqued. I watched him and sure enough I saw a furry face when he looked at me."

"Where did they go?"

"They didn't ask directions but rode straight on. There are many inns in the next few streets."

More coins. "Thank you, my good man. Please ask around to find where they are staying and I will be grateful." Then in a louder voice, "We'll search the inns here by the south gate first. My guess is that they're near the north gate, so we'll search there next. Failing that we'll go to the harbor and check the inns there. I want them found and we don't have much time before everybody locks up for the night."

Ferris could hear the sound of men mounting their horses and inwardly breathed a sign of relief. Then he heard something that chilled his heart. Teledon said, "You two men stay here and watch this gate. If they try to leave town, one of you follow them discreetly while the other comes to get me. If you see any of their party pass by, one of you must follow them to their inn while the other searches for me. Is that clear?"

"Yes, lord!" said two voices nearly in unison.

Ferris heard the horses trot off.

"You stay here and watch the gate," said one of Teledon's men. "I'll go in and get us each a mug of ale to make the wait go more easily."

I'm well known. If I attract attention ... He pulled his hood over his face and leaned against the window frame as if asleep in the shadows.

He heard the door open. He listened as the man ordered two ales in a loud, gruff voice. When the main door closed again, he listened until the outside chairs creaked and the men sighed and complimented the ale. Just to be sure, Ferris peeked out to see if it was all clear. He left his beer and walked leisurely to the back of the inn, suppressing an urge to bolt.

Our escape hangs by a hair. Falcor has to come through for us. We'll never outrun Teledon now. Ferris found a back door to a neighboring street and walked briskly back to the Golden Goose, hood drawn and worried that he would meet Teledon at any moment.

Ferris went upstairs and roused Arlana.

"There's no time to lose. Teledon has made better time than I expected. We must leave now."

He went on to knock on Dave's door. There was no answer. He went in. The room was empty. The window at the back was open.

Arlana stood beside him. Ferris looked at her. She was pale and her lips were trembling. "He wanted to see the town. We had an argument. I threatened to have the innkeeper take him to his room."

"A lie, Arlana? I've never heard you tell a lie before."

"Dave makes me so angry sometimes with his immaturity," said Arlana. "It was the only way I could think of to keep him here. It would have been better to be truthful and to have let him go. At least then I would know where he had gone."

"Well," said Ferris, "since Hanomer is not here, it looks like he went with him. Hanomer has more sense than Dave. I take that as a hopeful sign."

Ferris paced back and forth. Finally he turned back. "Arlana, Teledon is heading to the north gate, to check out the inns. If Dave has gone there, he will be caught. I will go there and check it out. You search the streets nearby. If you find him, or he comes back to the inn, take your equipment and horses to a boat called The Eagle. If you're stopped, ask to see Falcor, the captain, and explain you're with me. If I find Dave, I'll come back, get our supplies and make my way back to the boat. Without Dave, Teledon has nothing. Does this make sense?"

"Yes," said Arlana. "I'll stay close and check in the vicinity. May the Creator be with you."

"And also with you." They hugged good-bye and Ferris left.

"A wise decision, youngling." Dave could still hear Arlana's words ringing in his ears as he and Hanomer went back to their room after supper. *I wonder if she really could get the innkeeper and his buddies to restrain me?* Dave closed the door. He walked over to the window and looked out. There was a sloping roof just outside and he had the beginnings of a plan. Dave packed his gear and then wrapped himself in his cloak. "I think I'll lie down for a while Hanomer."

"I will do the same friend Dave."

Dave settled on his bed and pretended to be asleep. He could hear Arlana splashing in a bath in the adjacent room. Dave listened for Hanomer's quiet breathing and then crept to the window. Opening the window carefully, he looked back. Hanomer hadn't stirred. He climbed out, not daring to close the window again. Quietly creeping along the roof, he came to a drain pipe and climbed down to street level. There was no one around.

This will be much better than leaving by the front door. I'll be out and back in twenty minutes and Arlana will never even know that I was away. It will be my secret.

He thought about where to go. *If Teledon arrives late tonight, he'll come in by the south gate. To be safe, I'll explore the north end of town.* He saw the streets sloped down to Lake Tolbar. Now with his bearings, he headed for the north gate. He found the gate without difficulty. He had looked at a couple of the inns when he decided it was time to go back. He rounded a corner. Not ten paces ahead of him, Teledon and another man were talking to an innkeeper. Teledon looked up and shouted, "That's him."

Dave ran for it. He heard Teledon shouting, "get the others, I'll stay with him."

First, I have to break contact and then work my way back to our inn.

Dave rounded a corner and heard Teledon pounding behind him. *He's too close to lose him.*

Running as lightly and quietly as he could, Dave rounded another corner and stopped, his back pressed against the wall. When Teledon came around the corner, Dave caught him with a forearm to the mouth that completely knocked Teledon off his feet. *I've been wanting to do that ever since I heard you talk to Arlana as if you owned her.* Dave ran off before Teledon could recover.

He turned another corner and ran into the midst of a group of men. "That's him," one of them shouted and they all piled onto Dave. He was able to knock a couple down, but was subdued and tied up.

"Cantor," said the leader, "you guard the prisoner, while we find Teledon and the others. I'm pretty sure Teledon will want us to get the horses right away and leave tonight. The rest of you spread out and find all of the company and then get our horses and meet back here. I'll look for Teledon—he can't be far and then the three of us will guard the prisoner until you get back."

Dave was bruised and battered. *Why am I so stupid? Why didn't I listen?*

Cantor, apparently satisfied that Dave was tied securely, turned his back and kept an eye on the alley.

Just then a hand touched his arm and he heard Hanomer's voice in his head.

Friend, Dave, I'm going to cut you loose. Are you able to walk?
I think I am, Hanomer.

He felt his hands come free. Dave reached under his cloak and pulled out a small, well-concealed knife, then put his hands behind him and waited. His captor paced back and forth and then turned to look down the alley. At Hanomer's urging, Dave crawled into the shadows and with Hanomer's third hand pulling him, was guided up a stair, to a ladder and eventually to a rooftop.

He heard the shouting of many men in the streets below. Hanomer had him crouch in the shadows until the shouts and the running diminished.

Follow me, friend Dave. Walk softly!

How is a two hundred and thirty pound guy supposed to walk softly on a tile roof? Dave asked himself.

Hanomer led him across a set of houses that had a common roof. He then guided Dave to crawl down some ancient ivy to a lower roof and they were able to head in a new direction. Finally Hanomer brought them to street level. By now it was quite late and the streets were deserted. When they reached their inn, he and Hanomer had a whispered discussion about how to return to their room. Hanomer wanted to use the roof and the window and Dave finally agreed. The window was still open and Dave climbed in followed by Hanomer. Dave immediately went to the hall, glanced up and down. Seeing no one, he went to Arlana's door and knocked. No answer. He knocked again, more insistently. He looked up and down the hallway again and turned the handle. The door was open. The room was dark, but in the lantern light from the hallway, he could see that the room was empty and the bed had not been slept in.

He tried knocking on Ferris' door when he heard steps on the stairs. He dashed across the hall to Arlana's room and quietly listened as soft steps came up the hall.

Someone is trying to be very quiet.

The steps stopped at the door. In the dark, he could hear the scrape of a latch being lifted.

It was Arlana.

They said each other's names simultaneously. Dave pulled Arlana into the room. They both spoke at once.

"I've seen Teledon," said Dave.

"Oh, Dave ..." whispered Arlana.

"We have to leave immediately," continued Dave.

"I know," said Arlana.

"Where's Ferris?"

"Looking for you, Dave."

"I've really bollixed things up," muttered Dave.

"Dave," said Arlana, "Ferris left instructions and we have to follow them exactly."

"Instructions?"

"Yes, Dave. Gather your things. We have to take the horses and go down to the wharf to find a ship called The Eagle."

"Okay, what about Ferris?" asked Dave.

"When he comes back and finds the horses missing, he'll know I found you and will join us on the ship. Teledon needs you to make his case. He has no reason to detain Ferris. By the way, is Hanomer with you?"

"Yes he rescued me from Teledon."

Arlana breathed a sigh of relief. "Let's get going. Ferris paid in full so there's no tab to settle."

In a few minutes they carried their belongings down the back stairs to the stables. The stable was guarded by one of the inn servants, but he knew Arlana and let her take the horses.

In a short time, they were saddled and Arlana led them down to the harbor. They had to go up and down the wharf twice until they found The Eagle. The chain across the gangplank indicated that the crew was still in town, so Arlana unhooked the chain, opened the large hatch on the deck and led the horses into the hold where other horses were stabled. After replacing the chain, she hid with Dave and Hanomer in the cable tier along with their equipment.

After about an hour, Dave heard steps on the ramp. The hatch opened quietly and he heard Ferris whisper Arlana's name.

Ferris had spotted Teledon's people soon after Ferris had arrived near the north gate. The men were obviously agitated and were searching for someone everywhere. *At least they haven't found Dave.*

Ferris hid himself in the shadows and watched the search from a distance. After a few minutes, he decided that with the frenetic activity of the searchers, he was likely to be spotted. When he had a chance he left the shadows and headed west to search a different part of town. After about an hour he returned to the inn. Arlana and Dave's supplies were gone. He also left the inn with his saddle bags and made it to the stable. When he saw that the horses were also gone, he headed to The Eagle.

After Ferris found Dave safe and sound on the boat, he went upstairs and hid in Falcor's cabin and waited.

He roused himself when he heard loud voices and singing on the deck.

The door opened and he saw a big man silhouetted against the dim light, come into the cabin. He started unerringly toward the lamp, closing the door as he came.

"Brother I need your boat," said Ferris quietly.

The flint clattered onto the floor.

"I know that voice. What in the name of our western brethren are you doing here Ferris? Haven't you shortened my miserable life enough? Scaring a man half to death by sneaking into his cabin at night."

"I had no choice Falcor. I'm in trouble and I really need a favor."

"Trouble? Ferris, trouble is your middle name. I'd ask you 'what kind of trouble?' but I'm not sure I want to know."

"You're right. You probably don't want to know."

"How bad is it this time?" asked Falcor. "Is it 'losing your head' kind of trouble?

"No," said Ferris chuckling. "It's not quite that bad. It may be 'losing your boat' kind of trouble though."

"Oh that's a relief! My friendship to you will only cost me my dear Eagle and put me on the street. The Creator seems to have put me on this earth to rescue you."

"I seem to recall," said Ferris, "that I've done my own share of rescuing myself."

"So you have, so you have."

Falcor, rummaged around on the floor until he found the flint then lit the hanging lamp. He pulled out a bottle of wine, and poured a couple of glasses and gave one to Ferris.

After clinking their glasses he said, "What do you need my friend?"

"I need a trip up to the Northborough, no questions asked."

Falcor stroked his chin with his glass. "I told the boys I would give them a few days off and then we'd pick up a cargo here and head south to Shadowvale. I'll just tell them there's been a change of plan."

"One more thing. We need to leave tonight."

"Tonight? You really are in trouble."

He put his glass down and got up. "We've got a bit of a land breeze and that should get us out of the harbor."

Ferris heard some harsh words as Falcor roused the crew, but soon he felt the rhythmic motion of a ship under way. Ferris sipped his wine and waited for Falcor to return.

Presently Falcor returned, sat down and poured himself another glass.

"You should know, friend Falcor, that I'm not the only one on board."

"Quietly," said Falcor as he moved his chair closer. "The walls are very thin," he whispered.

Ferris touched Falcor's arm.

Falcor, I am not the only passenger on board.

I thought so, Ferris. I know my own horses and what I heard below decks was not one of them.

One can't fool a captain on his own ship. I have my cousin Arlana, a Hansa, and a friend of Arlana's called Rokodor on board.

You're not involving me in some love intrigue of that child Arlana are you?

No Falcor, it's nothing like that. We're going to Celyddon. If Arlana were eloping against her father's wishes, she wouldn't be running to her father's best friend would she?

I guess not.

Chapter 15

The Giant Steps

After three days in the hold, Dave insisted that he go on deck. Arlana hovered around him as if he were a newly hatched baby chick ready to fall into the water. First, he had to ask all kinds of questions about the use of boat weed in boats. Then Dave went to the bow. They were approaching a deep bay. Off to port, beyond the bay, he saw two rock islands with tall towers on them. A giant bronze chain bound to huge floating logs was stretched from the far promontory of the bay to the nearest island.

"What are those chains and booms for?" asked Dave.

"Ahead is the entrance to the Devil's Throat and the Giant Steps. The chain and those floating logs of boat weed prevent boats from drifting into the strong current of the Devil's Throat and thus over the waterfall into the gorge. Can you see that bridge spanning those two mountain peaks?"

"Yes, what is it?"

"That's the High Bridge. We have to travel across it to make our way down the far side to the cavern that holds our ships at the bottom of the falls."

Dave was silent and looked at the dark water of Devil's Throat.

How would I feel if I were caught in that current? We're much higher here than on the plateau when we were escaping the Halfmen. The plunge must be incredible. I think I can hear the rumble of the falls now.

Falcor came on deck and began calling instructions. The ship sails were reefed and The Eagle glided in under topsails only. With the timing of a seasoned seaman, Falcor took the way off her and kissed the wharf so that hardly a tremor was felt as The Eagle was made fast.

Ferris came forward. "We had better get moving. I hear Celyddon has an excellent table and I could use a good meal."

Arlana needed no further urging. She pulled on Dave's arm and dragged him below to get their things and the horses.

Northborough proved to be a walled town about the same size as Westport. Dave looked out from under his hood as the winding road climbed from the harbor into the foothills of the mountains. The two-storied row houses were of white plaster and the doors opened right onto the narrow street. The first and second story windows all had shutters and flower boxes. The mums in the boxes added splashes of reds and yellows to the white and green of the plaster and the shutters. Finally they reached the top of the hill where the row houses were replaced by much larger houses surrounded by walled gardens. Ferris turned left until they came to the end of the street. Ahead of them was an open space. They could hear the dull, muted roar of a waterfall. Ferris pulled on a bell cord next to an iron-bound wooden gate and waited.

"This is the home of Celyddon, my father's oldest and closest friend," said Arlana. "I do hope he's home."

Ferris, growing impatient, was about to ring the bell again, when a small door opened in the gate and two dark eyes peered out.

"Master Ferris!" said a voice. Lord Celyddon will be happy to see you!"

Arlana looked, if anything, more anxious at those words, even than she had before.

"I thought you'd be relieved?" whispered Dave.

"I am, in a way."

"What's the matter?"

"You try to explain to your father's best friend that he's adopted a son he's never seen before."

The door swung open. The door warden was a rotund man, slightly balding on his pate. When he saw Arlana he could barely suppress a squeal and ran to embrace her.

Arlana disentangled herself from the door warden. "Myrodon, these are my friends Rokodor and Hanomer."

Myrodon's eyes lit up at the introduction. He greeted Dave warmly. Then, turning to the *Hansa* he added gravely, "I have long dreamed of meeting your kind, Hanomer.

"But don't stand there, come in. My Lord Celyddon will be delighted to see you."

"Yeah sure, I wonder how delighted he's going to be when Arlana tells him I'm his new son. How do I get myself into these situations?" Dave wondered.

Arlana fell in beside Dave and whispered. "We have some explaining to do to Lord Celyddon. Please don't say anything unless he asks you a direct question."

He looked at her and her eyes were pleading. "Sure Arlana, even though I can't really see how you can get by without my expert diplomacy and winning ways, my lips are sealed."

"*Kree ah na koo*! May the Creator help me! Dave, be serious. This is important."

"I won't speak unless spoken to, Arlana. Satisfied?"

She didn't answer but instead gave him a skeptical look and then turned to rejoin Ferris.

Dave looked east and saw a heavy plume of smoke in the air. He caught the scent of burning wood. He followed the others across the gardens to a large building at the corner of the estate. The interior was well-furnished, with floors and columns of marble. Myrodon led them to a large room with glass windows overlooking a chasm. Dave could hear the faint roar of a mighty waterfall.

A man with long, wavy, white hair stood with his hands clasped behind his back staring out the windows into the gorge. He did not hear them come in.

"Lord Celyddon, we have guests. I was sure you would want to see them right away."

Celyddon started and turned around. His eyes widened.

"Arlana, Ferris—what a surprise. I'm delighted to see you."

He limped across the room, hugged Arlana and clasped Ferris' hand.

"Uncle Celyddon, are you injured? " asked Arlana.

"Yes child, I was severely wounded by the Halfmen when I set out to look for you and your father. I've only just been healed and I'm recovering my strength. It will be some days until these old muscles are strong enough to lead an attack."

Arlana's face clouded and she hung her head.

"Now, now child I was not chiding you. What you did was foolish, going after your father, but your actions were noble and motivated by your love for him. I was so worried. Imagine my relief when Sirona wrote that you were safe. Enough of that. Have you heard from your father?"

"No uncle, he has not returned. What is that smoke?"

"Yes, the smoke. The Halfmen have gone wild and are besieging us at every pass in the Barrier Mountains. They are burning the Guardian Forest in an effort to reach us. Each day when the wind is favorable they send flaming arrows into the wood to cut a path through."

"What has come over them?" asked Ferris.

"This has all of the telltale signs of a Bent One. I think one of the Bent Ones has come back and is using the Halfmen to attack us.

"Who are your companions? I don't believe we have been introduced."

"This is Rokodor, a particular friend of mine and that is Hanomer a *Hansa* traveling companion I met on my journeys."

At that moment, Hanomer stepped out from behind Dave. Dave saw Celyddon's eyes widen at the mention of *Hansa*, but he quickly recovered and clasped Hanomer's arm and then Dave's, and welcomed them. Dave, remembering his promise to Arlana, smiled at Celyddon and nodded his head in a bow, but said nothing.

"It is because of these two I have come to you uncle, but it is a long story."

"In that case I will hear it now. Myrodon, please have some refreshments brought in and make it known that I am not to be disturbed for one hour."

Arlana began her story, starting from when she had left Celyddon and headed east. Celyddon sat up straight and his eyes narrowed when she spoke of rescuing Dave and Hanomer from the Halfmen. When she finally came to her conversation with Sirona and Dave's healing, Celyddon jumped up and began to pace.

"Arlana, Arlana you have broken all of our strictest rules in healing Rokodor. You have given a great club to our enemies. "Now they're about to beat your father over the head with it."

"Uncle, I had no choice."

"No choice? Arlana, we always have a choice."

"Uncle Celyddon, those rules were made to prevent us from warping Ancients as the Bent Ones have done, not to prevent us from restoring Rokodor to his ancient heritage. His people were once like ours, before they were corrupted and weakened by the Bent Ones."

Celyddon ran his hand through his long, white hair and sat down heavily.

"What's done is done, child. That your friend survived what I would have deemed too dangerous, is encouraging. Perhaps he has a purpose in our plans that I cannot see. What can I do for you?"

"Lord Celyddon …" said Dave. Ferris put a hand on his arm.

"Lord Celyddon," continued Dave heedless of Ferris, "I need to get back to my people to warn them about the Halfmen. Just help me get out of your country, and then Teledon will have little evidence with which to build a case. Perhaps his club will break in his hand if he tries to wield it."

"Didn't you hear what he said Dave—I mean Rokodor," said Arlana. "The passes are all blocked."

Celyddon looked thoughtful and spoke quietly as if to himself. "Yes, the passes are all blocked, but the port caves are still open."

He looked intently at Dave. "Rokodor, the journey will be dangerous are you sure you want to go?"

Dave nodded emphatically, not trusting his voice.

"Myrodon, send word that my boat is to be made ready to sail."

Celyddon turned back to Dave. "Rokodor, you will not be able to sail on your own. My boat requires a minimum of three and the waters in the gorge at the base of the falls are not too swift, but there are many rocks."

"He's not going alone," said Arlana. "I'm going with him."

"Child, I cannot allow it!"

"I'm not a child!"

"Enough! Your father would never forgive me if I let you leave at a time like this. He trusts me. We've been friends since childhood and I know what he would say if he were here. I cannot let you go."

Arlana hung her head.

"I will go with him and so will Hanomer," said Ferris. "That makes three."

"That would be well, since hiring help would set tongues wagging," said Celyddon. "You know the passage through the gorge. Keep the boat until I can send some others to bring it back."

"So, that's settled," said Ferris. "We had better get some sleep; we have an early day tomorrow. We have to get the boat ready and our supplies loaded."

"Ferris," said Celyddon. "The Halfmen who now hold the heights above the gorge can reach you with their arrows."

"But the rocks in the gorge are too treacherous to try the passage by night."

"Ferris, our people now leave at dusk or in the early morning twilight. The Halfmen have trouble seeing you in the shadows. They still shoot, relying on chance."

The talk continued until Celyddon had to leave for another appointment. Dave was shown to his own room. He felt disappointed that Arlana was not coming.

Hanomer had asked to stay in Dave's room. "You seem troubled, friend Dave."

"I guess I am, Hanomer, but I don't know why. I'm heading home to my people and I ought to be happy. Maybe I'm worried about them."

"Leaving good friends is always difficult. Arlana, you and I have had many adventures together. We will remember each other in our songs."

"Yeah, Hanomer, you have enough to keep you composing for several months." Dave's despondency continued and it took a long time for him to fall asleep.

The next morning he was as gloomy as the night before and didn't want to get up. Finally Hanomer had to speak up, "Friend Dave, you Ill? If you don't get up, you will keep Ferris waiting."

Hanomer I don't actually care if I keep Ferris waiting—what's the matter with me?

"I know Hanomer. I'll get up."

Once he got moving his mood improved. Hanomer and Dave made it on time. They met Ferris outside a small postern gate on the north side of the estate. Ferris was holding their two horses and one of them had two packs strapped behind the saddle.

Dave was surprised to see Traveller. He had not expected to see him again. "Why do you have two packs on your horse, Ferris?" asked Dave.

"The second is Arlana's. No time for questions. I know my cousin well and all will become clear soon. Strap your packs onto Traveller. She passed me a note with instructions." Ferris pulled out the parchment and read it

"Ferris, I rescued Dave twice," Ferris read aloud, "and he needs me to look after him. I will at least give him Traveller since the horse has more sense than he has and will look after him. In any case Traveller has taken an unaccountable liking to him and would pine away if I didn't let him go. Please pick up my pack outside my room and take the horse to Dave. I'm sure you'll figure out what I plan to do—Arlana"

"There you have it. Now let's get moving," said Ferris.

With that he led them out the postern gate down a steep switchback to a road cut in the side of the cliff. At the edge of the gorge the roar of the falls was deafening. Mist shrouded everything and the road and rocks were slick. The road, cut out of the living rock at the edge of the gorge, descended at a gentle incline into the mist. Soon out of the mist Dave saw ahead of them a single arched bridge which spanned the gorge. They followed the road onto the bridge and Dave stopped to look back up to the lake. In the center of the bridge, the wind whistling down the gorge blew the spray away providing better visibility.

The bridge was high above the level of the lake. The water from Devil's Throat boiled over the edge and spilled down a series of steps each about one hundred paces in height until it emptied into the gorge far, far below.

Ferris led them into a tunnel on the far side. The tunnel was smooth and ten feet in diameter and led straight ahead. Dave felt his skin crawl. "Was this tunnel carved by rock borers?"

"Yes, Dave it was," said Ferris. "I take it you have encountered a rock borer before? Don't worry, there are none here now. Even if there were, you must realize we are their true masters and can rival Meglir in controlling them. Since you have been restored by the healing plant, you are not the same person you were the last time you met one."

They mounted their horses. They came to a small opening to their right, and turning their horses into it, moved down the tunnel. The clip clop of the horses' hooves on the stone echoed. They would hear others coming a long way off. The familiar green of lumi-lichen was sufficiently bright that with the visual acuity of an Ancient, Dave did not even have to bring out his light gourd. After about half an hour, during which the road continually spiraled downward, always turning to the right, they entered into a large cavern. The light of a large opening showed that half of the cavern floor was taken up by stone quays, but only a few had ships tied up.

Ferris said, "We have not had occasion to use the river much since we prefer to travel overland. The attack by the Halfmen has changed all that. Come, Celyddon's boat is this way."

Ferris led them to the end of the last jetty where a medium-sized vessel, made of boat weed, was tied up. They led their horses on board and placed them into a small pen under the bow. The horses happily began munching on hay. Ferris directed Hanomer and Dave to the largest of the three tiny cabins in the stern.

They spent the rest of the morning loading cordage and supplies from an adjacent storage cavern. Around noon a wagon full of food arrived. When that was stowed, Ferris sat on deck with his feet up.

"Why don't we go?" asked Dave.

"Didn't you hear Celyddon? The Halfmen hold the heights. It's much too dangerous to attempt by daylight. They'd shoot at us from above. When it's twilight or if it becomes foggy we'll head out safely enough."

Dave was just beginning to doze when he heard a horse galloping toward the quay. It was Arlana, her braid streaming behind her. She pulled back on the reins so hard that her horse pawed the air as the mare slid to a stop.

"We have to leave NOW!" said Arlana leading her horse at a run onto the boat.

Ferris and Dave were already loosening the mooring lines while Hanomer located the sweeps. With Arlana and Hanomer on one oar and Dave on the other, Ferris guided them towards the entrance.

"It's Teledon," said Arlana as she pulled on her sweep with all her might. "He commandeered another boat and followed us here. He means to capture you Dave!"

As if to underline Arlana's words, riders thundered into the cavern and began shouting. The three rowers redoubled their efforts. Dave, on one side, had to row hard enough to balance the other two. Ferris had the tiller and was guiding them out of the cavern.

There're only three of us. When they get moving, they'll haul us in quickly.

With the rising fear of capture, Dave redoubled his effort. The entrance was not far off. The boat slid into brilliant sunlight.

"Hanomer," shouted Ferris, "you keep rowing. Arlana, take the tiller. I need to get us ready for the arrows of the Halfmen."

Arlana took the tiller. The boat twisted as Dave's stroke overwhelmed Hanomer. Ferris ran to a locker at the back and brought out a rectangular shield which he fastened over Hanomer's head.

"See to it you stay under it."

The falls roared down around him, like an endless thunderclap. Dave thought he saw something fall into the water only ten yards ahead of them. Ferris put a longer shield over Arlana at the tiller and then did the same for Dave.

Plunk! The first arrow struck the deck near the bow. Soon, arrows began falling all around them.

"Arlana go below," said Dave.

"*Kree ah na koo*, I will not go below."

"Be reasonable."

"Why tell me to be reasonable when you should be telling me to be courageous?"

Dave saw Ferris roll his eyes as he took up Arlana's position at the sweep. The arrows were falling so heavily that it would have been dangerous to leave the protection of the shields. Dave glanced back and saw a larger boat leave the protection of the cavern. The fall of arrows diminished a little as more and more arrows were directed at the pursuer. Arlana guided them along the south edge of the gorge in the hope that any slight overhang would protect them.

"They're shooting fire arrows!" shouted Ferris.

Sure enough there were flames enveloping the bow and the stern of the pursuing boat. Dave glanced behind to see the oarsmen back water and attempted to return to the cavern. The water was moving more swiftly now, but now fire arrows began to fall on their craft as well.

"Keep rowing!" shouted Ferris. There were burning arrows stuck in the deck at the bow and the stern. Ferris, while staying under the shield, was throwing water with a bailing bucket to put out any fire arrows that landed close by.

"Luckily this green boat weed is not very flammable," muttered Ferris.

Dave didn't like how this was going. Maybe a Teledorian prison wasn't such a bad idea after all.

In ten minutes this is going to be all over.

"Arlana, head to the other bank," shouted Ferris.

Arlana put the tiller over and the boat began crossing the river. Dave saw what Ferris was aiming for: there was a small cove protected by a high rock abutment. When they reached this shelter, Ferris rushed out and doused the flames in the bow. Arlana handed Dave another bucket and then helped Dave douse the flames on the stern.

After twenty minutes the four of them sat down covered in grime.

"How bad is it?" asked Dave.

"Well, the bow and stern are both damaged. We'll hang on here until tonight and then creep slowly downriver to a place where we can repair the damage to the boat and let the boat weed recover. You're not going to get home as quickly as you hoped, Dave."

It was a week later when they finally left the great river and went up the tributary to Eleytheria. Soon after they entered the River Tor, Dave, who was on lookout in the bow, could see a smudge of smoke rising in the distance. It filled him with foreboding. *Have we come too late?*

"Ferris, we'd better pull into shore. Something's not right."

Hiding their boat on the western shore and climbing a small rise, the island of Eleytheria stretched out before them. The dwellings were smoking ruins and the fields were on fire. There were Apemen everywhere on the island.

Chapter 16

Besieged

Floyd Linder was peering west as he often did these days. He often wondered why he still had hope when it had been more than a month since Dave and Hanomer had left. Yet Floyd's heart would not let him give up all hope and he expected to see his two friends appear on the western shore. A sudden pang struck him. He realized that Pam and Al had probably been in Halcyon for a week now and he had not thought of them at all.

All my close friends are gone and I'm left here to look after all of these people who depend on my decisions.

Floyd heard a rustle behind him. It was Cordomer.

"Hello, friend Floyd."

"Hello, Cordomer. How are you?"

Cordomer bowed.

"Friend Floyd I have some grave news—our scouts have just returned to report that Meglir is approaching from the East."

Floyd swore under his breath. His throat went dry and his heart began to pound.

"How long do we have Cordomer?"

"The Apemen are moving slowly but Meglir has a band of men with him and they will be here much sooner. We have maybe three hours."

Why did this have to happen now? We've been expecting this for months and just when we started to feel safe, Meglir decides to attack. I could sure use Al and Dave.

"Cordomer, do you remember the plan?"

Cordomer fidgeted and hung his head.

"What's the matter?"

"Friend Floyd, I'm afraid of sending our little ones into the fortress of the Torburg."

"Cordomer, we've been through this before. I know that fortress has a terrible history, but that was a long time ago. We're not going very far inside. You and I both checked it out and there was nothing there to cause alarm. Whatever killed so many men and *Hansa* many years ago is not there now. Will you carry out the plan? I need you to do this."

"Yes, friend Floyd I will carry out the plan as we agreed. I will round up all the *Hansa* warriors and we will prepare to prevent Meglir from crossing to our island. I will get the eldest among us to move our women and cubs to the old fortress in the heights."

"Good. I'll do the same. I'll be a lot happier when all our mothers and children are safely up in the heights.

Floyd stood on a promontory in the foothills of the Torburg Mountain looking east. He had some reason for grim satisfaction. Torburg had been designed for defense, making use of the natural defensive terrain and modifying the fortress to make it almost impossible to take by storm. The route up to the fortress would hold surprises for Meglir if he ever crossed to the island. In a long vertical cleft of the mountain, the *Hansa* had rigged a series of three of their water elevators, to make the six hundred foot ascent to the Torburg plateau.

The water elevator was an ingenious device consisting of a large basket attached via a pulley to a counterweight. The counterweight consisted of rocks to offset the weight of the basket and a bundle of large hollow gourds which could be filled with water. When the gourds were full of water, the basket would descend. When the gourds were empty the heavy counterweight would drag the loaded basket up. As long as the stream from the snows at the top of the tower kept running, they could operate their elevator.

Floyd saw movement on the east shore of the river.

"Showtime!"

Cordomer, who was also watching the east bank, looked at Floyd. "Showtime?"

"It's an expression we use to indicate that the battle is about to begin. Let's stay hidden and see what they do."

Floyd watched as Meglir's men took up positions. All of them had either crossbows or regular bows. He knew they might also have guns, but he saw none.

Floyd watched carefully as they hid themselves along the shore. He would not have been able to pick out Meglir's men if he had not seen them go into hiding.

What are they going to do? What would I do if I was in their place? If I thought I had surprise on my side, I'd try a sneak attack—get a landing party onto the island and overrun it before the defenders knew I was coming. The best time would be to wait for nightfall.

Nothing happened for several hours. Finally, just as the sun was setting, Cordomer quietly approached. "Friend Floyd, a raft has left the shore upstream and they are poling across the river."

"How many are there on the raft?" whispered Floyd.

"About thirty."

"We'll make them pay for overreaching themselves. They should have waited until it was completely dark."

Floyd picked up his crossbow and moved silently through the brush to the river and then upstream under the shadow of the Torburg rising above them. Ahead the sheer cliffs of the Torburg plunged straight into the water. Floyd signaled for everyone to take cover. Soon he heard the splash of poles as a large raft, loaded with men, drifted into view. It was still a hundred feet offshore, but clearly they were aiming to make landfall where the shore became less steep–right where Floyd had hidden most of his men. It was a good plan for the Turncoats, if they were assuming that the villagers felt secure and didn't have a lookout keeping watch on the water during the supper hour.

They don't have a very high opinion of our watchfulness. They'll think differently after this is done.

Floyd nocked a bolt into his crossbow and shouted "shoot at will." A cloud of arrows flew at the raft. A few men fell from the raft into the water. The rest, shouting and cursing, tried desperately to get the raft away from the shore. The shower of arrows continued.

Floyd was puzzled. Even though the trap was well executed, far fewer of the Turncoats had been hit than he had expected. At this range the *Hansa* were particularly deadly. He had seen them hit Apemen with deadly accuracy at much longer distances. What was happening? He felt his features tightening as the realization hit him.

The bloody Hansa are deliberately missing the men.

Still, Floyd's Halcyonites were not aiming to miss. More and more men on the raft were hit and fell into the water. Finally the rest threw down their weapons and jumped into the river to swim back to the east bank. The *Hansa* stopped shooting. Floyd also stopped his own men since he didn't want to waste their arrows.

"So much for round one."

He felt the anger rise within him.

If Cordomer and the Hansa *had aimed to kill, perhaps so many of the men would have been killed that Meglir would have been thwarted. Meglir has many Apemen but only a few men that have rebelled against their own people in Halcyon. I bet without the Turncoats, Meglir is going to have a very difficult time bridging the river to assault us. Blast those* Hansa!

Floyd was just about to vent his anger on Cordomer when the men on the east shore began to shoot at them. The arrows left long flaming trails in the sky as they arced toward them. Fires sprang up among them and Floyd ordered the most dangerous fires put out. Soon the archers had changed their objective and were sending flaming arrows into the cottages and fields. Floyd could see Apemen arriving. Their awkward, ambling gait was unmistakable. The siege had begun.

Floyd looked at the faces around him. Every face was streaked with soot from the fires and every eye was dull with lack of sleep.

"We're not going to be able to stop their pontoon bridge. Their archers are keeping up a withering fire and I will not trade our people for Apemen."

"But what are we going to do?" asked one of the Halcyonites.

"We're going up to the Torburg. Up there we can hold out for a long time."

"You mean until our food runs out!"

"Yes until our food runs out. We have to start moving up supplies now. I want any remaining women with children in the fortification as soon as possible. The rest of us will stay behind and make them pay for every inch of lake they have to cross. Cordomer, you help move supplies up to the Torburg."

The battle had settled down to a routine. The Apemen never screamed or shouted, so the only sounds on Elytheria were the shouts of orders and the twang of bow strings. The smell of burning rafts mixed with the stench of burning flesh filled the air. While Meglir's Turncoats were building another pontoon raft, Floyd's men shot fire arrows to burn the bridge and take up a position on the bottom of the mountain. As the Apemen paddled the newly made raft into place to lash it to the end of the pontoon bridge, Floyd's forces showered them with arrows. Sometimes they killed them all and the raft drifted aimlessly. When that happened Floyd's men eventually set it on fire. Other times the Apemen succeeded in lashing the raft quickly to the end of the bridge. After securing the new pontoon, they doused it with water so that the incendiary arrows had no effect.

Finally the Apemen were only about a hundred feet from shore. They had built an extra-long raft to cover the remaining gap and storm the island in one engagement. They were setting a trap for the defenders. If Floyd kept a sufficiently strong force to oppose the landing, and if the landing was successful, most of those defenders would never make it to the heights. However, Meglir's men had not anticipated the defenses of the Torburg!

Floyd and his men shot every arrow that they had, but he could see there were too many Apemen. Meglir's forces had advanced onto the bridge and were shooting from behind improvised shields, so even Floyd's perch on the base of the Torburg was increasingly coming under attack.

"On the double now, head up to the Torburg in groups of three."

The first group started off. With the lull in fighting, some of the enemy archers gave up shooting and began hauling the final raft into position. With a whoop, Meglir's men leaped onto the raft and ran to the shallow water beyond.

"Okay everyone, let's make a run for it."

Floyd hung behind as the group sprinted along the cliff around to the center of the island. They entered a narrow cleft in the towering massif where a rope ladder was hanging from a ledge which formed an overhang to the cleft about a hundred feet up. The first men began to climb frantically while Floyd watched for the enemy. Finally, it was his turn.

Take your time. One rung after the other.

He reached the ledge. Although the ledge nestled as a natural notch in the mountain, closer inspection would show that it had been improved with excellent stonework to make it very defensible. Guards could shoot from cover anyone who tried to climb the wall in the cleft. A couple of his men were watching his back as he climbed, preventing any pursuit to the cleft.

"Okay, let's haul up the ladder and then we'll head up the rest of the way." The ledge gave a good view of the center part of the island.

Floyd stayed out of sight and watched as Meglir's troops systematically searched all the cottages and then torched the buildings and what was left of the crops. However, they had not found the Eleytherian's escape route. Perhaps they never would.

Finally Floyd's turn came to ascend further. At the back of the lower redoubt as they called the ledge, there was a rising tunnel that ran right through the Torburg massif. He gave final instructions to the *Hansa* lookout and then entered the tunnel that had been constructed long ago when the Torburg had still been defended.

After about a hundred feet, the tunnel opened into a room and then continued on in a different direction. After five tunnel segments like this, Floyd emerged onto a narrow ledge facing west. To his right the cliff plunged several hundred feet directly into the lake below.

Ahead of him another rope ladder swung in the wind. Floyd climbed up to the second redoubt. When he had climbed up, he pulled that ladder up. If he had had more men, he would have defended both redoubts, but now he couldn't afford to risk his people, so he left only a lookout.

He and two others climbed into the water elevator and opened the valves to let water out of the ballast gourds. The water drained out of the large barrel-sized gourds, and the elevator began to rise.

Floyd Linder walked around the outer parapet of the Torburg as he did every morning and evening. The parapet was twenty to fifty feet wide and girded the entire mesa including the broad column of rock at the center of the mesa they called the Tower. He and Pam had climbed the Tower shortly after they had arrived. At the very summit was a deep, snow-enshrouded lake that fed the stream that ran through the Torburg and down to the fields below. Water would not be their problem. They usually only stored a small amount of smoked meat in the Torburg. The rest of the food supply had been moved up here after Cordomer had warned of an attack. Still, they could hold out for a long time in a pinch. On the steep lower sides of the Torburg roosted hundreds of birds that provided a steady supply of eggs. They could also lower someone down to the water's edge on the sheer south side to set nightlines. The fish could be collected the next evening. However, long term food would be a problem and that's why he had called the meeting.

He completed his circuit and came to a large flat ledge about three hundred feet across that Floyd had dubbed The Parade Ground.

It was dotted with tents that clustered around a central pool since the *Hansa* did not want to enter the Torburg's inner fortifications. Cordomer was waiting for his return.

"Friend Floyd, the Council thought we should meet on the wall. The others have already arrived."

Cordomer led Floyd to the outer wall, which was raised about ten feet above the parade ground. Floyd marveled at the stone work. Every block fit snugly without gaps. As Cordomer had promised, the others were waiting on the wall.

The council members greeted each other, and Floyd gave a brief summary of his walk.

One of the new council members, Hosea Mbeni, who had replaced Dave after his disappearance said, "I'm glad nothing has changed."

"As Dave and Al proved at the City of the Dead, lumbering Apemen, despite their appearance, can't climb very well, and Meglir's men know they will be sitting ducks if we discover them during the climb," said Floyd.

"Sitting Ducks?" asked Keilomer, one of the *Hansa* councilors.

"Sorry," said Floyd. "'Sitting ducks' is an expression that means they would be easy to kill," said Floyd.

"So why all the secrecy about our meeting?" another of the council members asked.

"Well, I wanted to talk to you first before my thoughts became general knowledge, in case you disagreed with my ideas. I want us to settle on the best plan; not necessarily my plan."

"So what do you have in mind, friend Floyd?" asked Keilomer.

"As I see it," said Floyd, "we're okay for the present. Meglir cannot get to us. Still we're trapped. I think we ought to try to send someone to the *Hansa* elders, up at the City of the Trees, to let them know of our situation and what Meglir is doing. It's a very dangerous attempt, but I'm pretty sure I could make it."

"No, wait a minute," said one of the other council members. "You can't leave. With Dave and Al gone, you're our leader. You can't run out on us!"

Floyd felt himself grimacing and took a deep breath.

"I'm not running away—this needs to be done and it's dangerous. I'm sure Meglir is watching for this and would love to capture someone who might tell him the best way to take this fortress."

"Hosea is right, though." said Nils Sorengaard. "Let me go."

"You've never been to see the elders."

"Well neither have you."

Tranomer stood up and folded his hands behind his back, while gently waving with the hand on his tail, patiently waiting for the others to recognize him. Floyd turned to him expectantly.

"Friends," said Tranomer. "Friend Floyd has an excellent notion. We should tell the *Hansa* elders about Meglir. They will send us help or food. However, it is clear to us that *Hansa*, not friend Floyd, should go on this trip. This is *Hansa* country. We swim like fish and can easily greet our kin. Friend Floyd, you must stay here to shepherd your people." Tranomer sat down.

The discussion went on for some time, but in the end Tranomer's plan made the most sense. The *Hansa* began work immediately on a small, light, oval coracle. The skins were sealed with grease. That evening Tranomer was ready to go. How the *Hansa* decided on who would go was never clear to Floyd. Floyd had wanted them to use a part of the cliff that had not been used before, just in case Meglir had spies watching the winches currently in place. Floyd chose a section at the southern end of the island out of easy sight of Meglir's forces. They began to assemble the winches after dark. Cordomer wanted to test the lines before they lowered Tranomer onto the water. Floyd let Cordomer handle the winch ropes while he watched Meglir's camp on the eastern shore for any signs that someone had given an alarm. Everything remained quiet.

Floyd was startled by a tap on the shoulder. It was a sentry.

"Floyd, you had better take a look. Something is going on down below."

Oh no, they've spotted our winch and they're moving to intercept Tranomer. Floyd hesitated, reluctant to leave the winch operation. "I guess I'd better come and have a look." He followed the sentry until they came to a section of the wall facing northeast. The sentry pointed down to a steep part the cliff. Floyd saw nothing unusual.

"I don't see them."

"Keep looking!"

Sure enough, a patch of shadow seemed to be changing aspect ratio and was slowly creeping up the cliff. Once he knew what he was looking for, he spotted another and another.

"You're right; they're trying to surprise us. Quietly wake the men and the *Hansa*. I don't want the sentries to leave their posts—this may be a diversion."

Soon Matthew Odonahue, one of the platoon commanders Floyd had appointed arrived, followed by several of the men and *Hansa*. The men were cranky because they had just been wakened from their sleep. The mood quickly became more serious as Floyd explained the situation.

"I want to turn the tables on these traitors and capture them. The last two hundred feet are open to us and they will be exposed. Let's stay out of sight and then we'll tell them to surrender and let them up one at a time. Let's keep a lookout along this section of the wall."

Floyd left them to set up the ambush and ran back to see how Tranomer's sendoff was progressing. By the time he arrived at the winch, everything had been tested and they were all set to lower Tranomer and the coracle down to the water. They had decided to lower the two together to avoid giving Meglir any time for a response.

Floyd took the first winch down to a ledge about three hundred feet above the water surface. He carefully checked the water for boats and the rock face for intruders. Everyone waited for his command. He gave the "all clear."

They lowered Tranomer the last three hundred feet in the coracle down to the water, like a lifeboat being lowered from a stricken ocean liner. Tranomer then cast off and paddled quietly into the darkness. Soon even the faint whisper of a paddle striking the water faded into silence.

When Floyd returned to the parapet he saw that everyone was prepared. They crouched out of sight with weapons ready. A runner appeared from a distant observation post and whispered into Floyd's ear.

"The first of them is just crossing over into the kill zone."

He then went around and told the others.

Floyd spread his hand indicating five minutes.

When the time was up, Floyd crept up the parapet and peered over.

"Surrender and you won't be hurt."

"Okay, you got us. Don't shoot."

"Bring them up one at a time. When you check them for weapons, strip them naked. Don't take any chances—they may have concealed weapons. They're trying to trick us. This was too easy. You five follow me." Floyd ordered.

He headed off to the left, frequently looking over the parapet and planning to personally check with every sentry. Odonahue and Banomer also came to join him. He decided to reinforce the two sentries furthest from the diversion.

When he reached the part of the wall overlooking the village below, the sentry whispered, "Is there trouble?"

"Probably—we captured some Turncoats. The capture was too easy. I think there's another attack coming."

"What made you think it was coming this way?"

Floyd checked over the parapet and again scrutinized the mountainside.

"I figured the main attack would be as far away from the diversion as possible, but still readily accessible from the lower part of the island. Maybe I'm wrong."

"I'll stay here," said Floyd. "Matt, you and Banomer check with the next sentries in the circuit to make sure no one is sneaking up on them."

They ran off into the darkness.

Floyd became more and more worried. With proper timing, the main attack should have come shortly after the diversion surrendered. Too much time was passing. He heard Matthew bellow a loud 'HELP.'

Floyd raced in the direction of the sound. He ran as fast as he could. When he reached the site of the attack, he saw two camouflaged combatants sprawled up on the parapet. Crossbow bolts were skipping off the crenellations. Several sentries were trying to get a shot over the edge.

Floyd shouted, "Don't try to shoot straight down—they're too close. Just heave rocks over the side. You men, head farther down the wall and shoot at them from the sides."

The shouting became louder. Floyd climbed down some stairs to a platform of rock extending out from the rock wall and came upon Matt. He had two crossbow bolts sticking in him as he leaned over the parapet and fired another shot.

"They were just coming over the wall when we arrived," he sputtered, blood frothing from his mouth.

"Shoot them. Don't let them get established," said Floyd to the men that had followed him as he lowered Matthew to the ground. One of the arrows had evidently punctured one of Matt's lungs.

"Is it bad?"

"I won't lie to you Matt, it looks bad to me. You have been very brave. You saved us from being overrun."

Matt spat up some blood.

"Where am I going, Floyd. What's going to happen to me after I die?"

"I don't know Matt. I honestly don't know. I guess I always thought that when my body stopped working the part that's me ceased to exist. Once I'm gone there's nothing. But how can I really know? Al believes there's a God and that our existence continues after we die, but I just don't know."

"I hope Al is right," sputtered Matt. "If not—what's the point?"

Another fit of coughing brought up a huge gush of blood and Matt lost consciousness. Floyd rolled Matt onto his side to help clear his lungs, but couldn't detect a heartbeat. He picked up his crossbow and went to make sure Matt's sacrifice wasn't in vain.

It was all over. Others had come from the far side and the attackers had been hemmed in. None surrendered, but a few clambered back down over the wall. Floyd didn't have the heart to shoot them as they hung onto the cliff trying to escape.

"How many casualties?" asked Floyd wearily.

"Just two—Matt and Banomer."

Chapter 17

Kelldor

Dave watched with consternation the desolation of Eleytheria.

"Why are you so agitated, youngling?" asked Arlana.

"It shows does it? I guess I'm worried about my friends."

"The Torburg is very strong and has never been taken when defended. I think your friends will be safe."

"But I want to help them," said Dave. "Or at least let them know that Hanomer and I are alive."

"Be patient and don't do anything rash Dave."

Dave felt himself scowling.

"If Meglir finds out we are here," continued Arlana, "things will go very badly for us. Especially if he manages to capture you."

"Why me?"

"Because you're very special. You are a Lesser Man who has been repaired to be an Ancient. From what you've told me, right now Meglir inhabits Hoffstetter like a parasite. But Meglir's power is diminished because his host is a Lesser Man. If he could inhabit an Ancient, then he would achieve his full power."

"So you and Ferris are also at risk."

"First of all, since Meglir is a male, he can only inhabit males. So Meglir is not a danger to me in the same way. He could kill me but not possess me as he does this fellow Hoffstetter.

"Adult Ancients such as Ferris, my father Kelldor, and I are of limited use to Meglir. He would have to break us to get us to surrender to him. We have a strong enough will that has been trained not to be broken. We would die before we would break, and so our usefulness to him is limited. You, on the other hand, are an Ancient in body, but a child in mind…"

"A child in mind! You may be an Ancient, but you're about my age."

Arlana smiled mischievously.

"What are you laughing at?"

"Youngling, you are so easy to get riled. I quite enjoy it."

"In English that is called 'getting my goat.'"

"In that case," said Arlana, "I seem to be have captured of a whole herd of your goats."

Dave couldn't help but laugh. "Alright, you win this round. Tell me about your father, Kelldor."

"I do not say this as a boast, but state it as a simple fact: my father is a great man, the greatest man among my people at this time. He is almost six hundred years old now, but as a young man, he took part in the long war against Meglir. He rallied my people during the great plague and has watched over us during our long vigil in the plague lands. With his years he has accumulated great wisdom, lore and knowledge of our history. Now in the last few years he has faced opposition from Arachodor and Teledon. The siege of Gurundaria by the Halfmen will help Arachodor immensely since he will direct the defense, while my father is not home to help."

"What will your saving me with the healing plant do to your father?"

"Arachodor will try to use that against him. Since he doesn't have you to show to our people, his case is weaker. Still I cannot deny what I have done when I am asked by the Council."

"I'm grateful you did it, Arlana."

"Well youngling, in that case, don't give me any reason to regret it."

Dave felt himself turning red.

"Have I managed to find another of your goats, Dave?"

Before Dave could answer, Ferris returned with Hanomer. Both were excited and moving quickly, crouching and taking advantage of cover to avoid being seen by Meglir's sentries on the island.

"Hanomer has news—great news!"

"Friend Dave," said Hanomer, "a large force of *Hansa* is approaching on the west side of the lake. Our friends either sent word to the City of Trees, or scouts from the tree city saw what was taking place at Eleytheria. This will save us much time. We should go immediately to meet them and plan our next steps.

After traveling south for some time, Hanomer signaled a halt. "They are not far ahead now. I'm sure their scouts will have spotted us. Let's wait for them to approach."

They had only been sitting for about five minutes when an old *Hansa* wearing a green travel cloak embroidered with gold fringe, entered the clearing.

All four rose from their seats and bowed deeply.

"Welcome Granomer, Chief Loremaster of our people," said Hanomer.

"Greetings, friend Hanomer. May the Creator's bounty fill you with joy. Greetings, friend Dave. I am glad to see you well. You have journeyed far since we last met. And finally, greeting friends." said Granomer bowing in turn to Ferris and Arlana. "Our peoples have been sundered too long. It is good to see our friends and allies again."

"Greetings to you, wise one. We are more than glad to see you," said Ferris gravely.

"And is it not proper for a daughter to greet her father?" said a deep voice.

Dave saw Arlana become radiant with joy as she exclaimed "Father!" and rushed into his arms.

An old man, with a white beard and white hair, was leaning on a staff at the edge of the clearing. He wore the green, living cloak of the Ancients. He was tall and did not stoop, except to lean a little on his staff. He wore a long sword at his side, yet his face was a mixture of kindness on the surface with gravity beneath. He received Arlana into his arms and she nestled her head into his chest as if she were a little girl.

"I was so worried that you were in trouble, father."

"I was in trouble, my child, but that has passed now. Still, I see that if I made a list of all of my strict commands that you have disobeyed—that list would be very long indeed."

Dave saw Arlana, turn red.

Kelldor turned to Ferris. "Nephew Ferris, I thought you would have more sense than to let your cousin create the mischief she has done."

"Your daughter, sir, is a masterful woman, not easily deflected from her purpose, especially when she thinks her father is in trouble and in need of her."

"In need of her! My load would be so much lighter if I only have to worry about myself and my people and not my daughter as well. Enough said. We will speak of this another time. I have much to learn from you and much to tell. Tell me your story in detail…"

Here Kelldor looked long and hard at Dave, "…and then I will tell you mine."

Arlana and Ferris related their story to Kelldor and he listened intently. Then he questioned Dave at length, first about how Halcyon had arrived in Feiramar, and then the ensuing release of Meglir. Kelldor had many questions about technology. Even though he did not have the mathematical background or the grasp of chemistry to understand much of what Dave was saying, he had a remarkable facility to understand the implications of the twenty-first century technology. Dave could see the lines around Kelldor's mouth tighten as Arlana described Dave's healing and their escape from Gurundaria.

"Well," said Kelldor, after Arlana finished, "what's done is done. I think it was no accident that your people have reconnected with Feiramar after such a long sundering, and it is no accident that you were rescued by Arlana in the nick of time. There are forces in play, and this may yet work out for good. But matters hang in the balance. If Meglir appropriates your power of technology, as you call it, if he reunites with the Bent Ones in Abaddon. Worst of all, if he manages to get to your world where he can wield his influence, we could enter a dark period out of which only the Creator can see the time when we would be rescued.

"Father, what about your story?" asked Arlana. "I have been so worried. Why have you not sent word?"

"My story? It seems so long ago. I was about to turn home when I felt a prodding within me to go back to Arkand. It was there that I came across a trail that puzzled me. I followed it and came upon a band of Rokash and Wogogs…"

"Wogogs?" asked Dave.

"Wogogs are large, very intelligent wolf-like creatures that have been created by the Bent Ones as hunters."

"Oh!" Said Dave. "I think we call those Lupi. We ran into some once in the mountains and they killed several of my friends. I would not like to meet them again."

"Nor I," said Kelldor. "They are even more formidable when they are under the guidance of a Bent One.

"When I came upon this band, I knew I had to get help. A Bent One from the continent of Abaddon, across the sea, had landed and penetrated as far as Arkand without being spotted. Now he was already moving back into the swamp south of Arkand and heading for the coast. Bent Ones are not kept out of Arkand by fear of the city, as the Halfmen are, and this one had clearly been in Arkand. Whatever he had come to find in the libraries, he was taking back to Abaddon, so I had little time. Here, I made my great mistake.

"I had assumed there was only one Bent One and focused all my energy on pursuing him. I sent a messenger back to you dear Arlana to tell you of my delay and to summon more help, but I had not reckoned on a second Bent One mobilizing the Halfmen. The messenger never reached you or our kindred, and the Gurundarian Mountains were besieged by the roused Halfmen without warning.

"When I had assembled the Guardians scattered throughout Arkand, we pursued the Bent One to Goose's Neck and fought a battle there, even though we were badly outnumbered. We held our own, but I was wounded by a Rokash talon. I left the pursuit to my two lieutenants and I went to a Travel Oak grove near the place of my wounding and so traveled to the *Hansa* City of the Trees, where I was able to recuperate. It was there that I found out that Lesser Men had come back to Feiramar and that Meglir had found a new host. This troubled me greatly. I was torn between returning to lead the fight against the Bent One and the need to confront this new danger. When I heard that Meglir was besieging Eleytheria, I decided to come along with the relieving force."

"What are 'Travel Oak groves'?" asked Dave.

Kelldor stared at Dave with his deep blue eyes out from under his bushy white eyebrows. "Rokodor, you are now an Ancient. Perhaps, if I see fit, I may even approach my good friend Celyddon and ask him to adopt you."

Here he looked long and searchingly at Arlana who turned red again. "Becoming an Ancient is an unexpected gift to you. With that gift, however unwillingly you received it, comes grave responsibility. Travel Oaks are part of the hidden wisdom of the Ancients and we do not readily share that knowledge. The function and more particularly the location of Travel Oak groves is one of our most closely guarded secrets. Still, perhaps time for secrecy is passing.

"Travel Oaks or Whispering Oaks, as they are sometimes called, are a species of oak trees that grow in a ring or grove from a single root. If one of these Travel Oak stems is cut out of the ring and planted elsewhere, then the parent tree and the new grove that grows from the cutting are linked. It forever remembers its sire and its location. The Travel Oak in the Goose's Neck was a cutting from a Travel Oak near the *Hansa* village. By spending a night in the grove, I woke up in the other location."

"That's incredible. How can that happen?" asked Dave.

"I don't know," said Kelldor "How do birds find their way south in winter? Why is my spirit troubled sometimes when one of my children is in danger? There are many wonders that living things accomplish that I do not find surprising, only because in my mind they have become common place."

"Hmm," said Dave. "I can see what you mean. Can you only travel one way?"

"No, I can travel back. This particular Travel Oak grove is a dyad, that is to say only one cutting has been taken and replanted. Spending a night in this Travel Oak will take me back to the Goose's Neck grove. Some groves are triads so traveling from the parent grove will take one to the first daughter grove, whilst traveling in the first daughter grove will take one to the second daughter grove. Finally the second daughter grove will take a traveller back to the parent grove. As far as I know there are no quadrads, but if there were, in principle, they would work the same way.

"But enough of this talk. We need to get back to camp and then we must decide what to do."

The *Hansa* scouts led the way back through the bush by paths that were not visible from the lower reaches of Eleytheria. Finally they emerged into a small dell that had a rivulet running through it. Dozens of *Hansa* warriors were resting, waiting for their next orders. A murmur ran through the crowd and Dave could hear the words "Rokomer" and "Hanomer" whispered among them.

They didn't risk a fire during the day, but broke out provisions. The Old Ones bowed briefly in thanks and then the *Hansa* softly sang a song of thanksgiving.

Like all *Hansa* they ate with enthusiasm and laughed as jokes were bandied about. Hanomer seemed to be the butt of most jokes.

I don't know what they find so funny about our adventures, but I can tell Hanomer is never going to live this down.

Finally Dave saw Kelldor catch Granomer's eye and then Granomer nodded and rose to his feet.

"Friends and guests…"

The buzz of the banter ceased.

"Friends and guests, we must keep our fellowship time short since there are decisions at hand. We must determine what to do about Meglir and his forces as they besiege Eleytheria. Does anyone have wisdom to share with this gathering?"

A *Hansa* stood up. When Dave looked at him intently he recognized Tranomer from Eleytheria.

"Friend Dave and friend Hanomer, I didn't think you were coming back and now you're here. That is too wonderful for words.

"Friends of the council, I think Meglir has been given to us by this circumstance. He's trapped on an island away from his Death Plants. If we surround him now we could end this once and for all. We just have to hold the shore and keep him and his Apemen from escaping."

"He has men with him too. Would you also kill those?" asked Granomer.

"I don't want to kill them, but we can't let them continue to do evil because we don't want to hurt them. It seems to me they picked this path."

"Friends, may I speak?" An older *Hansa*, with graying fur stood up.

"Speak, captain Sheiomer," said Granomer.

"I have led our forces at the City of the Trees for many years. We have taken our turn in guarding Meglir's lair at the City of the Dead for time beyond our reckoning. Meglir is a crafty general; let us not now walk into one of his traps. We have emptied our city to help our brothers. We must proceed carefully. If we surround Eleytheria now, in our haste to capture or kill Meglir, we will find he has men waiting to ambush us. Let us take the time to scout the eastern shores before we pass over to that shore in force."

There was a murmur around the circle at Sheiomer's words.

"I have one final thing to say," said Sheiomer. "We all know the terrible history of the Torburg. Now, during this siege, our brothers and our friends have gone back to the Torburg. Have they reawakened the dread of that place? Are we even sure that they are still alive up in the heights? They should never have gone up there. The terror of that place must not be stirred again to life."

It looked to Dave as if Sheiomer's words were going to carry the day. Dave stood up. "Noble Granomer, may I speak?" He could see that Arlana was frowning.

"Noble Granomer, friend Sheiomer has made some important points. But I have friends and kin besieged on the Torburg and they believe me and Hanomer to be dead. I want them to know that we're alive and that Tranomer has been able to bring help. With your permission, I will climb up the Torburg and warn them that you are here. Then they can help break the siege. I can signal you that they are alive to allay Sheiomer's legitimate fears. From that height, we can even warn you if we see evidence that Meglir is planning an ambush. After all, if Sheiomer is concerned about the 'evil of the Torburg,' should we not do everything in our power to bring our kin down from the heights?"

Granomer, twitched his tail back and forth, opening and closing his third hand. Finally he looked at Kelldor and spoke again.

"And what do you say Lord Kelldor?"

Kelldor rose, leaned on his staff, and looked sternly around the circle.

"Friends, you have faithfully defended Meglir's lair for countless years. Without our help, you have remained faithful. Now the end of that long vigil may be at hand. Do not falter because of caution. A campaign without risk is a campaign that is lost before it starts. Send Hanomer and Rokomer to the Torburg. Surround Eleytheria swiftly. Once the trap is closed, we can follow Sheiomer's counsel and send scouts to warn us if Meglir can bring up strength either from the east or the south. I think we should send half of our force across the lake to the east bank before morning and I will go with you. Sheiomer can watch the west bank and so we will close the trap."

Granomer looked around and then spoke. "I think Kelldor's counsel is good. It fulfills our vow to oppose Meglir, yet I think it still exercises prudence. We can draw back if we find Meglir has strength to the east."

The talk went on for some time, but no one came up with a better plan than Kelldor had proposed.

Chapter 18

Hanging in the Balance

The evening was overcast as Hanomer and Dave set out for the south end of the cliff in a small boat paddled by two *Hansa*. They were heading for a small shelf at the bottom of a steep rock wall where the two used to go fishing. At the back of this shelf was a long crack that ran up about fifty yards. During one of their fishing excursions, Hanomer had climbed part way up without difficulty, but now they hoped it would carry them a good deal further.

They reached the shelf and unloaded their ropes and a couple of backpacks. Hanomer climbed up ahead. Instead of pitons, the *Hansa* used tough wooden stakes and a natural glue that set as hard as cement into cracks in the rock. Hanomer fastened the rope and Dave followed. His old fear of heights returned but he grimly carried on.

It was on the third leg when disaster struck. Dave was feeling his way up the cliff when he put his weight on a knob of rock. It gave way and he plunged fifteen feet before the rope pulled him up short. He slammed into the rock face, knocking the wind out of him. He bounced off and swung freely as the ropes constricted his chest so he couldn't breathe.

I have to get my weight off the rope.

He began to swing himself until he was able to grab a small edge. His toes groped for a foothold—any foothold. Finally he found one and pulled himself up.

"Friend Dave, are you alright?"

"Yeah, Hanomer I'm okay. I just feel stupid for leaving so much slack in the rope. I don't think I broke anything, but I'm gonna be sore tomorrow."

The rest of the climb went without incident. When they were within about two hundred feet below the crest of the Torburg, Dave took two light gourds out of his pack. He and Hanomer began to wave them.

"Who goes there?" said a puzzled voice.

"It's Dave and Hanomer," called Dave. "Is that you Watson? Call Al or Floyd and send us down a rope."

There was a whoop from the Torburg and the sound of running feet. In a few minutes, a light gourd appeared on the wall and a figure leaned over.

"Is that really you Dave?" It was Floyd's voice.

"Yeah, it's me. I can't wait to see your ugly face, Floyd. Send a rope down."

"Well I will be glad to see your ugly face. We'd given up hope and here you return in the middle of the siege."

A long rope snaked down and Hanomer scrambled up as fast as he could run.

Dave started to climb after Hanomer.

"Dave, tie yourself on. My grandmother can climb better than you. Come to think of it, even my great grandmother can climb better than you can."

"I didn't know you had a grandmother. I thought Al told me they found you under a rock."

The rest went quickly. Dave fended off the rock with his legs and they rapidly pulled him up to the top.

Dave was overwhelmed with joy when he reached the top and saw Floyd. He grabbed Floyd in a bear hug.

"Whoa Dave, you're gonna break my ribs."

"Floyd we need to talk."

"What's going on?" asked Floyd.

"The *Hansa* are here and gathering on the west shore. They're going to cross over to the east and if the coast looks clear, they're going to try to recover our island."

"Wow, that's better news than I could have hoped for. When is all this supposed to happen?"

"At dawn tomorrow. And another thing, if we could muster a sortie from the heights that would help them a lot."

Floyd thought for a moment and ran his hand over his clean-shaven scalp.

"We have some fortifications fairly far down that we abandoned as we retreated to the Torburg. I don't know if they've been occupied by the enemy. But we could try to retake them. That would bring a lot of the island under our fire. We'll try it. You and Hanomer get something to eat and grab a few winks if you need them, while I wake the guys and get ready to head down before it gets light."

It was about an hour before dawn. Up ahead, Hanomer, who was acknowledged as the best tracker and climber, was inching down the cliff head first. This posture was so unnatural to Dave that it made him cringe, but Hanomer had told him it was perfectly safe for a *Hansa* and allowed him easily to see what was happening below him. Hanomer was using the hand at the end of his tail to clasp handholds well beyond the reach of his other two hands. Dave saw him disappear around a wall of rock. Dave wiped his sweaty hands on his shirt, fearing the sound of combat if Hanomer were discovered. Silence. Minutes passed and he heard a distant cough from someone on the island.

Suddenly, below him he briefly saw a light gourd partially uncovered. This was repeated twice. He felt Floyd beneath him shake on the line for more slack as he began to climb down the narrow access crack to the flat walled terrace, which formed the lowest part of the Torburg defenses.

When Dave finally joined Floyd on the terrace, he looked out over Eleytheria. He saw three campfires with no one visible in the backdrop of the flames. He unwrapped his bow, set his quiver at his side and waited for dawn.

When it finally came, he saw three small camps near the three campfires with sentries standing about.

"Where have all the Apemen gone?" asked Floyd. "There were hundreds of them here and now I only see the Turncoats."

"Well the pontoon bridge is still there," said Dave. "Maybe they've spotted the eastern force crossing the river and have gone to meet them."

"Let's hope not," said Dave.

Just then, Dave saw boats come around the western cliff and land. *Hansa* and several Ancients climbed out.

"Who are the big people?" asked Floyd.

"It's a long story. I'll introduce you to them later."

"Dave …"

"What?"

"Your skin—it just went from whitish pink to dark brown what's going on?" asked Floyd.

"That's another long story and I don't have time to tell it now. We'd better get ready to help the *Hansa*."

With that, Dave fired off an arrow toward the leftmost camp.

When the men in Eleytheria saw what they were up against, several of them fired their rifles, and then ran for the bridge.

"Now to close the trap!" said Floyd.

"Now you know that's not going to happen," said Dave.

"Those blasted *Hansa*, said Floyd. "They're supposed to help us win this war, but every time we could deliver a killing blow, they let the enemy flee."

"I know," said Dave, "if our lives were at stake they would reluctantly kill the men, but almost nothing else will make them do it."

"At least I'll give them 'what for,'" said Floyd as he fired his arrows as fast as he could at the fleeing men.

"We may as well go down."

He lowered the rope ladder and began the final descent down to the flat regions of Eleytheria. They ran to the bridge and began breaking it up as soon as the east bank *Hansa* force was across since Floyd didn't want any chance of surprise attack.

Dave could have wept. Except for the three makeshift lodgings, everything had been burned: all the houses, all of the crops and most of the stores. A few supplies were found in the three huts that were still standing, but they would have to start over and rebuild their whole village and once again plant all their crops.

Dave wanted to introduce Floyd to Kelldor, Arlana, and Ferris. As they approached the group, they saw them all huddled around a still form. It was Ferris. Ferris sat up holding his arm. A trail of blood soaked through his fingers as he tried to hold the wound closed.

"One of their loud weapons damaged me."

The wound was only a flesh wound, and soon the bleeding had been stopped.

Kelldor said, "Nephew, you will soon be better, but you must stay here for a while until you're fit to travel."

When Ferris had been taken to a tent to lie down, Floyd wanted to know in detail what had caused Dave's and Hanomer's long absence.

Dave began at the beginning and explained their adventures step by step. When he came to the part where the Halfman cut off his arm, Floyd made him roll up his sleeve and checked his left arm.

"You're not pulling my leg. You say your arm was chopped off and then the Ancients healed you?"

When he came to the healing plant, Arlana demonstrated their control over their skin color by changing from her current light hue to dark brown.

"So now you're one of them."

"It's still me," said Dave. "I'm still the same guy."

Dave saw Arlana and Kelldor exchange glances.

Kelldor stood up and looked around the circle stroking his white beard.

"Friends, I have to go. I've given up enough time already."

There was a murmur of disappointment among the *Hansa* around the circle.

Granomer also stood, his tail swishing back and forth in nervous excitement.

"It seems to me, Lord Kelldor, that we ought to maintain our alliance now that your reason for staying away from Meglir's lair has vanished."

"It hasn't completely vanished," interrupted Kelldor. "Meglir still wants to capture Ancients. He probably can't break the will of an adult, but if he laid his hands on an Ancient child," here he looked at Dave with concern, "then he would have a much more powerful host than the Lesser Man, Hoffstetter, he now inhabits. His power might be too much for us. That must not happen!"

"I bow to your wisdom, Lord Kelldor, but the little wisdom I have still tells me we ought to work together, especially since Meglir's move to the island of Halcyon, must be stopped," said Granomer.

"Yes," said Kelldor, "if that's where Meglir's heading and if he defeats Halcyon, he will be double the strength he is now."

Dave stood up. "Meglir's next stroke will fall on Halcyon. I want to go with Kelldor to the coast and help get rid of this other Bent One from Abaddon, who's threatening our land. From there I would also like to warn Halcyon of the danger that's approaching.

Dave was surprised when Kelldor agreed with him, and even more surprised when he saw Arlana smile.

Dave bowed again to Granomer. "Granomer, send some of your scouts with me to aid Kelldor. Send also Hanomer with me. Then our peoples will again be working together."

The discussion, getting down to the details of the trip and the supplies needed, looked as if it would go on for some time, so Floyd took Dave by the elbow and whispered, "Let's go for a walk."

When they were out of earshot, Floyd turned Dave around and looked him in the eye. "Dave, what are you doing volunteering for this mission? I need you here."

"Floyd, Meglir has left and is threatening Halcyon. He's given up on Eleytheria. Someone needs to warn Halcyon—even though they probably deserve what's coming to them."

"But why does it have to be you?"

"Who else is there in our group? Besides, you heard what Kelldor said about Meglir trying to get back to our world. We as a people have been weakened so that Meglir and the Bent Ones can control us. What about our people back home? Hoffstetter must have had a plan or mechanism for getting back. I'm clearly the man for the job.

"By the way, that brings up another question; where are Al and Pam?" asked Dave.

"They left about a month ago to go back to Halcyon."

"Why would they do that?" asked Dave.

"I tried to talk them out of it, but I couldn't. Al can be really stubborn sometimes. He said that Pam had to go back and try to rescue her son, Little Thomas, from the Staycare Center. The funny thing was that he knew he and Pam would probably get caught, but believed he had to go anyway. He said something to the effect that he, Pam, and Thomas' relationship stretched beyond this world and even if he and Pam were caught, it was still important for their relationship."

"I see his point," said Dave.

"What's gotten into you Dave? What do you mean you see his point? Al and Pam are throwing their lives away. They can't help Little Thomas. Little Thomas is Bigelow's child. Why does Dave care about him anyway?"

"I'm seeing a lot of things differently, Floyd. I've kind of started in a new direction in my life, and I can see where Al is coming from. If I were in Al's shoes, I could see myself making this attempt to rescue Little Thomas even if I was to get caught as soon as I set foot on Halcyon."

Floyd looked sharply at Dave and then shook his head in disbelief. "Is the whole world going crazy? What do you mean, you look at things differently? You're not going religious on me are you?"

"Maybe I am. I've had a crisis of sorts. I've been looking for something and I may have found it."

Floyd turned away and ran his hands over his bare head. They walked in silence for a while.

"Look Dave," said Floyd. "You have experienced severe emotional trauma and a near death experience. People often have these kinds of conversions under those circumstances. When they're in trouble, they imagine there's a God and that He will somehow rescue them when they're helpless—it's a useful psychological crutch. That's all it is. But now that you're over it, set the crutch aside and return to reality."

"Floyd what you say makes some sense, but you're looking at it from the outside. From the inside, the experience looks very real and very connected to reality. First of all, I started thinking about these things before my arm was cut off. I'm a different person now. God seems more like a person than an idea or a concept."

"Of course you're a different person. The Ancients put you through that healing plant and who knows what that did to you. All that translates into a new life, but all this belief in God and that he came to the earth two thousand years ago is hocus pocus."

Floyd looked thoughtful. "Doesn't this new world challenge your faith at all? After all, why wasn't this place mentioned in the Bible? You believe this carpenter from two thousand years ago saves people. Does he save these people too? Don't you see how unexplained and unanticipated it is?"

Dave felt his heart sinking. Still, maybe what Floyd said was true. Perhaps he had been brainwashed into believing that everything had changed.

If there's one thing I've learned, I have to stay rooted in reality. If I'm fooling myself, I have to face up to the truth no matter how much I want it to be wrong or different.

"Maybe you're right, Floyd. Maybe this is all wishful thinking. It would be really sad if what you said was true. I was honestly beginning to feel as if I had come home and I had a true Father waiting for me there."

"You see, that's the problem," said Floyd. "You want the comfort of a father so badly that you're willing to believe this idea of a rebirth on the flimsiest of evidence, because you want it to happen and be true."

Just then Granomer came up and bowed to the two of them. "Friend Floyd", said Granomer, "I think you should go with Lord Kelldor as well. I will stay here and with my *Hansa*, help set your village right. Meglir will not come back and it would be a good opportunity to let someone else manage the reconstruction."

Floyd was about to protest, but seemed to change his mind. "Perhaps you're right Loremaster Granomer. Hosea Mbeni is more than capable of leading the reconstruction from our end, and someone needs to look after Dave so he doesn't get into even more trouble."

Granomer bowed and moved off.

The next morning, the party assembled on the west bank of Lake Tor. Floyd was riding Kelldor's pack horse. Dave finished loading his supplies onto Traveller and mounted. Arlana already had Hanomer on her horse in front of her. Additional *Hansa* scouts were to come later with Ferris. Kelldor led the party along the edge of Lake Tor and a trail that climbed up the ridge to the Lake of the Trees. Soon Kelldor guided them to a high pass that took them south. After two days of hard traveling they finally came to their destination, a high plateau. They traversed the rocky plateau until they came to an alpine meadow. In the middle of the meadow was a nearly circular pond, fed by a small mountain brook. In the center of the pond was a circular island. On the island was a grove of oak trees.

Dave could feel himself getting excited. "I've seen this type of grove before," said Dave. "in Arkand in a park. It was also on an island."

"We often put them on islands to keep people and animals away from them," said Kelldor.

"What's so dangerous about them?" asked Dave. A chill went through him as he thought back to Arkand.

"Come and see," said Kelldor.

Kelldor searched along the shore and then led his horse into the water. The lake was quite shallow at this point so that the water never reached up to the horse's fetlocks. The others followed and soon were standing in the middle of the oak grove.

"Now what?" asked Dave.

"We make camp," said Kelldor.

There was a small stack of wood and soon, Hanomer had a fire going. The grove was about fifty paces across. The horses began to eat the grass along the fringes. After a brief meal, Kelldor had all the horses staked in the middle of the grove and then he wrapped himself into a blanket beside Arlana.

He turned to Dave and Floyd. "Under no circumstances, wander out of the grove during the night. Stay in your position."

As Dave lay down in his bedroll, he thought about what Floyd had said before they left, and again felt a pang of regret mixed with doubt.

My heart really yearns for a Father. I wish there were one that would look after me and offer me a place to go home to.

Floyd's questions and assertions had really shaken him up. Still, there was a part deep inside him that told him Floyd was wrong, but he couldn't put the reasons into words.

He thought he heard frogs croaking and had the faintest whiff of rotting vegetation. Both the frogs and the smell had probably been there before. Maybe he hadn't noticed them because he had been talking. He fell asleep as he wondered what they meant.

Chapter 19

Goose's Neck

Dave woke to a strong smell of rotting vegetation that seemed vaguely familiar. It reminded him of the journey to the Worm Caves. He stretched his legs and saw that a thick fog covered the land. But the high mountains were gone. Kelldor was already up.

"What's that smell?" asked Dave.

"Reminds me of the time we looked for a pass over the coastal mountains," said Floyd.

"That is the swamp we call Morfen," said Kelldor. "We are on a long, thin rocky mesa, called the Goose's Neck, that separates Morfen from The Great Southern Fen. This is where I stayed behind after I was injured. The Gurundar have moved east to pursue the Bent One and his forces. Now we have to ride swiftly, to catch up with the others."

"You mean while we were sleeping we traveled here?"

"Yes, that's the secret and the danger of the Travel Oaks. That's why we keep a close watch on them and place them where the unwary will not wander in. Walking through them is not dangerous. The traveler has to spend many hours relatively still and then in the blink of an eye the party is transported to the other location. This particular tree is a cutting from the grove near the Lake of Trees and so the two groves are linked."

Dave looked around and saw a section of the grove missing.

"Kelldor, it looks like someone has dug up a couple of the stems on the periphery."

"That is a great problem and I believe is one of the reasons that the Bent Ones have come back to Feiramar. We have destroyed all the

Travel Oaks linked to Abaddon to prevent the Bent Ones from troubling our land. Now, if they take cuttings back, they can travel to all of these locations. We will either have to destroy these groves which have taken many years to grow, or risk having them used as entry points."

"Kelldor, there's something I should tell you. It seemed inconsequential to me before, but the grove I saw in Arkand had a cutting missing as well. Maybe that's what the Bent Ones are up to, setting up a bunch of entry points. How many combatants could they bring in?"

"Not many—it depends on the size of the two groves. The smaller the grove, the fewer that can travel and the longer the sending takes. However even the largest grove can only handle a small party. Still, that grove in Arkand is linked to a very young grove in the Barrier Mountains—so young that the dyad is not useable for anything larger than a scroll. Still, if the Bent Ones grow a cutting in Abaddon, they will eventually have ready access to Arkand and even The Barrier Mountains.

They made breakfast. The *Hansa* had given them a delicious dish made of quails eggs mixed with greens and back bacon, all wrapped in a thin unleavened bread. The *Hansa* took such great joy in skillfully preparing food that even a modest meal like breakfast was a delight.

After Dave finished his meal, he realized that something had been troubling him all morning. "Kelldor, I keep hearing about this Abaddon. What is that?"

"It is a word that is foreign to our language and comes from the past. In its original tongue, which has been long forgotten, it means 'the place of destruction.' Abaddon is a continent east of here across the sea. I have never been there; neither have any of our people now living. Our lore tells us that the continent is surrounded by a ring of very high mountains, but the continent itself sits far below the level of the sea. Only the mountains keep the continent from being flooded. Furthermore, because of the depth, the air is so thick in Abaddon, that to animals living in the interior, our air would be so light and thin that coming here would be like us trying to live on the highest mountain. The Bent Ones long ago moved to Abaddon to practice their black arts as they twist, mold and remake creatures. The few times our people traveled there, they brought back strange tales. The air is very thick. The thick air lets them make huge creatures that could not live here. For example, there are very large flying creatures, much larger than the great condor in Feiramar which has a wing span of eight paces. In our long history, evil has ever festered in Abaddon and then come to Feiramar to trouble us. We have had relative peace since the Great Plague and Meglir's imprisonment inside the City of the Dead. That time is now coming to an end. Many beautiful things will be lost before the evil that is now growing will be defeated again."

"What kind of animals are there in Abaddon?" asked Dave.

"Enough of questions. You're babbling my ears off. Our future hangs in the balance and I'm spending my time instructing you. Am I to tell you the long years of lore? What I've told you, young Rokodor will have to do for now. We have work to do. I fear for my small army of Guardians." With that Kelldor rose and summoned everyone to travel.

Dave noticed that Arlana sat by with an amused smile on her face. "Is your father always this testy?" asked Dave.

"Testy? Dave you weary him and me with your endless questions. He had more patience with you than he would have had with me. I guess he realizes you are a mere child in a man's body and so he indulges your questions as one would a boy of seven winters."

"And you, I suppose, Arlana, would have asked more intelligent questions?"

"Me?" said Arlana. "I would not have been foolish enough to ask a question on a topic I could have looked up in the libraries. Perhaps you should learn to do the same if you would like to move from being a child of seven winters to one of eight."

"Come on you two, quit bickering. You're nattering at each other like an old married couple," said Floyd.

Dave glared at him and noticed Arlana was shooting daggers with her eyes at Floyd at the same time. Floyd burst out laughing.

"Lord Kelldor is waiting for us," said Hanomer. Dave and Arlana hastily assembled their kits, saddled their horses and then followed Floyd and Kelldor out of the grove.

They were at the summit of a flat-topped hill. Kelldor descended the hill in a southeasterly direction. Dave saw that they were in a shallow stone valley with low ridges to the north and south of them. In the center of the valley was a broad ribbon of green. Kelldor picked out a rough trail that led in that direction. The green ribbon proved to be a band of low bushes at the fringe of a brook. Under the cover of the bushes was a path. Everywhere the bushes had been slashed and hacked and the reeds by the brook had been crushed and bruised. The damage was not just the passage of a large force, but rather it seemed as if the enemy had taken delight in laying waste to as much of Feiramar as they could.

"Everywhere they go," said Kelldor, "the Bent Ones leave a trail of destruction as if they were at war with all living things."

Dave fell in beside Floyd. Hanomer was riding with Arlana who had gone ahead.

"What do you think about this 'Travel Oak' business?"

"Hmm," said Floyd. "I would have said that was physically impossible. How can a plant connect two sites that are physically remote and then teleport visitors to that remote location? Even if it were possible, how does the plant know what goes and what stays? Why didn't the soil and the grass move? Why just us and our belongings?"

"I know, I don't understand it either. If I were to try to develop a physical explanation, I wouldn't even know where to begin. Still the whole system vaguely reminds me of a capacitor—it has to charge for a while until it has whatever it needs to transport everyone to the other location, and then when it happens, it's like the capacitor discharging."

"I see your point," said Floyd. "But it brings us back to my point—how in the world is this possible? I suppose, to be fair, plants and animals have accomplished some amazing things: nerve conduction, bird migration, and even electrical discharges in water by the electric eel. The trees pull it off, so there has to be a physical explanation."

"I know," said Dave, "the hard facts of reality, destroying another of our beautiful theories that says this has to be impossible."

They had been travelling east for about a week. Increasingly Dave had seen the after effects of battle. Here and there, a mounded barrow, marked with a small stone cairns and planted with yellow bog asphodel were found along the way. From time to time they came to the larger smoldering remains of a bonfire.

"We burn the remains of our enemies lest their corpses be taken to the death plants and made into Apemen. We do not have the heart to do the same to our kin," Arlana had said at one of these. "Alas, many have died and we are so few."

In the distance Dave saw a high rocky outcropping that stretched right across Goose's Neck while the road passed through a narrow defile. Up ahead, sentries welcomed Kelldor. Dave and the others hurried up to hear the news.

"How goes the pursuit, Cantor?"

"Not well, Lord Kelldor. We pressed the Bent Ones hard and thought we had them on the run, killing many Halfmen, Lupi, and even a few Rokash. However their flight was but a ruse, as we chased them through the Gizzard into ruins of the Kellburg, they ambushed us and many were wounded and killed. We hold the open country but they hold the old fastness of the Kellburg, effectively blocking our road east.

"I need to have a look at the tactical situation," said Kelldor. "Call my commanders to a council. The Bent Ones are stealing our Travel Oak cuttings to open up new gateways from Abaddon to Feiramar. We have little time to stop them."

Arlana, Dave and Floyd went looking for something to eat.

"Arlana, what is this business about the Kellburg that they're talking about?"

"Yet another question, youngling? Well I suppose I should tell you so that you don't make a fool of yourself in questioning Kelldor. Kell Ironfist, my grandfather was Kelldor's father. Ironfist had already been very old when he and his wife had Kelldor. When Meglir, set himself to evil and sought to subdue all of these lands, he sent to Abaddon for help and they launched a great expeditionary force. One of the forces tried to sail up the River Pichon to Meglir's aid, while the second was sent to Goose's Beak Harbor, which became a great base for them. They hoped to march up Goose's Neck and attack Arkand directly, effectively cutting our empire in two. While Kelldor was fighting Meglir, Kell defended the Kellburg at great odds and would not let this second attack succeed. After a long and valiant defense, the defenders numbers diminished until they were overrun. By then it was too late and the City of the Dead gates were breached and Meglir unleashed the Great Plague killing both Ancients and Bent Ones alike. Kelldor only escaped because he had been wounded in the siege. He went back home on the other side of the Guardian Mountains recuperating. Ever since, we have been cut off from the western lands and have stayed away from Meglir's Lair."

"What happened to the expeditionary force up the Pishon River?" asked Dave.

"They were defeated by Brandor in a river battle at Brandor's Bend. He caught them tacking against the wind as they rounded a sharp bend in the river and he sent hundreds of fire rafts among them. Many ships burned and others foundered as they tried to maneuver out of the way. The rest he fought with his small fleet. Brandor and his brave men were also lost as the plague was unleashed."

Arlana began to sing softly.

Their host was great
Their deeds were fell
The sky was red
Alone stood Kell

The way he barred
He stood alone
No help would come
To bring him home

The Bent Ones raged
The siege was fierce
Yet Kell still stood
With arrow pierced

Till plague did come
He held at bay
He died unyielding
He saved the day

The maidens sing
Kell's glorious deed
He gave his life
At greatest need

As Dave listened to Arlana's voice, he could picture the dark smoke-filled night as wave after wave of Halfmen assaulted the Kellburg and with Kell knowing that soon they would be overcome.

So much violence. So many valiant people dying. When will it ever stop? And soon we go into battle once more.

They talked for a while longer and then climbed into their bed rolls near the fire.

Dave was just dreaming of burning rafts and a sea battle when he felt a hand shake him. He was instantly awake to Arlana's voice. "Wake up youngling," whispered Arlana, "it's time to go to battle."

"What time is it?" said Dave groggily.

"It is still several hours before dawn. Kelldor wants us in position in the ruins of the west wall of the Kellburg while it is still night. It is cloudy tonight, very dark, and smells like rain. Follow me."

Dave collected his weapons and all the food he could gather from the remains of last night and joined Arlana, Floyd, and Hanomer. Arlana led them to a weapons cache and told them to pick up a shield as well as any weapons they needed. Dave picked up a battered shield with a golden lion embossed onto it. Arlana then led them to a group of men who were assembling. The four of them, taking their cues from Arlana, did not mingle with the other Guardians. Finally, as if by predetermined signal, the group of about fifty headed off into the rocks.

"The Kellburg fortress," whispered Arlana, "is really two mirror image fortresses on either side of a deep chasm that has a river of fire at the bottom. There is only one large bridge across the chasm. Our scouts tell us the west fortress, called the Westwall, is only lightly defended, presumably because it's very difficult to get a large force across the bridge if this position is overrun. We're to attack the northern end of the Kellburg Westwall." She picked up her bow. "Let's move off."

"How do you guys see where you're going? I can't see a blooming thing," said Floyd.

That's odd. It's dark but I can still make out the rocks well enough to keep going. I wonder what's wrong with Floyd?

"Floyd, grab onto my backpack. For some reason I can see well enough to keep from breaking our necks."

By now they were into a large valley and the group leader was leading them in a northeasterly direction. Up ahead, a broken wall loomed. On command, everyone in the company touched each other's hands. Dave heard the thoughts of the commander in his mind:

Fan out and climb as high on the rubble as possible, but watch out for sentries. May the Creator be with you.

Arlana, taking the lead, led them off to the left and climbed the pile of stone in front of them with sections of wall still standing like towers on either side. She reached the crest and kept pushing on. When Dave reached the crest, he was looking at a large rectangular courtyard about five hundred paces across and about a thousand paces long. The narrow valley was bounded by high rugged hills made of huge slabs of broken stone on the north and south side of the valley. A walled tower, built into the impassable living rock had anchored the wall on the north side. In the distance Dave could also see a similar tower on the south side of the broken wall. In the middle of the courtyard was a chasm filled with pale red light. Across a narrow part of this chasm, at the center of the courtyard was a large arched stone bridge. He could see figures running over the bridge. There were so many they looked like a river. Most were men bearing cudgels, swords and axes. But around them loped the dreaded familiar forms of the Lupi. Finally, here and there, he also saw several of the reptilian Rokash. The plan had clearly gone awry—instead of a surprise attack by the Guardians, the Bent Ones were dealing out surprises.

Just then he heard the nearby voices of Halfmen speaking the Common Tongue in their guttural dialect.

"Garn, they ordered us out without even a decent meal and a decent night's sleep."

"Shut yer mouth. You do as you're told see, or else you'll catch it."

Dave peeked over the rubble heap and saw a large band of Halfmen approaching, carrying torches. Just then an arrow thudded into the first Halfman and the others howled with rage and sprang to the attack. There were so many of them that they flowed through a gap in the broken ruin of the wall like a dark howling tide. Dave had no time to think, but along with his friends was fighting for his life. Three large Lupi bounded on a nearby broken wall. The leader spotted Dave, growled and leapt for him. Dave rammed his shield into its snout and thrust his sword into its chest. It didn't go in very far because he felt it hit a rib and almost wrenched the sword out of his hand. A bolt from a crossbow ripped into the flank of the creature as it gnawed and ripped at his shield.

"Fall back Dave!" It sounded like Floyd's booming voice.

Using all of his strength, he heaved the creature off and backed toward the sound of the voice. Suddenly he was pulled backward into an opening in the rubble. Outside it was all confusion.

"We're cut off from our friends," said Arlana. "We're too small a group to form a defensive line. Let's hope the main group beats them back."

"Where are we?" asked Dave.

"Friend Dave, I guess we are in the remains of a watch tower. There seems to be a tunnel that goes back into the mountain, but it is much plugged up with rubble."

"We're trapped in here, Hanomer," said Dave. "Let's back in as far as we can. Maybe the Halfmen won't see us. I think you killed that Lup and in the confusion we may have escaped."

"Let's hope," said Floyd. He didn't sound too convinced.

Dave followed Hanomer down a short passage way, strewn with rocks to the back of the ruined tower. There was a pile of rubble but he couldn't see what Hanomer meant by a tunnel. Suddenly Hanomer appeared behind a large block of stone and waved to him. Behind Hanomer was a narrow cleft that Hanomer climbed into easily.

That's too small, I'll never be able to follow Hanomer.

Just then, Floyd came racing into the room with Arlana.

"They're coming. I don't think they saw me, but they're coming."

"Arlana, follow Hanomer."

She didn't move. Dave picked her up and pushed her behind the rock, where Hanomer's tail hand grabbed her wrist and guided her through the opening.

"Now you Floyd."

"You go ..."

"Don't argue Floyd, just go!"

Dave saw torchlight shining through the room door and heard the harsh voices of Halfmen.

"Come on, Dave," said Floyd.

"I'm too big. I'll hide here and take my chances. Lead Arlana and Hanomer to safety."

"Dave take off your stuff and hand it to me. You can make it. Stop being a hero and do it."

"Dave handed his pack, crossbow and shield to Floyd's outstretched arm, then his belt and cloak."

"Dave," said Arlana. "Put this on." She threw him a small canister. It felt greasy to the touch.

He put the greasy cream all over his chest and back as quickly as he could. Then he took a deep breath and exhaled. Extending his arms he thrust himself into the narrow crack. He knew that the fit was so tight that he couldn't breathe and he would suffocate if he became stuck. His shoulders were stuck on the smooth rock of the opening.

Chapter 20

The Bladewood

Panic began to overwhelm Dave as he felt trapped. Murmuring a prayer, he searched with his fingers for a purchase, he found one and pulled with all of his might. He felt hands on his forearms pulling him also. Suddenly he was through the opening. They moved away to hide themselves, then Dave put on his shirt and buckled on his sword. He felt like he had taken most of his skin off.

Although the torchlight played around the opening, no head ever appeared to peer in. Still, from the torchlight, it looked as if some of the Halfmen were staying in the tower room. Dave felt Hanomer pull him back further into the pitch black passage so that the small amount of torchlight filtering through the opening became a tiny slit in the distance. Turning a corner, torchlight vanished from sight altogether.

Hanomer held up a light gourd that shone off the walls with a pale yellow-white light. They were in a well-hewn passage. Before them was a set of stairs that headed down.

"Now what do we do?" asked Dave.

"I think we ought to explore this. Maybe there's another way out and we might learn something useful," said Floyd.

"In that case, we ought to let Hanomer lead. A *Hansa* does not easily get lost underground."

With the others' agreement, Hanomer led them down the stairs. After several hundred paces, the stairs ended in a wide, straight passageway. The lumi-lichen gave enough light to see now. They were at a tee intersection with the stairs forming the stem of the tee.

Do we go left or right? wondered Dave.

Hanomer moved part way up the passage to the left, sniffing the air while he swished his tail back and forth, opening and closing his tail hand in rhythm. He then repeated this procedure by going part way in the right direction.

Pointing to the left, Hanomer said, "This way leads in the direction of our camp. There is air movement down this hallway, so it is possible that there may be an opening at that end. To the right we head for the enemy camp. Friends, which would you like to pick?"

Dave was surprised that they all looked at him. "If we want to be safe we would go left, but I think we ought to go right. We just got beat up on the Westwall and the Bent Ones will be even more on guard in the future. Maybe we can learn something that would help us. What do you think?"

"There may be some hope for you yet, youngling," said Arlana. "Some days you show a glimmer of thinking like a man."

"Coming from you, that's a compliment and I take it you agree."

With Hanomer leading they headed right. The passage remained broad as it curved. After a while, like a snake, the passage changed, bending to the left. After another hundred paces, Dave saw a red glow playing off the walls of the passage ahead of them, around the bend. Floyd grabbed Dave's arm and Hanomer hid the light gourd in his pouch. Dave felt sweat bead on his forehead as he held his breath, listening for the sound of tramping feet. There was nothing.

"I don't smell torches," said Hanomer. "The light is too steady." They crept forward and the red light grew brighter. Finally, they saw an opening ahead that led onto an arched stone bridge about a hundred paces across. The bridge crossed a crack that was illuminated by a dull red glow. When they reached the bridge, Dave peered over the parapet. The narrow crack plunged a thousand feet, like a knife thrust through the living rock, and there was a tiny red ribbon of hot lava at the very bottom. Even at this distance, the heat beat on his face.

"Look," said Arlana pointing to the right along the deep, narrow canyon. In the distance they could see faint daylight, mingling with the dull red of the lava. "This is the same chasm we saw in the middle of the Kellburg and morning has dawned."

They hurried across the bridge. The passage ran straight as a ruler due east by Dave's reckoning. From time to time there were smaller side passages and the occasional guard room, but it was easy for Dave to see that they were on the main road. Finally, the passage ended in a broad circular stair. They climbed and climbed, feeling a hint of a breeze. Finally, creeping with great care, they climbed out of a crack in the mountain wall high above Goose's Neck. Off to the west, Dave saw the eastern ruins of the Kellburg and just outside the wall was the crude camp of the Halfmen.

Dave knew they were all thinking the same thing. "Let's get back to Kelldor and tell him about this route before he launches another frontal assault."

Dave led on the way back. They traveled as quickly as they dared, hoping that the Halfmen had not discovered the way into the passage at the back of the guardroom.

When they approached the bridge over the fissure, Dave called a halt and wanted to go on alone.

"Friend Dave," said Hanomer, "I'm much smaller than you are. Let me go, and I'm sure even if those sharp-eyed Halfmen are there, they won't see me."

"But Hanomer .."

"He's right youngling," said Arlana.

"Arlana you stay out of this."

"They're both right Dave," said Floyd. "You should listen to them."

There was nothing more to say. Hanomer crossed the bridge and disappeared over the rise of the arch without so much as a sound. Soon he reappeared and waved to them. They crossed in front of the side passage that led to the guardroom and continued on along the same broad passage, this time running straight west.

Hanomer stopped. The broad passage continued on, but a side passage headed off to the right.

"Why are we stopping Hanomer?" asked Dave.

"Friend Dave, I'm deciding which way to go. Both ways have fresh air coming in, but I think this passage to the right is much closer to the opening. I think we will go right. It may be that going straight ahead will bring us out, but we might be far from the camp."

Dave followed Hanomer down the right hand passage, which shortly ended in a circular stairway. Hanomer led the way upward. After several hundred steps, Dave saw bright sunlight ahead. He emerged from an archway into a wood with huge, ancient trees. The trees had long narrow, shiny leaves about two feet long with two lobes at the stem that made them look like daggers. There was only grass underfoot. Hanomer had already disappeared among the trunks and Dave did not want to call for him in case the enemy was about. He walked one hundred paces ahead until he came to a steep rock wall that rose at least one hundred feet straight up. He leaned on the nearest tree to steady himself and looked up the rock wall to see if they could climb out.

"Ow!" Dave looked at his arm and saw a deep slice, with blood trickling out.

"What the heck?"

A blade of glistening blue metal protruded from a vertical split in the tree trunk. An unbound metal hilt above his head was free from the tree. He grasped it and pulled. The straight blade, a yard long, separated from the tree without much effort. It was wondrously light, but needed to have a handle bound onto the hilt. Dave ran his finger across the edge as lightly as he could only to draw blood again.

Arlana appeared and stifled a gasp.

"You're bleeding," she said gravely.

"Yeah, I guess I am." Dave found it hard to take his eyes off the sword in his hand.

"What's going on here Arlana? Why was this sword stuck in this tree?"

"I need to sew and bandage your wound. Hold your questions."

She worked swiftly and efficiently and had just finished when Floyd and Hanomer appeared.

"There's no easy way out," said Floyd. "This dell is completely surrounded by a high rock wall. What happened to you, Dave? Fighting with Arlana again?"

Dave harrumphed. "No, I was trying to see if I could get over the wall and leaned against this tree to look up and the next thing I know I have a three inch long slice in my arm. It came from this thing that was wedged into a crack in the tree."

Floyd picked up the blade and promptly cut his finger as he tested the edge."

"In the tree you say?"

"Here's another one," said Dave. From the other side of the same tree, he pulled a double-edged dagger of the same blue metal.

"This is an ancient Bladewood and these are Blade trees," said Arlana with wonder in her voice.

"Blade trees are named after the leaves?" asked Dave reaching out to the dagger-like leaves on a branch.

"No, they are named after the trees' function. From ancient times my people have used these trees to make blades of wondrous quality, better than any smith could make. The smiths of our race forge and craft excellent weapons, but none have an edge that never dulls, or blades that never break.

"To make these truly wonderful blades, a craftsman spends long hours making a fine, intricately crafted steel weapon. These manufactured blades are then imbedded in the living wood of a Blade tree. Over hundreds of years the tree changes the blade until it is very light, has an edge that never dulls, and cuts steel or iron as if it were a poplar wand. Since it takes so long for the tree to do its work, we pass these on as heirlooms. My father has one at his side. There are only five with our people right now."

"I bet a metallurgist would give his firstborn son to analyze the composition of this blade," said Dave. "Are these trees rare?"

"Yes, they are," said Arlana. The soil conditions to support a Bladewood are not easy to find, and all the old Bladewoods were destroyed during Meglir's War, as the trees were split apart, and the partially finished blades ripped out for the fighting. We have one Bladewood beyond the Barrier Mountains, but it is relatively young and we don't know yet if the soil conditions are good enough to produce first rate swords. This Bladewood is a great find."

Arlana carefully wrapped up the sword and the dagger. "We should go back and try the other passage." They retraced their steps until they came back to the main gallery. Turning right, they continued on for about four hundred paces, then again entered the circular stair of a tower. They soon found themselves on a high lookout platform with a view of the Guardian camp below them.

As Dave stood high up on the platform, he had not really realized until now, how much the terrain had changed. When he looked back the way they had come, most of Goose's Neck had consisted of two parallel ridges of rock with a shallow valley in the middle. At the Gizzard, the ridges had become low mountains and broadened out considerably. The creek had long since disappeared into the southern fen.

Hanomer again took the lead and, in the late morning light, found a trail that was well hidden, passed right under their lookout perch and then wound its way to the valley below. When they reached the valley, they were challenged by sentries. "Lady Arlana, where have you been? Your father has been looking for you, fearing that you were dead."

"May I ask your name ranger?"

"I am called Caledor. Are you or your friends hurt?"

"No Caledor, we're not hurt but we have urgent news for Lord Kelldor."

By the time they reached the command tents, Lord Kelldor had arrived.

He looked at them keenly. "I am glad that you're not hurt. But I can tell you have tidings for me."

"Yes father, but I think I will let Rokodor tell you."

"Lord Kelldor, we were holding the north flank of our line. As the Halfmen attacked our position in strength, we were separated from the others and driven into a ruined guardroom."

Dave went on to explain their discovery.

Kelldor said, "I knew in my heart all of you had a role to play in this battle, and my hope has been rewarded. Caledor, call the captains. It's still morning and we must get moving."

"Now show me the blades Arlana."

Arlana unwrapped the sword and dagger. Kelldor looked at them keenly. He pulled his own sword from the scabbard. It also had the same blue sheen. "These blades have come to you, young Rokodor, so they are yours to wield. I will respect that, even though there are great warriors among us who have to fight with inferior weapons. I will have one of our smiths fashion a worthy hilt. Later, we will see what other blades are in this secret wood. This wood will be a great boon for our people. My sire, Lord Kell the Ironfist, reaches to us from the past and brings help to us again."

Within the hour Dave and his friends were at the head of a long line of men climbing up to the high mountain entrance to the stair. Kelldor went with them.

"It looks like you are bringing most of your men Kelldor," asked Dave. "Isn't that risky?"

"Very risky. Still it's a gamble worth taking. The few men I have on the Westwall of the Kellburg are in very strong positions, particularly in daylight. Since the attack this morning ultimately failed, I don't think they will try it again. If I can get my men behind the Halfmen and cut them off, then I can prevent the Bent Ones from returning home. If I'm in time. If only I am in time."

Within an hour they emerged at the eastern opening and saw the crude Halfmen camp below. They had passed completely behind the enemy defenses on the eastern wall of the Kellburg. Hanomer had to search for a back way down to the woods beyond the Eastwall, since they needed to stay out of sight of the Halfmen camp. Still, the Halfmen had few sentries and slowly the Gurundar assembled at the edge of the forest at the foot of the mountain.

Finally, about mid-afternoon, Kelldor and his captains loosed the attack. The Halfmen, shrieking with rage and anger, fought ferociously. The Lupi also attacked, but were cut down by the ranger bowmen. At last they had had enough and scattered south, looking for any way across the broken crags of the Gizzard. The rangers hunted them until it grew dark. Few Halfmen escaped from that battle.

It was evening when the last of the Halfmen had been cleared from the ruins of the Kellburg Eastwall and Kelldor met with his captains.

"Tis as I feared," said Kelldor. "This was only a delaying action. The Bent Ones fled south while they used the Halfmen to cover their retreat. The Halfmen are tools crafted by the Bent Ones for their use. I need a company of our best mounted rangers as well as our best woodsmen. I want to leave tonight and try to catch the Bent Ones. The Bent Ones and their guards will be few now. They had counted on the Halfmen to hold out for a long time in such a well-fortified position. Perhaps, if we rush after them with a small, light force, I can steal a march on them and overtake them before they leave. There is hope yet!"

Dave stepped forward. "Lord Kelldor, let me come with you."

"Yes Dave, you may come. Your people had a hand in loosing this evil, and so it is only right that you have a hand in its remediation. But we leave within the hour.

They had ridden hard all night and Dave was dead tired. The scouts had seen no trace of the Bent Ones, although signs were everywhere that the Bent Ones had preceded them. Dave felt sorry for the horses. Finally, Kelldor had dismounted and crossed a ridge. Below them was a broad rocky plain and a harbor. Four ships with black sails had weighed anchor and were beating their way past the promontory.

"I am too late," said Kelldor. "They have achieved what they came for." He sat down heavily and wiped his brow.

"What is this place?" asked Dave.

"It's called Goose's Beak." said Arlana. "Can you not see how those peninsulas remind you of a goose's beak. It is the best harbor on the eastern shore. In the days of our might we kept many ships here."

"Let's make sure there are no enemies about and then make camp by the harbor. I'm sure the rest of the army will be here err nightfall," said Kelldor.

The rest of the afternoon was spent setting up camp. It was a pleasant place in spite of its forbidding appearance. There were woods off to the south and clean running water from the high crags, some of which were lofty enough to be snow covered.

When the preparations had been made, Kelldor beckoned them to come with him. He followed a path south through the cool woods and within a mile came upon a beautiful cove. Kelldor took an object like a flute out of his cloak, and stepped into the water. Lowering the end of the object into the water he blew some notes. Dave could barely hear the high-pitched whistle.

Kelldor returned to the shore and sat down.

"Now what?" asked Dave.

"We wait," said Kelldor and promptly closed his eyes. Within half an hour, a large marine mammal's head broke the surface and a chattering noise woke Kelldor. Dave saw that the mammal had an hourglass shape with a triangular snout. On top of the head were two bony projections almost like goat's horns with a fleshy appendage at the end. Kelldor waded out into the water, wrapped his living cloak close about him and sat on the mammal. He leaned over, spoke quietly, and then the mammal shot off at surprising speed. After about a hundred paces, Kelldor leaned forward and suddenly the mammal leapt into the air and then vanished with Kelldor under the surface.

"What was that?" asked Dave.

"We call them Dorai," said Arlana. "Just as the Guardians each have a horse that is bonded to them, they also come here to find their personal Dorai. I hope to find mine soon."

"What's that strange bony structure on the head?"

"The appendage is a special organ of hearing and touch. They can sense other fish—and us—at great distances. They also use the appendage as a sense of touch in dark or muddy water."

In about half an hour Kelldor returned. "The black ships have sailed east. They are beyond reach. Let's head back to camp."

When Dave reached camp, he was extremely tired. He could barely make it to his bedroll before he fell asleep.

Chapter 21

Hide and Seek

When Dave finally woke up, the sun was already high in the sky. He realized that he had not been woken for his early morning watch. He was just sitting down with the others to their noonday meal when the first army detachments arrived.

Curiously, there was a small party that didn't seem to fit, a young woman and child, accompanied by *Hansa*. Dave punched Floyd's shoulder and said, "If I didn't know better, I'd say that was Pam, and Ferris is with her."

"Pam, here? Your eyes are a lot better than mine if you can recognize someone at this distance."

"I'm thinking Dave is right," said Hanomer. "Rolomer is with them, so they must have returned from down river."

Pam came riding into their camp with a young boy on the horse in front of her. When she saw Dave and Floyd, her faced brightened. She dismounted, and lifted the boy off the horse. Dave and Floyd were already running toward her.

"Dave, Floyd—and Hanomer. Am I glad I found you at last." She burst into tears and ran to hug them. Her words came out in a torrent. "This is Little Thomas. Al has been captured and it's all my fault."

Taking a cue from his mother's strong emotion, Little Thomas began to cry.

Pam took him into her arms. "Shush, my love. Everything is going to be all right now. We've found our friends and they're going to help."

Arlana came over, took Pam by her arm, and gave her a hug. "I am called Arlana. I am cousin to Ferris whom you've already met."

Turning to Dave and Floyd, Arlana put her hands on her hips and said, "Men! Didn't your mothers and fathers teach you how to treat a woman and mother."

Putting an arm around Pam and the other around Little Thomas, she brought them to the fire. Let me get you some *Siph* that Hanomer has made for us, and then you'll tell us all about it when you're ready.

In a few minutes, Pam almost seemed her old self again.

"So what happened?" said Floyd.

"Al, in helping me and Little Thomas escape, was captured by Bigelow. Now I have to rescue him."

"Listen," said Floyd, "if we're going to help you, you had better go step by step and start from the beginning."

So Pam, in detail, recounted their trip to Halcyon, their near disaster with the swamp Krachodon, and then their sojourn in Halcyon until she had escaped."

"So what happened after you escaped?" asked Dave.

"Well," said Pam, "I wanted to go back to try to rescue Al, but Rolomer reminded me of my duty to listen to Al and to save Little Thomas." She then went on to recount their flight from Halcyon. Dave was so caught up in Pam's story that it seemed to him he was there with her, and seeing the events unfold through her eyes.

Little Thomas was sleeping in Pam's arms. Several hours had passed. Dawn had finally come. She looked back at the tiny, receding island of Halcyon. Rolomer made their reed boat maintain good speed on the starboard tack.

"Friend Pam, I see you sitting looking back at Halcyon. I have brought you some *Siph*."

Pam hugged Little Thomas to herself. "Oh Rolomer, Al tried to tell me it wouldn't work, but I wouldn't listen."

"But friend Pam, it did work. You rescued the little one."

"But at what cost?"

"Would friend Al not have thought it worth it?"

"Yes, I suppose he would have. I can't really explain it, but he seemed to adopt Little Thomas and love him. Perhaps, because of the similarity in names, he felt he was rescuing his own estranged brother Thomas when he rescued Little Thomas."

She seemed to shake off this line of thinking. "But what will they do to Al? Last time they had him locked up and drugged. I know you don't really understand what I'm saying."

"I understand that they treated Al badly," said Rolomer. "Still we must trust the Creator. If one does the right thing, and I think you did, then even though there may be some dark chapters in the middle of the story, one should expect the end of the story to come out well."

Rolomer stood up and pointed. "There's a sail coming around that point. Friend Pam, it is one of the Halcyon boats."

Pam shielded her eyes with her hand and looked at the boat in the distance. "Yes, Rolomer, it looks like a Halcyon longboat."

Rolomer shouted some orders and the *Hansa* scurried across the deck and tightened up the rigging. The breeze was quite light. Rolomer chose a course that put their reed craft on its best point of sailing.

Pam sat in the back of the boat and watched the pursuing sail. She could feel them pick up speed. Rolomer moved some of their stores to improve the trim. Still, the pursuing sail grew larger slowly.

"They are gaining on us. With a much bigger boat and a light breeze, their sail is catching more wind while the headlands and islands are stealing ours."

"What will we do? They mustn't catch us! Not after all we have gone through. Not after Al has sacrificed his freedom."

"The Creator will watch over us, friend Pam. I thought you would know that. Up ahead the Caiman Swamp is on our starboard. When they get close, we will dart in there and hide deep in the swamp. Even though they have a shallow draft, they are broad of beam and will eventually get stuck in a narrow channel or a mud bank. I don't think they will follow us.

"But what if we meet one of those monsters we saw when we came down? What did you call the creature with the head of a crocodile and a mouth ringed with tentacles?"

"We called it a *Krachodon*. Still, friend Pam, there are no safe paths. To stay this course is to invite capture. If you think it best, then we will continue the chase as long as we can. Perhaps the wind will change or they will hit a mud bank. Nevertheless, I would council we try the swamp."

"Rolomer, I will not make Al's sacrifice meaningless by giving up. I will take your advice, and we will take our chances in the swamp."

Pam looked back and the longboat was close enough that Pam could see the figures on board. An officer in the bow had his glass trained on them. The right bank fell away and the swamp began, but Rolomer did not change course.

"If I turn in too soon, then I can only turn to port when I am out of sight. I want to wait until I am further into the swamp."

Rolomer doesn't miss a trick. I hope our luck holds.

A rifle shot rang out and hit the water about twenty paces off the port bow. Rolomer tacked quickly and the boat darted toward the swamp. The longboat tried to tack immediately, but the sails were slow to be reset and she missed stays. Dead to the wind, the longboat began to drift downwind. The crew was scrambling to recover.

Good, thought Pam, *that will buy us some time. Oh no, they're launching a boat!*

The captain of the longboat knew his business and used the setback to launch a small skiff. The little craft would have no trouble following them, wherever they went in the swamp. Rolomer kept their speed up as the first island of reeds passed on their port side. He headed up a channel while maintaining all the speed he could. Finally after passing several possible side channels, he picked one on the starboard side, drifted around a large bed of reeds, then using the oars, backed into an overgrown cypress island surrounded by a tangle of vegetation. The *Hansa* unstepped the mast and spread out the boat weed skirt. Bandomer was in the water pulling the skirt down to the water level. Rolomer fastened a rope to a towering cypress beside them and hauled the bow around so that they were well into the reed bed.

They scrambled under the reed cover and waited. Pam was speaking softly to Little Thomas, praying that he would remain silent. She heard the bleating croak of a frog and then a loud splash in the distance. Time passed slowly.

Faintly, there were voices, as if at a great distance and her heart began to race. Oars splashed in the water. She gripped Little Thomas tightly. The splash of the oars now seemed very close.

Slowly they began to recede and Pam let out a sign of relief. Clouds covered the sun and a light rain began to fall.

"What do we do now?" whispered Pam.

"Do you think the men in the big boat will wait for us?" asked Rolomer.

"Yes, I'm sure they will wait."

"Then we must stay in the swamp and work our way upriver before we re-enter the main channel. We will wait until the small boat has left the swamp."

Hours later, with darkness surrounding them, Bandomer left the cover of the reeds and watched for the return of the boat. Pam was relieved that Little Thomas had fallen asleep.

Finally the *Hansa* decided it was time to leave. They left the reed covering in place and Rolomer swam to a nearby cypress grove and began warping the boat out of the reeds. They then brought out the oars and quietly began rowing up the channel. The three *Hansa* took turns perching on the bow and whispering directions to Pam at the tiller. It was painstaking work, but the *Hansa* had an unerring sense of direction in the swamp and they never reached a blind channel. Finally, after several hours of crawling through the swamp, Rolomer directed them back to the main river. When they exited the swamp, Pam looked with trepidation up and down the river. The fog was so thick that she could barely see twenty paces in any direction in the pre-dawn light. Nonetheless, Rolomer would not take any chances; he kept the craft creeping along the bank for another hour before he hoisted the sail and began to head up river.

They were finally sailing up the Tor River to Lake Tor. Pam couldn't wait to talk to Floyd.

With a pang of regret, she realized she hadn't thought about Dave for a long time. *I do hope he's back. He has to help me now.*

As they approached the Torburg, she strained her eyes looking for anyone she recognized on the shore. With a shock, she saw the smoldering blackened hulks of cottages, fields trampled and burned, and bodies of Apemen lying on the island. A bonfire was burning and the bodies of Apemen were being dragged there for cremation.

What has happened here?

As they neared the shore, several of the *Hansa* came to meet their craft along with a tall man with dark brown skin and his arm in a sling. Gradually, others came running until quite a crowd had gathered on the shore.

Pam climbed out of the boat scanning the crowd for Floyd or Dave. She saw Hosea Mbeni coming toward them. Pam hurried to meet him, carrying Little Thomas.

"Oh Hosea, am I glad to see you. Did Dave come back?"

"Yes Pam, Dave and Hanomer came back."

Pam breathed a sigh of relief. "I need to see Dave right away."

"I'm sorry Pam, he's left again."

"Left again. Where?"

"Pam, calm down. Let's get some *Siph*. I have a long story to tell you and you have a long story to tell me. Then we'll decide what to do."

Pam reluctantly agreed.

Things never seem to move as fast as I need them to.

Pam had finished her third cup of *Siph* by the time her story and Hosea's story had been told. She needed Floyd and Dave to help her rescue Al and now they were gone. She was nearly in tears.

I am not going to cry. I have to think. I don't care what it takes, I'm going after them and no one is going to stop me.

The stranger called Ferris, who still had his arm in a sling, and who had figured so strongly in Hosea's story about Dave, spoke. She was amazed at the quality of his English.

"I help perhaps. You ride?"

"You mean 'can I ride a horse?' Yes I can ride. How could you help?" asked Pam.

"My arm better now. I go to kinsmen to fight. I take you and boy to … to find friend Dave."

Pam felt herself break out into a smile. "You would help me?"

"Yes. We leave soon. We leave when sun comes up."

Chapter 22

Romulus and Remus

Pam concluded her story. "And so we've been following you ever since. Without Ferris I would never have known about the Travel Oaks. We would have been weeks on the road."

Dave came out of his reverie. "You know Pam, a war zone is no place for Little Thomas," said Dave. "Why not just send a message with Ferris. We would still have gone after Al, you know that, right?"

"Yes, I know," said Pam, "but make no mistake, I'm going with you."

Dave was worried. "You can't Pam. Who's going to look after Little Thomas?"

"He's going to come along," said Pam. "He knows how to keep quiet and I'm not going to be parted from him again."

"No way," said Dave. "This is no place for a child."

"I'm going along, and so Little Thomas has to come too. I'm not going to be parted from Little Thomas again and I will try to rescue Al."

"Pam," said Dave, his voice getting louder, "By insisting on coming you're putting Little Thomas at risk. Blast Pam, you're putting all of us at risk. At least stay here with the army. We'll let you know as soon as we find Al."

Dave could tell Pam was furious by the red color of her cheeks. Tears came to her eyes, but she did not break down and cry. "Dave, this is not up for discussion. I'm coming along. My mind is made up."

Dave threw up his hands in exasperation. "Pam you're impossible."

In response Pam wiped her cheeks and gave him a smile that did not quite touch her eyes.

"Hold it, you two, before it comes to blows," said Floyd. "Why don't we plan how we're going to pull it off, and then we can tell if it's even possible for Pam and Little Thomas to come."

Dave saw Pam look at Floyd as if her eyes could bore a hole through him. Dave took a deep breath. "Okay, let's do that. I don't think we can land on Halcyon Island itself and hope to remain undiscovered. So I have another idea. There are two small rocky islands off Halcyon's east coast, named Romulus and Remus. They are honeycombed with sea caves. I spent many hours exploring them since I like spelunking. Romulus, the larger rock closer to shore, actually has a large sea cave that could hold a sizable boat if we enter it at low tide. We could set up camp in the caves and use them as a safe base of operations. By my thinking we would only travel to and from Halcyon at night, when we would be harder to spot."

"If you were spelunking there before, what happens if someone is camping in the caves now?" asked Floyd.

"We never stayed overnight," said Dave. "Why would we? The outside is sheer rock and even as a lookout post, the mountain is much higher and more easily accessible. Anyway when we went spelunking, we would tie up in a small cove on the west side of the island and enter the caves from there. What I am proposing is much more dangerous, but would leave the boat hidden."

"That settles it then," said Pam. "Little Thomas and I can stay in the caves and be perfectly safe. We can help because Halcyon has changed since you were there last, and I can bring you up to date on the current situation. Face up to it, Dave. You need me."

Pam never gives up. She's as stubborn as a post when she sets her mind on something, thought Dave.

"Pam why not tell us now? It's too dangerous to take Little Thomas along," said Dave.

Arlana who had been listening turned to Pam and said, "Do all your men argue against women with good sense or is it just Dave?"

Pam smiled. "All of our men do it from time to time, but I think Dave has developed that particular art to a very high degree."

"I have noticed that," said Arlana. "He does it with me too. We will have to train him out of it if he is ever to grow up."

I'm sitting right here and they're talking about me as if I were a piece of furniture.

"I will also go along," said Arlana.

"Enough of this nonsense," said Kelldor. "My work here is done and I will join you too. Your people need some looking in to; I plan to do that before Meglir attacks them. You will be glad of my help before this adventure is done. Besides, if I don't provide you with a boat, how will you get there? Are you planning to build one?"

Dave looked helplessly at Floyd.

Floyd shrugged. "We need Kelldor's help. If he and Arlana want to come, how can we say 'no?' After all we'll be traveling in their boat."

Dave threw up his hands in frustration then stuffed them into his pockets and turned, trying to control his temper.

"How long will it take us to get a boat?" asked Floyd.

"We keep a few reed boats anchored in the marsh to the south. The boat weed keeps the craft in good condition."

Dave, Floyd, Arlana, and Kelldor made the short hike to the southern marsh. Kelldor pointed out a number of boat weed boats that were anchored in the reed bed. They selected one the right size and trimmed some of the foliage back. After cleaning the inside, they tested it to prove it was seaworthy. The mast was in good condition.

"Where are the sails and rigging?" asked Dave.

"That will be more of a problem," said Kelldor. "The Bent Ones set fire to all of our storage sheds before they left."

They headed back to camp and searched the smoldering ruins for cordage and sail. Eventually they found enough rope and sails to rig one boat. In two days they were ready to begin their journey up the coast.

The boat was barely large enough to house all of them. The *Hansa* volunteered to sleep on the deck and Dave did the same. Pam, Arlana, and little Thomas slept in the bow cabin. The deck was going to be crowded until Dave insisted that everyone, including the *Hansa* draw lots for the aft cabin. Hanomer, Floyd, and Kelldor chose the long straws and moved their supplies to the aft cabin. Dave placed his supplies on the quarterdeck next to the tiller. He figured he could hang a sheet over the tiller in a pinch if it rained.

They cast off with the ebb tide and a gentle land breeze, giving them barely enough way for steerage. The rocky headlands of the Goose's Beak bay surrounded a convex lens-shaped body of water. The northeastern mouth of the bay was guarded by two rocky massifs.

"What are those two rock formations at the entrance of the bay?" asked Dave.

"We call them Ton-Heimar, 'the Gateway of Home.' When the weather is stormy or foggy, we light fires on those heights to guide sailors home. Before Meglir's war, we kept constant watch on the Gateway Pillars. Now we are too few. The best we can do is send regular patrols this way to make sure the enemy has not gained a foothold," said Kelldor.

The wind had freshened, and soon they were cutting a bow wave as the boat heeled over. They made straight for the entrance and passed into the shadow of the rocky promontories. Soon they were through and reached the rollers of the open ocean.

"Friend Dave," said Hanomer, " make our heading three hands further north and then I will trim the sails. Steering on the ocean waves was tricky. The crests were high enough that they would lose way in the trough and regain it at the crest. This meant that Dave had to constantly make adjustments to the tiller.

Six days later, in the dead of night they were approaching Halcyon Island. The land loomed as a dark smudge in the distance in the pale moonlight.

"Can we head a bit further east?" whispered Dave. "The two small rock islands are on the southeast side of the main island.

Hanomer sniffed the air. "I think it best if we tacked and approached from the southeast, friend Dave. That way if we have problems we will drift away from the rocks."

They did as Hanomer wisely suggested. Dave sat in the bow looking for Romulus and Remus. Hanomer had been watching the tides and estimated that low tide would occur just after midnight. Dave heard the sound of breakers and saw the lights of Halcyon in the distance. The nuclear power plant at the south side of the island was also lit up and Dave used that to keep their heading toward the two rocky islands. He heard breakers quite close to the boat but still could see nothing. Finally he saw the island looming ahead, but they were drifting wide. The breakers began to recede again.

I was too cautious. We sailed by too far south.

Dave crawled back to Hanomer and explained the situation. Hanomer placed the boat on the other tack and shortened sail. Dave crawled back to the bow. This time a dark mass loomed up perhaps one hundred yards off the starboard bow. Dave guided Hanomer to the narrow channel between the islands. They dropped the sail and manned the sweeps, rowing up the channel, which was sheltered from the wind.

"There," pointed Dave, "can you see it Hanomer?"

"Yes friend Dave. We will have to take down the mast to make it in."

With Pam and Arlana gently rowing to keep the boat off the rocks, the others took down the mast and stowed it on the deck. Then they rowed into a cave until the bottom of the boat scraped on sand.

"Now for a light," said Dave. He pulled out a light gourd and stroked it to activate the yellow-white light. As the light strengthened, it played off the sea cave roof about thirty yards above the water. The entrance was only about five paces high. At high tide there would be no going in or out, although a careful observer would still be able to see the entrance.

"Come on," said Dave. He leapt out of the boat and placed the light gourd onto a rock while he moored the boat to a boulder sitting on the sand. He then walked to a narrow crack at the back and waited for the others. He led them up several passageways until he came to a sandy chamber high up on the rock.

"I think we should make camp here. There are fissures in the rock that let light and air in during the day. We should post a lookout to warn us if any boats are coming, especially during low tide."

"This could work, said Floyd. "Let's get the supplies up and then get some sleep." It took only ten minutes to get their supplies to the cave. They had a cold supper and unbundled their sleeping bags.

Dave walked over to Pam and said quietly, "Pam we need to talk."

"Dave if this is to change my mind and urge me to go back, it won't work. Don't you see I have to do this?"

"Pam, you and Little Thomas are my responsibility now. It's just not safe here. A party of spelunkers from the mainland could arrive here any minute or I could be detected on Halcyon just like Al was, and then all of us would be captured."

"Dave that's just a chance I am willing to take."

"But what is Al going to say to me when he finds out I let this happen?"

Pam's tone softened. "Dave, Al knows what kind of a stubborn, ornery woman I can be. He'll know you were overmatched and just had to go along with my plan. Besides, Arlana and Kelldor have given every indication that they plan on staying, so there is no boat going back. This whole discussion is moot."

Dave shook his head and went back to his sleeping area. He had chosen a cave high up in the honeycombed rock that had a small fissure that gave him a view of East Harbor in the distance. He looked with apprehension for the first hint of a boat lamp that would indicate visitors.

The next morning dawned as a dull drizzle; Dave went down to the main cave only to find the others already gathered there. Most were dressed. Arlana had her long golden braid wrapped in a towel as if she had just had a bath. Just then he saw Hanomer enter carrying a heavy load of driftwood that he added to a pile. Dave still marveled how the extra hand on his tail helped him to carry a relatively large load for his small size.

"Only a cold breakfast," said Floyd, "we can't risk a fire since the Halcyonites may see the smoke."

"Good idea," said Dave grumpily.

"What's eating you?" said Floyd.

"Oh, I don't know. I didn't sleep much last night." He sat down and leaned his chin on his hands. "I also haven't figured out how to get back to the main island without being seen."

"I've been wondering that myself," said Floyd. "If we take the boat during the day, they are sure to see us. If we go at night, we'll be going blind since I don't know this part of the coast as well as the north."

"I've just realized, it's worse than that. Since the cave opening can only be used at low tide, there will be days where we can only leave in daylight."

"Why don't you swim Dave?" asked Arlana.

"I've been thinking about that. I'm pretty sure I could make it even though there can be a fair current through the channel between Romulus and the main island. But during the day someone will see me for sure. If I wait until tonight, then a boat may be better."

"No, I mean swim the whole distance underwater. I did it this morning."

Dave felt his mouth drop open and he closed it.

"You did what?" said Floyd.

"I swam the whole distance underwater."

Floyd scratched his head. "Tell me Arlana, how long can you hold your breath underwater?"

She thought for a moment. "I would say about sixty of your minutes."

Floyd whistled.

"You seem surprised. Did you not see my father go for a deep dive with his Dorai. You must be more like the Halfmen, who can only hold their breath underwater for a short time."

"But we have to get Dave over there."

"But don't you see," said Arlana. "Since Dave has been healed, whatever organ the Creator gave us to swim long distances under water has been restored and repaired in Dave. Dave, have you ever tried swimming under water since the healing?"

"No I can't say I have." Dave could feel himself getting excited. "This could work."

He ate a hurried breakfast, and then assembled a waterproof bag. He wanted to leave from the island side of the rock, but thought he ought to try swimming under water first.

Kelldor came to the water's edge and sat down.

"Dave, I need to give some instruction on how your body works. Your new body stores what you call oxygen, not only in the blood but also in a layer under the skin. When you enter the water, that extra oxygen is used to keep you alive. But after you have been under water for an hour or so, all of the reserves are gone and it takes several hours to replenish your supply. Once it is used up, you will only be able to stay under for minutes. Longer, of course, if you have had a few minutes to replenish your oxygen store."

"I get it Lord Kelldor. I have some kind of oxygen reservoir which I can draw on, but need to refill before I can use it again."

"So be careful."

"I will."

"I'm going with you," said Arlana.

"Now wait a minute."

"Don't be such an obstinate child, Dave. I have swum across already. I am used to swimming under water—you are not. At least not like this. I'm coming and that is all there is to it."

"Suit yourself." Dave stripped down to his bathing trunks and stepped into the water. It seemed cold but that passed quickly. He dove in and tested the bag to see if he had put enough rocks in to get near neutral buoyancy. It seemed pretty good.

The best way to answer these women is not to fight with them. I'll be across before she has time to get changed.

He heard a splash and a long lithe body shot past him, circled around and grabbed the other end of the bag.

Arlana touched his arm and he heard her voice in his head.

How are you doing, youngling?

I'm fine Arlana. I should be gasping for air but I'm not. I can't believe it. And another thing, I don't have my swim goggles but I can

see quite well without them. Much better than I could before. Dave thought back at her.

Let's go then.

She let go of his arm and headed out of the cave pulling on the dry bag. Dave kicked his legs and caught up with her. Brilliant sunlight shone around them as they swam into the channel between the two islands. Arlana headed right and skirted the rocks.

Dave marveled that he felt no shortness of breath and that his body had adjusted to the relatively cold water. He had expected to be shivering by now as his body fought hypothermia. They headed across the main channel toward Halcyon. Arlana was confident about the direction they should be heading, so they stayed about six feet under the surface. The water here was very deep. Dave saw a school of mackerel swim by in the depths but nothing else. After about ten minutes, Dave could see the bottom and knew they were approaching the shore. Arlana changed direction and Dave could hear the faint gurgle of water tumbling over rock. Arlana tugged on the dry bag and pointed to the surface. Dave broke the surface and anxiously looked around. Arlana had guided them to a heavily wooded creek.

Arlana climbed out of the water and sat on the shore gently kicking her legs in the water. She wrung the water out of her braid.

Dave found her presence intoxicating. He found it difficult to keep his mind on his work and his eyes stole back to watch her sunning herself, apparently unaware that he kept looking at her. He had taken his buckskin clothes out of the dry bag and laid them out on some bushes to keep them dry.

"I have to change."

"Oh," said Arlana. "I will climb up the bank and keep watch. I will whistle like a woodpiper if someone comes."

Dave didn't know what a woodpiper sounded like, but said nothing. He changed quickly when she disappeared through the brush. After wringing out his bathing suit, he stuffed it into the dry bag and hid it under a fallen log. He gathered some dry branches and made a mound over it so that it was no longer visible.

That ought to do it.

He climbed up the bank following Arlana. He found her at the top of the bank looking north.

She turned and smiled. "There is no one in sight. Be careful. I don't know how you will manage without me to look after you. You'll probably lose control of your skin color and be caught within the hour and then I will have to rescue you."

"Arlana, you should head back to the island. Don't even think about rescue. You don't know our customs; you would have no chance. The first time someone would recognize that you don't know what a flat screen or a telephone is, the jig would be up."

"The jig would be up?"

"It means your deception would be found out."

"Be careful, youngling." She gave him a peck on the cheek, climbed down to the shore, and then dove in.

Dave felt relieved. He took one more look around. He had an idea. He took out his hunting knife and cut down a long straight sapling and stripped off the branches. He got up and carried the stick like a fishing pole. First he cut through heavy brush to meet the road. Then he headed north toward East Harbor.

He began to pass the fields of the experimental farm and some of the workers waved to him. He waved back. When he got to East Harbor, he hid his fishing pole behind a shed and walked around the warehouses that were used for fish cleaning. He didn't know what to do. He saw some workers lining up. He lined up as well, hoping to fit in and earn a little bit of money while talking to his fellow workers to find out what had been happening. Halcyon had used as much of their American currency as they had in circulation. They supplemented that with a credit system. If he was going to eat or buy supplies, he would have to earn some of the money.

The student admitting people said, "Do I know you?" to the fellow at the head of the line.

"Probably not," said a scruffy looking youth. "My name is Glenn Wilcox. I'm just down from Wood Island and I wanted to earn a few extra bucks while I'm in town."

"Already blown your whole allowance while you're in town. Well, we can use all the help we can get. People hate the smell of fish guts and so there are never enough to get all the fish cleaned. The coveralls are just inside the door. Pick one that fits."

A few more logged in and then Dave was at the front of the line.

Now I find out if I asked Pam enough questions, to get me by.

"Name?" said the clerk.

"Donovan Barclay."

The clerk looked up.

"I'm also from Wood Island."

"You guys," said the clerk. "After weeks of cutting lumber and ferrying it back here, you're given a wad of cash and you seem to blow it the first couple of days."

"I'll know better next time," said Dave.

Dave cleaned fish all day and talked to everyone who was inclined to converse. Wood Island was a large island up the coast beyond the Halcyon River mouth. Since the mainland was off limits because of the Renegades, Halcyon had established a lumber camp there and ferried lumber back to the university. They had converted part of the Hobbes dormitory into a bunkhouse for these transient workers, so Dave had a place to sleep without having to go back to his old room.

The Hobbes dormitory was on the east side of campus, not far from East Harbor. He went there first to rent a room.

"You have some kind of nerve coming in here wearing your smelly fish-cleaning coveralls. Come back after you've cleaned up," said the woman behind the counter.

"I'm really sorry," said Dave, "I'm from Wood Island and I wanted to rent a room during my stay here. I have to go back and clean some more fish. Just give me a room and I promise I won't go up there until after I've cleaned up."

"You wood-cutters are all the same. You blow all your money as soon as you get back into town. Put your name here. Here's a piece of paper with your room number on it. We don't give out keys since they tend to walk, so just be aware anybody can get into your room. Take your money along with yuh whenever you go out."

Dave thanked the clerk and then went back to clean more fish. He saw several people in buckskin and so he figured he wouldn't be as conspicuous as he had feared in his travel clothes. After he had worked the rest of the afternoon, he showered, changed into his buckskins and moved his few belongings to his room. He then ate some of his provisions and waited until the sun began to go down.

He figured that Al was probably locked up in the old biology building, which had a lot of animal cages. A small structure (which had been converted to a pub) was across from the biology building. There he nursed a cup of Halcyon tea while he watched the entrance across the road. A few prisoners were escorted in by security but no sign of Al.

This is not going to work. It was a long shot anyway. Think, Dave, think!

He reviewed the situation.

Halcyon probably has a lot of prisoners by now, some political like Al and others who simply persist in being a public nuisance. But as a society they are still struggling to survive so they can't afford to just lock people up like we did back home. They will have to make them work. Where could they safely allow prisoners to work where they couldn't do a lot of damage? The experimental farm or the fish factory.

Dave decided to check out the experimental farm the next day. He hadn't seen anyone that looked like a prisoner at the fish factory but maybe they were in a separate building. He would check that option next time he went to earn some money. He decided he would head back to the cove where he had landed. He returned to the fish factory and picked up his fishing pole and headed down the road. He had to double back to find the trail from the shore. He used his pole to keep the bushes out of his face in the gloom under the trees. Eventually he reached the shore and found the rock where he had agreed to leave his message. He took the paper with his message out of his pocket and stooped to place it under the rock.

"Dave, is that you?"

The sound of the familiar voice lifted his heart. "Arlana, is that you?"

A dark shape rose from the brush and came toward him.

"How long have you been here?" asked Dave.

"I followed you to the road and then watched you as long as I could. I figured, youngling, you would need me to rescue you before the morning was out."

"I'll have you know," said Dave, "that I was enormously successful. I think I missed my calling as a spy. I also found a safe place to stay and I have the perfect cover story ..."

"Cover story?"

"A story invented to avoid suspicion. They have opened up a new island to supply wood to Halcyon and they have a constant stream of visitors coming to the mainland. So I pretended to have spent all my Halcyon dollars in wild living so I have to work at the fish plant to earn enough to keep me fed. I'm as safe as a mouse in a blind man's house."

Arlana was scowling and had her hands on her hips.

"Even a blind man may keep a cat."

"What I want to say," continued Dave, "is that it would be much safer if I didn't report in."

"Then how shall we know that you are not in need of rescue?"

"Arlana I can take care of myself."

"Youngling, you are like a bumbling child. I am sure they will have found you out within a week."

Dave felt himself getting angry. "Give me a week, Arlana. If I haven't come back by then, you'll have to make other plans. The best would be to give up on Al and head back to defend the Torburg."

Arlana crossed her arms and looked into his eyes. She bit her lip as if she were going to say something and changed her mind. Like a storm passing, her face changed and a tear glistened in the corner of her eye. She unfolded her arms and leaned forward to kiss him on his cheek.

"Be safe Dave." With that she turned and silently walked back to the shore.

Dave caught himself staring after her open-mouthed.

What was that all about? And I thought our women were strange!

He walked back to his room, trying hard to appear the weary fisherman at the end of the day. The room was sparse and the bed was the usual dorm bed, but Dave slept soundly, happy for a reason he couldn't explain.

Chapter 23

Trouble in Halcyon

Dave woke early the next morning. He headed off to work at the fish plant. A trawler came in and emptied its hold. The smell of fish was very strong in the air, but he had grown used to it.

I will probably never get a date and not even know why. I'm sure I smell to high heaven. After about an hour of hard work he spotted a face that seemed vaguely familiar. *Who is that?*

Dave didn't want to be caught staring so he chose to work on moving fish. This let him look at the newcomer. He was in blue coveralls, probably in his early twenties, but a thin beard and mustache made him look older. The most striking thing about him was the dark brown mass of curly hair, cut as an afro, that crowned his slender frame.

It's the beard. He never had the beard and mustache when I last saw him. It's Tom Chartrand.

Dave decided to take a chance. Tom apparently was checking the haul for new species, so Dave picked up a small three foot fish with a mass of tentacles around the mouth and carried it over to Tom.

"Is this a new species, sir?"

Tom looked up at Dave. His eyes were puzzled for a moment, and then went wide in recognition. He looked over his shoulder to see if they were being watched, then took the fish from Dave and examined it carefully.

"This is definitely an interesting specimen. What's your name?"

"My name is Donovan Barclay. I'm in from Wood Island, working to make ends meet, until I head back."

"Nice to meet you. I notice you take an interest in fish. You wouldn't happen to like fishing, do you?"

"I love to fish," said Dave.

"Great," said Tom. "Not many here do. Would you like to come along with me? I can show you a great spot."

"I would love that," said Dave.

"I was planning on going this evening. If you're interested, care to join me? When are you off your shift?"

"I'm only working half a day today. We could go this afternoon if you're free."

"I'm free Donovan. How does one o'clock sound?"

"I'll meet you here by the fish plant."

"Done."

At one o'clock Dave was lounging around the fish plant with his fake fishing pole waiting for Tom to show up. Soon after one, two figures carrying fishing poles approached. They were dressed in grubby coveralls and both had floppy hats that covered their faces.

That can't be Tom. Surely he didn't tell someone else.

It was Tom's voice that said. "Let's walk. I'll explain as we go." They walked in silence. When they were clear of the building, Tom said, "I'm sorry to spring this on you Dave, but I had to get you to meet Edward Makalo." His dark face, grinning a broad, white toothy smile, looked out from under the floppy hat. Makalo was a heavy set, short man.

"Good to meet you," said Makalo. "I made Tom bring me to you."

"You made him bring you to me?"

"He owes me a favor and I need to meet you."

Dave was annoyed and exhaled. "O-kaaay." He really didn't know what to say.

Tom took up the conversation. "It's extremely dangerous for you to be here Dave. Bigelow definitely doesn't like you. But I'm pretty sure you're here taking a chance because Pam sent you back to rescue Al."

Dave groaned inwardly.

Tom's expression changed as he watched Dave's face. "Don't worry Dave," said Tom. "Makalo is in on it, and knows about our search for Al."

Dave looked intently at Makalo. He seemed vaguely familiar. Dave pulled his thoughts back to the topic of conversation as he processed Tom's last statement.

"You mean you don't know where Al is?"

"As you probably know, Al was captured as Pam escaped with Little Thomas. Dwight and I had to lay low because we were afraid that Blackmore and his cronies knew that we had helped Al. We changed our appearance and stayed with friends most of the time, hardly ever going back to our official lodging. Still, we've been keeping an eye out for Al. At first, they made him work in the fields as part of a chain gang and fishing was our way to keep walking by without rousing suspicion. Then about three weeks ago he disappeared. He was no longer on the chain gang, but we don't know where he is."

"Did they send him off the island, do you think?" asked Dave.

"I can't be sure, but Dwight has hitched a ride up to Wood Island to see if they took him there. I kind of doubt it."

"So now what do I do, when you can't even find him? Pam will kill me and then try something stupid," Dave said half muttering to himself.

"Don't give up hope, but trust us," said Tom. "We're working at it as has hard as we can. You have really helped our planning by showing up since we didn't know how to manage Al's escape when we do find him. He couldn't stay here and we had no place to send him. Now we do."

"So how can I help?"

"The best thing is to stay out of our way. We'll keep searching and keep you informed. The longer you skulk around here, the greater the chance someone who knows you will report you to Bigelow."

"You mentioned Bigelow before. What's he got to do with this?" Dave remembered the confrontation he and Al had had with Bigelow on the mainland exploration trip.

"Bigelow has worked himself into chief honcho of our police force. He's a tricky piece of work and he's the one who ferreted out Al and nearly caught Pam and Little Thomas. Bigelow never forgets a slight and he knows you."

"Yeah that's bad news. Really bad."

They had left the road and were walking through a wooded area. The well-used path was still wide enough for them to walk abreast. Dave was thinking furiously.

If Bigelow has the network to keep tabs on Halcyon and found Al, he'll find me sooner or later. My guess is sooner. I have to play along and trust Tom.

"Okay Tom I'll play it your way."

Tom exhaled as if he had been holding his breath and Makalo flashed another dazzling smile.

"Good, good," said Tom. "Now for the reason I brought Makalo."

"Dave," said Makalo, "I had to come when Tom told me you're a relative of O'Reilly."

"I am," said Dave slowly. "Edward, do I know you?"

"Dave, call me Makalo—all my friends do. Do you know me? Well, I know you, Dave. I was trapped in the stockade at Botany Bay with your uncle, O'Reilly. I was the sentry that spotted the message you threw over the wall. If it weren't for you and O'Reilly, I'd be dead now."

Dave didn't know what to say.

Makalo continued. "He also said that you saw Hoffstetter soon after the explosion—is that also true?"

"That's right. I was with my uncle when the Dislocation occurred and we went to visit Hoffstetter in the hospital. What's this all about?"

Makalo glanced back to see if they were being followed and then pulled a piece of paper out of his breast pocket. "Did you by chance see this object?"

Dave handed his fishing pole to Tom and unfolded the paper. It was an image of a black object about twenty inches long judging by the pencil in the background. The object had red lettering on it.

"Yeah," said Dave slowly. "I remember this. Hoffstetter put it away just as we entered his room in the hospital right after the Hoffstetter Field Generator overloaded in the experimental area. I didn't get a good look at the lettering, but his secrecy piqued my curiosity as my uncle questioned him. I would say that's it."

"Do you know what Hoffstetter used the object for?" asked Makalo.

"No, I don't. But I remember, it sounded as if Hoffstetter were chanting or talking to someone when we were standing outside the door. There was no one else in the room and no other exit. I did not hear any other voices either, but still it was curious enough that I remember it now."

Makalo smiled. "Thanks, Dave. I am a physicist and was asked by Blackmore to study Hoffstetter's notes in order to try to get us all home. I found this object in Hoffstetter's safe—we had to break the safe open. The object seemed out of place right from the beginning. It felt like a heavy stick. So why would Hoffstetter keep a stick in his safe unless it had some extraordinary value?"

Dave grew very interested. "Go on."

"With Blackmore's backing, I could commandeer pretty well any analytical equipment still operating at Halcyon. I used X-ray, Magnetic Resonance Imaging, and high resolution neutron beam diffraction to analyze the object, as well as everything else I could use without destroying it. What I found was simply astounding." Makalo smiled broadly and showed the excitement of a boy with a new toy at Christmas.

Dave became impatient as the suspense built. "Come on Makalo, what did you find?"

"The stick is wood, but a kind of wood I have never seen before. The cellulose and DNA never matched any wood types we had in our catalog. Although the wood is very old and has not been exposed to water or sunlight for a long time, micrographs indicated that the cells in the wood were still alive."

"What?" said Dave. "How can that be? That has to be impossible."

"I'm just reporting the data Dave. To be honest, I thought so too, so I kept replicating the experiment and verifying it by other tests until I convinced myself. This wood is not like any other wood. It has unique structures in it—we can see them on electron micrographs."

"What kind of structures?"

"There are peculiar long carbon structures grown by the tree embedded in the cellulose. It almost looks like a nerve network except they're some kind of carbon nanotube—you know graphite wrapped into a cylinder. There's more. Let me give you a bit of background. I work with integrated circuits in silicon. This wood reminds me of them. I used a nanoprobe to test electrical properties. I identified conductive carbon nanotubes and other carbon structures that, from their voltage-current behavior, act as transistors. These structures are carbon-based transistors and there are millions of them. Bottom line–this plant grows natural integrated electronic circuits made of carbon allotropes."

"Allotropes?" asked Tom.

"Allotropes," said Dave, "are different versions of the same element with widely varying chemical and physical properties. They differ because the bonding between the atoms varies. Graphite and diamond are both allotropes of carbon. Bucky balls and carbon nanotubes are also allotropes of carbon."

"So let me get this straight," said Dave turning back to Makalo. "You're saying this wood from some kind of a tree, managed to grow carbon-based integrated circuitry."

"That's right."

"Are you kidding me?" Dave said softly, growing introspective.

"No I'm deadly serious. Physicists have used silicon and sometimes germanium for integrated circuits for many years. Carbon is in the same group in the periodic table. That means that carbon will have very similar electronic characteristics. Unfortunately, although we have tried, we have never succeeded in making practical integrated circuits from carbon. We have known for years that carbon nanotubes have semiconductive and conductive properties. But now, as always, nature's designs are so much better and more elegant than anything we can construct."

"But how can that ancient relic be alive?" asked Dave.

"Don't know. I was hoping you could tell me. It's puzzled me too. These organoelectronic structures penetrate all the way through this piece of wood and somehow play a role in keeping the wood alive, even when cut off from the rest of the tree."

Dave's mind was whirling.

Black wood. Meglir's obelisk deep in the cave at the City of the Dead. Trees that somehow connect to trees far away and let you travel large distances while you camp there. There must be a connection. Do I tell them? They'll think I'm crazy.

Dave chewed his lip and decided he wasn't going to put his cards on the table just yet. "Makalo, you said this wood has stayed alive without water or sunlight. How can you be sure of that?"

"Oh easy, Dave. I thought the micrographs were fooling me, particularly after the carbon-14 dating indicated that this piece of wood was at least seven hundred years old. To prove things one way or another, I sealed the wood in a long glass tube. I placed a wireless analytical microchip inside, so I could get a full analysis of the inside atmosphere without breaking the glass seal. With no air or water entering, the mass of the tube must stay the same. I accurately weighed the sealed tube and placed it in the dark and then later weighed it again. The tube continued to get heavier and heavier. There was more water and carbon dioxide inside. It had to come from somewhere else. Of course, I also ran a control. Ordinary wood, even if I used a live sample, showed no increase either of mass or pressure inside the tube."

They walked on, Dave lost in his thoughts, and entered a small glade in the forest. The path was cut by a small brook that bubbled and gurgled amid the long grasses and sedges. Dave concentrated on where to put his next step. On the other side, Tom left the trail and cut across the glade to enter the forest well to the left of their original heading. The dense brush and the narrow path gave Dave some hope they would not be followed. As a precaution, Tom stopped them—by raising his fist—every few minutes so they could listen for the sounds of anyone who might be following them.

When they finally reached the coast, they baited their hooks, put their lines into the water and huddled together. Dave had taken some fishing line from Tom, to make his pole look more like a real fishing pole even though he didn't have a reel. Dave could tell that Tom had a number of questions.

How am I going to answer him without jeopardizing the whole operation? What if they get caught?

"How did you get here Dave?" asked Tom. "Did you really come via Wood Island?"

"No, that's my cover story. Pam found me and told me about Al's capture. We came by boat and we have a hideout."

"You said 'we.' Do you mean Pam and Little Thomas came with you?"

Dave nodded.

"That woman! When she gets something into her head, there's no stopping her," muttered Tom.

Tom continued in a serious tone. "Listen Dave, you and Pam need to stay away from Halcyon. If Bigelow sees either of you, our only chance for Al's rescue will be lost. Ever since he captured Al, I'm pretty sure he's been waiting for Pam and her friends to make a move to rescue him."

"But Tom, Pam will never buy that. We didn't come all this way to stay away. Surely after all this time Bigelow's guard has dropped a little?"

"Let Dwight, Makalo and me do the leg work. Dwight should get back from Wood Island any day now. With any luck, Al will be there and the rescue should be easier since Bigelow's eye is squarely on Halcyon."

"In any case, you need to stay away at least until we figure out where Al is being kept."

"So how do Pam and I stay in the loop?" asked Dave.

"We'll use fishing," said Tom. "Where are you hiding?"

Dave hesitated. *I have to trust them.*

"We're hiding in the caves on Romulus."

"Great idea," said Tom. "That actually makes my plan easier. Every day either Makalo or I will go fishing within sight of Romulus. Not too close since we don't want to attract attention to the site. If we have news and want to talk, we'll hang our coat in plain sight. When you see that signal, take all due precautions. Make sure you're not followed, but come and see us after dusk. We'll give you the information."

"That should work."

They talked a while longer, then Dave bid them goodbye and headed south. Heeding Tom's advice, Dave did not return to the main road, but took a trail that skirted the shore. After a while, he came upon a path that he recognized and headed to the shore near the islands of Romulus and Remus. He looked around expecting Arlana to be waiting, but he didn't see her.

I guess she's gone back.

He found his cache, stored his work clothes, changed into his bathing suit and quietly entered the water. He swam all the way to the island under water. He had grown used to his new ability. When he finally came out of the water at the beach inside the cave, Pam was waiting for him, with Little Thomas standing in a small patch of sunlight from a crevice in the roof. She searched his face expectantly.

"I'm sorry Pam," said Dave, "I still haven't been able to locate Al." The disappointment in her face was evident. A tear began to form in the corner of her eye. "However, I made contact with Tom and they're already looking for Al. I'm quite encouraged now that they're involved."

Arlana joined them, a look of concern on her face. She handed Dave a towel and he sat down drying himself off. He told them the whole story from the time he had left for the main island. After he had described his meeting with Tom and Makalo, he said, "So you see, there's a good chance that Al has been moved to Wood Island—this new island they've discovered. If that's the case, it will be a lot easier to help him escape since, according to Tom, they don't have nearly the security there that we would encounter on Halcyon."

Pam brightened. "Tom and this new fellow Makalo have obviously been searching pretty thoroughly for Al on Halcyon, so it makes sense he was moved, as part of the work gang, to Wood Island to fell trees. That's good news."

"There's something else," said Dave. "I think this is actually why Tom took the chance of introducing Makalo to me. Makalo is a physicist who has been working to understand Hoffstetter's notes. Do you remember when I told you and Al about the day of the Dislocation?"

"Vaguely."

"Well when my uncle, Chancellor O'Reilly, and I went to see Hoffstetter at the university hospital we interrupted him as he was chanting. He had this odd object with red letters on it. I only saw it briefly as we came in, before he hid it away. Later, Al told me that he had heard the same weird chanting while Hoffstetter was camped on the wall of the City of the Dead before the expedition moved to occupy the citadel."

"Yes, Al told me about that as well," said Pam.

"Well, apparently, either Hoffstetter had a second version of that object or the object was returned to Halcyon. Anyway, Makalo found a similar object in Hoffstetter's safe at Halcyon."

Pam's eyes widened and Dave saw Arlana lean forward with interest.

"There's more. Makalo began to investigate the object. He said that it was in some ways like a piece of wood, but it also seemed to have natural carbon-based electronics grown into it."

"What?" said Pam.

"I know this is incredible and we've encountered some pretty amazing life forms in this world, but this has to take the cake—plant-grown, organic integrated circuits, based on carbon. But there's more. Makolo says the piece of wood is still alive. He sealed it in a dry tube and saw evidence for respiration with carbon dioxide and water building up. The tube gained weight as if water, oxygen and nutrients were coming in from outside, even though the wood was sealed inside a tube of thick glass."

"That makes no sense," said Pam.

"Perhaps It does," said Arlana. "You have seen Travel Oaks that brought us here." Dave nodded. "Travel Oaks use their ability to displace objects far away to share nutrients." A piece of Travel Oak would remain alive as long as the rest of the tree survived and had nutrients to share."

"But isn't that wood white?" asked Dave.

"Yes," said Arlana, "but there's another tree that I have read about called a Black Swamp Oak that has similar properties but is made of black wood—wood as black as night. It is said that Meglir's pillar is made of that black wood."

Chapter 24

Disappearances

"Dave. Dave." The words made Dave come wide awake from a deep sleep. The end of a long braid tickled his face. In the illumination of the light gourd he recognized Arlana.

"What's wrong?" said Dave, alarm filling his stomach with the hollowness of dread.

"Hush," said Arlana. "I don't think anything is wrong. Your friends Dwight and Tom are already at the fishing spot and I think they must want to talk. I thought I should wake you."

Dave was about to leap out of his blankets, but thought better of it. "I had better get dressed."

"Yes," she said the hint of a mischievous smile touching the corners of her mouth, "you had better get dressed little brother."

"I'm not your brother," said Dave. He could feel the color rising on his face. *I hope she doesn't see this. She's just trying to get my goat.*

"You're too immature to look after yourself, and so, as your adopted big sister. I have made it my mission and duty to look after you."

"You're neither big, nor my sister."

She laughed gently. Dave was delighted by the sound but tried valiantly to be infuriated by her insistence on managing his life like a big sister.

Arlana rose. "I'll keep an eye on your friends while you get ready to swim."

Dave threw off his covers and changed into his swimming trunks. He went directly to the cave that served as their beach and plunged into the water. The water was bracingly cold at first, but his body adapted quickly. He was able to see under water as if he had swim goggles on, and could see quite well even in the dim, scattered light of the underground passage.

He swam the whole way to the shore under water without his air reserve running out and emerged from the small creek. Searching in the dense thicket, at the edge of the creek, he found his work clothes and fishing pole and changed. Emerging from the thicket, he made his way casually along the shore.

When he joined the others, they said "hello" casually but Dave could see the look of surprise in Tom's eyes. Dave flung his line into the water and settled down between Tom and Dwight.

"I don't think we've been discovered or followed," said Tom.

"That's a relief," said Dave without looking at Tom. "It's great to see you Dwight."

"Wow, what a surprise to see you," said Dwight. "I've missed your homely face."

Dave laughed. "And here I thought it looked masculine. I've missed you too, Dwight."

"Listen Dave," said Tom, "Al isn't—and has never been—at Wood Island."

"Where is he then?"

"We think, he must still be here," said Tom. "Just before he attempted to leave with Pam, we helped him sneak into the primate area of the biology building." Tom told Dave about the captured Renegades and how Hyperhap was used to convert them into Bezerkers that could be controlled by voice command.

"There's something else," said Dwight. "I made friends with a former prison guard on Wood Island. He told me that Bigelow has a hidden compound near South Mountain. He uses it to train Renegades to become super warriors using Hyperhap injections to control them."

Dave felt dread wash over him. "Surely even Bigelow wouldn't do that to Al." Right after he had said it, he knew that's exactly what Bigelow would do if he had the chance.

Dave ran his hand through his hair as he tried to think about what to do next. "I'll have to go and check it out."

"Why you?" said Dwight. "It's too much of a risk."

"I have to tell you what has happened to me since we last parted." Dave told them the full story of how he met Arlana and how he had later been transformed into one of the Ancients. They were astounded.

"So you see, I'm going to go at night because my night vision is a hundred times better than yours now with my new and improved body, and if I'm spotted, I can always escape to the sea. If you're caught, Bigelow will have you doped up before you can say Abraham Lincoln."

Tom and Dwight looked as if they didn't believe Dave, but said nothing.

"Watch!" said Dave. He changed his skin color from his light tan to a darker brown.

He saw their eyes widen.

"Good grief," was all that Dwight was able to get out.

"Your story's incredible," said Tom.

"You're really determined to go?" added Dwight quietly.

"Yes I am. You'll see it's for the best. Dwight do you have any idea where the compound is?"

"No, other than it's somewhere on South Mountain."

"Well that makes my job difficult. Maybe I'll climb up the mountain at night and if I'm lucky, I'll see the lights of the compound and find them that way."

"So when do you plan on doing this?" asked Tom. "And how do we find out the results?"

"I'll go tonight. So let's meet here for fishing again tomorrow morning."

It was dusk when Dave again emerged from the water and donned his work clothes and headed through the bush. When he finally left the trees that blanketed the east side of the island of Halcyon, he followed a path crossing the fields that produced many of Halcyon's vegetables and grains. The workers had all left for the evening. South Mountain loomed ominously ahead of him. It would be unusual for anyone to go hiking on the mountain at night, so he looked around for suspicious eyes. On this cloudy night, someone would have to be quite close to see him. He had to remember the others didn't have his night vision, what appeared like twilight to him was really 'night' to everyone else except the Gurundar like Arlana. For a big man, he could move very quietly. He began to climb the mountain, heading for a lookout he knew on the north side. It was off the main path, but walking around South Mountain had been one of his favorite activities. He remembered this lookout because, with his fear of heights, it had frightened him badly when he had emerged from the game trail to a sheer drop appearing suddenly at his feet.

Thank the Lord I'm mostly over that fear now.

It hadn't come easily, but he had to force himself to confront the fear by little steps until it gradually subsided. After about twenty minutes he came to the place where he had to leave the path. Everything looked different in the dark. The path ended and he stood on the edge surveying the island of Halcyon. Down below and off to the left he saw a faint glow of artificial light. It came from a narrow ravine formed by two spurs on the north side of the mountain. The nearest spur started at the bottom of the cliff. He didn't relish climbing down in the dark, even with his improved night vision. The more distant spur would be much more accessible. He would have to make his way through the woods to reach it.

He worked his way through the dense forest. A fox ahead stopped unafraid. Dave smiled.

The fox doesn't know I can see him.

The fox vanished into the woods with only a light rustle. Dave finally made it to the top of the spur and climbed his way down. He felt much more exposed on the rocky ridge and knew if someone had night glasses down there, they would spot him. No alarm sounded. He finally edged over a ridge to look into a lit ravine. Figures were moving around in a fenced area. There were two kinds of people. The handlers wore uniforms; Dave could hear them issue commands to the Bezerkers. The Bezerkers had bulges on their arms—presumably the modified remote controlled insulin syringes that the handlers activated to achieve compliance from the Bezerkers by injecting doses of Hyperhap along with the commands.

Dave took his binoculars from his back pack and examined each Bezerker carefully. No Al.

Maybe they haven't brought him out yet.

Dave was very tired from his long vigil. It was about three o'clock in the morning. From time to time they brought out new Bezerkers for exercise. At the end of the night, they had a review and emptied the barracks for inspection. Dave could hear a handler call out that all the special forces were present and accounted for. Still no Al. Dave was disappointed; Al was still missing and he was running out of places to look. But he was also relieved; as long as he couldn't see Al, he assumed his friend hadn't been turned into a Bezerker.

After the lights in the compound had been shut down, he made his way carefully up the spur, rejoined the trail and walked back home. He was almost sleeping while on his feet. The trail came out of the woods and edged toward a cliff. He froze in his tracks as an icy hand seized his heart. Down below him in the narrow ravine he saw six lumbering shadows carrying a prone body like six pallbearers at a funeral.

Apemen! Meglir is already here.

His thoughts raced as he imagined the Apemen creeping up behind him, trapping him on the cliff. He prayed a silent prayer, asking for strength and courage. He felt no different, but he knew what he had to do to fight his fear—start doing his duty and he would feel better.

He dragged his thoughts away from his fear and decided he had to see where the Apemen were going. He crept along the edge of the cliff, keeping them in sight. The Apemen, with their burden, lumbered up the steep-sided ravine until they came to a rock fall. Dave lost them among the van-sized boulders. He waited to see if they would re-emerge, but none came out.

He waited until the first glimmer of dawn. No additional parties of Apemen appeared and he suspected any ambushes the Apemen had set, would be abandoned if Meglir wanted to keep his presence on the island a secret. Nevertheless, Dave watched for every possible ambush site and tried to think of where he would run at the first sign of trouble. He finally left the mountain, and with fear of discovery relegated to the back of his mind, Dave went straight to Tom and Dwight's dorm. The front door was open but no one was up yet.

Dave went up the side stairs and knocked on Tom's door. There was no sound and he knocked again. He finally heard a muffled "hold your horses" and heard movement within. The door opened to reveal Tom in his housecoat.

Tom's eyes widened and he pulled Dave into the room, looking up and down the hallway to see if anyone had seen him. Dwight, just coming out of the bathroom, stopped when he saw Dave.

"Dave—what are you doing here? I thought…"

"Guys, I've seen Apemen. I had to come over right away."

"You've seen Apemen," repeated Tom trying to shake off his lethargy.

"Yes, I've seen Apemen."

"Where?" said Dwight.

"Here on Halcyon—on South Mountain. They were carrying a body."

Tom collapsed on the bed. Dwight leaned against the door frame.

"What are we going to do now?" moaned Tom.

Dave sat on the bed beside Tom. "Look guys, I know this is a shock, but we still have time to make a difference. If Meglir was ready to attack, he would have attacked already. It seems to me he's building up his numbers by capturing some of our people. He must be waiting for something."

Tom sat up. "This doesn't make sense. Why would Meglir risk tipping us off even if he swells his own ranks a little? The missing people must be reported. I know some are out at Wood Island, but someone would notice it and report it. The head of security would know."

"Bigelow!" said Dwight venomously. "Biglow must know Meglir is here. I'm sure reports will come to Bigelow, he'll pretend to investigate and complete the necessary paper work, but it won't go any further."

Dave stood up and began to pace. "Things are worse than I thought," he said. "If Bigelow is a fifth column within Halcyon, then we have almost no chance to defend ourselves. Our only hope is to convince Commander MacDonald that there's an imminent threat and get him to check it out by himself. Tom you need to go see MacDonald as soon as possible. But do it quietly."

"Hmm," said Tom. "It makes sense. I'll go right away. Wait a minute. You haven't told us about Al. Was he at the camp?"

"No," said Dave, "I checked the camp out thoroughly. They exercise the Bezerkers during the night. Al wasn't there, so I'm pretty sure he's not in the camp."

"If Al's not on Wood Island and he's not at the camp, where is he?" asked Dwight.

"He's either in the holding area in the biology building or he's on the mainland," said Dave quietly.

"He can't be on the mainland," said Tom. "Sure Bigelow may know about Meglir and maybe a couple of his close confederates may also know, but if a Bezerker who's being charted by the whole medical team were to disappear, everyone would ask unpleasant questions."

"Maybe Bigelow has handed him over to Meglir and he's already an Apeman," said Dwight.

That possibility shocked Dave to his core. "We don't know if that's the case. Bigelow may deliberately be using Al as bait to lure us to him. Bait has to be recognized by the victim to work. Still, if Bigelow has Al drugged in the biology building, it may only be a matter of time before he delivers him to Meglir. We have to move fast."

"Besides," said Tom, "Bezerkers may be of more use to Meglir in the long run than Apemen. He doesn't have a supply of Hyperhap, nor insulin injection devices right now, so he has no way to control the Bezerkers. Still, I'm willing to bet my last Halcyon dollar that Bigelow will have the Bezerkers fighting for Meglir when the attack begins."

"Okay," said Dave, "I'm going to have to report to the gang on Romulus, but tonight I break into the biology building and follow in Al's footsteps. Al has to be there—we've looked everywhere else."

Tom looked at Dwight. "Not without us you're not. I have Sturgeon's passkey remember."

"Okay, okay, I'll be back just before dark."

"This is really a dumb idea," said Dave to the cloaked figure at his side.

"Someone has to look after you, little brother."

"I keep telling you I'm not 'little,' and I'm not your brother."

Arlana looked up at him and smiled. Dave found it absolutely infuriating but what could he do about it? A troubling thought struck him. *I have made a career out of needling and aggravating my friends. Now Arlana is giving me my own treatment in double doses. Am I taking my own medicine?*

"I'm surprised your father is letting you go," said Dave.

"My father has taken his Dorai back to Goose's Beak."

Dave knocked on the door and Tom's face peered out at him. When he saw Arlana next to Dave his eyes widened. "Come in," he said hastily as he opened the door.

Dave and Arlana went in and Tom waved them to a couple of chairs. He also sat down; he didn't say a word but looked intently at Dave.

Dave didn't know how to begin, so the silence grew awkward. Finally Tom said, "Do you mind telling me what's going on?"

"Where's Dwight?" asked Dave.

"He's over at Sturgeon's office checking out a few things."

Just then the door opened and Dwight came in. He shut the door and said, "We should be good to go ..." when he saw Arlana sitting in the corner. He froze.

"This is Arlana," said Dave. "She's a friend of mine."

"Hello Arlana," said Dwight awkwardly. Dwight sat down and Dave looked from one to the other. Both their eyes were riveted on Arlana. She had taken off her cloak and wore a dark green ranger's outfit that fit her snugly. Dave had to admit she was beautiful even in that very practical garb.

What's with these guys? Why are they staring at Arlana is if they were shipwrecked sailors who hadn't seen a woman in ten years?

Arlana looked at Dave as if to say "Well aren't you going to explain things? Or will I have to do it?"

Dave spread his hands in exasperation. "You're probably wondering why I brought Arlana over." He saw Arlana roll her eyes. "Actually I didn't bring—she insisted on coming and I would have had to tie her up to stop her."

"Well Arlana," said Tom. "It's a pleasure to meet you. Dave told us the story yesterday, but he didn't tell us how beautiful you were. I think he's trying to keep you for himself."

Arlana smiled and Dave could feel his face grow warm.

"And so when I went back to Romulus after our last meeting, I told Arlana about my plans. I knew if I told everyone, then Pam would insist on coming and I couldn't have that. So Arlana insisted on joining me and threatened to follow me if I tried to leave her behind."

"Unbelievable!" said Tom.

"I know what you mean" said Dave. "How could she come along and threaten the whole enterprise?"

"No, I meant about what you told us yesterday about the Ancients who live hundreds of years, this ability to swim under water for long periods of time, and this plant that grew your arm back."

"May I see you change your skin color?" asked Dwight. "If I'm not being too rude or too personal."

"Of course you're not being rude," said Arlana in perfect English. She rapidly changed her skin color from very pale tan to a dark chocolate brown.

Dave tried to do the same. He had learned to keep his former skin hue, but couldn't change with the ease or precision of Arlana. He obviously did enough to startle Dwight and Tom. Even seeing it for a second time, they were surprised.

"Unbelievable!" murmured Tom again. There was stunned silence.

"So when do we begin to look for Pam's Al?" asked Arlana sweetly.

"This is not a good idea," said Dwight.

"Shall we tie her up until we get back?" asked Dave eagerly. Arlana shot him a blistering look.

"Arlana, would you be willing to stay here until we get back?" asked Tom.

"I will go wherever Dave goes. If he stays here, I will also stay here. He needs someone to look after him. He's not very sensible in a dangerous situation."

Dave threw up his hands in exasperation.

"We may as well let her come," said Dwight thoughtfully. "This scheme is hare-brained enough, without trying to restrain Arlana. We'll take her along and take a chance that unfamiliarity with our customs won't give us away."

Dwight looked at his watch. "Okay let's go. Everyone except the night watch will have gone home and we should be able to check out the facility without too much interference."

"What happens if we find him?" asked Dave. "How do we get him out?"

"Al's not that big," said Tom. "Dwight and I will head down first and we have a wheel chair hidden in Sturgeon's office. Even if Al is drugged, you and Arlana can manhandle him into the dumbwaiter and then Dwight and I should manage to get him into the wheelchair. We'll wait until you're down and then head out together. We have a boat hidden just off Romulus to row him over. We'll get it back tomorrow before it's missed."

"See Dave, it's good that I'm along; you would never manage to load Al yourself," said Arlana.

Dave grunted in disagreement. They headed out and walked as casually as they could over to the biology building. The parking lot was deserted when they came to a side entrance. Dwight had a keycard and the lock clicked. Dave and Arlana followed Dwight, while Tom watched from the shadows to see if anyone had observed them. Apparently satisfied, he entered and closed the door behind them.

"Won't the opening of this door register on the security guard's station?" asked Dave.

"If the system hasn't broken down yet, I would say 'yes.' However, Dwight and I often work this time of night, so I don't think this will raise undue suspicions."

"Can they shut us down and lock us in, if they get suspicious?" asked Dave.

"I don't think so," whispered Tom. "All the doors can be opened from the inside in case of fire. Also, I learned when I read his personal journal, that Sturgeon had insisted on a master access card with a chip, so he could rescue any of his grad students if they got into a dangerous situation. I guess he argued that if he was going to be responsible for their safety, he had to have access to whatever room they had to be working in. So this access card apparently overrides the security shut off, so they can't shut us out unless they've changed the system. I don't think the higher ups even know about this arrangement."

They came to Sturgeon's office and Dwight opened the door. After locking Sturgeon's outer office door from the inside, they used another door in the office to access Sturgeon's lab. From the lab they could access the feed storage area that had the dumbwaiter that they needed.

"The big fish tanks that we regularly service from here are downstairs," said Dwight, "so for us to be going upstairs to the primate holding area would appear unusual to anyone who knows our work pattern well.

"I'll go up first," said Dwight. "If it's all clear, I'll send down this feed bucket. Tom and I thought long and hard about whether we should all stick together or leave you here. If we all go together, we can search faster, and if we have to escape another way, at least we leave together without stranding you two."

Dave nodded as Dwight climbed into the dumbwaiter. Soon the feed bucket came back and Tom followed. Arlana was next and finally Dave. Everyone was crouching behind a lab bench when Dave slid to the floor. Dwight skittered forward in a crouch until he came to the door. He waved and stood up. They entered the large room that held the holding cells.

"You and Arlana check the holding cells in this room," whispered Tom. "I'll check the pen and Dwight will check the associated rooms."

Dave looked around. In the center of the large room was a smaller room which looked like a fully equipped operating theatre. It was empty. He touched Arlana's arm and motioned toward the bank of cells around the outside.

They found Al in the second cell. Obviously sedated, he had the orange hue of a Happenone addict. Dave immediately went to him and tried to wake him. No response. There were two feeds into the IV, one was Happenone and the other was likely a sedative, although Dave didn't recognize the name.

Dwight and Tom appeared with Arlana.

Good girl! She found the others. I can always count on her to do the right thing in a tight spot.

Tom came over directly and lifted Al's eye lids.

"Dwight, he's pretty heavily addicted already, judging by the eye color. Pam is going to have to figure out how to detox him. Find as much Hyperhap as you can, some sedative and Sedovarin. Hopefully that's all she'll need. I don't want to come back up here after tonight." He unhooked the IV bag from the stand and Arlana took them from his hands. Dwight and Dave carried Al, while Tom led the way with Arlana keeping pace. Al was surprisingly light. They placed Al on the floor.

"Keep the IV about this height Arlana," said Tom and then he climbed into the dumbwaiter. When the dumbwaiter returned, Dwight followed. They next loaded Al into the dumbwaiter and placed the IV bags on his chest. Arlana and Dave were able to follow without any problem. When Dave arrived in the lab, they already had Al muffled in a cloak in a wheel chair with the IV bags hanging unobtrusively from the back.

"Okay let's go," said Tom. "I'll push. Dwight you check if the coast is clear."

They exited the building and made their way across the parking lot.

"We have a borrowed electric car around the corner," whispered Dwight. "It won't hold five of us though." Dwight rushed ahead and looked around the next corner. He waved the all clear.

"STOP!" The shout chilled Dave to the bone. He turned around and saw four campus security guards moving toward them from the biology building. Tom and Dwight had already pushed Al around the corner of the building.

Maybe they haven't seen the wheel chair. I've got to buy them time!

He ran down a side street and emerged in full view of the guards. He heard Arlana following him. The guards pointed at them.

"Run for it!"

He sprinted looking back. Arlana was keeping pace and it looked like all of the guards were following them.

Break contact, go to ground, and then calmly walk back to the shore.

"Can you run faster?" gasped Dave.

In answer Arlana sprinted faster. Dave also increased his pace. He took them through an alley to the chemistry building he knew well. He saw what he wanted. He climbed up on a dumpster and helped Arlana up.

"Up on that low roof," he whispered as he helped her climb up to the roof. He jumped for the roof and pulled himself up by main strength and then pulled her flat onto the middle of the roof. In a few seconds he heard the pounding of feet. The sound receded. The men were breathing hard.

He listened for any sound. Since his hearing was much more acute than it used to be, he figured would hear breathing if they were close and were trying to surprise him. He crawled and peered over the edge of the roof. It was all clear. He let himself down and then helped Arlana down as well.

We've got to find people and disappear in the crowd. The Student Union Building and the pubs there will still be crowded.

He put his arm around her waist and pulled her close. She looked up at him. "What are you doing?" she whispered.

"We have to be lovers on our way to a night out at the pub. That's why we're out so late."

She put her arm around his waist and snuggled close. *Wow, it feels good to have her so close. Keep your mind on the business at hand, Dave!*

They reached the Student Union Building and went inside to the engineering pub. He found them a table one row from the window, and ordered two beers. He watched the door. He saw no sign of the campus patrol.

Finally, he saw what he was waiting for: a large group of people rose to leave. Dave quickly left some of the money he had earned at the fish plant on the table. "Come on. We have to go." He followed the group out the door. Most of the others knew each other. He put his arm around Arlana and pulled her into an embrace, waiting while the group members said "good-bye." Some of them headed in the direction of the dorms near East Harbor. Dave again put his arm around Arlana's waist and sauntered after that group. They eventually dispersed and Dave began to breathe a sigh of relief as they were quite a distance from the biology building.

He rounded a corner and his heart caught in his throat. Four campus patrol men were waiting for him with stunners drawn.

"Dave Schuster," said Bigelow's voice. "Fancy meeting you here."

"Run!" Dave pushed Arlana back around the corner and lunged at Bigelow. He felt the searing pain of one stunner hit but he didn't go down. A second stunner hit him as he landed a crunching fist in Bigelow's startled face. The last thing he remembered was the crackle of a third stunner bolt.

Chapter 25

The Winds of War

Glenn MacDonald, the acting naval commander of Halcyon, was not happy. His sources had informed him that several of his men had disappeared. When he had talked to Stan Bigelow, the head of the campus patrol, he had been told that they were following leads, but that some of the missing people had left Halcyon of their own free will.

MacDonald had just come back from a meeting with Nevil Sanderson, the official head of the navy station detachment, and now an elected member of the Halcyon Senate. Sanderson had looked like he had aged thirty years and had effectively told MacDonald to mind his own business, and leave things in Bigelow's capable hands. However, MacDonald thought the situation stank so badly one could smell it upwind in a hurricane, but all he kept hearing was "mind your own business."

There was a knock at the door and Anders Norgaard, his Chief of Staff poked his head in.

"What is it Anders?"

"Sir, Tom Chartrand is waiting to see you. He says it's of the utmost urgency."

MacDonald ran his fingers over his eye brows. "Chartrand—where have I heard that name before?"

"He was with us at the Battle of City Point."

"Oh yes, now I remember. I guess I should see him. Show him in."

Norgaard brought Chartrand into the room. Chartrand's clothes were rumpled and he looked like he hadn't slept or showered in a couple of days. MacDonald rose, came around his desk and offered his hand.

"Commander MacDonald, good of you to see me without an appointment," Tom said as he shook MacDonald's hand firmly.

"Not at all, Tom. I am still grateful for the brave role you and your friends played in extricating us all from that nasty encounter with the Apemen in the City of the Dead. We might all be Apemen now, if you and your furry friends—what were they called?"

"*Hansa.*"

"Yes, *Hansa*, had not come to rescue us from that attack through that tunnel under the water."

Tom appeared relieved. "That's why I've come, Sir. The Apemen are back."

MacDonald felt a cold fist grab his heart. "What do you mean 'they're back'?"

"They've been seen," said Tom, "on South Mountain. They're grabbing people again and converting them to Apemen."

"How did they get to South Mountain?" MacDonald couldn't keep the dread out of his voice.

"My guess is they are using the same trick that we observed at the City of the Dead, directing a Rock Borer to tunnel under the channel."

"But that's at least six miles." MacDonald stopped himself, straightened up in his chair and began again. "Look Tom, you had better tell me the whole story from the beginning."

Tom took a deep breath. "Sir, do you remember after the Battle of City Point how some of our company went upriver to found a new colony?"

MacDonald smiled. "Yes of course."

Well," said Tom. "They discovered an island and founded a colony with the *Hansa* called Eleytheria." Tom went on to tell about Al Gleeson's capture, their search for him, and Dave's discovery of the Apemen.

"So that's the whole story Sir," said Tom.

"That's quite a story containing some very serious allegations," said MacDonald, "Al Gleeson seized and drugged with Happenone against his will. Bigelow with a personal vendetta against Gleeson. These new people, the Ancients. And now Schuster and this Arlana disappearing after Gleeson's rescue.

"You haven't told me where Gleeson is now."

"That's true Sir. He's in hiding. I've made a promise and much as I'd like to, I can't tell you where he is right now."

MacDonald could feel himself getting annoyed. "So what am I supposed to do? I can't just go on your word, much as I'd like to Tom."

"I know some of the things I've told you are hard to believe—perhaps impossible to believe. I'm hoping you'll suspend your disbelief in those parts of my story long enough to investigate some of the things I've said about Bigelow and Apemen on Halcyon for yourself, Sir. That's all I'm asking."

MacDonald steepled his fingers and thought briefly again about Bigelow and his evasiveness about the disappearances. "Alright, seems fair. Leave it with me. How do I contact you?"

"I'm going to be lying low Sir. I have a locker at the gym." He slid a piece of paper across the desk to MacDonald. "If you drop a message into that locker, I'll arrange for a meeting, either here or somewhere else. Other than that, now that local cellphone service has been restored, I'll turn on my cell phone from time to time and call you from a location where my call won't give anything away." Tom rose and shook MacDonald's hand. "Thank you, Sir, for hearing me out."

"This conversation never happened. Look after yourself, Tom," said MacDonald.

After Tom left, MacDonald called Norgaard into his office. "Anders, I have to go out. Do we have any fuel left for the Boston Whalers?"

"I've kept some in reserve for an emergency, Sir."

"I think this qualifies Anders. Would you get a boat ready? I want you along and two others—veterans of the river expedition. Can you do that?"

"Yes, Sir!"

"And another thing, Anders. I'm going over to the detention center. Isn't our naval medical officer assigned over there?"

"Yes, Sir. You must mean Dr. Kherry Carter."

"Please call him and let him know I'm coming. I want this to be an unofficial visit."

"Yes Sir. Right away, Sir.

When MacDonald reached the outside of the detention center, he called Carter's extension. "Hello Kherry, this is Commander MacDonald."

"Hello Commander, I've been expecting your call. There's no need for you to check in at reception. I'll meet you at the employees' north entrance."

There were a few electric cars in the parking lot. Most had a badly painted Campus Patrol insignia on them, indicating they had been commandeered after the gas powered vehicles became useless. The flower beds were mostly infested with weeds and cracks were beginning to show in the pavement.

The detention center was a square building next to the campus patrol main building. It had previously been an office building for the parking authority, which had been a division of the campus patrol. Now apparently the offices had been converted to cells and guard stations. He wondered how they managed bathrooms when the building hadn't been designed for self-contained cells.

When he rounded the corner he saw Kherry Carter. His chocolate brown face bore a pair of heavy glasses and his expression was serious, even worried. He was wearing a white lab coat and saluted as MacDonald approached. "Commander!"

"At ease Lieutenant," said MacDonald. "Might we go to your office?"

"Of course Commander. This way." Carter held the door for MacDonald and then went up four flights of stairs. His office was on an outside wall, facing north."

MacDonald followed Carter into his office. Carter looked even more serious as MacDonald closed the door.

"May I sit down Kherry?"

"Of course, Sir."

MacDonald took the visitor's chair and gestured Carter to his own chair behind the desk.

When they were settled, MacDonald leaned forward. "Kherry, I'm responsible for the safety of Halcyon. I'm talking to you in that capacity now."

"Sir?"

"In the early days of the Dislocation, Commander Sanderson had control of both the naval station and the campus patrol, but now Commander Sanderson is taken up with his duties in the Senate. I am responsible for our naval forces, and Bigelow is effectively in charge of the campus patrol."

"But both are under Commander Sanderson."

"Correct," said MacDonald. "I am saying this to remind you that you are a naval officer and that you are still under my command even though you have been seconded to Bigelow. Is that clear?"

"Yes, Sir!"

Beads of sweat had begun to appear on Carter's face. MacDonald pressed on. "As I said, I have responsibility for the safety and security of Halcyon and the questions I'm going to ask you are motivated by that responsibility even though I cannot fill you in on the details of my concerns at this time. Understood?"

"Yes Sir!"

"There have been some mysterious disappearances from Halcyon. Have you heard of them?"

"There has been no official communication from Bigelow, Sir, but there has been scuttlebutt in the hallway."

"What have you heard Carter?"

"The word is that Bigelow isn't too concerned about the disappearances. He thinks they're people who have gone stir crazy being cooped up on Halcyon and have stolen boats and are camped out on the Channel Islands or one of the islands on the Halcyon River. Once they get hungry and tired of their camping trip, they'll be back. Apparently several boats are missing."

"Did you know that a couple of our people are among the missing?"

"No Sir, I did not."

"Well they went missing overnight—it's highly unlikely that they stole a boat to go fishing on a lark."

"I agree Sir. I unfortunately don't know anything about the other disappearances. Normally for ongoing investigations, I would hear more details than I have for this one. I think Bigelow is being rather tight-lipped."

MacDonald sat back in his chair and steepled his hands as he thought about this. He didn't like the sound of it at all. *Just too much mystery and secrecy.* He had a bad feeling about this and his feelings were usually right.

He leaned forward again. "Another thing Carter, I heard that a man and a woman were taken into custody yesterday. Do you know anything about that?"

"Oh you mean the squids?" Carter's face lit up with enthusiasm.

"Squids—as in Navy? What do you mean?" asked MacDonald.

"Oh, I see the confusion. It's just a nickname the medical staff gave them because they can change skin color like squids."

"You'd better tell me the whole story," said MacDonald leaning back in his chair again.

Carter cleared his throat. "I guess it was fairly late about five days ago when Bigelow came in with a couple of prisoners. The prisoners had been stunned and were unconscious. Bigelow was furious…"

Carter broke into a long laugh. "His face was swollen the size of a melon. Apparently Dave Schuster, the fellow they had brought in, had to be stunned three times before he went down…"

"Are you sure?"

"I'm sure."

"I've been hit by a stunner …"

"Believe me Sir, I'm sure." MacDonald gestured for Carter to go on. "Well apparently Schuster, even after the second stun had made it up to Bigelow and landed a wallop. Schuster must carry some punch—Bigelow is a big guy.

"Anyway it was late and they were carried into their holding cells. Everyone except me and a few of the night guards went home. I went into Schuster's cell, worried that three stun charges might have seriously hurt him. I lifted his eyelid to check his pupils' response to light and his skin color went from white to dark brown like mine. It freaked me out.

"I went over to the other cell to look at the blonde bombshell, I mean the woman prisoner, and she had the same response when I illuminated her pupils. Well the scientist in me was intrigued. I had really stumbled onto something new. I took advantage of their unconscious state, and with a couple of nurses, took blood samples, and completed Magnetic Resonance Imaging as quickly as possible. I also sent their blood samples for DNA sequencing."

"So what did you learn?" asked MacDonald.

"Well, those two may look human, and for the most part they are, but they have a few organs and structures that we don't. For example, just under the skin they have what are called chromatophores, bundles of pigmented cells controlled by muscles. When their skin is white, the pigmented cells are all contracted into a dot so that all you see is the non-pigmented region as you would in a Caucasian that doesn't have a tan. However when these muscles elongate or expand, the pigments spread out over a large area, giving dark brown coloration. I think Schuster and the woman (her name is Arlana) can control their color when they're conscious. They've stayed the same color ever since they woke up. I don't think they know that we know their secret. These structures have been seen before in cephalopods. That's why the nurses and I have been calling the two of them squids."

"That's unbelievable!" said MacDonald. "Schuster's one of us."

"There's more. They have another deeper layer under their skin and also a layer around their liver which looks like a biopolymer of hemoglobin."

"Okay do you know what that does?"

"I'm guessing, but I would bet if you tried to drown them, they could hold their breath a lot longer than you or I could. They have all this excess oxygen stored up the way we store glycogen in the liver to replenish our glucose in a long distance run. They can replenish the oxygen in their blood stream from their reserve."

"Anything else?"

"Well the cephalopod connection made me look for other related structures. They also seem to have photophores just as squids do. There's a chance they can produce bioluminescence although I haven't seen it."

"Anything else?"

"That's all I have now. I'm waiting for the DNA results. I would love to put them under for more tests, but now that they're conscious I would have to ask their permission and I'm pretty sure they wouldn't give it. I suppose I could force them to undergo the tests, but in the face of a denial, I think that would be unethical."

"Carter, I reminded you before that you are first and foremost a military officer."

"Yes, Sir."

"I want you to keep this quiet, especially from Bigelow, on my order. Is that clear?"

"Yes, Sir. Absolutely."

"Don't conduct any more tests on either of them. Schuster is a personal friend of mine. He saved my bacon at the Battle of City Point so I owe him one. Is that also clear?"

"Yes Sir!"

MacDonald rose. "You've made a stupendous discovery under very difficult circumstances. You are to be commended." MacDonald saluted and then let Carter show him out the side entrance. He took his electric car directly to the naval station on the south side of the island. When he arrived, the Boston Whaler was ready to go. The breeze was coming from the northeast. He had the crew head north, wanting to let the boat drift past the shoreline directly across from South Mountain. As the sun went down, they put on their night vision goggles and used the motor to get them into position. When MacDonald saw that they were close enough, he had the motor cut and let the wind carry them in. For an hour they saw nothing, then they passed a rocky promontory on the mainland just opposite South Mountain. Just past this promontory MacDonald caught a glimpse of movement. He increased the magnification of his night vision goggles.

Hidden in the woods, behind the promontory so that they would be invisible even to observers from South Mountain, MacDonald could see the construction of a fleet of longboats. The figures around the boats were Turncoats—members of his own team that had gone over to Meglir. He kept looking and he was sure he also saw the lumbering gait of Apemen as they dragged up logs for the construction. He kept watching for another two hours and then gave the command to start the engine as they slowly edged back to mid-channel and home.

When he reached the naval base at South Harbor on Halcyon, he went straight to his office. Anders Norgaard was already at his desk.

"Anders, arrange a meeting for me with Commander Sanderson and Blackmore. Tell them it's priority one."

"Yes, Sir."

"And Norgaard, this is urgent. Don't take 'no' for an answer. Is that clear?"

Norgaard gulped and turned a little paler. "No Sir, I won't take 'no' for an answer."

"I'm dead tired so I'll sleep on the cot in my office. Wake me as soon as you find them. I don't care where they are or what they're doing. Wake me when you get the appointment or failing that, find out where they are!"

Chapter 26

Traitor for a Higher Cause

The knock on the door woke MacDonald from a sound sleep. His groggy mind processed his surroundings and then he remembered last night. He shot up and opened the door. It was Norgaard. "What time is it?"

"It's ten hundred sir."

"Norgaard, what took so long."

"Sir, shall we move so I can explain on the way?"

MacDonald looked at his sweaty, rumpled fatigues.

"Do you need to change sir?"

"No, let's go; this can't wait."

As they walked to the electric car, Norgaard began his explanation. "Sir, I called Blackmore's office right away. Blackmore's executive assistant wanted to book the appointment tomorrow and I told her you needed to see Blackmore and Sanderson immediately. She wasn't happy and she hung up. I finally sent two sailors to her, to stand over her desk. I wanted to go myself, but I thought I needed to be here to explain our status. One of the sailors just called me. Blackmore and Sanderson are in a Senate meeting and will come out briefly when you arrive."

MacDonald swore under his breath. "Unbelievable! Do they think I'm making this fuss without reason?" He had said this before he realized he was speaking out loud. "Bring a couple more men."

Norgaard drove the e-car to the main administration building. MacDonald ran up the steps two at a time and the others hurried after him. Slowing down before he reached the outside of the Senate chambers on the second floor, MacDonald straightened his uniform as well as he could. He realized he looked a mess.

One of Blackmore's lackeys waited outside the Senate. "I'm here to see Chancellor Blackmore and Senator Sanderson on urgent business," said MacDonald.

Blackmore's official looked Macdonald up and down, a hint of disdain touching the corners of his mouth. "I'm afraid the Senate is still in session, Commander MacDonald. They will see you as soon as there's a break."

MacDonald exploded. He filled the air with expletives he hadn't used since he was a midshipman. MacDonald looked around and saw that all of the sailors had followed and had their arms crossed with scowls on their faces. The man blocking the doorway blanched and edged out of the way. "I need to see them now," said MacDonald. "Not ten minutes from now, but now. Either you open that door and call Blackmore and Sanderson out, or I'll go in myself and make a scene. Take your pick."

The official scurried through the heavy oak doors, producing a solid thud as they closed behind him.

MacDonald was just about to go in himself when the official, Blackmore, Sanderson and Bigelow came storming out of the council chambers. MacDonald sighed inwardly. He didn't want Bigelow part of this conversation. He just didn't trust the man.

Blackmore's brow was creased with fury. "What's the meaning of this, MacDonald? What are you doing disrupting a Senate meeting?"

"Meglir's Apemen are on the island," said MacDonald coldly and deliberately.

"What?" said Sanderson, growing alarmed.

"Have you actually seen Apemen on Halcyon Island, or is this somebody's hare-brained report?" asked Bigelow.

MacDonald looked at Bigelow coldly and then turned to Sanderson. "Sir, I completed a reconnaissance last night of the coast opposite South Mountain. I saw Turncoats and Apemen with my own eyes," said MacDonald.

"So you haven't seen them on Halcyon," said Bigelow a gleam of satisfaction in his eyes.

"No," said MacDonald, "the sightings on Halcyon are reports, but given the disappearances of people from our midst, and my sightings ..."

"The disappearances are being investigated by my people and they're not due to Apemen," growled Bigelow.

"So what do you suggest we do?" asked Blackmore as he turned from Bigelow to MacDonald.

"We need to put a protective cordon around South Mountain immediately. We also need to prepare for an attack on their settlement on the mainland to take out their ships before they can attack us."

"Wait a minute," sputtered Bigelow.

"This is not your decision Bigelow, this is a military matter," said MacDonald.

Bigelow shut his mouth. Blackmore pulled on his goatee in thought. MacDonald looked at Sanderson who appeared uncomfortable and averted his gaze.

What's wrong with Sanderson?

"I think," said Blackmore slowly, "that your idea of a protective cordon around South Mountain is a good precautionary measure. Draft up a plan for your attack and present it to Commander Sanderson and me for consideration. But under no circumstances proceed with the attack until you receive our approval. Is that understood?"

MacDonald looked at Sanderson questioning. He said nothing.

"Is that understood?" asked Blackmore again with venom in his voice.

"Understood," said MacDonald. He turned and walked away.

"What are we going to do sir?" asked Norgaard.

"I want an immediate cordon around South Mountain. When we get back we'll look at the map. We'll put up barriers, find all the reserve personnel we can and man the access points."

"I don't know if we have enough for such a large area."

"We won't, Norgaard, and I don't want our people alone. Have them doubled up—so they'll be spread even thinner. Our main objective is to keep Halcyonites away from the mountain. Since we can't cover that much territory, make sure our people at least block the roads."

They passed the gym complex. "Listen Norgaard, you take the e-car and head back to the base and get started on the deployment. I want to head over to the gym and I'll walk back to base."

"I'll send a driver back for you sir to meet you on the road."

"Good thinking Norgaard."

MacDonald walked into the gym complex and looked for the locker number Tom had given him. He wrote a brief note and slid it through the slot. The gym was only sparsely populated. He wondered how long it would take to get a response.

He began to walk back toward the base. He needed time to think. Halcyon was facing the biggest threat in its brief history, and all the help and direction he received was "go slow—don't do anything rash." Walking helped clarify his thinking. He knew what he had to do.

Chapter 27

Unleashing the Dogs of War

Bigelow waited in a ravine at the foot of South Mountain. He had been here for over an hour. *What's keeping Meglir?*

Just then he saw the corpulent figure of Hoffstetter approaching with half a dozen Apemen and two Turncoats. Bigelow stepped out of his hiding place.

"What do you want?" asked Meglir with Hoffstetter's voice.

"MacDonald knows about the Apemen and the fleet you're building at camp," said Bigelow.

"Does he now? Did he tell Blackmore?"

"Yes, but Blackmore is being cautious as ever; he told him to barricade the mountain but hasn't given the go ahead to attack your camp."

"In that case," said Hoffstetter, "I'll keep the Apemen back so none of them are killed. With no bodies, MacDonald's fears will look like paranoia. Having MacDonald know about our fleet is bad news. I'll have to see about setting extra guards."

"Those are good ideas." Bigelow couldn't help letting a smile break out on his face at the prospect of making MacDonald look like a fool.

"But I want you to do more. We're almost ready with the ships. I want you to arrest MacDonald."

"Arrest him?" said Bigelow alarmed, "On what charge?"

"Make up a charge; plant the evidence, then blame him for the disappearances."

"But it will invite scrutiny and it won't stick," protested Bigelow.

"It doesn't matter," said Meglir. "I want you to provoke a civil war pitting your police force against the navy. I want the navy so busy fighting you that they won't have time to think about striking our shipyards. After you arrest MacDonald, go after his lieutenants. Keep going until either civil war breaks out or you have so emasculated the navy leadership that it is in complete disarray. Then we'll strike."

"What about our allies?" asked Bigelow.

"We have been out of communication, but according to our timetable they should already be underway. I need maximum chaos as we prepare to invade. Is that understood?"

"Understood."

Chapter 28

Chaos

MacDonald headed to the gym. The barricades around South Mountain had been set up within a day, so at least that threat was contained to some extent. Now he had to decide what to do about the force gathering to attack Halcyon from the mainland. He opened his locker and noticed a folded sheet of paper. He looked around to see if anyone was close to him then read the note.

> Ready to see you.
> Go for a run on the East Coastal Road.
> T.

MacDonald carefully folded the sheet of paper, changed into his athletic shorts and then headed out of the building. It was a warm December day. A couple of other runners also left the building and then dispersed. MacDonald and another runner headed toward East Harbor. MacDonald picked up his pace and easily outdistanced the other fellow. When he reached East Harbor, he turned south with the fields of the experimental farm, now fallow in winter, on his right and the coastal forest on his left.

He looked back and saw the other runner stopped and talking on his cell phone. MacDonald was making his way toward the part of the coast opposite Romulus and Remus, scanning the forest for a sign of Tom. He heard the sound of an e-car. He edged over to the left to let the car pass, but the car screeched to a halt and blocked his progress.

There were four men in the car. He saw Bigelow's face through the window. Opening the door, Bigelow tried to get out, but MacDonald slammed it shut and darted into the woods. He heard the phtt of a stunner blast hitting the trees. He was already tired and they were gaining on him. Suddenly Tom appeared in front of him and dragged him into some brush at the foot of a small rock formation. He had what looked like a stunner, but not standard issue.

Tom put his finger over his mouth for silence. The four pursuers arrived in the area and stopped.

"He's gone to ground. Find him," said Bigelow. "Stun him if you see him. He's been too much trouble already."

Tom leveled his stunner at the nearest stalker and pulled the trigger. MacDonald, heard the phtt, and felt his skin-tingling as the stunner blast past him and felled the pursuer. The pursuer dropped like a sack of potatoes and his stun gun rolled forward. MacDonald lunged out and grabbed the stun pistol.

"There he is!" someone shouted. MacDonald fired at one of the patrolmen. When he looked for more he realized he could see four figures sprawled on the ground

MacDonald stepped out onto the path and collected two stun pistols from the prone figures of two of the guards. Tom walked up the path to collect the fourth stun pistol from Bigelow who had been hit as he was trying to flee. Tom, returning, was joined by two others.

"Commander MacDonald, these are my friends, Dwight Larsen, and Pam Gleeson," said Tom.

MacDonald shook hands. "I'm much obliged. You saved my life and maybe even Halcyon."

"We were just waiting up the road when they arrived," said Dwight. "Your quick thinking gave us just enough time to try to head you off. We figured you'd keep to the trail since the brush is pretty dense around here."

"Why did you want to see us?" asked Tom.

"I wanted to let you know that I found Dave and Arlana. I also wanted to tell you not to try anything stupid such as attempting to rescue them. Leave it to me; I'll take care of it. What are those stunners you're using anyway?"

"Oh they're animal control stunners from biology," said Tom, "which reminds me that we ought to get going. The charge is designed to knock out small animals so these guys will start to wake up any minute."

MacDonald tried to think. "I would love to arrest Bigelow. He's too heavy to drag back to the e-car. Maybe I'll stun him again and have my men pick him up." He looked up the path. Bigelow was gone.

"He's gone!" said Tom, "He can't have gone far."

"No time for a manhunt," said MacDonald, "Here you take three of their stunners and I'll keep the fourth in case I have any more trouble. I'm going to take the e-car so they'll all have to walk back to base."

"At least I brought Bigelow's cell phone," said Tom handing it to MacDonald.

"Good thinking, said MacDonald, as he bent down to collect the other three cell phones and the car keys, and then headed back to the road at a fast trot waving 'good-bye.'

MacDonald drove the e-car on to the small naval base at the south side of the island and immediately summoned Norgaard. "I want to issue a full mobilization. Everyone—and I mean everyone—is to be ready for extended sea duty. I want all personnel ready to go in four hours."

"Sir?"

"Norgaard, Bigelow is leading a coup against Halcyon and just tried to take me out on my run after he realized I was on to the Apemen. I barely escaped. He'll probably go after all of our senior officers to cripple us. I want control of the sea and I want a fighting force available to defend Halcyon, where he can't reach us. Now get going."

"Yes, Sir—Sir we don't have enough ships for all of our personnel. Also what about the barricades?"

MacDonald thought for a moment. "This base is defensible. Have them fall back here and hold it. We can re-supply them by sea if they're besieged. I don't think Bigelow has the firepower to break through a determined defence and it gives us a critical foothold on Halcyon."

"I apologize, Sir—I need orders about where the men are to rendezvous."

MacDonald pulled out a map. "We'll meet here by the Channel Islands at the mouth of the Halcyon River. I know those don't offer very good shelter in case of a storm, but we need them as our home base close to Halcyon.

"Another thing Norgaard, I need twenty men, heavily armed, and ground transport. I have something I need to do. Leave one boat for me and the twenty."

Chapter 29

War

Dave woke with a massive headache. He was lying on a cot that was too small for him and sagged under his weight. The room had no outside window, but a small opening into a hallway was set with bars.

He rose to use a latrine in the corner of the room. The room had an antiseptic smell. A face looked in the hall window and promptly disappeared. A few minutes later he heard voices. "Shall I get the guards?" said a tenor voice.

"No, not yet," answered a deep voice. Maybe he'll cooperate and we won't need the guards. Why don't you go back to your duties. I can handle it from here."

A dark-skinned, honest face appeared at Dave's window. "Mr. Schuster, my name is Lieutenant Kherry Carter. I'm a medical doctor reporting to Commander MacDonald."

"Where am I?" said Dave.

"You're in the detention center." After a pause—"How are you feeling?"

"I have a massive headache."

"No wonder," said Carter, "you've taken more stunner hits than any person has a right to take, and you still slugged Bigelow hard enough to give him a mighty tender jaw."

"My heart bleeds for him," said Dave venomously. "Where's Arlana?"

"Oh, the beautiful blonde woman who was with you? She's here in one of the cells. She's safe. Unfortunately she clobbered one of the guards and tried to break you out, so we had to restrain her. She's quite a wildcat—a beautiful wildcat."

"Don't I know it. So why don't you let us go? We haven't done anything."

Carter looked up and down the hall and then said softly, "I report to MacDonald and I think he would like to let you go. He remembers your service at the Battle of City Point. But Bigelow controls this facility and he's pretty keen on keeping you locked up."

"So where do you fit in?"

"As I said, I report to MacDonald, but I've been seconded to Bigelow. Unfortunately, Bigelow's word here is law."

"Can you get word to MacDonald?"

"I can try. May I ask you a few questions?"

"You can always ask," said Dave.

"While you were stunned, I ran a few tests and completed some imaging. Here's what I know. You're not the same person that left Halcyon about a year ago."

"What do you mean?" said Dave, alarm tinging his voice.

"Well, while you were out, your skin color changed from the light color it is now to a very dark brown. It, er, rather surprised me. I have discovered that you have special pigmentation cells under your skin that let you do that. You also have a special layer under your skin that contains a bound form of hemoglobin. I would guess you could survive without breathing for a considerable amount of time. You also have photophores under your skin as squids do."

"What are photophores?" asked Dave surprised.

"Photophores enable organisms to produced bioluminescence. I take it you didn't know about those."

"No, I didn't." Dave's mind was reeling. *What else don't I know?*

There was a long pause. "Well," said Carter, "that's all I know so far. There's probably more, but I haven't found it yet. But here's the clincher. Your DNA is not exactly the same as human DNA. You still have 23 pairs of chromosomes, but you have less resemblance to the higher primates than you should have. I'm not saying there isn't a lot of commonality—there is, but there is less than there is for a *Homo Sapiens*."

"But it's still me," protested Dave. "I have the same memories—I'm the same guy."

"Sure you have the same memories, but you're not the same guy."

Dave realized there was no point in protesting.

Carter continued, "So who is Arlana?"

"You already pointed out that she's a beautiful, blonde wildcat. That's the most important thing to know about her—especially the wildcat part. She's 'sudden death' with either hand."

"I'll try to remember that," said Carter. "Well she's physiologically exactly the same as you …"

"Exactly?" said Dave smiling.

"Well, she's obviously a woman …"

"Obviously."

"But she has similar DNA and those same weird organs. When she was unconscious, she also changed her skin color."

There was a long silence. Carter continued. "Dave, there's so much we could learn from you. Won't you cooperate?"

"So why do you want to know? I'm locked up. Why should I trust you? Why should I even help you?"

"I'm a military doctor," said Carter. "I've never seen anything like you two. Of course I'm curious."

"Let us out of here and then we can talk."

"I wish I could Dave, but that's not my call."

Dave thought long and hard. *I have some leverage. How can I use it?*

"Look Carter, Arlana is probably frightened out of her mind, so why not bring her here so I can at least reassure her that things will be okay?"

"She doesn't seem particularly frightened," said Carter, a puzzled look on his face. "She seems more worried about you. By the way, how did she learn to speak perfect English?"

"She has a natural gift for languages," said Dave. "Well how about bringing MacDonald in and letting me talk to him?"

Carter looked hard at Dave. He seemed to be weighing the consequences of Dave's request. "Alright," he said at last with a sigh, "I'll see what I can do. If you change your mind, let the guard know."

Dave began to pace the room, trying to think of a way to escape. Three steps, turn, three steps. *I need to get out of here—but how?* A short time later a small door opened in the wall and a tray of food appeared with a sandwich, no utensils and a plastic cup. He ate ravenously.

Dave awoke to the sound of a commotion in the hall. He heard Carter's voice. "He's down the hall here."

A familiar voice said, "Open the door." The door opened and the face of Commander MacDonald looked in. "Schuster, are you alright?"

Dave smiled, "I think I am now, Sir."

"Well let's get going before Bigelow catches wind of what's afoot."

As Dave left the room, he saw Arlana being released from her cell, which had been next to his. She ran to him and gave him a hug, burying her head in his shoulder. "I was so afraid they had killed you," she whispered." Dave felt his face turning scarlet.

MacDonald smiled. "Let's move!"

MacDonald led the way down a side stairwell to the back of the building. Several trucks in camouflage waited for them.

"You have the trucks running again?" asked Dave.

"Yes we were able to convert them to run on ethanol. If you're wondering what we're doing, we're going to defend Halcyon from Meglir and not let Bigelow just hand us over. We're heading to the harbor."

Without further talk, MacDonald, Dave and Arlana climbed into the back of the nearest truck. MacDonald pounded on the cab and the truck started to move. When the truck stopped, they climbed out to see West Harbor stretched out before them.

MacDonald beckoned them to follow him to the nearest Viking longboat. As soon as they embarked, the lines were cast off and the boat made for the harbor entrance.

"Where are we going?" asked Dave.

"We're going to take as many of the boats as we can. We're going to set up our base on the Halcyon River Channel Islands. We're also going to try to hold the naval base at South Harbor."

"Can you realistically do that?" asked Dave.

"If Bigelow wants to throw all his resources at the naval station, he might get it, but we would make him pay. In any case, we will leave enough boats there to evacuate if we have to."

When they arrived at the nearest Channel Island, which had been designated Jersey, Dave saw that it was already inundated with boats of all descriptions. Many were Viking longboats; there were a few powerboats and many of the smaller dinghies.

After a quick meal they embarked and headed down the coast in a small flotilla of boats. Dave and Arlana joined MacDonald in one of the larger powerboats. The crew was tense.

"May I ask where we're going?" asked Dave.

"We're going to give Meglir a bloody nose," said MacDonald.

Dave and Arlana exchanged looks. They moved to the bow.

"Little brother," whispered Arlana, "should we not ask to be taken back to our friends? They will be worried."

"Arlana, although I trust MacDonald, I don't want to give away our hideout. We don't know how far the information will travel, and if Bigelow hears about it, our friends will be lost."

"But we have to get back."

"We should try to get back to South Harbor. From there we're pretty close to Romulus and Remus, and we could even swim it if we had to."

A crewman approached. "Excuse me Sir, Ma'am. Commander MacDonald would like to meet with you in the aft cabin."

Dave and Arlana followed the crewman to a ladder at the back of the boat, which led to a low room with a desk and a couple of chairs.

MacDonald dismissed the crewman and indicated the chairs to his guests.

"I'm afraid I have to ask you a few questions."

Dave groaned inwardly. He had been afraid of this. He deliberately did not look at Arlana. "Of course, how can we help?" was all that he said.

"Carter has told me some rather interesting stories about you two. I wanted to hear it from you personally. So Arlana, who are you and how do you fit into this picture? Are you human?"

"Human?" asked Arlana.

"He means are you like us—people" added Dave unhelpfully.

Arlana gave Dave an annoyed look. "My people are called the Gurundar which means 'guardians' in your tongue. We watch over this country, although until recently, we have stayed away from Meglir and this part of the coast."

"So you're people like us?" asked MacDonald.

"Not exactly," said Arlana. "You are what we call Lesser Men. You have been changed. The Bent Ones of old experimented with our people. We were too hard to control, so they weakened us by mixing us with the apes. You had a bit of mixing and we call you the Lesser Men. You are still sentient. More mixing gives the Halfmen. They have lost almost all of the spark of the Creator. They are cruel but cunning. Finally there are what you call Apemen. They are like machines that can be commanded."

MacDonald looked incredulous. He started another approach. "We've been here more than a year, why haven't we met you and your people before?"

"Meglir, whom you know, unleashed a plague on this land hundreds of years ago that killed almost all of my people. We are a remnant. Until recently, we avoided this coast and the City of the Dead, afraid that the plague would begin again. We could do that since Meglir was trapped inside the City of the Dead. Now that he has been released, we cannot stay away any longer."

MacDonald looked troubled. "Well that brings me to you, Dave. What's happened to you?"

Dave took a deep breath and related the whole story of his capture, the fight with the Halfmen, and the risky procedure to heal him. He ended by saying they had returned to Halcyon to rescue Al, without indicating the help that he had.

MacDonald's penetrating gaze told Dave that MacDonald knew he was holding back. MacDonald turned to Arlana. "This is an awful lot to take in, but what I really need to know right now Arlana: are your people on our side against Meglir or not?"

"I cannot speak for our leadership, but I can say we have always opposed Meglir and continue to do so. It is our turn to wonder if you are truly on our side. Your people seem to be helping Meglir a great deal."

"Fair enough, I'll have to think about what you told me. I'm sure I'll have more questions later. Right now I need to plan our attack."

It was dark and the clouds added to the gloom. The water lapped against the side of the boat. A leadsman in the bow quietly passed the sounding to the helmsman. Dave could smell pine, so he knew they were close to shore. Up ahead a fire burned. When the boat ground to a halt, Dave, Arlana and the rest of the crew leapt off. Soon they were among a series of partially finished longboats on wooden rails. Dave carried bundles of straw and a can of ethanol. They heard the sound of a clash in the harbor as the other boats attacked enemy craft already afloat. "Now!" came the command and Dave lit his bundle of straw and threw it into the nearest boat. Soon every boat was blazing. Now they had to defend the boats until the fire was far enough advanced that it could not be put out. Soon Apemen lumbered toward them and Dave, along with the rest in his company, formed a line in front of the burning boats and shot bolts from their crossbows to bring the Apemen down. They had wanted to throw the bodies into the fires, but too many of them were attacking. Finally the command came for them to retreat back to the boat. They ran into the surf, pushed their boat free and then were pulled aboard. After a quick headcount, they headed out to the rendezvous. They hadn't lost a man. Looking back,

Dave saw that the boats on the shore were ablaze. He smiled. *That should set Meglir back.*

The next day, Dave awoke early. His tent was on Jersey, the largest Channel Island, in the mouth of the Halcyon River. In sympathy with the more famous Channel Islands off the coast of Normandy, the other four inhabited islands were named Guernsey, Sark, Herm, and Alderney. All of these Halcyon outposts were rocky outcroppings and reefs that had accumulated silt from the river and though they possessed excellent soil, were less than suitable as naval bases. The water was brackish, so the one solar desalination unit had to be augmented with regular trips up river or to a nearby creek to provide the large naval contingent with adequate drinking water. Still, it had to do, and Dave was impressed by how much the facilities had improved from more than a year ago when Halcyonites had first begun farming here. Dave saw a curious boat coming into the marginal harbor with another craft in tow. The first boat looked like it was overgrown with brush and was manned by *Hansa*. His visual acuity was unsettling—another consequence of his healing. Before, he could not have seen this much detail without binoculars. *What are* Hansa *doing towing a boat?*

There was no point standing here, so he decided to find the mess tent, then head to the harbor to discover what was going on. As he searched for the mess tent, he wondered how Arlana was doing. She had been indignant at the Halcyon egalitarian idea that she be forced to share quarters with a bunch of men. After threatening to sleep out in the open, the powers had eventually relented and taken her somewhere else. Dave congratulated himself that he was finally away from her sarcasm, jibes, and cutting remarks. Still he didn't feel the elation that he had expected at the prospect, and that puzzled him.

Dave had just finished his first plate of fish (he didn't really like fish for breakfast, but he was hungry enough not to care) when Arlana strode in, spotted him and gave him a scowl that would have curdled milk.

"Where are your manners, youngling?" demanded Arlana.

"My manners?" mumbled Dave.

"Don't speak with your mouth full."

Dave waved his fork in acknowledgement.

"Here I am, alone among these hostile people and you abandon me. Would I have done the same to you? Where is your loyalty to family? Where is your—she groped for words—your chivalry?"

Dave's mouth was empty but he thought it better to pretend he was still chewing. After all, Arlana was on a roll. She looked at him again and almost started to laugh, then sat down and smiled.

Women! I'll never understand them.

"If you're hungry, there are plates over there and the food is free," said Dave pointing to a line of people at the back of the mess tent.

"I am hungry," said Arlana. "Might I get you anything?"

"No thanks," stammered Dave, still stunned by the change in the conversational weather.

Arlana returned with a plate full of food, briefly looked toward her home, bowed her head in thanks to the Creator and began to eat.

Dave, finding the silence oppressive, after the initial verbal deluge, ventured a comment. "I saw a curious ship coming in towing a small boat. I want to go to the harbor after breakfast. Would you like to come?"

Arlana smiled that disarming smile of hers and said "Sure."

They headed down to the wharf. Both the small craft and the boat covered with masses of reeds were just pulling into shore. Dave, recognizing the people, said "Come on Arlana," and began to run.

A bedraggled and bearded form stumbled out of the craft. He looked vaguely familiar. "Glenn is that you?"

The tired eyes looked up at Dave. They brightened with recognition. "Dave is that you? Thank the Lord!" It was Glenn, his roommate who had been left at New Jerusalem.

"What's going on Glenn? Why were you out in a craft alone? What's happened?"

"He needs a drink of water," said Arlana. Always thinking ahead, she had filled her water skin before leaving the cafeteria.

Glenn drank greedily.

"Not too much," said Arlana. "It may make you sick."

"Thanks," said Glenn. "You're an angel."

"What's an angel?" asked Arlana, puzzled.

"Never mind," said Dave to Arlana, then looking at Glenn. "Remember you're married now. What would Sonja say if you're praising beautiful women as angels?"

Glenn started at Sonja's name. He grabbed Dave's arm. "Sonja is in trouble. You've got to help me. That's why I was trying to get to Halcyon. We've been overrun."

"Slow down Glenn. Take another drink and tell us what happened."

Just then a group of *Hansa* approached. Glenn started.

"Hanomer!" said Dave. "What are you doing here?"

Friend Dave, I have been patrolling the coast with my friend Bandomer and his reed boat. We were hoping to bring back word of you to Pam. We saw this man alone in a boat. We gave him water, but he was so frightened by us that we thought we had to bring him in for his own safety."

Just then Commander MacDonald approached with a group of armed men. He pushed his way through the crowd that had formed around Dave and the *Hansa*.

"What's going on here?" MacDonald asked.

"You remember my friend, Hanomer, from the Battle of City Point?" asked Dave. Hanomer bowed and said in perfect English "Pleased to meet you again, Commander MacDonald."

"Pleased to meet you too, Hanomer. What brings you here so—unexpectedly?"

"We have been patrolling the coast in our boat, when we rescued one of your people."

"One of my people?" said MacDonald puzzled.

"Commander MacDonald, let me introduce Glenn Thompson, my former roommate. He is part of a splinter colony residing in a place on the mainland they call New Jerusalem. They've had trouble of some sort. He was just going to tell us about it."

MacDonald turned to Glenn. "This should be interesting." MacDonald sat down on a bench at the wharf, expecting a detailed account.

"About a month ago, we saw this ape-like creature amble up Botany Creek to our front door." He looked at MacDonald's puzzled face. "Let me tell you about New Jerusalem. New Jerusalem is a perfectly round impact crater, with high unbroken walls all the way around. At the west end, Botany Creek is dammed up to form a pond. We have a fortified wall and a drawbridge. We call this our front door. We live inside the crater in safety and are self-sufficient.

"Anyway, back to the ape-like creature. Some of our people were at the Battle of City Point and recognized it as an Apeman and so we knew that Meglir, or possibly one of his lieutenants, was nearby. We also knew we were in trouble, so we closed our spillway and flooded the whole entrance to the front door by expanding the size of the pond. We put patrols up on the high rim wall. We saw no more Apemen, but we did see the large wolves, the Lupi, skulking in the woods.

"When nothing happened for a couple of weeks we thought we were safe, and that Meglir had decided that we were too tough a nut to crack—but we were wrong. One night we heard screams. The Lupi had killed one of our families living away from our village, on their farm plot in the crater. Everyone who could, ran for the safety of the caves in the eastern rampart, since the Lupi were now inside. They had found a way across the rim wall. We had been too few to guard the long expanse of the rim adequately.

"About twenty of us, including Sonja, my pregnant wife, were too far from the caves when the attack came, so we took refuge in the main stone building. We were trapped. Finally, in desperation, one dawn a few days ago, we made a run for the caves to join the others. We were cut off by the Lupi at the lake. Our leader, Dalrymple kept us from routing and gave us the courage to fight. We would have been lost if some of our missing friends hadn't sortied out of the caves and driven the wolves off. Still, the Lupi came back in greater numbers just as we were climbing to safety. Dalyrmple and several of our men gave their lives, holding the Lupi at bay, while the families escaped up to the caves.

"We had some supplies in the caves, and the caves themselves were defensible, but we were running out of food. Since I knew the way better than anyone else, we agreed that I should get help. We had one boat for emergency purposes in the cave and I took it down Botany Creek. Luckily, I didn't encounter any Lupi. Even so, I would have died trying to cross over to Halcyon if these *Hansa* had not rescued me.

"Will you help me? Will you get my people out?"

Dave watched MacDonald's face. It had the look of one who had to deliver bad news. "I'll go," said Dave.

"As will I," added Arlana.

"Friend Dave, our boat is available for your use," added Hanomer.

"Hmm," said MacDonald. "It seems to me you have no chance if you try to go overland. Either the Renegades will get you—assuming any are still alive, or the Lupi will hunt you down, especially if you have women and children along.

"I don't think you can use Botany Creek again—it's too close to Meglir. The only reasonable solution is to imitate what Glenn did but use another creek. If you can identify a route on our maps, perhaps we can help. We don't really have the resources to mount a rescue, but maybe I can give you a longboat and one of the hybrid outboard motors to get you there. I'll even ask for volunteers for a skeleton crew. You'd better come with me to the map room and see if you can find a viable route."

Glenn insisted that after a drink of water and some food he was ready to look at maps, so an hour later Glenn, the *Hansa*, Arlana and Dave were looking for a route.

Glenn pointed to a small creek emptying into the Halcyon River with its headwaters further south. "When the survivors from the Battle of City Point joined our colony, they told us they had found a deep creek without any rapids that let them navigate many miles inland so that they only had to trek across country about five miles. Maybe this is the creek here."

"Friend Glenn," said Hanomer, "if what your friends say is true about this creek, our boat can go much further than even your shallow draft boats."

They argued back and forth about the feasibility of Glenn's proposal and Hanomer's modification for another twenty minutes, but even though this plan had many deficiencies, no better approach emerged. They agreed that they would give it a try and leave first thing the next morning.

Chapter 30

Rescue

After an early start and a long day, at four o'clock in the afternoon, Arlana, Dave, and Hanomer left Glenn and the other *Hansa* at the creek in the reed boat. The water level was quite low and the longboat had bottomed out about five miles back. Glenn was completely exhausted. The others had convinced him to stay with the *Hansa*. Dave was worried that he wouldn't be able to find the secret entrance to the caves, but they had no choice. Glenn could barely stand. The prospect of carrying him was worse than the prospect of spending extra time searching for the secret entrance without Glenn there to point it out.

As they headed across country, Dave felt his fear of the Lupi returning. He remembered the pervasive dread and impending sense of danger he had felt at every step, as their expedition had headed down from the Lupi Pass. However, he was quite a different person now than he had been then. It seemed like a lifetime ago, but it was only last year.

They left the reed boat on the southern shore as the creek bent west towards the mountains. The boat looked like a patch of shrubbery with its blanket of boat weed spread out. The shore climbed rapidly to a low ridge covered with tall cedars. Dave loved the smell of cedars. He saw Arlana, wearing her dark complexion, her living cloak wrapped tightly around her, inhale deeply then turn and smile at him. Hanomer was ahead since, he was by far the best scout. They moved silently, with Arlana watching to the right and Dave watching left and behind. He had a rifle but hoped he wouldn't have to use it. A rifle shot would let Meglir know that Halcyonites were on the mainland.

After reaching the ridge, the unmistakable circular rim wall of New Jerusalem loomed ahead of them. From this side it looked to be about two miles distant. The rim rose steeply some two hundred meters from the surrounding forest. He could see the rim quite clearly but could detect no movement on the top.

Hanomer came up and quietly touched Dave's arm, telling him by contact telepathy that he wanted to scout ahead all the way to the small pond at the south side of New Jerusalem. By Glenn's description, they both knew that the passage had to be there. Dave crouched down and watched as Hanomer quietly entered the woods on the far side of the ridge. Dave had a hard time following him, even though he knew where to look.

An hour later Hanomer reappeared and motioned to them to follow. The route Hanomer had chosen provided maximum cover; even someone high up on the New Jerusalem rim would have found it very difficult to see them. They reached the small pond at about six in the evening. The rim wall rose right out of the western edge of the pond. Dave could see by the color of the water that it was very deep right next to the wall. About halfway across, the water was disturbed as if an underground river emerged deep under the water surface. Hanomer pointed to a small ledge about twenty feet up from the pond surface. Dave could just see the head of a lookout, who turned his head from time to time to scan the whole valley before him. Hanomer led the party to the sheer cliff wall. He began to wade in the water just off the vertical cliff. Dave joined him and saw to his surprise that there was a three foot wide ledge just under the surface before the rim wall plunged deep into the watery depths. The lookout had stood up and Dave waved to him and then indicated silence by putting a finger to his lips. The lookout complied. When they were directly under him, Dave saw that what had looked at a distance like a crack in the rock face was really a cave, but the cave angled in sideways so that the open entrance was practically invisible from either side. A rope ladder snaked down, Dave climbed up first, followed by Arlana, and then Hanomer. He recognized the face of Hugh Matthews, one of his comrades at the Battle of City Point. "Glenn sent us," said Dave.

Matthews' face brightened. "He made it then. Thank the Lord. Where's Glenn? Sonja is anxious to see him."

"He's nearby but was too exhausted to come the last stage. Who's in charge?"

"Shepherd Dalrymple is dead," said Matthew heavily. We don't really have anyone to lead us anymore. Sister Sonja has been keeping our spirits up."

Just then, Hanomer touched Dave's arm and pointed. On the south side of the creek, a large wolf-like shape emerged from the woods and drank from the creek. It peered up at their lookout and then disappeared into the woods.

"They know about this back door then," said Dave.

"Yes, it's not as heavily guarded as the inside, but they seem to check both sides of the pond regularly," said Matthews.

Matthews led them up some roughhewn steps into a large storage cavern. Most of the shelves were bare and all of the barrels had been opened. Dave could hear voices. Matthews took them down another passage until they came to a large room that was filled with about forty people, mostly women and children. When Sonja saw him she rose quickly and came over to him. She was probably in her sixth month of pregnancy. She looked at him intently.

"Dave? Dave Shuster is that you? You look different."

"Hi Sonja," said Dave, breaking into a broad smile and looking at her distended tummy, "you look different too!"

"You are being very rude, youngling," said Arlana glaring at Dave as she came up to join them.

Sonja smiled at Arlana and then her face clouded. "Have you seen Glenn? Tell me he's alright? He took a big risk to make it back to Halcyon."

"Yes, he made it. In fact he's waiting not too far from here."

"Why didn't he come? He would have come. Is he hurt?"

"He's fine," said Dave. "He had rather a rough journey and needed to rest. He wanted to come but we wouldn't let him."

Sonja seemed to see Hanomer for the first time and her eyes widened.

"Let me introduce you to a couple of friends, Sonja. This is Hanomer, one of the *Hansa*. Matthews may have told you about how they helped us win the Battle of City Point."

Hanomer bowed deeply and said "Pleased to meet you, friend Sonja."

Sonja smiled. "You are the first of your people that I have had the pleasure to meet. Your people's bravery at the Battle of City Point is known even to us."

Hanomer bowed again.

"My other friend has already introduced herself by insulting me. This is Arlana. She is also native to this world. Her people are the Gurundar, the Guardians in our tongue."

Arlana threw her braid behind her, stepped forward, and shook Sonja's hand. "I am glad to meet you Sonja."

"Come, have something to eat," said Sonja.

"We know you're low on supplies, so we'll eat our own provisions. Then we'll have to figure out how to get out of here."

While they were eating, Sonja told them in more detail about their current plight.

"It all began when our scouts told us a great force was coming over the pass that you and your friends discovered," said Sonja.

"So that road, which we found at the head of the pass, actually leads to the City of the Dead as we had always suspected," said Dave more to himself than to anyone else.

"So it seems, youngling," said Arlana quietly. She turned to Sonja, "What else did the scouts see?"

"We were torn between hiding in New Jerusalem behind our mountain walls and quietly shadowing this army across our land. In the end, our shepherd, Brother Dalrymple sent a few of our best scouts out to follow the army. The army brought a black, hideous statue with three symmetrical faces down the pass and through the forest. They were cutting a road as they went, so they obviously planned to move a lot of stuff. Finally they also brought a huge worm strapped to two joined wagons through the pass. After that report, Shepherd Dalyrmple had heard enough and ordered all of the scouts back home, but it was too late. The Lupi had nosed out our scout's trail and followed it back to New Jerusalem. The next thing we knew, Apemen were guarding the entrance. The Shepherd ordered the walls watched and the west canyon flooded to protect our main entrance. Still the Lupi prowled the woods around the crater walls looking for a way in. For a while it seemed we would be safe. But eventually, the Lupi found a way through and we had to flee to these caves. The men held off the Lupi, so that the women and children could make their way back here. Finally, Shepherd Dalrymple held off the Lupi alone, so that the last of the men could climb up to the ledge on the inside without the Lupi pulling them down.

"Shepherd Dalrymple gave his life for us."

Dave was deeply moved by Dalyrmple's sacrifice. Whatever pain he has caused Al and Al's brother, in the end Dalrymple has fulfilled his duty as leader and shepherd by giving up his life for those in his care. "I'm determined that Shepherd Dalrymple's sacrifice won't be in vain," said Dave. "We're going to get you out of here."

"There's only three of you. How are you going to accomplish that?"

"We've got a boat north of here. We've got to get everyone there as quickly as possible."

"But there are about forty of us," said Sonja, "can your boat hold so many?"

"No," said Dave. "We'll put the women and young children in the boat, the rest will have to walk."

They spent the rest of the evening debating various plans, but all depended on not being spotted by the Lupi.

Hanomer went out each day on scouting expeditions. Meanwhile Dave went to the cave opening on the inside of the New Jerusalem rim. Lupi were on patrol everywhere. They had no fear of the trapped people and kept a close watch.

On the third day, Hanomer said it was time to go. The wind was coming from the north and so any Lupi ahead of them would be upwind. Everyone had to travel as lightly as possible—only weapons and a little food and water.

Dave climbed back up to the ledge on the inside rim. When he thought of his friends. who had died in the jaws of the Lupi, his anger still smoldered.

This move to distract the Lupi, I like.

He set up well back from the edge of the ledge and targeted the nearest Lup with his rifle. The rifle discharged and he felt the recoil on his shoulder. The wolf jumped two meters into the air and ran into the brush. He found another target. They were all trying to locate him. He fired again, hitting another. The Lupi were in a frenzy, running this way and that. He kept firing until he had no more targets and then he carried his rifle into the cave mouth and through to the back door. Hanomer had left an hour ago to make sure the route was safe. Arlana was leading the whole band in a long line back along the way that Hanomer had initially brought them. Dave climbed down the rope ladder and followed them. Part way up the trail, Dave saw the carcass of a wolf with Hanomer's black feathered arrows protruding from its side. *Black feathers—Hanomer was using poison to bring down the beasts.*

After two hours they reached the reed boat. There were far too many of them to all fit into the boat. The children and the pregnant women were placed in the boat to capacity. Everyone else had to follow the creek on foot.

Finally the base on the island of Jersey was in sight. As they drew closer, it became clear that something was amiss. The harbor was full of boats of all sizes. The Navy had pulled boats in from as far away as Wood Island. The wharf was busy with activity. Everywhere boats were being loaded with supplies. When they finally reached the harbor, the only quay available was the farthest one from the settlement. As Dave disembarked, a naval officer was waiting for them.

"Commander MacDonald wants to see you right away."

Dave looked at the others. Seeing no one else was making a protest, he said "But, we have women and children we just rescued. We have to get them settled. Can't it wait?"

The officer looked at Dave with the bewilderment of one who had just seen water run uphill.

Collecting his thoughts, the officer said, "No, it can't wait. I'll get someone to take care of the refugees. Commander MacDonald meant now."

Dave, Arlana, and Hanomer followed the officer to headquarters where they were shown into a large room filled with maps. MacDonald was poring over a large map of the Island of Halcyon. He looked up. "Ah you're here at last. Have a seat." He gestured to a group of chairs near his desk in the corner.

Dave led the group to the desk and sat down. MacDonald's desk was cluttered with maps. MacDonald grabbed an armful and put them on a chair behind his desk. They slipped to the floor, but MacDonald ignored the sound and sat down heavily on the edge of his desk. Dave looked at him. He had rings around his eyes as if he hadn't slept in days.

Never one for small talk, MacDonald launched right into the meat of the discussion. "I've decided we need to take back Halcyon right away from Blackmore and Bigelow."

Dave felt his eyes go wide and the hairs on the back of his neck rise. He saw MacDonald's eyes focus on him intently. "I know what you're thinking," said MacDonald, "we can't possibly be ready and if it comes to a fight, a lot of our fellow Halcyonites will be killed."

"But here's the situation. First of all, we haven't crippled Meglir's fleet nearly as much as we had hoped …"

"Maybe we can hit them again," said Dave.

"Not a chance," said MacDonald. "We pulled it off because we had surprise on our side. This time, they'd be waiting for us. But there's more. My inside people tell me that Bigelow is taking more and more control of Halcyon and we have to assume he's in Meglir's pocket. I just heard he's going to begin deploying the Renegades onto the campus proper any day now. When he does that, he'll have his own private army, and will effectively be in control—or I suppose I should say Meglir will be in control."

"A friend of mine, Al Gleeson had been captured by Bigelow and escaped. Have your sources heard anything about him?" asked Dave.

"I remember Al Gleeson from The Battle of City Point, of course," said MacDonald. "I have not heard anything, either about his escape or recapture."

MacDonald looked searchingly from face to face. "I don't expect you to tell me everything, but I figured you must have a base of operations somewhere. I may be slow, but I usually figure things out eventually. For example, I've noticed you've been doing a lot of fishing off the east coast, near Romulus and Remus, in fact. Now if I were looking for a safe base, I would consider using the caves there. So just in case I might stumble onto something I'd rather not find, I've deliberately kept my guys away from the caves in Romulus and Remus because we didn't want to draw the attention of Bigelow to them. I suppose I could have tried to check the caves out at night, but if there were someone there, they would probably flee at the first opportunity once they knew they were discovered. We'll just have to hope Gleeson is safely holed-up there."

"I could go," said Dave.

"You're here, Schuster, because I need you for something else."

Dave felt deflated. He was really worried about Al and now MacDonald wanted something else. He looked MacDonald in the eye and felt his face harden.

MacDonald waited for Dave to speak. When he realized Dave wasn't going to say anything, he went on. "I need you to help Norgaard take control of the underground Command Center in the main administration building. I want him to take over and use the public address system to order all of the Halcyonites indoors to avoid as many casualties as possible. Also, many of the video cameras are still working, so you can keep an eye on Bigelow and see where he sets up his troop concentrations and then feed that information back to me by cell phone. Finally, depending on how many troops Bigelow has in the administration building, I want you to help Norgaard surprise and capture Blackmore."

MacDonald went on gesturing to the pile of papers on the floor. "I don't have a building plan of the administrative building. What do you remember of the Command Center?"

Dave took a pad of paper and began to sketch. "It's one floor down from the underground parking lot. Chancellor O'Reilly, my uncle, took me there when the Dislocation first occurred. We left the facility to go to the underground garage, so we could drive to the bridge and confirm what we had seen on the video cameras. I'll describe what I remember of the route."

He sketched a number of entrances to the building from the garage. "I'm pretty sure this is the one we used to enter the garage."

"Okay," said MacDonald. "So what's the layout inside?"

"Inside there's a stairwell. We go down one flight, then down the corridor to the right and the entrance to the control center is here. But all the doors have electronic locks."

"It's probably only a four digit combination," said MacDonald. "We have a device that can figure that out in short order. If not, we'll blow the lock with plastic explosive. That will give us away, but we need to get in quickly."

MacDonald leaned back in his chair. "Good! Here's the plan. Dave, you get some rest tonight. You'll have a long night tomorrow, or more properly, a very early start to the next day."

He picked up a map from the floor and unrolled it. "We're going to land a strike force under Norgaard on the north side of the island at 0300. Do you know that part of the island well?"

"Yes," said Dave. "I also used to fish up there."

"Good," said MacDonald, "Then you help Norgaard lead them through the woods to the edge of campus." He traced their progress on the map. "Make straight for the administration building. Norgaard's men will override the lock or force their way in. Then straight down to the Command Center and neutralize any opposition. Once you have control, Norgaard will take over, call my communicator and guide our operations using the tools you have available. At that point he'll make a decision, based on how strongly the admin building is defended: whether he's going to hunker down and protect the Command Center or if he'll try to capture Blackmore."

"What happens if we're spotted?" asked Dave.

"The team will carry stunners and neutralize anyone who sees you. But here's the key point. We're building up a large force at the naval base on the south side of the island which we still hold. While you're seizing the Command Center, we'll simultaneously land at East Harbor and West Harbor and move to control three objectives: South Mountain to cut off Meglir, Bigelow's headquarters to take out his command center, and your objective, the main administration building."

"And if we can't reach the Command Center?" asked Dave.

"Well, I'm hoping, of course, that doesn't happen. But if it does, then you'll help us by being a diversion and drawing Bigelow's attention away from the landing sites to the center of campus. Don't get caught!"

"Youngling," said Arlana, "I'm coming with you."

"Arlana, don't start in now. You should go to Romulus and tell them what's happening."

"Our friends on Romulus will be safe. You are a cub, youngling, and will get into all kinds of trouble if I'm not there. I'm still learning English—did I give you the wrong impression that I'm making a request?"

Dave looked at MacDonald pleading for help.

"She's your problem, Dave. I have no objections if she goes along with you."

"Arlana, you are the most annoying, stubborn woman ..."

She broke into such a big, exasperating smile that Dave couldn't even finish his diatribe. He threw up his hands. "Have it your way."

Chapter 31

Commando Raid

The reed boat under Hanomer's guidance crept up the very creek Al had once used to land at Halcyon. Dave leapt ashore followed by Arlana. He tried on the night vision goggles, but decided his night vision was so good, that he could see just as well as without them. He quietly worked his way through the brush until they came to the main trail, grumbling to himself about the noise, created by the sailors behind him.

Why couldn't I get a company of Green Berets instead of a bunch of bumblers who can't walk through brush without snapping every twig?

When they reached the path, he whispered to Norgaard. "I'm going to go up ahead about twenty yards to make sure that we won't be surprised. Arlana will come with me. I'll send her back to tell you to take cover if I encounter anyone."

"Here, take a stunner," whispered Norgaard.

Dave took the stunner, checked the settings, and then headed up the path followed by Arlana. The path was clear. The way was familiar and Dave led them unerringly to the edge of the campus. Rather than following the streets, he kept them to the woods and green spaces and finally brought them close to the administration building.

He gathered the group around him, and pointed to the nearby entrance to the underground parking lot.

"Okay," said Norgaard quietly. "I'll lead. Stay together. We move fast, but quietly." With that he started off at a run. Dave and Arlana hung back to the end, checking if anyone had spotted them. The entrance was an unlocked steel door and led to stairs with a landing halfway down.

A second door opened onto an empty parking lot. Dave took the lead again and guided them to the secure entrance. One of the soldiers placed a flat device over the keypad and numbers flashed as it worked through the combinations.

"Come on, come on," said Norgaard. "There ought to be hundreds of combinations that work."

There was a reassuring "click" as the lock retracted. Norgaard breathed a sigh of relief as the door opened.

Dave again led the way down the stairs to a second secure door and the procedure was repeated. This time it took even longer. When the door opened, Dave put a finger to his lips and led them to the control room. The door was open. The room was empty except for one man in front of the big wall-sized screen at the front of the room. The man had his feet up on the console and was asleep.

Sloppy, thought Dave. Norgaard pushed past Dave and fired a brief stunner blast at the fellow. Two of the sailors lifted the unconscious man and unceremoniously dumped him in the corner on the floor.

Norgaard gave orders and the sailors took up positions with several manning the consoles and others heading back out to the hall on guard duty.

"Can we lock the door?" asked Norgaard.

One of the men looked at the door. "It's a heavy door, Sir, with an electronic lock. We can always open it manually from the inside. Do you want me to lock it now?"

"No, leave it open until we have trouble. Then lock it as a last resort after the others have retreated here."

The men at the consoles had brought up several cameras, one of the naval station at South Harbor, two more of East and West Harbor and also two of Bigelow's headquarters. "Quite a number of the cameras are dead Sir, so we can't always pick the angle we want."

"Do the best you can, Walters. Any evidence they're waiting for us?"

"Quiet as a morgue at 0300, Chief."

Norgaard called MacDonald on his cell phone and briefly relayed their status and Walter's report. "Well things ought to be happening now," said Norgaard.

On the screen, the gate at the naval station opened and a series of vehicles, everything from electric cars to small trucks crammed with men, poured out of the gate. Some headed toward the center of campus, while others headed to South Mountain. On two other screens, a couple fast boats roared into East and West Harbor respectively and discharged their men. The slower sailing craft were making their best time trying to get into the harbor. West Harbor was going to be a problem since the wind was against them. When they couldn't make the narrow entrance to the bay called The Lens, the sailboats veered off and began discharging sailors by longboat off the west coast.

"Something's up," said Walters. "They know we're here." Dave, from his vantage point at the back of the room, could see a few men leaving Bigelow's headquarters. Several of the dormitories also had men leaving in significant numbers, heading mostly in the direction of East and West Harbor.

Norgaard called MacDonald to let him know. When he finished his call, he said to Walters, "Can you put me on campus-wide broadcast?"

"Sure thing Sir."

"On behalf of Commander MacDonald of the Halcyon Naval Defense Forces, I urge everyone to stay in their dormitories as the campus is under martial law. I repeat, do not leave your dormitories until you receive further instructions."

When Norgaard was finished, he asked Walters to use the internal cameras to make a quick scan of the administration building. "Look especially for Blackmore. I have my doubts he would be here at this time of night. Still make your check thorough. He may have gone to ground after our announcement."

Dave turned his attention to the main monitors around the campus. The most serious fighting was taking place at the South Mountain perimeter. A group of combatants in black uniforms and helmets charged out of the woods with ferocity and fell on the sailors as they were putting up their perimeter. Several of the black clad combatants fell to gunfire, but the rest, undaunted by their wounds, rushed the sailors with terrifying speed, mowing everyone down in their path with two-handed swords. The sailors ran for their lives.

"Bezerkers!" muttered Dave. "Bigelow has unleashed the Bezerkers."

"Find me another camera," said Norgaard. "Get me those Bezerkers back on screen. I need to know where they're going." Dave saw him pull out his communicator. "It's dead," he muttered. "They must have shut off the communication towers figuring it would hurt us more than it would hurt them."

He turned to Dave. "Dave, I need to ask you a favor. You have the best chance of getting through. Can you head over to the Bigelow's headquarters and warn Commander MacDonald that the Bezerkers have broken through. If he's not there, find out where he is, and report my message."

Dave picked up his crossbow and set off at a run. He took the steps up to the parking lot two at a time. After a quick scan for opposition, he sprinted to the parking lot exit ramp.

I don't know the combination to the door. I'll never get back in if I get into trouble.

He ran quickly onto the street and to a small park, where he ducked into a grove of trees. He had decided to avoid the open areas, and to take a longer route that took advantage of cover. Some of Bigelow's men still had rifles and he didn't want to get shot while running up the street. He hadn't thought about it before, but he should be more tired than he was. *There's a lot about being an Ancient that I don't know yet*, he thought.

Just ahead was Bigelow's headquarters. The area was quiet—too quiet. Where was MacDonald? Just then, he saw movement to the south of the building. MacDonald was marshaling his men for the assault. He thought his back was covered. Dave had to warn him or else they'd be a grape smashed between the hammer and the anvil.

Dave headed east to stay out of sight of Bigelow's headquarters. *Try not to get yourself shot by MacDonald's men Dave.* He moved rapidly for the first part of his flanking run, then used all of his skills at woodcraft until he came upon a sentry. He was about twenty yards right in front of the sentry. He put his hands up and stood up in full view. "I've been sent by Norgaard. I have a message for MacDonald." The surprised sentry raised his rifle in panic, and Dave watched his trigger finger, ready to dive into cover.

Recovering his composure, the sentry took his finger off the trigger. "I remember you. Walk ahead of me though, just following orders. MacDonald's with the main group."

Dave walked rapidly in the direction that the sentry had indicated. *I'm in a hurry; he can just hurry to keep up.* He entered a clearing, where MacDonald was studying a schematic of the building with his squad leaders around him.

MacDonald looked up in surprise. "Dave, what are you doing here?"

"Norgaard, sent me Sir. The Bezerkers have broken through in the south and they're coming up on your back."

MacDonald swore, tried to use his communicator and realized it was dead.

"It's not just your communicator, Sir. They've apparently shut down all of the signal towers," said Dave.

"Okay," said MacDonald, "Johnson, I want you to dig in here. Keep a lookout for our reinforcements from East Harbor. The rest, including you Dave, come with me."

They left the grove of trees and came out onto the main boulevard running toward South Mountain. After a short distance, they reached a square with a large statue of Atlas holding up the world. It was surrounded by benches and fountains, which had long since run dry. MacDonald positioned his forces at the edge of the square. They tried to pile anything loose into a crude barricade.

Within five minutes Dave saw movement across the open common. He could tell they weren't ordinary Halcyonites by the speed of their approach and that they cleared benches and bushes by leaping over them with ease. "They're coming," he said to the squad leader next to him.

The squad leader pulled out his binoculars to look and said, "You're right!" Then he elbowed his second in command, "Head down the line. Tell everyone to take cover. Go quickly and make sure MacDonald knows."

The sailor saluted and moved down the line. His squad took cover. The squad next to them went to ground almost at the same time.

The mad rush of the Bezerkers had slowed down. Dave could see them sneak up the center of the common. They, or their handlers, seemed to know what was waiting for them. Then all of a sudden, the Bezerkers gave out a yell and charged the middle of MacDonald's line. A few shots were fired and Dave saw several Bezerkers fall, but the main body of Bezerkers swept into the sailors' line. At close quarters the sailors were no match for the Bezerker juggernaut. In the distance Dave also heard yells and shouting in the direction of the Bigelow's headquarters. They had launched a coordinated counterattack.

Stragglers from the middle of the broken line began running through their ranks, followed by Bezerkers, swinging their two handed swords at anyone they could catch. A sailor just ahead was decapitated from behind by a Bezerker. Dave fired a crossbow bolt into the Bezerker's chest and pulled out his sword from the Bladewood. He wished he had brought a spear; he didn't have the reach of a Bezerker swinging his heavy, two-handed sword. There was nothing for it, but to move into the trees where the two handed sword would be a disadvantage. Another Bezerker charged and swung his sword. Dave stepped out of the arc of the swing, heard the sword thunk into the tree trunk and then he drove his sword into the Bezerker's heart. Another Bezerker swung at him. This time he met the Bezerker's blade with his own and to his astonishment, Dave's blade cut through the Bezerker's steel. Dave's next stroke killed the Bezerker as he was reaching for Dave's throat. The onslaught continued. He was growing weary. The road behind them and the edge of the common were littered with bodies, but the steel of the Bezerkers were no match for Dave's blade.

In the distance, he saw a group of enemy combatants moving south. After they had left, Dave realized that the Bezerker attacks had stopped.

I thought they had us. Why did Bigelow call them off?

Now that the tension of the battle was over, Dave felt extreme weariness descend upon him. He leaned against a tree to keep from falling over. He heard a shout behind him. *Now what?*

He saw sailors coming through the trees, weapons at the ready. Finally the reinforcements from East Harbor had arrived. Dave followed them into the killing ground in the middle of the line. MacDonald, on the other side of the breach, had a bandage on his arm, but was still giving orders. Dave sat down, spent. He heard MacDonald tell the reinforcements to pursue the Bezerkers, but under no circumstances to approach South Mountain until further notice. It looked like they had most of Halcyon back, but at what cost?

Chapter 32

In the Eye of the Hurricane

Dave rejoined MacDonald, whose face wore a tired smile. "We did it. We have the island back."

"That's great," said Dave. "Did you get Blackmore?"

MacDonald's eyes took on a troubled cast. "No," he said. "We had hoped to snag him at his home, but he wasn't there. Norgaard, did not find him at the admin building either. We assume Bigelow was able to get him before we did and dragged him to South Mountain along with most of his men."

"So we still have a big problem," said Dave.

"Yes we still have a big problem, but at least we have Halcyon back. Now Meglir is going to have an awful fight on his hands if he tries to take over."

Dave was not as sanguine as MacDonald about their prospects. "Mind if I go to check on Al?"

"By all means, go ahead. Thanks for your help." MacDonald turned his attention to a courier.

Dave went looking for Arlana. He had left the Command Center so suddenly that he had hoped that he would have disappeared before Arlana had realized what was happening. Given her character however, he knew she would try to follow as soon as she realized he was gone. He had not seen her since the control room. However, the Bezerker attack had caused so much confusion that he worried that she might have still been caught up in the fighting and been hurt.

On the way back to the administration building, Dave was relieved to see her striding toward him, a scowl on her face that would cause fresh lettuce to droop.

With one hand on her hip, she looked up at Dave and waggled her finger in front of his face. "What you did youngling, was very foolish—running off from the Command Center like that. Don't ever, ever do that again."

Dave beamed broadly. "I was trying to protect you, Arlana. You don't …"

"Protecting me! You're the one who needs protection!"

Dave put up his hands in protest. "Shouldn't we continue this conversation while we head to Romulus?"

Arlana calmed down. "Yes, we will do that. Don't think you'll get off because of this sensible distraction."

When they returned to Romulus, they found Ferris, Pam, and Al waiting for them anxiously. "Thank the Lord you're alright," said Pam. "When we saw all the trucks and people moving, we knew something big was up. We were just deciding if Ferris should go over there to find out if you two were all right."

"We're fine," said Dave. "I take it Al's here?"

"Yes," said Pam.

"How did Tom and Dwight manage to get him here?"

"They borrowed a fishing row boat up the coast that they knew about and rowed over at night. After they dropped Al off along with the medical supplies, they returned it when they went back."

Without answering, Dave went over to Al and looked at his eyes. They still had an orange hue, but it was clearly fading. "How are you, Al?" he asked gently.

Al smiled weakly. "I'm better now, thanks to you, Arlana, and the others. Still, an hour doesn't go by when I don't crave Happy Berries or Happenone. However, the Sedovarin keeps the worst of the cravings at bay." He looked at Dave. "You've had this, Dave. How long are the cravings going to last?"

Dave remembered his own struggle with Happy Berries, and he felt fears forming in his mind as he thought back to that terrible time. "The worst will be over in a month. Keep taking the Sedovarin without fail. Then it's best to stay as far away from Happy Berries as you can and keep busy."

"That long, huh?" said Al.

Dave clapped Al on the back and turned back to the others. "Sorry, I just had to find out how Al was doing. You were asking about what happened on Halcyon—MacDonald has taken control of the island back, Bigelow has been driven to join Meglir on South Mountain, and Blackmore is missing. Everyone is celebrating a great victory."

Dave grew somber.

"What's wrong? Why aren't you happier about our victory?"

Dave looked at Arlana. "We're happy enough. No doubt winning Halcyon back is a great victory, but it still doesn't make sense to us. Why didn't Meglir attack MacDonald's men to support Bigelow? In fact, why did he call Bigelow back, if this contest was game, set and match? What's he waiting for? Meglir is no fool. Is the storm over, or are we just in the eye of the hurricane?"

"Let's hope for the best and plan for the worst," continued Dave. "I wish there were some way that we could let Kelldor know what's happened here, but we have no way of contacting him."

"You're right," said Ferris. "Even though Kelldor sees many things others do not, he needs to be informed of these developments. I'll go back and let him know, in person, what's happened here."

"But we don't have a boat," said Dave.

"We Ancients have a great love of our special animals. When we are on land, our horses are never far away. On the sea we have our Dorai, and they are also never far away. Sigor, my Dorai has been close for the last few weeks. He will bear me back to Goose's Neck."

"Arlana, you should go with him," said Dave. "Your father will be worried."

She smiled her mischievous smile. "You will not get rid of me so easily. My father knows I'm committed to being a shield maiden and has resigned himself to the fact that I will often be in danger."

Dave felt himself getting exasperated, but strove to put it behind him.

"What about you, Dave?" asked Al. "What are you going to do?"

Dave took a deep breath. "I'm going to go back to Halcyon. I met a physicist called Makalo. I want him to have a look at my sword from the blade tree. This sword"—he took it out of his scabbard—"cut through Halcyon steel sword as if they were sticks. Maybe we can learn something useful about what makes this sword so incredibly strong and sharp. I also have some things niggling at me about the Dislocation.

"Maybe Meglir wasn't just after Halcyon to get our technology as we thought. There's an even more important reason. Remember Al, when we were in the prison pit at the City of the Dead, how Meglir in Hoffstetter's body sneered that Hoffstetter had been *called or sent for* from our world into his. Why did Meglir want him? There's something about Hoffstetter's plan that we're missing. If Meglir orchestrated the Dislocation through Hoffstetter, what is his grand plan? Until I know that, I'm going to be very uneasy. I want to go over Hoffstetter's personal effects and lab notes. Maybe there's something that will pop out at me."

Ferris gathered his belongings and went to the cave with the underwater entrance. He took out a long, curved flute-like object and placed the end in the water and played a tune. To the listeners, it was not very loud, but had a haunting quality. Soon, a grey head, much like an oversized dolphin's, broke the surface. Ferris stroked the head affectionately and quietly spoke to the creature as he straddled its back. Then waving 'good-bye,' he held onto the bony projections on the top of Sigor's head and was pulled under the water and out of the cave. After Ferris had left, the friends on the shore went to the upper caves. In a few minutes, at the edge of his greatly extended sight, Dave could see Ferris, riding Sigor, heading south much as one would ride a horse.

Dave knocked on the office that had a paper label 'Makalo' taped over the name plate.

"Come!" said Makalo.

"Ah David," said Makalo as Dave entered the room. "Come, sit down. It's good to see you again."

"Thank you, Makalo. I'm here, looking for your help."

"What can I do?"

Dave unwrapped a bundle he had been carrying. Makalo gazed in awe at the beautiful, gleaming sword, with its intricate scroll work on the blade and a beautifully crafted hilt. Dave kept the cloth on the blade and handed it hilt-first to Makalo. "Be careful—it's razor sharp."

Makalo, his eyes bright with wonder, admired the sword. "I have never seen such a fantastic sword. Where did you get it?"

"It's a long story. I want you to analyze it—X-ray, scanning electron microscopy, and anything else you can throw at it. This sword will cut through most other swords as if they were wood. It's virtually unbreakable and doesn't need sharpening. It's just come out of battle with the Bezerkers and doesn't have a mark on it, even though it cut through several Halcyon blades."

After several hours, Makalo was looking at the results. "So you really got a sword out of a tree, a blade tree?"

"Yes, the hilt, of course, was added later."

"Look at this," said Makalo, thrusting a micrograph a Dave. "The metal is an unknown alloy—mainly iron, but also manganese, cobalt, copper, carbon, and zinc. Here, see this very thin layer, this is a diamond allotrope of carbon perfectly bonded to the metal layer. Normally they would separate. I think I could bend this blade 180 degrees and it would not break, yet it cuts through steel if the blow is strong enough. These Ancients use plants to do metallurgy beyond anything we can do."

"You know what the funny thing is, Makalo? They understand the plants, but they don't understand the metallurgy. They're like a plumber using a wrench and pipe without knowing anything about the materials in those tools."

Makalo looked at the micrographs again, tracing the layers with his fingers. "You know Dave, we couldn't make this either, without the plants. We just don't have the kind of molecular control you need to assemble these layers so precisely. The plant must take the basic steel blade and gradually replace the iron and carbon with these components, and so the overall shape doesn't change, just the molecular structure."

"Dave, let me change the subject before I forget. You wanted to look through Hoffstetter's notes while I did the analysis. Did anything show up?"

"As a matter of fact, something curious did show up. Hoffstetter organized a complete turnover of staff after the building of the experimental field was about three quarters complete. In the official records, it looks as if he only bought enough equipment to conduct the experiment, but in his personal records, it's clear he bought much more."

"Where you going with this?"

"Well, what might Meglir want? At first I thought he wanted Halcyon itself to get our technology, which made sense. But our infrastructure is slowly falling apart. The real technology gold mine is back home. I think Meglir wants to get there. He would have both an army of Lesser Men to control and the technology to boot."

"But he would have no chance against us back home would he?"

"Maybe he would and maybe he wouldn't, but he may think he has. One of us is underestimating the other and I'm not sure Meglir is the one with the false estimation."

"So what do you conclude?"

Dave took a deep breath. "Hoffstetter bought enough equipment to replicate the Dislocation event and get us home and we have to figure out where he hid it. He built the storage facility and then fired the whole crew that knew about the construction and the equipment orders. Then he hid the duplicate equipment, hired a whole new crew to man the facility and took them along with the Dislocation. The new crew was never allowed to learn about the duplicate equipment because they would have tried to return home right away. So where would Hoffstetter have hidden it?"

Makalo stroked his forehead and leaned forward on his desk, his eyes closed in thought. "We have the power plant and could jury rig the cameras to know when the field had expanded beyond the bridge. So he would only need the equipment that was destroyed in the explosion and all of that essential control equipment would fit into a small room."

"Where would he put it? Where would I put it so no one would become curious?" Dave got up to pace around the office deep in thought.

Makalo snapped his fingers. I have it! Of course, under the control building that was destroyed! Hoffstetter would have complete control of that site before and after the Dislocation. It would be off limits to everyone else. Also, transporting a lot of equipment off site would create suspicion. The closer to the experimental field control center the better."

Dave held up a key. "This key was locked inside Hoffstetter's safe. Every other key had a label except this one, but it was in a special box as if he didn't want to lose it. My guess would be that if we can find the door that's unlocked by this key, we'll find what we're looking for."

They headed off to the equipment room that contained the field generator equipment destroyed in the Dislocation experiment. The control room housing the staff and the monitoring equipment was about fifty yards distant and had not been much affected by the explosion. The room had been cleared, mainly under Hoffstetter's supervision after the Dislocation. They searched the room thoroughly for forty-five minutes and found nothing.

Makalo stretched and yawned. "I'm not surprised we didn't find the door. I work here most days and would have known if there were an obvious additional door that was never used."

Dave motioned at a large piece of damaged equipment. "Have you ever moved that thing."

"What the Temporal Qualifier? No it was here right after Dislocation."

"Can we move it?"

Makalo obtained a small hydraulic lift with which he lifted the equipment then wheeled it away.

Dave looked eagerly at the floor, but disappointment washed over him—there was no trap door.

Dave sat down heavily. "I thought that was going to be it."

Makalo said nothing but got down on his hands and knees. He grabbed a broom and began sweeping the floor. Dave went over to kneel beside him.

"What is it Makalo?"

"Makalo pointed to a faint square outline. The concrete's not the same, Dave. It's poorly finished."

He got up and came back with a crow bar and hammered it into the floor. The concrete broke easily. After five minutes, they were looking at a steel door with plastic tape over the lock to keep it clean. The key fit.

"So what you're telling me," said MacDonald to Dave and Makalo, "is that you found all the equipment you need to replace the stuff burned out during the Dislocation experiment, in a buried room under the wreckage of the Field Generation Unit. It's been there the whole time, because Hoffstetter put it there." He leaned back, rubbing his eyes.

"That's right," said Dave stolidly.

"And then you tell me Dave, that the reason you think Hoffstetter kept this a big secret rather than take us straight home, was because he was talking to this Meglir guy through a big stick…"

"Not an ordinary stick, sir. This stick had bio-microcircuity…" MacDonald put up his hand and Makalo stopped talking.

Dave was beginning to get angry. He knew what he had heard and seen. MacDonald should listen to him. He sat up straight, pursed his lips and looked MacDonald straight in the eye.

MacDonald looked long and hard at Dave's determined face. MacDonald looked away and continued in a more conciliatory tone. "I'm just trying to show you how ridiculous—implausible your theory sounds."

"Sir," said Dave, "the story doesn't matter. The equipment find matters. Do we try to get back home right away or not?"

"You're quite right, the equipment find matters and yes, we'll try to get back as soon as possible. Makalo, get your team together and make this your top priority."

"What about Meglir and the Apemen?" asked Dave.

"I'm not going to have my men killed trying to dig them out of their maggot holes in South Mountain. If they want to come along for the ride, we'll deal with them with the resources we have back home. They won't stand a chance."

Dave wasn't so sure. Taking Meglir where he wanted to go, sounded dangerous.

"Alright, guys. I know I was pretty hard on you with my response to the Meglir theory. I was just rehearsing for the grilling I'm going to get when I get back home and try to make this implausible story sound sane. I do know, regardless of the reason, I can't thank you enough for finding the hidden storage area. You may have saved all of us.

"Dave, one more thing. Someone needs to travel up river and tell your friends at Eleytheria that we're going home. They all have amnesty. I don't know when we'll be ready, but we won't wait for stragglers."

Dave and Makalo said their goodbyes and left.

Walking back toward the experimental field, Dave asked, "Do you really think you can take us home?"

"Dave, I have not told you this, but I have been working on the theory behind the Dislocation. I have equations for the worlds. There are actually three."

"Three!" said Dave alarmed.

"Yes," said Makalo, "our world, this world and a third."

"Won't we then jump into the third world?"

"My calculations say 'no.' When atoms and molecules absorb light, electrons move from one orbital to another. We have equations, called transition integrals that tell us if that jump can happen. I developed similar equations for jumps in time dislocation. The integral to the third world, which trails this one time-wise, is what we call a forbidden transition, since the integral is nearly zero, so we'll skip over it. I think if we were in the third world, we could leave it, but not get back to it."

"One other curious thing comes from the equations—time differential between worlds change periodically in complicated cycles. My best guess is that, about two thousand and again about six hundred years ago, the time differentials between this world and our home world were very small. The different worlds' time envelopes bump into each other, but can't cross, so they mix and repel."

"What does that mean?" asked Dave bewildered.

"I'm not sure. Maybe for a time, when the times are mixing, there are portals, or places where one can cross over from one world to another. I'm still trying to understand the physical meaning of the calculations. Portals would develop where worlds were most similar in density and composition. Maybe in the next few hundred years we will see these portals appear."

"Wow," said Dave, "what would we do if suddenly we could bring a whole infantry division from home into this country?" Dave didn't like the possibilities.

The next few weeks were filled with frenetic activity. Al, Pam and Little Thomas had left for Eleytheria as soon as Dave had told them. Makalo and his team were working around the clock to be ready to try the experiment. They were about a week away when disaster struck.

Dave and Arlana were out for a walk along the East Harbor road. Dave's mood was somber. For some reason, going home should have filled him with delight, but he realized he would miss this place.

"Youngling, you seem sad," said Arlana.

"I'm wearing my feelings on my sleeve, am I?"

"Wearing your feelings on your sleeve?" repeated Arlana, puzzled.

Dave smiled. "It means you know what I'm feeling because I'm not able to hide my feelings."

"Why would you hide your feelings?"

"Oh, I don't know. People have power over you if they know you want something, are afraid, uncertain, or care."

"And you don't want to give them that power because you don't trust them—because you don't have faith in them."

"I guess that's it," said Dave.

"Why don't you want to go home to your family? Why would you possibly want to stay?"

Her tone was so unusual that he looked at her. Even in that evening light, he could see that there was a longing, a hunger in her eyes. *What's eating Arlana?*

"I do want to see my family. I miss them very much. But on the other hand, I guess I'm worried I won't fit in. I'm not the same person since you and Sirona healed me. They may even seize me and use me as a guinea pig to figure what they can learn from my new and improved biochemistry."

"A guinea pig?"

"An animal to try experiments on," said Dave.

"They would do that?" Her eyes were wide. "Your people are bent. You must stay here."

"I'm torn, Arlana—I really am. I'm longing to go home, but I will miss this place terribly if I go. What if I go and long to come back but can't?"

Something caught Dave's eye. They were walking north toward East Harbor and it was after midnight. The night was dark. Dave stopped and pointed out to sea. A chill of foreboding gripped his heart.

"Arlana, what do you see?"

She looked and gripped his arm. With trembling voice, she said, "Oh no, no! The black fleet of the Bent Ones. They've returned."

Dave used his cell phone to try to call MacDonald. There was no answer. He tried a few other numbers without success. "Where are they? Why isn't anyone on alert?" he muttered.

"We have to warn the others," said Dave. "I'll run to headquarters, and you keep trying to call anyone who will answer on my contact list. He thrust the phone into her hands and rushed off. "Clear out before the Bent Ones land," Dave shouted over his shoulder as he ran toward the center of campus.

Dave hadn't sprinted more than two hundred yards before he saw the lights of one of Halcyon's ethanol-powered trucks approaching. He jumped into the middle of the road, wildly waving his arms. The truck screeched to a halt, its horn blaring. The driver jumped out of the cab, furious and ready to throttle Dave.

"We're under attack," Dave shouted pointing east. "Take me to MacDonald."

The driver looked east into the dark night and, of course, could not see anything. But apparently Dave's demeanor had convinced him he ought to take Dave seriously and his anger evaporated as he said, "Hop in."

The driver put the truck into gear and mumbled to himself about how he was going to take Dave apart if this turned out to be a drunken prank. Dave said nothing. Within minutes, the truck screeched to a halt before headquarters and Dave jumped out calling 'thanks.' The driver, still surly, said nothing but drove off, tires squealing.

Dave ran into police headquarters expecting to find a duty officer at the front desk. There was no one. He saw him in a side room, with a cap pulled over his face, asleep. Dave shook him.

The duty officer, was startled awake. "What the hell…"

"Get up," shouted Dave. "We're under attack." Finally he was getting through.

The duty officer, still groggy, stumbled back to his desk. He tried MacDonald and swore when there was no answer. He called another number and told the listener to wake MacDonald now. "We're under attack."

"What to do? What to do?" said the duty officer to himself, in near panic.

"Call the Command Center in the administration building, they can monitor the invasion from East Harbor. Alert the naval base and the perimeter forces around South Mountain. I'm heading to admin. What's the pass code?"

"Disabled," said the duty officer absently. "Just walk right in."

The duty officer began punching in telephone numbers and Dave rushed out the door and ran to the Command Center.

He arrived there, just as another groggy serviceman was on the telephone, while wildly trying to bring up the necessary screens. Dave saw a blanket lying in the corner beside four chairs that had been arranged into a rough bed.

Another watcher, asleep on the job, he thought ruefully.

He studied the large wall-sized monitor, now displaying many windows from cameras all over the island. He found East Harbor and what he observed dismayed him. He saw the lumbering forms of Apemen, leaving the black-sailed ships on the quay. Then he saw the more rapid strides of Halfmen, carrying their crude weapons. Finally he saw black-cloaked shapes also disembarking. The hoods of the cloaks completely shrouded the faces of the Bent Ones.

So these are the Bent Ones that I've been hearing so much about. The first one he saw was riding an enormous Lup, one of the large wolves Dave had encountered in the Quarry Pass, which led to the City of the Dead. The ridden Lup, controlled by the cloaked figure, was accompanied by a pack of Lupi. He could hear the barks as the Lupi spread out for action.

What happened next, dismayed him even more. From one of the ships that had disgorged its Apemen, came an ominous shape he recognized all too well—a Rokash. The reptile stood eight feet tall at the shoulder. Unlike the Rokash he had killed to earn his *Hansa* name, Rokomer, this *Rokash* had a saddle and a harness. In the saddle sat another Bent One.

A soldier broke cover, trying to run back to his company. The Bent One touched the side of the Rokash's neck and the monster leapt, pinning the hapless soldier to the ground, dismembering him with the first bite. The Bent One howled in triumph and then guided the Rokash back to the Apemen.

What he had witnessed filled Dave with nausea. He willed himself to study his adversary. This Bent One, with a cloak of a different shade (although he couldn't tell the color in the dark) had an air of command. A line of Halcyonites had finally formed and thrown up a crude barricade. The bodies of lumbering Apemen, felled by crossbow bolts, littered the road. Suddenly the Bent One on the Rokash approached and extended his hand menacingly. He could see the defenders quail, then throw down their weapons and run back toward the center of campus. Dave thought back with a shudder to the time in the cavern at Fort Linderhof, near the City of the Dead, when they had first encountered the lieutenant of Meglir and the horrible assault of fear that had paralyzed him. This time there were no *Hansa* to sing their way through the terror. He could see the same fear in the actions of the fleeing combatants.

But not everyone fled. The right flank held and kept up a withering fire into the ranks of the massed Apemen and Halfmen. Suddenly a pack of Lupi emerged from the attackers' line and they were among the Halcyonites in a moment. The firing dwindled away as the men were fighting for their lives; the hordes of Apemen overran this part of the line as well.

He looked for camera views of South Mountain. He found one. What he had dreaded was also happening here. Meglir had assaulted the defensive line around the mountain. Dave could see a wedge of Bezerkers bursting through the barricades.

I've been such a fool, he thought. *It was all right in front of me and I missed it. And now I've helped them get what they want.* He knew what he must do, but did he have the courage to do it?

But before I do that, I have to get Arlana out of here. She's a prize the Bent Ones covet.

As if summoned, Arlana came into the room.

Dave grabbed her arm and hauled her out the door. "Come on, Arlana, we have to go!" She didn't resist. Dave headed toward the center of campus at a trot. "Arlana, you have to get off the island. If Meglir catches you, you may end up like Hoffstetter."

"Meglir, a male, can't use a female host," said Arlana.

"Okay," said Dave, exasperated, "so you'll be host to some female Bent One."

"None of us are allowed to leave Gurundaria, until we have the strength of will to resist the possession."

"You and I both know, Arlana," said Dave scowling at her as he ran beside her, "you left without permission."

Arlana grimaced but didn't say a word. They came to the experimental field.

Dave stopped and grabbed Arlana's elbow and made her face him. "Arlana, I have to destroy the Dislocation equipment—that's what Meglir is really after. I can't let him get back to my world."

She nodded.

"But even more important to me, I need to get you to safety." Now he had her attention. She looked up at his face, her eyes widening.

"I couldn't bear it if you were captured. I think I'm a big enough fool to have fallen in love with you. Will you promise me, you'll get off the island?"

"I will promise what you ask Dave. I will be ready when help comes." A shadow of a smile crept across her face. "I will also consider your proposal for marriage most earnestly."

"My proposal for what? Never mind. Just get off the island now!"

Arlana leaned forward, kissed Dave gently on the cheek, and then melted into the shadows as she headed southeast towards Romulus and Remus.

Dave shook his head in confusion and then remembered what he had come to do.

How am I going to destroy that equipment? If I had C-4, I could blow it up. If I had a sledge hammer, I could smash it. In the end he decided, rather than search for a sledge hammer, he would build the biggest fire he could inside and rely on the heat and smoke to destroy as much of the equipment as possible. He opened the door to the building and threw what papers he found lying around onto the middle of the floor. He ran outside and found some lumber and sticks and dragged them in. He crumpled and threw the papers into a small pile, pyramided the sticks against them and lit the papers at several places. The flame leapt up. He stacked the two-by-fours on top and even rolled one of the operator chairs over hoping that it might catch. He ran out the door to get more wood and collided with a Bezerker. The force of the collision knocked the Bezerker down. A second Bezerker raised his sword, but a bellow stopped him. "Don't kill him. He's mine," said a familiar voice.

It was Bigelow. "Tie him to that tree," commanded Bigelow, pointing to a tree at the edge of the experimental field.

Dave heard the soft hiss of the injectors as each command by Bigelow was emphasized by an injection of Hyperhap into the Bezerkers.

Just then Bigelow noticed the smoke pouring from the building and swore as he rushed in with the other Bezerkers to put out the flames.

Dave was dragged to the edge of the experimental field. Suddenly, one of the Bezerkers fell with an arrow through his heart. Another arrow felled the second Bezerker. Arlana stepped out from behind the tree.

"Come suitor," said Arlana. "I can't have the first man who proposed marriage to me killed so soon after the event. What would that do to my reputation?"

Dave looked back at the building. Smoke was still pouring out the door. There was nothing more he could do. They had to go.

Chapter 33

Fugitives

Dave and Arlana sat on the lookout rock at Romulus. Dave was peering anxiously for any sign of a boat approaching. He turned to Arlana who was sitting with her legs drawn up and her arms folded around her knees, her wet braid over her left shoulder. "We can't stay here Arlana. Several people know we've been hiding here now. Meglir and the Bent Ones will find out if they don't know already."

"I know Dave. But what frightened the others? Why did they leave? Where did they go?"

"I don't know Arlana, but it could have been many things: the black ships approaching, the fires on Halcyon, the sound of gunfire in the woods—but all that doesn't matter now. We need to decide what to do next."

"I have an idea," said Arlana. "My people, when they travel great distances on the sea on their Dorai, often need to rest. There are small floating mats of weeds called *Sorgai*. They provide a dry place to rest and even can be used for food. We need to search for one, then use that as a hiding place, or how do you say it, for a base of operations."

"Well, we could try that," said Dave in a skeptical tone.

Arlana, lost in thought, continued. "Our best chance would be when the *Sorgai* drift in with the tide. We should go to the northern side of the island where the coast is most rugged and few people go."

The next tide found them swimming off the northern coast. The sea was choppy as if a storm had churned up the water far from land. On the crest of a wave, Arlana pointed to a small mass far out in the ocean. "We could ride it until we come close to shore," suggested Arlana.

"It's a long way off, and it's only the first one we've seen. Let's keep looking."

The next hour only produced sightings which were even further away. Dave was just about to suggest Arlana had been right, when he spotted a floating mat west of them. Arlana saw it at the same time and they swam for it.

The mat was a rough disk about three meters in diameter. It consisted of a mass of fibrous air bladders and tough vines in a compact mass. On top, completely out of the water, a second layer of vines like ivy, filled the surface with leaves. Shrubs, extending up to two meters into the air, gave the mats the appearance of a miniature forest.

"Let me show you how my people use these mats," said Arlana. She took out her belt knife and cut an opening into the fibrous matt. "There are several living things that come together as a *Sorgai* mat," she explained.

"I think we call them symbiotes," said Dave.

"It's important to only cut the top layer and then one can use the mat as a floating tent."

Arlana, rolled the foliage she had cut into a cylinder. She did this four times and then crawled through the hole she had made. "I will need your help, Dave."

Dave followed her in. There was a gap between the floating bladders and gourds, and a layer of fibrous plants that grew on top. Light filtered through the dense foliage above them. In the semi-darkness he brushed her calf as he followed her in. He felt a thrill at the contact.

"Dave, please push up on the roof plants."

Was there a change in her voice? Was it just the acoustics of this enclosed space?

"I need to place these pillars upright to make a space, like a tent."

Dave pulled himself back and pushed with all his strength. The gap between the layers widened and he was surprised how easily he was able to lift the roof. Soon Arlana had all four pillars secure, and a space, about one-and-a-half meters by two meters had been created. There was not enough room to sit up.

"Why don't you get some rest, Arlana," said Dave gently, "I'll keep watch and see if we have an opportunity to snag the shore."

"That might be best," said Arlana.

Dave climbed back out and folded his arms around his knees. *Did she want me to stay?* He felt his desire for her well up inside him. *Maybe I could find some fruit on some of these plants and just see if she's hungry? I'm kidding myself. But on the other hand, she figures we're betrothed—it doesn't really matter does it? After all God is a forgiving God and loves us.*

I'm thinking with my gonads. God knows my secret thoughts better than I do. But on top of that, I will know and Arlana will know. We may both want it, but after the moment of pleasure has passed, how will we feel then? No, this won't answer. We'll either start this relationship properly or not at all. He looked for something to take his mind off Arlana.

He looked at the fine material of his living cloak. Arlana had made if for him from his living blanket and pulled it out of her pack when they were deciding what to do on Romulus. The cloak was wonderfully warm and easy to swim in. Every time he touched it, it reminded him of Arlana.

The wind was veering around to the north. At the risk of being seen, he took off his living cloak and stood at the south end of the *Sorgai* and spread his cloak wide, hoping to make as much leeway as possible.

After about ten minutes, he saw what he was looking for, an uprooted sapling that had drifted down the Halcyon River and was now at the mercy of the tide. Dave plunged into the water and dragged it back to their raft. He opened the waterproof bag he had acquired in Halcyon for his frequent swims to Romulus and pulled out his sword. *This is a waste for such a good blade.* He began slicing at the sapling, first trimming off the branches and then hacking off the roots. The sword was unbelievably sharp taking deep bites with every stroke. When the ten foot pole was finished he tried to decide if it was better to use as a mast or as an oar. He decided he would try it as an oar. He wrapped the oar with wiry vines to act as an oarlock and then swung it back and forth like a gondolier.

Twilight began to settle in. He knew there were rocks off shore just ahead. He dove under the raft and saw many roots hanging down, including three or four thick, very long roots that acted like a keel and kept the raft from flipping. He took one, as thick as his arm, and pulled it over to the rocks that were only twenty feet off shore in a shallow bay. He dragged the end of the root ashore wedging a portion of the length into a split that had rent the rock in two. On the other side of the rock, he wound the end of the root around an oblong stone, the largest he could lift, and placed the stone in the shallow water on the landward side of the rocky reef. He surveyed his work. The crack in the rock would keep the root from fraying on the surface of the reef. The loops around the stone would prevent the raft from pulling away. As long as the drifting of the raft didn't sever the root, the raft would stay. In a heavy sea, it wouldn't have a chance, but for most moderate seas, the shallow bay would provide sufficient protection.

To be safe, we had better hide our supplies on land whenever we head out.

Dave was crouching on the hill overlooking East Harbor. He could just make out the experimental field. There was a lot of activity and he thought he saw Hoffstetter. *What if my fire hadn't worked? What if they were ramping up the generators even now? Shouldn't I send Arlana away? Yeah right.*

There was another problem. Hoffstetter's crew had carried several crates off the ships. The crates were made of slats and they contained brown objects like coconuts. The crates were heavily guarded by a Bent One on a Lup and many Halfmen. The boxes were finally moved into a warehouse near the East Harbor quay. Why would the Bent Ones disperse cargo over many ships? Why guard coconuts? He and Arlana would have to find out. Arlana joined him wearing her cloak. As always, he only saw her because she was moving. Those cloaks were remarkable; they would be counting on their invisibility tonight.

He and Arlana decided to have something to eat before they started out. Yesterday Arlana had found some shellfish and he had caught a few small fish with his fishing line. Their meal had been cooked on a small fire on the shore last night, but the remains still tasted good cold. He drank some water from his water skin. Arlana had told him they could drink sea water, since their bodies could process the salt, but he hated the taste.

They began their journey down the hill to East Harbor. When they left the trees, they wrapped their cloaks tightly around themselves. Dave checked that his sword was free in its scabbard. They headed for the water tower near the wharfs, since they needed to use the stairs for their plan. The night was very dark and the streets were deserted. Their biggest concern was being smelled by the Lupi. When they reached the upper landing of the water tower, Dave climbed over the railing and leapt lightly to the nearest warehouse rooftop. Arlana waved off the rope he proffered and leapt, equally lightly, to join him. She didn't make a sound.

Bending low, he led the way across the roofs, since all the warehouse sheds shared adjoining walls. When he finally came to the one he wanted, he went to a ventilation window and, using his Swiss Army Knife, he unscrewed the screen. Inside, it was pitch black. He pulled out his flashlight and shielding the light with his body, shone the light into the cavernous room. It was empty except for a small stack of the coconut boxes near the entrance. Putting his flashlight on its lowest power setting, he snapped it to his belt and swung onto the ceiling strut. Carefully moving along it to the wall, he was able to work his way down the corrugated side using a support post. Arlana was close behind him. He heard her gasp as she approached the stacks of crates. He saw now that most of the crates contained what seemed to be half coconuts. Only one box contained the joined halves of a full nut.

"What are they, Arlana?"

"They are Swamp Oak nuts. They come in pairs. Most of these boxes are Swamp Oak halves. The other halves have probably been planted in Abaddon, and these are to be planted at the travel destination. These others are the full acorns with two halves and can be used to found a whole new connection."

"What do you mean?"

"Swamp Oak only grow in swamps and fens, but act like our Travel Oaks. The fully grown trees are only big enough to take one or two people, but unlike the Travel Oaks, they grow fast. There are many hundreds here. If these halves are planted in a swamp, the Bent Ones could bring a raiding party through."

Dave put one full acorn and a half acorn into his knapsack for study.

"They must want to take these to my world." said Dave, "Then they could go back and forth. We don't spend much time in swamps, but they could use them as a base of operations."

"We could come back later and destroy them," said Arlana.

"We have to destroy them now." said Dave, "What if the Lupi smell us and they know we were here. Then they would guard the Swamp Oak acorns carefully and we wouldn't get another chance. No, I think whatever we're going to do we have to do tonight.

"We have to use fire," said Arlana, "but it has to burn quickly or else the enemy will put it out."

"Halcyonites have been using ethanol and biodiesel as an alternate fuel for the boats. Maybe there's some stored in the other warehouses. Let's break these boxes apart and spread the acorns out. We can use the wooden boxes as kindling."

The plan quickly became unworkable. Although Dave could pull the slats off the boxes by hand, without tools, it was too slow. In the end he used the boxes he had pulled apart to make a pile and dragged the other boxes around the kindling stack. There was a door to the adjacent warehouse. It wasn't locked. He found some papers, a few oily rags, but the rest was machinery under repair. The next door proved more helpful. There were several Jerry cans, some labeled "ethanol" and others labeled "diesel." Dave grabbed the diesel first, carefully climbed up to the top of the pile, and drenched the acorns and boxes with the fuel. He sent Arlana up to the roof (of course she didn't listen to him, and waited in the rafters).

Dave decided only to pour out some of the ethanol. He was afraid of a fireball or an explosion if the vapor built up. He put the opened cans into the center of the pile and left them there. Taking a wooden slat and wrapping an oily rag about it, he climbed up to the rafters near the ventilation exit. He lit the torch with a lighter and tossed it onto the pile. Even before it hit, the vapors blazed up.

They raced across the rooftops. The light was already showing in the ventilation window. *We certainly left our calling card.* When they had climbed down, Dave already heard shouts and snarls. He and Arlana sprinted for the trees. Dave saw a black shape streak toward him in the dim light. He turned and pulled out his sword and swung just as the large shape launched itself for him. The blade bit deep into the Lup's neck, severing the massive head from the body. Still the weight of the carcass drove him to the ground. He shoved it off, and covered with gore, wiped the wolf's blood from his eyes and resumed his sprint into the trees.

Then they heard it. The sound of a battle horn.

Chapter 34

The Battle for Halcyon

"Well now we've done it," said Dave, "we've roused the whole camp."

Arlana was listening intently. "No, I don't think so," she said. "Those are the battle horns of my people. They must be attacking! They probably began to attack without warning hoping for surprise. When my people realized the surprise had been lost, they sounded the battle horns to let everyone know stealth was no longer required."

It became clear to Dave: he may have fouled everything up. The Gurundarians, under Kelldor, were attacking. Arlana and Dave, in burning the warehouse, had roused the whole camp and taken away Kelldor's surprise advantage.

Dave's recriminations were bitter, but a part of his mind told him he couldn't possibly have known about the attack. He knew what he had to do.

"You head back to the *Sorgai* raft, I'm going back." In the dim light, he could see her lips tremble. She put her hand on his arm. "I know what you're thinking, my betrothed. You blame yourself for rousing the Bent Ones. You couldn't have known. Don't rashly throw your life away. There's one who couldn't bear the thought of being alone without you."

He put his arms around her waist, pulled her toward himself and then realized he was covered in blood from the Lup. He stopped, but she rose on her toes and kissed him lightly on his lips. He pushed her back and looked at her now blood-streaked face, and the Lupi bloodstains on her outfit. He ran his hand over her face. "I love you, Arlana."

"I know," she said as she kissed his hand and it touched her cheek. "Let's go together and help in whatever way we can."

"Alright," said Dave. They returned to their lookout post and picked up the extra weapons they had hidden there. Dave looked back at the warehouse, which was completely engulfed in flames. On the shore he could see upright figures—riding what must have been Dorai—approach the shore and then leap off. A reed boat full of diminutive figures also pulled ashore, then they attacked the ships of the Bent Ones.

"The *Hansa* are also here!" exclaimed Dave. "Kelldor must have summoned all of his allies. He's really brought everyone. We have to get back to the field generation building. They ran under cover of the trees, getting as close as possible to the experimental field. They saw surprisingly few people. Most were running either south or west. Arlana and Dave moved quietly from building to building, counting on their cloaks to hide them. Finally they reached the perimeter of the experimental field. In the very center stood the field generation building. At first glance, there appeared to be no sentries. Then an Apeman ambled out of the open doorway of the field generation building and began patrolling the grounds.

Dave didn't know if killing the Apeman would alert whomever was controlling him. He decided not to take that chance. The Apeman was slow, his circuit predictable, so Dave knew he and Arlana simply had to be patient and wait until the Apeman wandered to the other end of the experimental field.

As the Apeman disappeared into the shadows of a storage shed, Dave and Arlana began their approach. All of the rubble had not been removed, so there were still piles of debris that made a sheltered route possible. Their final dash took them within twenty yards of the field generation building. After checking for other sentries, Dave and Arlana sprinted to the entrance and stepped inside. Four Apemen were standing motionless. A black-robed figure was working on the open panel of a machine across the room.

As soon as they entered, the four Apemen began to move toward them. The Bent One turned and raised his gnarled hands, contorted into two claws. Dave felt a wave of fear sweep over him just as he had when he had encountered the black statue at the Battle of City Point. He tried to raise his hands, but the terror had immobilized them. He looked at Arlana. If he didn't act, she would be killed. Cold wrath welled up within him. The torrent of fear snapped like a chain bursting. He had his sword out and had killed the first Apeman before the creature could grasp and rend Arlana. The other three Apemen turned towards him as the Bent One pulled out a black blade covered with a white oil. Arlana seemed frozen, unable to move.

Dave attacked the three Apemen and killed them with three rapid strokes.

The Bent One swung his blade. Dave's life was saved as the black blade caught a light fixture that deflected the killing stroke. Dave's blade struck the black metal and sparks flew, but his blade did not cut through the Bent One's steel. He was clearly out matched. The Bent One was mouthing incantations that chilled Dave to the bone and robbed him of strength. His foe was playing with him now, tiring him out. Dave could see a confident leer grow on the Bent One's face under his cowl.

Help me!

Suddenly the Bent One staggered, an arrow buried to the feathers in his chest, his red blood staining the cloak. The black sword fell from nerveless fingers as the robed figure fell on his face.

Dave turned to see Arlana leaning against the door frame, tears welling from her eyes. "Dave, I'm so sorry. I was paralyzed. I was so terrified, I couldn't move."

Dave took her in his arms and cradled her head on his shoulder. "I know, I felt it too. But you saved me in the end. He was just playing with me, enjoying my terror. I knew I was outmatched and beaten. Toward the end he could have killed me at any time."

Dave looked out the doorway. "We have work to do," he said. "Arlana, let me get rid of the bodies. You stand watch."

"Be careful of the sword, Dave. That milky oil is poison." Arlana ran out the door. Dave dragged the Apemen's corpses outside and hid them behind a pile of rubble. The still form of the Bent One, limbs splayed, lay before him on the floor, blood congealing in a small puddle. Dave dragged it to the rubble pile.

Arlana came back as he was finishing with the Bent One. "For now there's no movement out there," she said. "What should we do next?"

"If we lock ourselves into the control room and Kelldor doesn't win, we're finished," mused Dave. "I think we will be more effective if we're free to engage the enemy. But I have to disable this unit in case our side loses."

He ran back inside and looked at the module with the back off. With a screwdriver, he loosened the control panel on the unit, unplugged the cables and carried it with him. "Maybe this will disable the unit."

"Are you sure that's enough?"

"Nope. It will just have to do."

By now, the sky was growing lighter, and Dave felt much more conspicuous as they left the building. He led Arlana to a copse of trees. In the center of the copse was a gigantic oak. Dave, clutching the rough bark, pulled himself up into the branches. He climbed as high as he could until he had cleared the other trees and could see the field generation building clearly. He looked east and could see the glow of the warehouses still burning. Now there were additional fires—the Black Fleet was ablaze.

In the distance, Dave saw a steady stream of men, Bent Ones and Lupi heading west. Soon he noticed men, hard to see because of their living cloaks, advancing and harrying the enemy. The *Hansa* were even harder to see; they advanced under cover faster than the Ancients, got behind enemy lines, and then used their arrows on their retreating enemies. No one had re-entered the field generation building. Now all they could do was sit and wait, while on guard.

By late afternoon, Dave saw three ships with black sails leave West Harbor. They had been hidden by the hill that shielded the quay from the main campus. Was it over? Had they won?

Dave climbed down when he saw a group of *Hansa* approach The field generation building. He and Arlana went over and were delighted to find Hanomer at the head of a band of *Hansa* warriors. Dave knelt down and hugged his friend.

"Hanomer, it is so good to see you."

"And you friend Dave. I am thankful to the Creator to see you well."

"Hanomer, have you seen Al, Pam, and Little Thomas? We couldn't find them at Romulus."

"Yes, friend Dave. A black ship discharged troops onto Halcyon just off Romulus. I counseled them to leave right away and we sailed toward the Goose's Neck only to meet up with Kelldor. Kelldor would not let Al join the fight. You will see him soon."

"Hanomer, where is Kelldor now? I want to let him know Arlana is safe."

"He is fighting at East Harbor. I cannot guide you since we still have to hunt through all of the buildings to make sure that all of the enemy has fled and that the buildings are safe."

Dave returned the control unit to the field generation building and then he and Arlana headed off towards East Harbor. As they approached the harbor, Apemen and Lupi were still fighting. A lup came toward them. Arlana shot it with an arrow and Dave finished it off.

They were by themselves. If the enemy saw them, they would be quickly outnumbered. Suddenly a group of Bent Ones appeared, one riding a Rokash. Several Gurundarians appeared with archers shooting from behind and swordsmen fighting in front. Suddenly the Rokash with its rider leapt and grabbed a swordsman in its jaw shaking him like a terrier shakes a rabbit. The valiant swordsman tried to stab the beast until the end but then went limp. Arlana shot an arrow at the rider. Dave charged in and swung with all of his might at the neck of the Rokash as it tore at its hapless prey. The sword cut the head off in one stroke and the beast fell over, blood spurting from the severed neck. Ahead, a group of Ancients in chainmail armor and living cloaks charged the Bent Ones. Sparks flew as their swords collided. None could withstand the leader. He cut down four Bent Ones. The others fled. He turned and looked at Dave and Arlana and took off his helmet. It was Kelldor.

Kelldor took a long look at his retreating foes, shouted commands to his companions and then rushed over to Arlana with a broad smile on his face. "Daughter, daughter" was all that he could say as he gathered her into his embrace.

Although Dave had tried to clean the dried blood off his clothes, he was still a mess, yet Kelldor hugged him next. There was a merry twinkle in his eye. "Come behind this tree," he said. "They still have archers loose."

When they had taken shelter, he smiled again. "Everything has gone well, very well indeed. We have dealt the Bent Ones a sharp blow that may give us peace for some time and, even more importantly, we may have prevented a great disaster.

"Come and rest for a minute. I need a drink. Would you like some?"

Just then Ferris arrived. "Lord Kelldor, the enemy has been routed and driven into the sea. We still have pockets of fighting."

"Well done Ferris. I think I can leave this in your capable hands. I need to go back to camp and look after the wounded."

He led them southwest to the fields of the experimental farm. "Tell me what happened here," said Kelldor, "since I left to gather our forces."

As they walked, Arlana related their adventures since Kelldor had left on the Dorai. Kelldor beamed at news of the rescue of the trapped people at New Jerusalem and then of the assault by MacDonald to retake Halycon. Ferris had already told Kelldor much of this news. Then

Arlana told her father about Dave's attempt to destroy field generation equipment, his rescue, and their guerilla warfare from the *Sorgai* raft. At this, Kelldor looked sharply at the two of them, but said nothing.

When Arlana related the discovery of the Swamp Oak acorns and their destruction of the warehouses, Kelldor murmured "So that was you two."

"I'm sorry Sir," interjected Dave, "I realize now that I alerted Meglir's forces just as you were attacking and took away your surprise."

"You did well, young man," said Kelldor. "You had no way of knowing of our attack and the fire did distract Meglir enough to help us build momentum. He defended to the south and east when we were mainly attacking from the south."

"Did you capture Meglir, sir?" asked Dave.

"No," said Kelldor wistfully, "it seems Meglir, and most of the Bent Ones—except the few we killed—escaped from West Harbor. They did not land on the mainland, nor head up river. Our *Hansa* allies chased them and they were clearly heading back to Abaddon. We did however capture two of Meglir's lieutenants and that will bring down to three those still holding the City of the Dead. We still cannot take their cavern, but their hold is much diminished.

"What about our friend MacDonald? Did you find him?"

"Yes, this camp we're now occupying had been used to hold many captured troops. They were sleeping on the ground and the perimeter was guarded by Bent Ones and Apemen. The Hansa had scouted ahead under cover of darkness and brought us the information. We were afraid Meglir would kill the prisoners once he found we were attacking, so we sent a force ahead and scattered the Bent Ones and the Apemen. Once free, Commander MacDonald took his men to the west side of the island and drove the enemy up the coast on that side, freeing up our people for the attack on the main campus. He should be back soon."

They arrived at the perimeter of the camp. The Gurundarian archers, patrolling the perimeter, greeted Lord Kelldor. In the center was a large hospital tent and a smaller pavilion, flying Kelldor's headquarters' flag. Kelldor took them to the pavilion and beckoned them to a couple of chairs, A servant brought them something to drink. "But let me tell you my story briefly. After I left you on Romulus," said Kelldor, "I gathered our army as quickly as I could. We landed in the south and on the mainland in force, and attacked South Mountain and the tunnel entrance on the mainland side. There were two lieutenants of Meglir, one inside South Mountain and one in a cavern on the mainland. They were too far apart to help each other, and we were able to subdue their fear—just barely—by the singing of the *Hansa* and the power of the council. All the Lupi and Halfmen were with Meglir, so with the lieutenants neutralized, the Apemen stopped their concerted opposition, sometimes attacking us, sometimes wandering aimlessly, and other times attacking each other.

"It was at that point that we approached the main campus buildings. It was hard to maintain contact between our force and MacDonald's. We had bypassed the naval base in the south because it was too well defended. We had collected a third southern force to attack the naval base when the fires started and many rushed out of the base to defend against that attack. That's when we sounded the horns and took the South Harbor without much trouble. The main campus was another matter. From then on it was a slow, tough struggle, but I think the will to fight went out of them when Meglir, who I think was in charge, decided he could not risk being caught. With the leadership fleeing on the ships, the Lupi, Halfmen, and a handful of Bent Ones fought with terrible ferocity, determined to kill as many of us as possible. The Bent Ones are dead, the rest we are still chasing down."

"What about the Bezerkers?" asked Dave.

A sad look crossed Kelldor's face. "Of all of our enemies, they were redeemable if only we could have captured them. Perhaps, that hope, on our part made us reluctant to kill them. They were vicious and killed many of my people. In the end we had to kill them all, since they fought with such ferocity. It fills me with great sadness at the loss of life—both ours and theirs.

"Come, enough of talk. You look famished and need to eat." In typical Gurundar fashion, Kelldor rose to serve them. At that point Hanomer appeared and, of course, was delighted to partake in a meal.

Kelldor excused himself to visit the wounded in the hospital tent. Arlana, Dave and Hanomer spoke of the peace this victory would bring, the opening of the road, past the City of the Dead—its power now diminished—to the coast, and the reforging of the alliance of *Hansa* and Gurundarians. Dave started to nod off. When Kelldor returned, he offered Dave a tent to sleep in, but Dave asked to return to his dorm room.

Hanomer went back with him. They walked in silence. Dave stripped off his clothes, set them to soak in water, showered and then dropped into bed.

It was the following morning when he awoke to find Hanomer quietly sitting in the corner, nursing a cup of *Siph*.

"Friend, Dave," said Hanomer, "Come have a cup of *Siph*. Soon we will send the second of Meglir's lieutenants to a watery rest."

"What are you talking about Hanomer?" said Dave stretching and then yawning.

"We are going to drop Meglir's lieutenant into the sea, far from land."

"Why not destroy the statue?"

"We discussed that possibility, thinking we could use your explosives to blow the stone casing apart. Then, we'd burn the Swamp Oak within. But Kelldor argued that both lieutenants were great men, before they were corrupted. It is not for us to take life needlessly. Perhaps after long thought, even these may turn and repent of what they have done.

"It would be too dangerous to sink two such powers together, so the *Hansa* loremasters and the Council went out with the first this morning. We will discharge the second into the depths this afternoon, well separated from the first."

After lunch, Dave changed into his best buckskin outfit, took his sword and his crossbow and went with Hanomer to East Harbour. The black, hideous statue, with the three terrible faces looking out, had already been made fast to the barge. Dave joined the council, Arlana, Ferris, and MacDonald on the barge. One of the fishing trawlers towed them out to sea, toward the south. After several miles, when the depth was more than two thousand feet, they left the barge. MacDonald set off some charges that scuttled the wooden vessel. As the barge filled with water, they saw it roll over and the statue sink into the depths.

"It is done now," said Kelldor. "We can relax our vigilance. He has sunk far enough into the depths that he can no longer threaten us with fear."

He turned to Dave and whispered. "David, do exactly as I tell you and act like you're meeting your adopted father."

"Rokodor," said Kelldor in a loud voice. "I have a surprise for you. Your adopted father is here."

The man, whom he had met briefly at Giant Steps, clasped his arms around him and said, "My son, it is so good to see you safe. I have heard from my life friend, Kelldor, of your exploits and I could not be prouder as a father." Celyddon seemed to be genuinely proud of him. Out of the corner of his eye, he saw Arlana turning red and behind her another superbly dressed man with a scowl on his face, standing with Teledon.

Great, thought Dave, *I hardly know these people and I'm already making powerful enemies.*

But he said, "Thank you, father. It is so good to see you too." Dave then initiated another hug so he wouldn't have to say more.

Kelldor grasped Celyddon's arm in his right hand and Dave in his left. He said, "I'm sure you have many things to say to each other in private." He led them to the stern and left them.

Celyddon whispered, "We'll talk later Dave, and decide what to do. We're being watched by Arachodor's people. They're still hoping to use you against Kelldor and me."

They stood together for the voyage home, with Celyddon asking Dave to repeat his exploits of the last few days. After about half an hour, Arachodor, scowling at the turn of events, was called away to a meeting.

When they docked at the quay, Arlana came up, looking more frightened than Dave remembered since their near disaster at the city of Arkand. "Dave," she said with trembling lips, "I need to talk to you, now."

"Yeah, me too, Arlana. Let's go for a walk." They were first off the boat, afraid that someone would stop them. They walked north at a brisk pace.

Dave broke the silence. "You know, Arlana, if the equipment at the field generation building is functional, MacDonald will try to take Halcyon back."

"I know," said Arlana. Her voice was almost a whisper.

"I'm not going back."

"Oh!" said Arlana. Silence.

"Aren't you going to ask me why?" said Dave at last.

"Why aren't you going back, Dave?" another tentative whisper.

Dave took a deep breath. *Here goes.*

"I have two reasons, Arlana." He tried to sound as matter-of-fact as possible as he continued. "Both reasons are important, but one is much more important than the other."

Arlana looked up at him, but said nothing.

"First, the lessor of the two reasons. I'm not the same person I was when I left. To my people back home I'm a freak now. A freak who can see in the dark, change skin color, swim under water a long time, and one who can drink sea water without killing himself. I wouldn't fit in, and frankly, much of our government is like Blackmore and Halcyon. They'll want to study me for the good of the State. My life would be hell."

"That's a pretty important reason. I can see why you don't want to go back."

Dave turned toward Arlana and took both her hands. "But the main reason I want to stay is that I love you, Arlana, and I want to marry you."

"You love me," said Arlana, tears welling in her eyes. She thought of something and then smiled mischievously. "You know I will be a very difficult wife."

"Yes," said Dave breaking out into a smile himself. "I'm counting on it."

"I will be correcting you all of the time."

"Yes," said Dave rolling his eyes, "and you know I will be ignoring most of your corrections."

"We will probably be fighting constantly."

"Yes, we will," said Dave, "but making up should be fun."

"David Schuster, you are the most exasperating man I have ever met, but I can't bear to be parted from you, so I accept." She rose up on her toes, put her arms around his neck and kissed him. Dave returned her kiss, tenderly.

When they finally separated, Dave said. "Well, you didn't exactly melt into my arms when I proposed to you."

"Do I strike you as 'the melt in your arms' type?" she asked.

"No, I guess not."

They started to walk back to the quay. She took his arm and leaned her cheek against his shoulder in a brief hug. "We need to go straight back to father and Celyddon. They're probably hoping that you're going back with Halcyon to get out of this difficulty about Sirona healing you at my instigation."

"Really? What happens if the Council turns against me?"

"We go into exile with the *Hansa*."

"You would do that for me?"

"Of course. You belong to me now and I belong to you. We're one. That can never change."

"If that happens, your father would be devastated."

"And so would I, but you have also left everyone for me. Let's hope it doesn't come to that."

"So you want to get married," mused Kelldor as he paced back and forth. "I knew something like this was up when I looked at you. What do you think Celyddon?"

"It may help us Kell. Our people regard marriage very highly. It will make Dave one of us and unite our two families in the struggle to recognize him. Anyways, it doesn't matter what we think. These young people are determined to marry. We must fight and win, or else my adopted son and your daughter will be exiled."

"Do you, Dave Schiller Schuster, take Arlana da Kelldor as your lawful wedded wife?" said Commander MacDonald.

"I do."

"Do you, Arlana da Kelldor, take David Schiller Schuster as your lawful wedded husband?"

Arlana turned and smiled up at Dave. "I do."

"You may exchange rings."

Arlana accepted a ring from Pam while Al gave Dave a ring. Dave and Arlana placed the rings on each other's fingers.

"By the promises, vows, and covenants before God you have made to each other, and by the authority invested in me by the university and independent colony of Halcyon, I pronounce you husband and wife. You may kiss the bride."

Dave felt an incongruous mixture of panic and joy. Panic because a door had closed on his past life that could never be reopened. Joy because he couldn't imagine living life without Arlana. After the kiss, Dave shook hands with Al, Floyd and Hanomer. Arlana in turn hugged Pam and the two other bridesmaids.

"I hate to hurry things up," said MacDonald, "but we're scheduled to dislocate in two hours. If you're leaving, you need to go now."

They hurried to West Harbor and boarded one of the reed boats readied by the *Hansa*. With a brisk wind they headed over to the nearest channel island to watch the dislocation.

"Did the Dalyites find New Jerusalem livable, Hanomer?"

"Yes, friend Dave. The Lupi were all gone and we helped them reinforce the breach in the outer wall where the Lupi had gotten into the crater. They seemed happy to be back home."

"I suppose they would be. They really didn't want to go back to our home world."

Dave looked at his watch. If they're on time, they ought to be starting now. Out of the clear air, dark clouds began to form above the center of Halcyon Island. The clouds grew in intensity and then lightning began to strike the island in rapid succession, bolt after bolt.

A shimmering semi-transparent sphere began to expand outward as the lightning barrage continued. It expanded to the edge of the bridge and then the sphere turned coal black. Halcyon was gone and in its place was a low rocky island with a sandy beach all around. A loud splash sounded as a piece of bridge fell into the ocean.

"Wow, they let the sphere get a little bigger and cut a piece off the bridge from our world and brought it back," said Dave. "I guess that piece of bridge means that they made it."

"It's time we headed home. Now we will have a Gurundarian wedding to plan," said Kelldor.

Gurundarian tradition demanded that the bride and groom be separated for at least thirty days of contemplation after betrothal, to see if they really wanted to enter into marriage, so Dave and Arlana traveled in different boats. Dave directed Hanomer to head deep into Caiman Swamp to an island with a rock that looked like a fist. Here he planted his half of the Swamp Oak acorn he had taken from the warehouse.

"Is this wise, friend Dave?" asked Hanomer.

"I don't know, Hanomer. I didn't ask for permission from Kelldor, but I have this feeling, I may want to find out some day what the Bent Ones are up to. If they do come to this place, they'll find this is a most unpleasant swamp and may find it difficult to get out of here."

Chapter 35

A New Life

Dave sat on his veranda overlooking Lake Tolbar. It had been six months since he and Arlana had been married in a second wedding ceremony that would have been fit for royalty. Although he had been very uncomfortable with all the pomp, Kelldor and Celyddon had known what they were doing. By making it a spectacle that all the Gurundarians talked about, that event had made it relatively easy to get Dave accepted as an Ancient. Only Arachodor and his closest allies had objected. Dave, conscious that he and Arlana had made many enemies, decided to lie low and so had deliberately built their house near the tree line in a secluded place above Kelldor's home. Dave, feeling as if he were half *Hansa*, had spent two weeks searching the mountain side for just the right place. He eventually found what he was looking for. The cottage was built right into the mountainside and covered the front entrance of a cave he had discovered. The cave opened up a honeycomb of passages and was quite deep. Dave only had the ability to explore the outer reaches of the system. The front chambers, he used for storage and sealed off the rest with a stone wall and a stout door.

As he was reflecting on the house and their second marriage ceremony, he remembered he needed to check the grove. He walked up a path that climbed up to a small bog in a mountain meadow surrounded by the steep walls of a blind canyon. In the center of the bog, he and Arlana had planted one half of a Swamp Oak acorn. The cocoon-shaped swamp oak was now only about one foot in diameter, but they had sent the second half with Al and Pam. Dave had placed a note in the box and checked every few weeks to see if the Swamp Oaks were big enough to complete the transfer. As Dave parted the branches, he was surprised to see a different box sitting there. Eagerly he opened it and found a letter with a gift.

> Dear Dave and Arlana:
> We made it back home without incident. Well almost without incident—Makalo, wanting to err on the side of conservatism, allowed the sphere to expand a little further than before to make sure everything came back. As a result, there is about a twenty foot gap in the bridge. Halcyon University has been seized by the government for research and everything is off limits to us and the general public. We had many long, grueling sessions of debriefing where our stories were checked and rechecked.
>
> We had left our Swamp Oak acorn half in the caves on Romulus and were able to retrieve it after the interrogations were complete.
>
> We have settled down on an acreage in South Carolina, and I'm teaching chemistry at a small college. I have reconciled with my brother Thomas, and I'm attempting reconciliation with my father and step-mother. Little Thomas seems content. Pam and I couldn't be happier.
>
> Pam and I are glad Bigelow is permanently out of our lives. His body was never found, so I think he must have escaped with Meglir and Blackmore.
>
> If he were here, Pam would worry he would come after Little Thomas. More later. Let me know if this gets through.
>
> Pam sends her love,
> Al

Dave showed the letter to Arlana with the pictures they had sent. Maybe someday, when the Swamp Oak grew large enough, they might even visit them.

The End

Glossary

Abaddon (A-bah-don): A continent to the east of Halcyon that consists of a continent-wide crater surrounded by a ring of tall mountains. The bottom of the crater is about 16 kilometers below sea level. The high air pressure at this depth and the warm temperatures sustain many large and unusual life forms that cannot survive at one atmosphere of pressure. This is the home continent of the Bent-Ones. The word in the language of the Ancients means "the place of destruction."

Ancients: A race of beings that inhabit the continent of Feiramar. These people were separated by the Great Plague unleashed by Meglir. The Guardians or *Gurundar* live east of Lake Tolbar and are not permitted to cross over to the western shores. West of Lake Tolbar live the *Naromundar* (the pure ones). The two sundered peoples only meet on the Callabar Islands in the middle of Lake Tolbar. After one of these infrequent meetings the *Narmundarians* who met the *Gurundarians* must stay in quarantine on the islands for three months before they can return home.

Ap: Hansean for "son of." This designation is used instead of a surname.

Arachodor (err-RACK-oh-door): Kelldor's chief rival on the Council of Thirteen, the governing council of Gurundar. Arachodor believes Lesser Men are not much better than Halfmen and need to be exterminated for the safety of the Guardians.

Arkand (ARE-kand): A great city that was the former capital of the Ancients before the capital was moved to Tar-en-Nar. It is guarded by the *Gurundar* for it contains many libraries and much knowledge. It is also the name of one of the mountains behind the city.

Arlana (ARE-lahn-uh): Arlana, a *Gurundarian*, is the daughter of Kelldor, the chief of the *Gurundarians*.

Bandomer (BAND-oh-mur): One of the *Hansa* members of the Council at Eleytheria. He accompanied Al and Pam back to Halcyon to rescue Little Thomas.

Barclay, Donovan: Dave's pseudonym while in Halcyon, searching for Al.

Bent Ones: Bent Ones come from the continent of Abaddon off the east coast of Feiramar. The Bent Ones only come infrequently to Feiramar. They are Ancients who have given themselves over to evil. They bend and shape living things, through their arts, in support of evil.

Boat Weed: A living plant used by the *Hansa* and the Ancients to build boats. A boat frame of cut reeds or wood is constructed and then planted with Boat Weed. The plant takes on the shape of the boat and makes it watertight while acting like camouflage.

Bog Asphodel: A yellow flower used by the Gurundar to mark barrows.

Brotas (BRO-taz): A travel bread which does not go stale and is nourishing for long journeys.

Celyddon (SELL-e-dawn): Best friend of Kelldor, and adoptive father of Dave. He is also a member of the Council of Thirteen.

Council of Thirteen: the ruling council of the Gurundar or Guardians.

Cordomer: The *Hansa* who traveled with Floyd to search for Dave and Hanomer.

Da: Word in the Old Tongue meaning "daughter of."

Glossary

Donovan Barclay: Dave's pseudonym while trying to locate Al on Halcyon.

Dorai (DOOR-eye): Aquatic mammals that Ancients ride when they travel over the sea or up rivers.

Erand Gabur (ERAND ga-BUR): A fortress belonging to Kelldor's chief rival Arachodor. Arachodor believes Lesser Men are not much better than Halfmen and need to be exterminated for the safety of the guardians.

Falcor: Captain of the brigantine the Eagle and Ferris' friend.

Feiramar (FAIR-a-mar): The name of the continent that contains the *Hansa* and the Ancients. The island of Halcyon is off the east coast of this continent.

Garandar (GARR-an-dahr): "The contaminated." A pejorative applied by the Naromundar to the Gurundar.

Granomer (GRAN-oh-mur): Chief Loremaster of the *Hansa*. Loremasters store up knowledge for the *Hansa* since the latter keep few written records.

Guardians: Also called *Gurundar*. They are the remnant of Ancients that guard the plague lands. They avoided Meglir's lair in the City of the Dead since only through them could Meglir capture a new body and be freed from his pillar prison under the mountain. For this reason, the *Hansa* thought the Guardians had all left and had abandoned the fight against Meglir.

Guria: (GUR-ee-ah): A generic name in the Old Tongue for the family of guardian plants that can live either outside or underground. They recognize non-Ancients and emit defensive secretions that prevent trespass.

Gurundaria (GUR-rund-DARR-ree-ah): The homeland of the Gurundar or Guardians behind the Barrier Mountains on Lake Tolbar.

Halfmen: Halfmen are short, powerful bipeds with long arms. They crudely speak the Common Tongue and use weapons, including short bows. They have been created by the Bent Ones from captured Ancients, by hybridizing them with apes so as to weaken them and make them susceptible to suggestion and control. Unlike the Apemen, who must be controlled directly, Halfmen act on their own, often fight among themselves, and have an abiding hatred for most living things.

Hansa (HAN-suh): *Hansa* are furry bipeds that have a prehensile tail that ends in a hand. Although not overly intelligent, they are given to music and poetry. They have a highly developed sense of honor and justice, and are self-sacrificing in their service to others. There are left-handed and right-handed *Hansa,* depending on the handedness of their prehensile tail.

Hanomer (HAN-oh-mur): A *Hansa* chief and friend of Dave Schuster.

Happenone (HAPP-en-own): The compound name given to the active ingredient in Happy Berries, which led to Renegades.

Hollidor (HAUL-i-door): Kelldor's brother, father of Ferris, and fellow member of the Council of Thirteen.

Hyperhap (HIGH-purr-happ): A derivative compound of Happenone used to control Renegades. Hyperhap injections turn Renegades into strong, fearless soldiers called Bezerkers who can be controlled by voice commands.

Kelldor (KELL-door): Kelldor is the leader of the Guardians and father of Arlana.

Kilk: The *Hansa* name for Apemen.

Koi-Banthu (coy-BANN-thew): Life-changers—Ancients who had developed the skill for modifying organisms.

Krachodon (CRACK-oh-dawn): A large crocodile-like creature with ten tentacles around the mouth to capture prey.

Kree ah na koo (CREE AH NAH COO): An exclamation in the Old Tongue, which means "May the Creator help me."

Lake Tolbar: The long lake that separates the western lands from the eastern plague lands. In the middle of the lake are the Callabar Islands, the infrequent meeting place between East and West.

Le Blanc, Bernice: Blackmore's executive assistant.

Little Thomas: The son of Pam Lowental and Stan Bigelow. He is kept in the Staycare Center. In principle, Pam is able to visit him whenever she likes.

Lore Masters: *Hansa* who specialize in remembering the past and lessons from ancient times. They teach other *Hansa* their traditions and history.

Lumi-Lichen: Lichen that coats most caves in Feiramar. It gives off a pale green light.

Lupi (LOOP-eye): Very large, intelligent, wolf-like creatures that can plan and coordinate attacks. The singular of Lupi is Lup.

Northborough: The village of the Gurundar near the Giant Steps and the nearest village to Celyddon's home.

Matthews, Hugh: The lookout at New Jerusalem. He was a participant at the Battle of City Point, and decided to join his cousin at New Jerusalem.

Mbeni, Hosea: A member of the Eleytherian Council who replaced Dave Schuster after he disappeared. Mbeni's family had immigrated to the United States from South Africa.

Meglir (MEG-leer): Meglir, a great king of the Ancients who grew corrupt and became a tyrant, re-opening ties with the Bent Ones who live on another continent called Abaddon.

Morfang (MORE-fang): Morfang is a Bent One who traveled to the ruined city of Arkand to seek knowledge from the great libraries in this city. He was discovered there by Kelldor.

Mindtalk: A name for the contact telepathy practiced by the Ancients and the *Hansa*.

Myrodon (MY-roe-dawn): Celyddon's door warden in the town of Northborough at the Giant Steps.

Naromundar (Nahr-oh-muhn-dahr): "The pure ones." The name given to western Ancients sundered from the Gurundar. They were never exposed to the great plague and forbid Gurundar from approaching their lands.

Odonahue, Matthew: Platoon commander guarding the Torburg. He was killed defending the Torburg against attack.

Pishon (PEESH-hawn): The *Hansa* name for the Halcyon River.

Plague: Some 500 years ago, Meglir unleashed a plague that killed most of the Ancients and all of the Lesser Men besieging the City of the Dead. Meglir retreated into his obelisk, as his host also died. The Gurundar were sundered from their western brethren and they declared the City of the Dead "off limits" in case the plague should reoccur.

Rangers: Rangers are Guardians who travel alone to scout out and observe the vast territory under their guardianship from Lake Tolbar to the Eastern Sea. They are the elite of the Guardians.

Rickets: A small lakeside village near Arlana's house.

Rokash (ROW-cash): A large bipedal reptilian carnivore about ten feet tall.

Rokodor (ROW-ke-door): Ancient name that Arlana gave Dave as she came up with the idea to make Dave, Celyddon's adopted son.

Rokomer (ROW-coe-mur): Dave Schuster's *Hansa* name bestowed on him after he killed the *Rokash*.

Rolomer (ROLL-oh-mur): One of the three *Hansa* that accompanied Pam and Al to rescue Little Thomas.

Sigor: The name of Ferris' Dorai.

Sheiomer (SHY-oh-murr): The captain of the Hansa forces from the City of the Trees.

Siph (SIFF): A golden-colored drink made by the *Hansa* that can be drunk cold or hot.

Sorgai (SORE-guy): Small floating rafts of seaweed that are used by the Gurundar for refuge and rest when on the ocean.

Staycare Center: A 24-hour nursery and daycare center for mothers at Halcyon University. Women at Halcyon are encouraged to continue their studies and their work and to leave the raising of their children to professionals. Mothers are permitted to visit their children whenever they like, and to stay overnight with them.

Squids: The medical team assigns this nickname to Dave and Arlana because of their ability to change their skin color, reminiscent of cephalopod color changes. To be distinguished from the pejorative term "squid" used for sailors.

Sugar Gum Bush: A bush that grows to five feet with variegated leaves. The root is used by the *Hansa* to make *Siph*.

Tar-en-Nar (TAR-en-nahr): City of Light. The ancient name for the City of the Dead before Meglir corrupted it.

Tar-en-Gorg: (TAR-en-ghorg): The City of the Dead. The name for Meglir's city once the great plague was unleashed, killing most men east of Lake Tolbar. Meglir and his lieutenants ruled through the Apemen.

Taromer (TAR-oh-mur): The third of three *Hansa* companions accompanying Al and Pam back to Halcyon to rescue Little Thomas.

Teledon (TELL-e-dawn): The son of Arachodor and suitor of Arlana.

Thicket Islands: Small, low islands, covered with brush at the mouth of the Tor River, which obscure the Tor River from the Pishon (Halcyon) River.

Trail Talk: A method of communication used by the *Hansa* where directions and intentions are marked on a stick. Trail Talk sticks are usually left by an abandoned camp fire.

Ton-Heimar (TAWN-HIGH-marr): The rocky prominences guarding the entrance to Goose's Beak. Means "Gateway of Home" in the Old Tongue.

Tranomer (TRAN-oh-mur): The *Hansa* warrior who left in a coracle to report to the elders about the siege of Torburg.

Tranquor (TRANK-qor): A custom of the *Hansa* that everyone should be allowed a time of quiet reflection in the morning before being interrupted by the day's tasks and worries.

Traveller: The name of Dave's bay (reddish-brown) stallion.

Wogogs (WOE-gogs): The name for Lupi in the Old Tongue.

Wood Island: An island up the east coast that Halcyon began to use for timber when the mainland became too dangerous because of the renegades.

Acknowledgements

A multi-year project like *The Battle for Halcyon* confronts the author with many challenges: writing an exciting sequel, managing character development, staying consistent with the earlier works (I count *Questioning Your Way to Faith* as an apologetic prequel to *The Halcyon Dislocation*).

This process was helped immeasurably by a number of people who contributed their time, their skill, and their enthusiasm to make my work much better than I could have accomplished on my own.

First and foremost, I would like to thank my two editors: Stephanie Paddey and Patricia Paddey. They untiringly worked to remove extraneous material, make sure the characters remained consistent and to correct obscure or wordy passages. Their emendations proved invaluable and measurably improved the book.

John Greenhorn, Doug Paddey, and Phil Kazmaier meticulously read early drafts of *The Battle for Halcyon* and identified obscure passages and readability gaps. For their diligence I am deeply grateful.

I am also grateful to my other beta readers, who read early drafts of *The Battle for Halcyon* and provided excellent feedback on the overall readability of the manuscript and continued to encourage me to bring the manuscript to completion. Therefore I give a special 'thank you' to Mark Jokinen, Darren Kazmaier, Mike Kazmaier, and Ben Schmidt.

My monthly writer's group, "The Egglestonians," led by Don Martin helped smooth the rough edges off my writing. Particular thanks are due to Ian MacLeod, Brian Meyer, Zinta Meyer, Bruce

Soderholm, and Bonnie Beldan-Thomson for their constructive comments on the manuscript as I read portions to them.

I would like to thank the many readers of *The Halcyon Dislocation* who encouraged me to complete the sequel. Your interest in finding out "What happens to the University of Halcyon?" kept me writing.

I would also like to thank the staff at Word Alive for helping with the details of the publication process. Wholehearted thanks to Jen Jandavs-Hedlin, and Amy Groening.

As a Christ-Follower I claim no special aid or guidance in this work except in the most humble sense. I can see how following the Lord Christ has helped me grow as a person. Without His grace, and the people He has used to encourage me, I don't think I would have had the courage to attempt the audacious feat of writing a novel. Still, I readily acknowledge that no work is ever perfect or complete, and this story is no exception. Those who have worked with me have helped to make my book better, and for that I am deeply grateful.

About the Author

The Battle for Halcyon is Peter Kazmaier's third book and the second in *The Halcyon Cycle*. In this work he has been able to pursue a lifelong dream of writing fast-paced novels that explore the intersection between adventure, science, faith and philosophy.

    J. R. R. Tolkien's *Lord of the Rings* , C. S. Lewis' *The Chronicles of the Narnia* , Stephen R. Lawhead's trilogy, *Song of Albion*, and Robert Jordan's series *Wheel of Time*^{TM} are among his favorite and best-loved books. He also very much enjoys science fiction classics such as Robert Heinlein's *Tunnel in the Sky*.

    Dr. Kazmaier has spent most of his scientific career as a research scientist in industry. He was appointed as an Adjunct Professor of Chemistry at Queen's University in 1999. He has published more than sixty scientific articles in refereed journals and was awarded the Arthur K. Doolittle award for Best Paper by the American Chemical Society in 1993. Cited as the inventor or co-inventor on more than 175 patents, his strong background in science enables him to bring authentic scientific insight to *The Halcyon Cycle*.

    Dr. Kazmaier joined the *American Chemical Society* in 1976, the *Chemical Institute of Canada* in 1980, and *The Word Guild* in 2004.

He was married to Kathryn in 1976 and they live in Mississauga, near Toronto. They enjoy spending time at their cottage near Seeley's Bay, Ontario on the Rideau Canal.

He blogs regularly at www.peterkazmaier.com and welcomes feedback from his readers.

www.ingramcontent.com/pod-product-compliance
Ingram Content Group UK Ltd.
Pitfield, Milton Keynes, MK11 3LW, UK
UKHW022214230426
12048UKWH00016BA/832